DOMESTIC VIOLENCE: A THRILLER

"*Domestic Violence* is an ambitious and broad-based debut novel introducing protagonist Mike Paxton and author Chuck Edmonds who both appear destined to carve out their place on the bookshelves of political thriller fans. Edmonds displays a deft understanding of global political intrigue and populates his book with characters readers will love to love or love to hate. Climb aboard and buckle up."

—Mike Murphey,
Award-Winning Author of the Physics, Lust and Greed Series

"*Domestic Violence: A Thriller*. Cinematic. Intelligent. And a sobering reality check. A well-orchestrated covert assault on the American homeland yields the greatest fatality toll for a single event in recorded human history, and it prompts the hunt for a multi-generational cabal of bankers, clerics, and global money managers determined to cripple the U.S.A. on the world stage. This cautionary tale reminds us no one is exempt from the evil that is terrorism, but neither is anyone exempt from the pursuit of justice by a presidentially-appointed cybersecurity expert and his team, no matter how long the task might take. Kudos to author Chuck Edmonds. Five-plus stars for *Domestic Violence: A Thriller*!"

—Laura Taylor,
6-Time *Romantic Times* Award Winner

DOMESTIC VIOLENCE

A THRILLER

CHUCK EDMONDS

ACORN PUBLISHING

FROM THE TINY ACORN . . .
GROWS THE MIGHTY OAK

www.AcornPublishingLLC.com

For information, address:
Acorn Publishing, LLC
3943 Irvine Blvd. Ste. 218
Irvine, CA 92602

Domestic Violence

Cover design by Damonza.com
Interior design and formatting by Debra Cranfield Kennedy

Printed in the United States of America

ISBN-13: 979-8-88528-016-7 (hardcover)
ISBN-13: 979-8-88528-015-0 (paperback)
Library of Congress Control Number: 2022907667

To Carolyn

and of course, James, Millie, and

Charlie, whose lights shine brightly

1

No Accident
Agnew

1140 hrs. CDT Agnew, Texas
Friday, October 25

The sweltering humidity, unseasonable this time of year in the south-central Texas farming community of Agnew, made the scorched air feel close to a hundred degrees. For the overflow crowd in the aged gymnasium, it was stifling. The community-wide pep rally was a welcome respite between harvesting soybeans and pulling cotton bolls. Everyone hoped their undefeated, six-man football team could do what had not been done in two decades: win tomorrow's game and play for the state championship.

Signs and hand-painted banners urging the team to victory hung on every surface in town, from storefronts to churches, the co-op grain elevator, and even the fire station. Nine-year-old Emma Bergsten and her classmates sat atop the foldaway bleachers, screaming cheers and singing songs. Her older brothers were team stars, her sister the head cheerleader, and her three cousins played in the band.

Hearing the whistle of the train on its way through town, Emma glanced out the gym's gaping double doors just as the landscape of Agnew and the lives of everyone she knew changed forever.

The colossal explosion from its payload ammonium nitrate bomb obliterated a box truck near the railroad crossing. In an instant, the first of five engines pulling the hundred-car Union Pacific Eagle Ford Shale crude carrier plunged into chaos as the eruption thundered all around.

Screaming at supersonic speeds in every direction away from the explosion's core, the shockwave freed its unbalanced energy in a microsecond. Driven by molecular nitrate collisions at the nanoscale, the invisible, vibrating force smashed tsunami-like through massive concrete cylinders at the grain elevator, destroying the cotton gin, sheriff's office, and volunteer fire station in seconds. Intense wind followed, sweeping the debris into a destructive wake. The concussion shattered the cafeteria windows. It triggered such biological havoc in the bodies of the three cooks, and they died before the glass hit the floor.

Jolting through the adjacent gymnasium, the devastation continued, windows shattered and shards of concrete from the elevator scythed the roof. Survivors scrambled over tubas, trombones, ceiling fragments, and each other in their efforts to escape.

Find Mommy, Emma thought as she fell from the top of the foldaway bleachers.

The old building shuddered and collapsed. As the explosion subsided and the smoke cleared, only a portion of the south wall remained.

Maria Valdez's four-year-old screamed, "Look out, Mama! Look out!" as the blue car crossed the centerline. Tires screeched as the driver pulled back into his lane, over-corrected, slid off the shoulder, and jerked back onto the road. The oncoming car swerved again, missing them by the narrowest of margins. Maria jammed the accelerator of her old pickup to the floor and pulled off to the shoulder.

Her entire body trembled. Sitting on the edge of her seat, she gripped the steering wheel with both hands. She took several steadying breaths, then looked at her daughter, who sat quivering beside her. "You okay, Pumpkin?"

Her sobbing daughter freed her booster seat belt, scooted closer, and burrowed like a puppy into her mother's arms. "He about hit us!"

Holding her close, her mother kissed her forehead and whispered, "Honey, he came close, but we're okay."

"Why was he driving like that? Was he mad at us?"

"Maybe he's going to the hospital. I'm sure he was not mad, just in a big hurry." Trying to distract her daughter, she said, "Tell you what, after the pep rally I'll invite Shelly and her Mommy for lunch. We'll have cookies and ice cream for dessert. I bet you'll feel better!"

Calmer now, the little girl nodded. "I'd like that."

They held their embrace as Maria scolded herself for letting her mind wander on this isolated road. She thought then about the pep rally and the team uniforms she'd picked up at her sister's cleaners in Pearsall. Before the near collision, she'd considered speeding to the rail crossing in town to make it to the pep rally in time for the team to wear their jerseys. Now, she took her time, looked both ways before pulling back on the road, knowing they wouldn't arrive on time.

She made a mental note about the vehicle: *Dark blue Toyota Camry, like Mary's new car. Green license plate with a white number six and the letter T in the middle. It had to be going a hundred miles an hour. Who'd be so irresponsible on this narrow two-lane farm-to-market road? Not even that wild Jenkins kid from over in Karnes City would drive so recklessly.*

Whoever it was, isn't a local, she decided.

Tank car after tank car buckled like an accordion stretching a half mile back through town, some upright, most on their sides. Oil gushed from fissures in car walls. Sparks emitted from the wreckage ignited the low flashpoint crude. Rapidly growing pools generated a huge fireball twice the height of the grain elevator. The first of five explosions registered 4.8 on seismographs in Austin, Houston, and Albuquerque, shaking every structure in town and alerting the residents in a twenty-mile radius to what many believed to have been an earthquake.

The initial concussion from the blast shattered businesses and most of the homes closest to the tracks while others crumpled and ignited. Menacing flames destroyed everything in their wake. Those trapped in their homes died as their skin melted. The town burned in a sea of red, yellow, and orange.

Flames erupting from ever-deepening fuel lakes the length of the train created giant curtains of fire. Fire begat fire. Fresh combustion-devoured oxygen twisted and danced skyward to a pounding rhythm of its own making, belching mounds of ugly, black, boiling smoke, which obliterated the midday sun's brightest rays.

The stench of burned hydrocarbons, cars, houses, businesses, and human flesh, combined with the heat and the roar of the fire, made the remains of the community of Agnew unbearable. The penetrating heat ignited the combustible wheat dust inside a grain elevator silo. A yellow-orange fireball leapt into the sky, blowing several large holes in the silo's cylindrical concrete sides and those of two adjoining silos, killing the work crew of four. The process repeated in an adjacent silo where tens of thousands of bushels of wheat provided ready tinder, which, when combined with the trapped air in the confined space, exploded.

Most of the eighty-three derailed cars suffered a breach, releasing more than two-and-a-half million gallons of crude into an ever-increasing firestorm. The somewhat viscous fluid found its way into the storm sewer and emerged as exploding manhole covers and fireballs erupting in the streets throughout the village. Craters large enough to consume half a city block appeared on several streets where, moments earlier, the town's sole focus had been on winning tomorrow's football game. Oil and vapor infiltrated the wastewater system as explosions lifted commodes off their fittings and fire emanated from residence sinks throughout town. The city pumping station was demolished as the blaze expanded.

In just minutes, the town of Agnew was gone.

Four miles west of Agnew, mere moments earlier, the engineer had throttled back the big diesel engines, slowing the train as he discovered the air compressor had failed. "No brakes!" Looking at his on-board conductor, he ordered, "Radio dispatch. Makes no sense. I checked them before we left. Nobody better be screwing with our equipment. We're ridin' a damn powder keg, gotta be able to stop!" Trying the brakes again, he throttled back even more, reducing his speed to within accepted limits, but still faster than he wanted with school letting out for lunch.

"Dispatch says to pull on the siding east of Gonzales and roll to a stop. They're sending a crew to meet us," said his companion.

Agnew, southeast of San Antonio and two hundred and fourteen rail miles from his destination at the Royal Dutch Shell refinery on the Houston ship channel, differed from other hamlets along his route by a long northern turn east of town. He knew every inch of this route, estimating he'd hauled half a billion gallons of Eagle Ford Shale crude in the year of making this run.

A half mile from the rail crossing, the engineer spotted a box truck. *What's it doing so close to the track?* he wondered. He pulled long and hard on his whistle, hoping to rouse the driver.

"Check out those homemade signs. Community pride's a great thing.Big school or small, everybody wants to be number one!" He laughed as the town slid by on their right.

Resigned to waiting for the train at the crossing, Maria caught the last tanker cars when the shockwave struck her pickup, shoving it as if hit by a crosswind, cracking her windshield, and breaking out her windows. "God help us! What's happening?"

Huge explosions, fire, and billowing black smoke terrified her daughter, who again clutched at her mother. Tank cars derailed. A twenty-foot wall of fire engulfed the train. She slowed, u-turned, and sped away to escape the firestorm. Smoke hot enough to scorch her skin invaded the pickup's cab. The reek of sulfur overwhelmed her nostrils, dominating her every breath. Bitter bile burned her throat, racking her chest into a coughing fit. Tears streamed down her cheeks from her burning eyes. The roar of the flames resembled the sound of an aircraft engine. "It's okay, Pumpkin. A terrible accident happened." She struggled for calm. "We're safe! We'll find daddy and the girls, then try to help everybody."

"Mama, I can't breathe," her daughter cried.

"Keep your head down, put your dress in front of your face, and breathe through your mouth. It'll help. I'm going as fast as I dare."

Grabbing her phone, she videoed the bedlam, narrating as she went. "Train cars jackknifed . . . Oil's everywhere! Fire thirty feet high as far as I can see. Driving upwind to the Bergsten place. Whole town's on fire . . . Can't breathe . . . Call 911! San Antonio Fire Department. Find help!" she screamed before sending it to her sister.

2

Fire

1210 hrs. CDT Agnew, Texas
Friday, October 25

The Bergsten family, among the first to settle in Agnew, was known for their integrity and firm belief in Agnew's future prosperity. A third-generation Bergsten, Jim farmed more than three thousand acres with the help of his two sons, nephew, and brother-in-law. He was first to discover oil on his property. In addition to farming and ranching, he and his family continued to own and operate several businesses founded by his father. Few could remember when Jim had not helped them or a neighbor during a difficult time. For years, he and his wife, Ole Mae, hosted the Fourth of July community barbecue and reunion in front of the elementary wing of the all-grade school until her health began to fail. He'd served as mayor for more than twenty years and enjoyed a well-deserved reputation as a good, honest man.

He and Ole Mae lived in a modest single-story home on four hundred eighty acres three miles west of town. Two Quonset huts with concrete floors housing large John Deere tractors sat a short distance behind the house. Loaders, plows, cultivators, and various other farm implements were parked between the two buildings. A shed housed a workshop, a tractor, and various farm tools used to plant his two-acre garden and complete other projects around the house.

The garden consisted of corn, squash, carrots, cabbage, beets, peas, radishes, lettuce, cauliflower, and potatoes, most of which they gave away in town. An apple and grapefruit orchard and several raspberry and blackberry bushes were also free for the picking. To the west of the shed were two elevated five-hundred-gallon tanks, one gasoline and one diesel; to the east sat a brick smokehouse used to cure beef, lamb, pork, and fish. Behind were stock pens, feeders, water troughs, loading pens, and hay barns sufficient to run a two-hundred-head cow-calf operation.

Every building in town's burning, Maria Valdez thought as she drove upwind to the Bergsten farm, hoping to find others seeking sanctuary. Air brimming with not-yet-combusted hydrocarbons made it nearly impossible to breathe. Turning off the road, she saw five pickups parked close together in front of the house; they provided a semblance of a heat shield where a group of older neighbors and farmers working the fields had gathered. Her jaw ached from the tension, noise, stench, and fear. Red-eyed and coughing, Maria's daughter pleaded, "Mama, I can't breathe. My eyes sting. Can we please go home?"

Maria's eyes moved from face to face in the assembly. She finally spotted Carlos, grabbed their daughter, and ran to him. Together they held their four-year-old, already fearing the loss of their second- and fourth-grade girls at school.

Jack got out of his soot-covered pickup.

"I called Mary," Maria said as Jack approached them. "She's contacted San Antonio. They're on their way."

"You were gonna drop those calves at Mike's. Is there a building left standing in town?" Carlos asked Jack.

"All gone. Part of the gym's south wall is all that's left," he replied.

His hand on Carlos's shoulder, Jack closed his eyes and took a deep, deliberate breath. Then, for a few moments, he stared at the house where he'd grown up. Wiping his face on his sleeve, he pulled his powerful six-foot-four frame into the bed of the middle pickup and turned, raising his voice to address the gathering. "Look around! We're almost everybody who's still alive. Can't wait for help. If we don't stop it before it gets to the pumpjacks, all hell will break loose. Cellphone service is out. Maria's sister called San Antonio. They're on their way."

Pointing to several older men in the crowd, he sent them to neighboring communities in search of help. "Mr. Martinez, can you check on the outlying farms and see how they're doing? Anybody needs anything, send them here. The rest of us, let's get to the Schneiders' with tractors, blades, plows, backhoes, whatever, to start a fire break and keep this thing contained."

Restricted to a walker, Jack's mother had known she couldn't attend the pep rally and have any hope of going to tomorrow's game, so she'd stayed home. "Mom, Dad," Jack called as he, Maria, and her four-year-old walked through the kitchen door.

"What's happened? What's on fire? I was sweeping the kitchen when we heard the first explosion. Why is everybody in our front yard? You look like you've seen a ghost! Dad and I can't breathe, what's going on?" she asked in a rush.

"Mom," he stammered, holding her in a tender embrace, his face pale as he focused on his mother. His eyes narrowed, angry, afraid. "The train derailed. Oil exploded. The pep rally was on when the gym collapsed. No one had a chance . . ."

The dispatcher's message had been vague: an oil fire of unknown magnitude, involving an oil transport derailment. Nothing more.

Adrian Uribe, Chief of Emergency Services District 3, Bexar County, hated responding to isolated flare ups in remote hamlets because carelessness outstripped a town's capability. On the horizon two-dozen miles away, though, he saw black smoke churning skyward as he sped toward its source, knowing this was real. People had died; homes had been lost. The town of Agnew was in peril. Five miles out, fireballs surged and plumes of smoke belched ever upward, the indisputable stench of crude oil ablaze. Calling his dispatcher, he requested more help.

Assessing the scene upon arrival, the fire's enormity shocked him. In all his years, he had never witnessed anything comparable. City Hall, the Sheriff's Office, and the adjacent US Post Office buildings were reduced to seared concrete slabs, most of their bricks vaporized. Steel frames of cars, trucks, and farm implements lay twisted, scattered in all directions, interiors and tires ravaged by the inferno. The school gymnasium smoldered. Its collapsed roof revealed the remaining portions of its back wall. Fire raged unsuppressed.

The chief had surveyed the situation, established a command post two hundred yards east of the railroad crossing, spoken with the Department of Public Safety Officer in Charge, and was concluding his call with his dispatcher when Jack Bergsten approached, removed his well-worn straw hat, wiped his brow with his sleeve, and extended his hand and managed a meager smile.

After introductions, Jack spoke. "Chief, pushed dirt for a fire break. Patrolling the perimeter to keep the crops safe. No need setting half the county on fire. Got two of our guys at the end of the train spraying water on the two tank cars closest to the fire, trying to keep them cool enough they won't explode. We've all got wells and will be glad to shuttle water here or take you to our wells and fill your tankers if it's faster."

"You guys have done a remarkable job," the chief replied. "Impressive. Very impressive, indeed. We've shut down the municipal water on the town site fire. Can't use it because of contamination. Need to put out any hot spots and cool the vicinity, not feed 'em. Appreciate your offer for more water. If we can refill a tanker, we should be able to stay ahead of any town site problems unless the wind whips up. Even though you guys have worked this from the start, I can't let civilians within five hundred feet of the fire due to the possibility of another explosion. I'll send two men to relieve your guys. Smart but dangerous to keep those cars cool. Couple of my guys have farms. If you'll let 'em use your tractors, they'll uncouple those last few cars and drag them out of danger. If you and your team will move 'em half, three quarters of a mile back, it'd be helpful."

3

Going Fishing

0600 hrs. MDT Boise, Idaho
Friday, October 25

Morning in Boise dawned clear and crisp, cooled by a brisk north wind. Don Plummer, Deputy Director of the Idaho State Police, had arrived at his office at six o'clock. Wearing khaki pants and a long-sleeve camo shirt, instead of his customary uniform, everyone knew he would be in for only a few minutes before leaving to go fishing at his ranch near Mackay. He made the rounds, checking with John Tilden, the Watch Commander, reviewing overnight activity, and talking to the squad leader whose team had busted a meth lab at 0340 hours. His last stop was his own desk where he found a post-it note. His friend and fishing partner, Mike Paxton, was on an international call and didn't expect they could leave before ten.

Don spent this unexpected time focused on his illicit drug money interception task force. Pocatello had been identified as the primary port of entry for drugs into the state. Eighteen months later, he now had three undercover agents paying cash for larger and larger quantities of cocaine. They had tracked the money to Salt Lake and Denver but no farther.

As he concluded his call with the French Minister of Defense, Mike's cellphone pinged with a text from his cousin, Jack:

> Can't believe you bailed. Largest terrorist attack since 9/11. French government vs. Agnew's state playoff game. Worried about your priorities. Bought the 60 heifers. Brought in 45 yesterday. Unloaded the rest on the back quarter of your home place. Dropped the trailer behind the house. Running late. On my way to the pep rally.

Smiling to himself, he responded:

> Killin' me. Didn't think we'd close this French power grid thing this fast. Let 'em know I'm thinking of 'em. Better win. See you next week.

Hitting send, Mike closed his office door and hurried out, his phone showing ten minutes after ten. He felt proud of what they'd accomplished. The French minister was effusive with platitudes. In two and a half days, Mike, creator and owner of Zia Cybersecurity, and his team had identified and repaired an electrical power grid software glitch, which instigated a power outage for all of Paris and the surrounding region. In the process, they'd identified those responsible.

Don had been waiting a few minutes in Mike's downtown building's parking garage when he walked up. "Sorry for the delay. Finishing Paris's national power grid hack and blackout from Tuesday."

"The City of Lights suddenly dark," Don responded with a laugh. "Interesting tactic. I mean, targeting a city's infrastructure puts the public at risk. International flights, traffic lights, public transportation, elevators, hospitals, supply chains, industrial production units of all shapes and sizes. Lose power or water, and you're in big trouble. Serves as a warning to a lot of countries whose electrical grids are at risk. This is a new level of terrorism. An entire city, a nation, impacted. Your teams finding them in less than forty-eight hours indicates they're not professional criminals. Was it sanctioned by a known terrorist group?"

"No one's taken credit," Mike replied as he and Don transferred his gear into his new Cadillac Escalade. "Takes me back to 9/11. Bin Laden targeted our military, form of government *and* economy. Not sure what these guys are trying to say. But enough business," he said with a laugh. "Good morning! Weatherman says snow should hold off till late Sunday. When it comes, supposed to bring a foot or more. I've caught lots of fish as the pressure falls ahead of a cold front. Not true for everyone." He slid into the driver's seat, pressing his key fob to lower the tailgate behind their packs. "Pack your long johns? Snow or not, it's gonna be cold."

"What's the deal? You've had this beauty for two weeks, and you're ready to take it on a fishing trip in bad weather? Still got that new car smell," Don mused, taking a gratuitous sniff as he buckled his seat belt.

"Bought it to hunt and fish, not to see and be seen. If the weatherman's right, we'll discover how it does in a good snow."

"Won't quibble. Looks good, bet it rides even better. Packed my wool socks and rain gear, so I'm ready. Even for a Paris do-over. We've got redundant power sources on the ranch," he explained as he glanced around. "Man, this is nice. Heated and cooled seats, voice command radio. Looks like it can do everything but drive itself and cook your breakfast." Don smiled in approval.

"Thanks. Got the radio, if you wanna listen to some country music when we're out in the middle of nowhere."

"You've got Wi-Fi—all the bells and whistles. Should've called. I'd have driven while you took your morning call, and we'd have our hooks wet by now." Don laughed. "What time did you go in last night?"

"A little before three to refine our presentation. Worked with the Pentagon and State Department to ensure the security of data transfer lines and started the call at six."

"What are they, seven hours ahead of us?"

"Eight."

"So, it was two o'clock, Friday afternoon in Paris when you started? Glad they didn't put themselves out while you solved their problems."

"One of the joys of international clients. Been workin' this case nonstop since Tuesday." Mike checked the road before pulling out of the parking garage and into the morning traffic.

"What are you, a full-service bank? Thought you were cyber specialists."

Maneuvering through light traffic, Mike turned north onto Orchard. "Taking care of business. They provided a persons-of-interest list. Once we discovered and repaired the infraction, we used their cellphones to track their locations. Turns out none of their suspected bad guys were involved. We've helped governments around the world with hundreds of terrorist encounters in the last eighteen-plus years. They always leave an electronic trail. In this case, they made no attempt to hide their tracks. Focused on achieving their goal and didn't seem to care if they got caught."

Staying in the left lane, Mike made the light, passed under Interstate 184, turned onto the feeder ramp, and entered northbound Idaho Highway 20/26. "I enjoy raging at you about being a prepper, but this attack could prove you right.

You've been at it awhile, and from what I've seen, you're as prepared as anyone for an infrastructure attack. How'd you start that, anyway?" Mike asked.

"It starts with a list. Do you have water, food, power, gear, a clear path to safety, and transportation? A pocketknife leads to a survival machete, a flashlight to a lantern and on to survival candles. Before long, you've got food for six months, a way to stay warm, water plus access to more, and the ability to make do in any circumstance."

"You're in pretty deep. How'd you get Nancy to buy into all that?"

"She's from Pocatello; her grandparents owned a hundred-acre place near Preston. She loved going there as a girl. We both have Mormon roots and believe in the storage of foodstuffs, basics. Our place is a working ranch, and I used to kid her that she married me to spend time there. When the kids finish college, if we're not too old and decrepit, we'll retire there."

Don laid out why he'd invested most of his inheritance, savings, and a large portion of his disposable income in his retreat. The house, made of reinforced concrete, slept ten with a pantry stocked to feed them for a hundred eighty days. Additional storage in the basement provided foodstuffs for another two years. With solar panels, gasoline and diesel-powered generators, and a wind-powered operation enough to keep his surveillance and communications systems operational indefinitely, he was power independent.

"Each year, chains of interdependence lengthen," he continued as the city began to disappear behind them. "Most kids today think milk comes in plastic bottles. They've no idea what it takes to put it on their table. They don't grasp that most of what they eat, wear, or own comes from supply chains thousands of miles long, creating an alarming vulnerability to disruption. No one cares except at Christmas. Lynchpin is the grid. Without functioning power grids, modern industrial societies will collapse within weeks."

Nodding his agreement, Mike added, "Look at France. International travel, their airports, train stations, their stock market, food, and hospitals. Every part of their lives was impacted. It'll take months for them to return to last week's functionality."

Don held court. "Global economies and interdependence, we lose electricity, access to clean water, communications, transportation—any of our infrastructure—and it would impact our lives for years. It's planning, study, and practice. For Nancy and me, our Achilles heel is the distance between where we live and where we need to be if disaster strikes. Having multiple roads to access our rescue house helps.

Preparedness isn't just accumulating a pile of stuff. You better know how to use it."

"One caveat might throw a wrench into your plan," Mike warned. "As Deputy Director, you hold a lot of responsibility within the state government. I can't think of a scenario involving an act of terrorism or a natural disaster where you and Nancy, with her obligations at the hospital, wouldn't play essential roles in dealing firsthand with the disaster. You two are poster children for 'stay the course, fight the good fight.' What would you do if Boise were in imminent danger?"

"You're right. We've thought it through and know we'd stay to the bitter end. Still, when we'd done all we could do, this is where we'd come," Don added.

Thirty minutes into their trip, they fell silent. Don worked on his laptop and his money-laundering task force. Mike thought about that morning's text exchange with his cousin and his conversation with the French Defense Minister. He'd been packed and on his way to the airport when the call came in from Paris. He would call his cousin and reschedule his trip for the coming week.

"Thank you, Dr. Paxton. You and your Zia Cybersecurity company have gone above and beyond this time," the defense minister had said. *"We're grateful to you for the quality and speed of your help. We'll be telling many others of your good work."*

He was pleased all had gone well, and he'd shared the minister's comments with the project team. He'd also received a personal email from the minister soon after the formal conclusion of their meeting, saying France would donate a million dollars to the Jessica Duncan Paxton Foundation and that similar contributions would be forthcoming from several French corporations and private industrialists.

He remembered a conversation with Sally three months before their wedding, which reinforced how far they had come.

"If we stay in New York, Daddy can provide all the legal help we need. He's the managing partner and knows a lot of influential people. He can help us start," she'd said.

"I don't doubt it for a second," he'd responded. *"New York's your home, and a happy wife makes a happy life and all. I'm going to marry my best friend, a beautiful girl who's way smarter than me. What I love most about you is you think things through, trust your own ability, and work hard to achieve your goals. Zia's our dream. I'm asking you to jump into the deep end of the pool. The one thing your Dad can't provide is talent. Silicon Valley's home to the best and the brightest. I can recruit them, but they won't move to New York. Zia's built on a solid concept, so if we work hard, it'll grow beyond our wildest dreams."*

Zia, started in San Francisco in a rent-free space provided by his uncle, began to install cybersecurity systems for industry, education, and local government agencies. Mike's world swung from development to production to sales, back to production, and then back to development. It was a wild ride, but in three years they'd acquired clients in government, the private sector, and the international marketplace. Everyone was getting hacked, and nobody wanted to be next. IBM, GM, Ford, ConAgra—everyone afraid their competitor, or the French, Chinese, or Russians could break through their electronic firewalls and steal their trade secrets, client lists, or their next, best idea.

As Mike drove, the sheer vastness of the mountains and the glacier-created valley, so different from his native Texas, prompted his recollection of his decade-old arrival in Boise. He'd met Don, a then forty-eight-year-old, tall, easy-going lawyer-turned-policeman, while he shopped for proper gray wolf ammunition. New to town and a novice wolf hunter, he'd appreciated Don's willingness to share his insight into the hunt.

Over coffee, Don had immediately recognized the name Zia Cybersecurity. "We use you and have recommended you to the governor and every agency and local police department in the state," Don had volunteered before asking how he'd come to Boise.

Mike had shared how a senseless traffic accident cost him his wife and parents on the same day their infant daughter hadn't survived a heart transplant. "I'll admit," Mike had said, "I was pretty undone after the funerals. My in-laws were very gracious and encouraged me to bury my wife and baby in our family plot in Texas. Sally was their only child, and it was hard for them. I'll forever be grateful. San Francisco's many benefits, including its proximity to a major talent pool, meant moving Zia wasn't an option, but I was surrounded by memories."

His need for a respite had inspired his search for a place with a strong work history, progressive city leadership, and a diverse economy. He found it in Boise and relocated the administration, sales, and service of Zia there. He'd also been impressed with Don's insight and his kind words about his newly formed foundation in his daughter's name.

"Boise's open and inviting and a complete change from the dense, compact city by the bay," Don had advocated. "It offers a new environment, new people, and an option for your employees. You also have easy access to the outdoors."

"You work part time for The Chamber of Commerce?"

Don chuckled. "No, raised here and enjoy the challenge of hunting and fishing, time alone in nature."

"Hunted coyotes as a kid, appreciate the wolf tips. Caught a lot of bass, but I'm struggling to learn to fly fish."

Thus began a great friendship.

4

Ana

1730 hrs. GMT Hanoi, Vietnam
Friday, October 25

The broad orange sun was setting as Ana Saleh stood before the floor-to-ceiling windows of the president's office on the fourteenth floor of the Capital National Bank Building in Hanoi. The street below remained a scene of seeming mass confusion. Cars, buses, bicycles, motor scooters, pedestrians, and taxis proceeded in protracted Brownian motion, ebbing and flowing through the intersection while darting to the next, where the process repeated. Sidewalks were covered with parked, stalled, and broken scooters, and people made their way as best they could around repairs impeding lanes of traffic.

A statuesque Ana Saleh smiled as she sat on the couch. "I appreciate you meeting with me this late in the day." Slender, dark-haired, and striking, Ana was, in fact, Rebecca Adichie, CFO of Algoa Construction of Port Elizabeth, South Africa.

"It's a pleasure to see you again, Miss You know your company is our largest client. We're eager to help in any way we can."

"Thank you," she said. "I'll come right to the point. We've been awarded three major contracts and are interested in moving 3.65 billion US dollars through your bank over the next nine to sixteen months. This bank will be the primary bank for deposit; however, we would benefit from including your branch banks and your subsidiary in Singapore. It will come through in bank-to-bank transfers, checks drawn on international banks, and lesser amounts for our subcontractors will be in cash. These funds may be held by you for as long as thirty days. Will this pose a problem for you?"

Ana had chosen this bank, knowing it was fraught with regulatory and management weaknesses, carried an overabundance of non-performing loans, was non-compliant with International Basel III standards for capital adequacy, stress testing, or market liquidity risk, and lacked international auditing. It had eighty-nine branch banks and an overseas subsidiary in Singapore. Trained in international law, she had learned from following in her father's shadow how to evaluate banks and the people who ran them. Not comfortable with any relationship, she vetted all facilities, did not let a single arrangement account for more than 10% of her portfolio, and moved accounts on a regular basis. She believed banks were living organisms with their own cultures and environments.

"You say the funds will arrive in US dollars?"

"Yes."

"And we will hold them for as long as a month in our branch banks and our bank in Singapore?"

"Yes, and of course we will pay our usual negotiated fee."

"I see no problem whatsoever. It will be our pleasure to work with you." He smiled. "Do you have plans for dinner this evening? I know you enjoy classical music. We have tickets for tonight's special performance, including the English violinist Claudette Sinclair, American pianist William Linden, and our symphony orchestra. Later, our best Vietnamese entertainers will be performing traditional songs and dances. My wife and I would count it an honor to have you join us."

"It sounds wonderful, and I would love to. Unfortunately, I have an important meeting and must go. Thank you, maybe next time." She extended her hand. Leaving his office, Ana headed to the airport and a sixteen-and-a-half-hour nonstop flight to Vienna.

5

Up In Smoke

1430 hrs. MDT Mackay, Idaho
Friday, October 25

Don's ranch, bounded by Salmon-Challis National Forest and Bureau of Land Management tracks, included over a mile of the Salmon River. His unremarkable turn off could be easily overlooked. Arriving after two o'clock, Don and Mike unpacked and made lunch before going to the river. Don fished downstream, Mike up. Working his way along the bank, Mike felt sure a gyrfalcon soared sixty yards above him. A natural arctic or subarctic species, the gyrfalcon and other raptors had been forced by the scarcity of food over the last four years to range as far south as Idaho's Bitterroot Mountain range. Its plethora of ground squirrels, field mice, rabbits, and other indigenous mammals served them well.

Mike, fishing with deliberate steadiness, stilled in a squat, refrained from looking up, and waited instead of stepping into the clearing ahead. With incredible quickness and efficiency, the world's largest falcon, among the swiftest birds of prey, descended upon a pocket gopher twenty yards to Mike's left, grasped it in its powerful, curved talons, ascended, and disappeared. He smiled. *Oh, that we could learn what nature has to teach us. There's life and there's death, ever in balance, never to excess.*

"Nerds and birds," he remembered his late wife saying. Watching the gyrfalcon, he thought of how Sally had kidded him at the start of the company: "Those are the people you work with. The nerds are super smart. Best left alone to stare at their computer screens. The birds are everybody else: hardware, sales, accounting, all buzzing around to make Zia the company you want it to be."

Mike tried hard to stay buried in his work, using hunting and fishing as a crutch. He knew he could not catch a fish or bag his game while thinking about anything else. Times like this, surrounded by the natural beauty of nature, he missed Sally so much he ached.

Gathering himself, he stood, took a long drink from his water bottle, refocused on the task at hand, and, staying in the shadows, stepped to the water's edge. The pool, eight yards long, was wedged between back-to-back sets of rapids. Thick pickets of Douglas fir combined with early evening shadows provided constant shade, making it harder to see into the water. Casting his fly above the upper rapid, he let the water churn it through the spillway, past a large boulder, and deposit it into the calm water on the downstream side of the obstruction where rapid flow mixed with slower, deeper water. He watched the big rainbow trout's slow rise to the surface as he took it. A flick of his wrist and the hook set. The fight was on.

They were big on catch and release, but Mike kept this one for dinner. They'd brought food for all remaining meals. Tomorrow, Don would grill NY strips with dirty rice, corn on the cob grilled in the husk, and peas. Tonight, though, Mike cleaned and wrapped bacon around their trout, readying them for grilling on cedar planks with crab stuffing, red potato mash, and black bean and basil salsa with a side of asparagus sautéed in lemon butter. And for dessert, the last of Don's fresh-picked raspberries and cream. No one lost weight on their outings.

Back from his garden where he'd gathered lettuce, carrots, radishes, and onions for their salad, and the raspberries, Don flipped on the television. "Man, you were right about the fish biting as the pressure falls ahead of the cold front. We killed 'em. Bet my smallest fish was fourteen inches. You?" Don dropped his vegetables in the sink and began to clean them.

"It's the same before a heavy rain. Maybe they sense the insects will temporarily disappear and they won't have anything to eat," Mike agreed, taking the fish-laden cedar planks out to the grill on the patio. "I kept my first one. Everything else was way more than I can eat."

"Returning to our top story," the CBS anchor said as she stared into the camera, "as we have been reporting all afternoon, an attempt on the president's life was thwarted today when terrorists tried to expose her to a cocktail of biologic toxins, including botulism, anthrax, and coronavirus delivered through the White House ventilation system. Authorities are looking for at least one man described as Hispanic, in his early twenties, five feet eight to five feet ten inches tall, about one hundred fifty pounds, wearing blue jeans and a black t-shirt, speaking with a Panamanian accent.

"Once again, the president is safe, never in any danger thanks to the work of a White House employee, the FBI, and the Secret Service. Tune in tonight for a one-hour CBS Special Report when we will bring you the latest on who may be behind this attack and why. That's tonight at 9:00 Eastern, 8:00 Central."

A single "crazy" or part of some bigger plot? Don wondered.

"We go now to our CBS affiliate KNES-5 in San Antonio and Valerie Paul on location."

The television image shifted from the New York City studio news anchor's desk to a veteran reporter standing nearly a hundred yards from an incredible inferno. "Eighty-three train cars carrying crude oil derailed in this small Texas town, causing a massive fire to spread across this community and destroying every building. Authorities are not sure what caused the accident, although some suspect an external explosion of some kind. The scene here's like a warzone. More than eight hundred people are confirmed dead, making this the worst rail disaster in our nation's history. Officials continue to look for survivors. We're behind police barricades, five hundred feet from the fire and the heat. Incredible noise and the smell of asphalt and sulfur make it unbearable. Hospitals in the nearby towns of Victoria, Corpus Christi, and San Antonio are on standby to care for the injured, but there have been none."

"Valerie, how long before it's out?" Mary Ann Holland, the CBS News anchor, asked.

"Firefighters as far away as Houston have come, bringing fire-retardant foam. But with water supply and pressure at a premium, we're told the best option is to let these fires burn themselves out, which could take as long as a week."

"Thank you, Valerie."

Don turned off the water, dried his hands and focused on the television, where the reporter was mid-interview with a survivor, whose face was streaked with tears.

". . . I don't have any words. I was working my cattle when I saw the flames roaring in the distance. Headed to town, it was a big curtain of fire. Lost my wife, my kids, parents, brother, and my two sisters and their families. House is gone. Everything, my friends, neighbors, all gone. I don't know what's gonna happen. All

I've got are memories. I'll trust the Lord and go back to work. It's all I can do."

"Thank you, sir. I'm so sorry for your loss." Looking again into the camera, Valerie continued, "Bret Donnelly, an environmental advocate in San Antonio tweeted, '*Rail or pipelines, there's a safety issue in this country. Another example of government, big oil, and railroads continuing to put profits ahead of public safety.*' This catastrophic fire's the immediate issue. Environmental problems from the contamination of benzene, polycyclic aromatic hydrocarbons, and arsenic might pollute the Edwards Aquifer, the 8,800-square-mile underground lake providing water for two million people, including San Antonio, could have a much greater impact."

"Reporting from Agnew, Texas, back to you . . ."

"Hey, Mike . . . Agnew, Texas . . . isn't that where you're from?" Don asked as Mike returned.

Sitting in Don's study, Mike spent the next hour on the phone with his uncle and cousin. "Jack. Just off the phone with your dad. Told me Cindy and the kids, Sammy Joe, Barb, their kids, even Aunt Connie and the whole Müller tribe are all . . ." He took a deep breath, pinching the bridge of his nose as he struggled to continue. This kind of loss was utterly unimaginable. "You, your Mom, Dad, and Grandma are all that are left. Damn. I'm sorry. Said you've been bustin' it building a fire break. Wish I was there—I will be there tomorrow."

"Whole town's gone. Elevator's a shell, south wall of the gym . . ." Jack sighed. "The gin and the first few cotton modules on the yard are gone. It all happened so fast. Heard the first explosion when I was dropping the trailer at your home place. Looked up. Pitch black smoke boilin' straight up. Drove as fast as I could to see if I could help. Everything from the Culpepper place on inta town was on fire. Mike, you can't imagine. Nanaw and Grandpa's house, Aunt Connie's . . . burnin' like candles. I was by their houses within five minutes of the first explosion. They were gone. Fire like you couldn't believe. Half mile, however long the train was. Hot. Loud. Smelled awful. It happened so fast. Pitch black smoke. Couldn't see. Nothing I could do. No town left. Headed to Mom and Dad's and as I passed a burning tank car, whole damn thing explodes, dug a hole twenty feet deep, swallowed the car and the two on either side it. Scared the shit outta me. Lifted the backend of my pickup clear off the ground, shattered the back windshield, slammed my head against the steering wheel. Stunned me for a minute, little pieces of glass cutting my shoulders and back of my head. A minute earlier, it woulda got me . . ." He fell silent.

"I was headed to the airport when the Paris call came in. Ten minutes later and I'd have been on the plane and there with you. We'd have used your trailer and mine. Brought those heifers in yesterday and both been in the gym this morning," Mike said.

"The Bexar County fire guys have given it their best but haven't made a dent," his cousin said, changing the subject. "They're considering dropping retardant from a helicopter. Otherwise, they're guessing it'll take a week to ten days to burn itself out. Built a fire break, patrolling the fields. No need to lose the crops or let it take a pumpjack. This sucks. Smells. Hot. Can't believe the heat. So damn loud. Can't hear yourself think, can't catch your breath, everybody's dead . . ." Jack's voice trailed off again.

"You've got to be exhausted. Your folks, Nanaw, they're looking to you to make it better. Reach out to them. It'll help them and keep you from collapsing from your own loss. Hey, why not bring in truckloads of dirt, fifty, hundred yards back, and push it forward with a dozer or bucket and smother the damn thing? Start on both ends and use the dirt as a heat shield. Ain't even close to high tech, but putting it out has gotta be better than letting it burn. Hundred and fifty, two hundred truck loads and two or three dozers. Bet it'll be out this time tomorrow. It's worth a try. Two hundred loads, a lot cheaper than a helicopter and could have it out before they have the paperwork done."

"Damn, you always come up with a simple solution. I'll talk to the fire marshal soon as we hang up. Been on autopilot. With all there is to do, I haven't even let myself think of Cindy and the kids. Tonight, in my big, old, empty house, gonna be hard . . ." He paused. "It'll be good to see you tomorrow. You lost your family and have gone on to do well. Not sure I'm as strong."

"You are," Mike assured him. "Right now, nothing makes any sense. Everything you believe in has been knocked over. Don't let mortality cripple you, or you can't see what's coming. Your dad sounded okay, but I know it's kicked a hole in his gut. Are your folks and Grandma all right?"

"As good as they can be. Like Dad said, Aunt Connie and all the Müllers were in the gym. They're gone. Good thing Mom brought Grandma over to their place this morning before the pep rally. Can you believe it? She's ninety-six this year, and her world's turned upside down. Both her daughters, all the grandkids and great grandkids gone, 'cept for you and me." Jack tried to be matter of fact. "Can't be more than three or four from her generation left. This may do her in. Everything and everyone she loved . . ."

"I can attest to how hard it is to lose your family. Hadn't been for Toby, you and your folks, it would have been darn near impossible," Mike said. "Where are you now?"

"Headed back to the folks' house, coming back from Carlos and Maria's. The ranking DPS officer, guy named Griffin, and Chief Uribe want several of us to meet at Mom's house in the morning to map out the town and do our best guess on the number of casualties. I may stay there tonight," Jack said.

"We've focused on helping the first responders, trying to stay busy," he continued. "Dad's seventy-five and has spent part of every day for the last sixty-plus years working his land. All he's worked for his entire life has changed forever. He misses you but knows you're doing what you do, and he's proud of ya. But it's our brothers he misses most. They were good farmers. When the reality of this sinks in, it may kill us all," Jack added. "It's like a bully punching you in the gut, watching you gasp for breath and punching you again. Schneider's, Valdez's, your home place, Hettler's, the outlying farms are all that's left. I heard over 860 dead . . . so far."

"You've got to be exhausted. Try to rest," Mike said. "The next weeks to months will be tough. Surprised me, wrapped the Paris attack with the French government this morning. When the game dropped out of the equation, came fishing with a friend. Pretty much out in the boondocks. I'll cut this short and be back in Boise by noon. I'll find a flight and see you tomorrow night. Text you with my flight information."

6

Loss

1930 hrs. MDT Mackay, Idaho
Friday, October 25

The Panamanian-flagged, Singapore-owned ship, *Martina Southampton,* whose cargo included 5,600 tons of ammonium nitrate in 165 containers, docked at the Houston Ship Barbours Cut Container Terminal. Unloaded overnight, it would be refitted in the morning and on its way by noon. Used as a component of fertilizer, the ammonium nitrate—the bills of lading indicated—was bound for commercial nurseries and custom seed producers in Indiana, Tennessee, and Colorado, with significant portions earmarked for the Texas Tech University Agriculture Extension Program and the Iowa State Department of Agriculture. The ship's registration and other papers were in order.

Although Don's dining room could seat twelve, he and Mike ate their now warmed-over dinner while seated on bar stools at the island in the kitchen. Mike, sipping a scotch, picked at his food.

"You know, if the first Paris call had come an hour later, I'd have been on the plane to Texas and in the gym with all the others," he told Don. "I lost sixteen kinsmen today. My ninety-six-year-old grandmother, my aunt, uncle, and a cousin are all that's left. If it's all the same, I'd like to be back in Boise and on to Texas by tomorrow night. Sounds like everything is gone, but I'll want to check fire damage at the cemetery. Our plot includes my great grandparents, my grandfather, my folks, my brother Toby, and Sally and Jessie."

They sat in silence for a few minutes, Mike's mind a million miles away. Discussion over dinner focused on the fire. How could this happen? Was it an accident or a deliberate act?

"Was it as bad as the news made it sound? I can't imagine what it's like to lose the friends and places you grew up with. Must be tough. What's it been, eight or ten years since you lost your wife and baby? Didn't you lose your parents then, too?"

The questions hit him like a slap across the face—more reality than he could process in the moment. A shocked Mike stood abruptly, walked outside and around the outbuildings for fifteen minutes or more. The yard lights led him back to the patio. He sank into a lawn chair.

Don, two glasses of Glenmorangie in hand, joined him. "Mike, I apologize. That was tactless of me. You're a good friend, and what happened in Agnew is unfathomable. I can't believe I was so insensitive."

"I shouldn't have let it get to me. It's been a long day. A long week . . ." Mike's voice sounded low and flat.

A few minutes later, the darkness and the evening chill drove them back inside. Don sought to shift the mood as they settled into easy chairs in the den. "Changing the subject . . . tell me about Maggie. Where'd you meet her? She's a classy lady with an easy, graceful way about her."

"Thanks, she is," agreed Mike, permitting himself a slight smile. "My Dad's sister, Barbara, married Bob Mutschler. They have three boys. As their bachelor uncle, I've spent lots of time with them. Last December, one of their boys married. Maggie is a family friend, and her string quartet provided the music for the wedding. I hosted their reception."

Mike leaned back in his chair, the strain of the day's news easing as he began to wander through older, happier memories. "Maggie and the San Francisco Symphony Music Director met their counterparts with the Boise Philharmonic to share lessons learned for increasing corporate support and expanding their repertoires to include more contemporary music this past May. You first met her when I hosted the four of them, you, and Nancy for dinner at my house. I got the impression it was a positive experience. They've extended an invitation to her to perform . . . Bach's "Cello Suites" and Franz Schubert's "Trio" in . . . umm "E-Flat" for a chamber music concert in January," he said.

"On another positive note, it's been a busy week," Mike continued, the alcohol lowering his guard. "On Tuesday, I received notice from the California Court of Appeals. They found in our favor and upheld our 84.4-million-dollar award from the medical equipment and emergency generator manufacturers in Jessie's case. Our foundation's endowment now exceeds 261 million. I'm confident in the next few years we can grow the permanent fund beyond 400 million. When we do, I'll quit all this and work full time for the foundation."

Turning his chair toward the fireplace, he continued, "I appreciate you serving on the advisory board. The foundation, as you know, is dedicated to research and education and finding applications to complex questions that directly improve people's lives. We need bright guys like you. Guys 'in the trenches' who know the issues and can identify realistic and creative ways to improve. A wise man once told me the best thing to do with money is give it away. If you don't, it's like fertilizer. It piles up and stinks. We have a scientist in San Francisco, who researches the projects you guys suggest. She's current in the scientific literature and does site visits to meet people and comprehend their issues."

"Does she work alone, or does she have a staff?"

"Fair question. My uncle, Bob Mutschler, builds skyscrapers in the Bay area. He serves the foundation as our president and CEO and provides her office space and administrative support. We've funded projects for five years and are pleased with the outcomes."

He continued, "Science is funny. Researchers drift around in deep water without a rudder, believing they're going in a specific direction. One day they stumble onto an unexpected, related finding, and it's not unlike finding dry land; it's a path through the desert. All at once, isolated facts, dissimilar concepts, and ideas running contrary to the logic of the day come together. At once they have a solid footing to build the next step in their search. We want to provide the rudder and help bring their ideas forward for public consumption where they can make a difference. The progress we make won't be left in the ivy halls of academia. Whatever good comes of this will be measured by the impact it has on improving people's lives."

Mike stood and poured himself another eighteen-year-old Glenmorangie. "More?"

"The same," Don said. "Man, it must have been tough, all you've been through. How do you find the courage to care when you've endured all that heartache?"

"Baby Jessie's death has kept me going. I don't ever want another parent to experience what I've gone through. It sucked. It still does. There are times I can't think about her. It hurts too much. It cuts you to the core, makes you come face to face with who you are and your own mortality. You've been a real help. New friends, seeking personal growth, new challenges, sailing, hunting, fishing. I compete with myself and can always do better. It's a choice: grovel in self-pity or make your life have meaning. I'm all that's left to achieve for us. It's why I established the foundation and am dedicated to making this world a better place." Suddenly exhausted, he said, "It's been a long day."

He washed out his glass and headed down the hallway.

7

A Cacophony of Chaos

How Big Is This Thing?

0330 hrs. MDT Moab, Utah
Saturday, October 26

Brought together to fight the Russians in their native Afghanistan, Hashem Nazari, Abed Javadi, and Nifi Mahta met as teenagers. The experience hardened them beyond their years and formed a bond stronger than family. After all their campaigns, hardships, and loss, the three remaining members of their combat group had come together for, what they hoped, would be their last operation.

Nazari flew from Athens, Greece to San Francisco, connecting on to Salt Lake City. Renting an SUV, he drove southeast to Moab and secured a room at the Super 8 Motel. His California driver's license was legal, except the photo was of neither himself nor the victim of the identity theft a year earlier. Javadi had flown from Cairo to Denver and rented a car with the credentials of a man living in San Diego. After driving for over six hours, he registered for the night at the Comfort Inn and Suites in Durango, using another false name. Mahta used yet a third false identification for a flight to Albuquerque and a drive northwest to Farmington, New Mexico, in a rented, blue Nissan pick-up with Colorado license plates.

Each of their remote villages in Afghanistan had received a gift: the restoration of the local Mosque for one, renovations and supplies for their schools for the other two. They practiced their English while memorizing the position and order of the dials and switches on a mockup of the device control panel. They also familiarized themselves with American currency, intending to pay their expenses in cash. Men of honor, they would complete their mission.

Rising at 3:30 am, Nazari found his bearings and prayed:

"Oh Allah, protect me from the front and the back, from my right and from my left and from above, and I seek refuge in Your Magnificence from being swallowed from below."

Annoyed with the overnight snow, Nazari drove to the self-storage unit, entered the access code, moved to unit 312, and loaded two large suitcases. With the help of a dolly, he moved a 320-pound wooden steamer trunk into the SUV. Now empty, he wiped the entire unit for fingerprints, took the lock and pushcart, and left.

Driving southeast from Moab to Durango, he met Abed in the Denny's parking lot at 5:15. Ten miles south of town, they found a dirt road, stopped, unrolled their *namazliks*, and prayed *Fajr*, their remembrance of Allah. They traveled another hour south before meeting Mahta behind the Walmart Supercenter on East Main in Farmington.

The Agnew fire, loss of his bloodline, and little sleep hit Mike hard. Neither he nor Don realized the threat posed by the weather. Heavy snow fell in the higher elevations. The ranch at six thousand feet was surrounded by the White Knob and Lost River Mountains, with towering peaks over a mile above the rooftop.

Don's phone erupted with a piercing sound at 3:47 a.m.

Watch Commander John Tilden had electricity in his voice. "I hate to wake you at this hour, Don, but there have been attacks on the Burlington Northern/Santa Fe and Union Pacific rail lines."

"What? Where?" Don answered in a voice thick with sleep. Sitting on the edge of his bed, he grabbed his glasses and focused on the words of his watch commander.

"BNSF reported a derailment crossing the Lake Pend Oreille Bridge, south of Sandpoint an hour ago. They've identified outages ahead of and behind the derailment. Their equipment's marooned. They lost the engineer and on-board conductor, three engines, and thirty-two of eighty-one cars in eighty to a hundred feet of water."

"Did you call the—" Don began.

John interrupted. "I've already notified our dive team to recover the bodies. They'll start at first light. A Union Pacific train derailed forty-five minutes ago when the engineer was unable to stop as he came on a grade-level bridge with one end destroyed five miles west of Bonners Ferry. I put both ops managers on a conference call; they've shut down operations statewide. They're mobilizing additional personnel and equipment to check for other disruptions. I called NTSB. UP says every grade-level crossing they've encountered has been tampered with. Apparently, the attackers have focused on bridges, overpasses, trestles, anything taking an engine above grade. Don't yet know the extent of it. The director's at the gang violence conference in Boston. You're the senior man. With your permission, I'll mobilize as many men as we can and ask for local law enforcement support in Sandpoint and Bonners Ferry."

With his phone wedged between his ear and his shoulder, Don pulled on his pants as he answered. "You have my authorization and full support. Have the rail guys give you a list of their outages and tell our people to be ready to go at first light. Start with sections accessible by car to get a handle on the scope of this. Have BNSF and UP talk with their counterparts in Utah, Montana, and Washington to see if it's contained here or if we have a national terrorist attack. I'll call the director and have him contact the governor. Sounds like you're on top of it. It'll take me thirty minutes to rouse the troops and be on our way." Don shifted his bleary gaze out the window. "Looks like we got a heck of a snow last night. How's it on your end?"

"Size of the storm surprised everyone. Downed power lines have half the city without power. Upwards of thirty inches in spots between us. Weatherman says the storm's going to intensify and move east. Expected to hit Chicago by Thursday, the East Coast next weekend. Be safe. Lots of unplowed road. We need you here."

Don stood at the bathroom sink, splashing water on his face. "Hope to be in the office by 0900 at the latest. Phone reception is spotty between here and there. Keep me posted. If it's more than a local issue, mobilize as many people as you need. Oh, and John, tell everyone, especially the locals, to treat it all as a crime scene, because it is. Tell 'em to tape it off, not to stomp around in the snow. We'll process everything."

Mike and Don grabbed trail mix, peanut butter crackers, a can full of mixed nuts, apples, and a thermos of hot coffee. Eighteen minutes later, they closed the house. Heavy snow still falling and the Escalade's heater on high and gas tank full, Mike drove the Escalade in four-wheel drive and with the lights on low beam as he pulled away from the house.

Tilden called back, reporting that the railroads had disruptions everywhere they looked, the current count of thirty-four sure to increase. He had mobilized all available personnel and requested that all local authorities in towns across the state join the search. Burlington Northern/Santa Fe and Union Pacific were having similar problems in other states, including the UP loss the day before in Agnew, Texas.

"Haven't had a headache like this in a long time." Don frowned. "If you want me to drive, just say the word. I've had more sleep than you the last two days."

"I'm all right. You'll need space to orchestrate this, but ride shotgun. As hard as it's snowing, an extra pair of eyes is good. Doubt we'll see a car, but won't be surprised at a deer or some other critter. We're not setting any land speed records going back," Mike warned.

Try as they might, there was no reception. Then, Don unexpectedly got through. "Where are we? What's the count? Is it confined to the western states? Is California involved? The coast? Sorry, we hit a dead spot and couldn't make contact. Snowing to beat the band!"

As John Tilden started to speak, the connection dropped off. Seven minutes and four miles later, Don's phone rang. Tilden.

"Bad news. It's a national attack. Texas was the first of many. The Federal Railroad Administration's Positive Train Control System, the national tracking system's been activated. Every train in the country's at a standstill. They've launched a full inspection of all mainline tracks from St. Louis, west."

John's delivery sounded erratic as he pushed forward with the details. "Right now, the east coast doesn't look too involved. Disruptions everywhere north and west of New Mexico have been reported. NTSB, FBI, and Homeland Security are aware. I pulled a big state map into the conference room and have red pins for BNSF, blue for Union Pacific, and green for Amtrak. Our outage count stands at forty-six, but it could expand into the hundreds. Besides Sandpoint and Bonners Ferry, we have interruptions along the south route via McCammon, the east fork, Pocatello to Dubois, and west American Falls all the way to Caldwell. This was a coordinated attack. We have unsubstantiated reports that Long Beach, LA Port, Los Angeles, San Francisco, and Seattle have all been hit. Apparently, they've tried to close east-west traffic nationwide. Be safe, but hurry!"

"Coming as fast as we can. This snow is fierce. I'm sure there'll be a lot of residue from the explosion sites. Identify one or two of the more promising sites, and have our forensic team start processing at first light, even in the snow. There may be residual particulate matter trapped by the snowfall. I talked to the director; he'll call the governor. Expect to hear from him. It's snowing hard. It'll be later than nine before we get back."

"Be safe. I'll keep you posted."

"Will do, thanks." Hanging up, Don turned to Mike. "You're not gonna believe this . . ."

8

TLS, The Three-Legged Stool

1130 hrs. CET Salzburg, Austria
Saturday, October 26

Outside the downtown Salzburg sandwich shop, the gusting wind, dim light, and steady rain made the fifty-one-degree temperature feel like sub-zero weather. Inside, Omar Saleh, a medium-sized, swarthy-complected man with wide eyes peering out behind steel-rimmed glasses, sat across from his contact in a booth at the back of the depleted sandwich shop where a few midmorning weekend tourists had braved the brisk weather. At the corner of the bar, within earshot, Jamal Shehadi, executive director of TLS, an international money laundering organization, sat in a booth and read the *Financial Times*, a cold glass mug of golden yeasty liquid in front of him.

Although not a native speaker, the contact, a dour and imposing man, spoke clear English. "A million, two fifty. Euros, five and a half percent, three days."

"Euros, five and a half, four days. The local bank is being audited. Can't risk using them," Omar countered.

"Need it in three days. What can you do?"

"Six and an eighth, euros. Our Bangkok bank, tomorrow late."

"Done. Not happy with the rate. Still, time's critical this time around," the contact conceded.

"We'll make it up to you when the local bank audit is complete."

"I know you will. What's it been, fourteen years we've used you? You've always been fair."

"We have a new counting place. The Schwannhein Chocolate Shop on Zugallistrasse. Ask for Tobias. I'll let them know you're on your way. What currency is it in now?" Omar queried.

"Small denominations of Ukrainian hryvnia, Turkish lira, Georgian lari, and Armenian dram."

"We'll pay the exchange rates into euros."

"Good to see you, Omar. You've got capable people, but it's good you work in the field. It keeps you connected to what's going on." The client smiled as he rose to leave.

Dozens of similar transactions were taking place in Salzburg and in hundreds of other cities throughout Europe, Asia, Mexico, and Central and South America. Later, among the thousands of separate transactions in fifteen Salzburg banks, 9.8 million dollars were deposited and transferred to the CTE Banka CZ, a leading Czech Republic commercial bank. The next morning, 1.25 million dollars transferred, bank to bank, to a Vietnamese bank in Hanoi and on to the second largest bank in Bangkok. Fee extracted, the remainder was exchanged into euros and held for retrieval by the client's designee.

Jamal and Omar had started the day in Innsbruck and would leave Salzburg on separate trains for Vienna and a meeting with Jamal's cousin, Parsa Shehadi. Although their organizational responsibilities were at the highest level, they made a point of working in the field at least once a month. Jamal had shadowed this client for an hour prior to his meeting with Omar to ensure there was no compromise. He observed their transaction from the bar two booths away and then followed the client to the bus stop, watching him board. Entering the corner pastry shop, he bought a croissant and black coffee before sitting at a window table to read his incoming email message:

> "Geraldo Lucero, our Barcelona conduit for funds from Spain, Portugal, and Morocco, has put his hand in the till for more than $600K this quarter. $238K for a yacht, an anniversary present for his parents. Remaining funds in three Portuguese and one Brazilian bank. Will extract money from them tonight. Sufficient funds to cover the cost of yacht and our efforts to untangle his mess. Will recover them as well."

The email from Nandi Zola, cybersecurity and communications chief for

TLS, came via their high-speed onion routing at the network layer, (HORNET) VPN, and a twenty-first century software upgrade to the electro-mechanical rotor cipher device based on the World War II German Enigma capable of detecting any unauthorized activity. HORNET was secret, anonymous, encrypted and routed through multiple destinations, making it nigh impossible to know where messages originated. They suspected US authorities were aware of TLS, but they made a point not to provide them with any reason to initiate an active investigation.

"Thank you. I'll take care of his transgression." Jamal pressed the send button.

9

Race Day

0630 hrs. EDT Dover, Delaware
Saturday, October 26

The antique school clock on the Dover Mayor's office wall clanged at 6:30, forty-five minutes into the morning meeting. Finishing his report of the first day's activities of the International Speedway's NASCAR Xfinity Series three-day event, the Police Chief recounted, "At 9:36 yesterday morning, Event Security discovered a brown paper bag in a stall in the men's restroom in Section 245 of the Earnhardt Grandstands. He called for backup from a uniformed officer, who cordoned off the zone while the State Police Bomb Squad removed the item. Late last night, the white powdery substance was determined to be a combination of powdered sugar, granular sugar, salt, and talcum power. Someone's sick idea of a joke. No fingerprints, no witnesses, chances of finding the culprit are slim to none. Other than that, it was a good first day. Twenty-nine drunk and disorderly, two broken car windows, fifteen misplaced phones, pretty routine."

"Thanks. How about you?" the mayor asked, turning to his Director of Public Works. "Have all your volunteers and weekend part timers shown up? Be succinct, please."

"A good first day, Mayor."

"What's your day look like?" the mayor then asked the Operations Director for the Dover International Speedway.

"Bank deposit last night was a record first day for any event ever here at the Speedway. From the 11:00 practice through the Series Qualifying starting at 12:10, to the start of the race at 3:30, we'll be hustling. Tom, you and your team do a great job of working with the drivers and keeping this circus on schedule," he concluded, pointing to the Director of NASCAR operations.

"Thank you all. A few of our city leaders argue the Speedway attracts rowdy drunks and caters to a bad element. We host over a hundred and sixty thousand people when the Speedway hosts this event. I assure you, the City Council, county officials, and I recognize the economic impact of the races, and we continue to find ways to make the events as safe and fan friendly as possible. Let's go out and have another great day. I'll see you here again in the morning."

The sun began its ascent as Nazari, Javadi, and Mahta drove west to Shiprock and on toward Kayenta. Winding dirt roads splintered off the state highway and snaked across the snow-dusted, rugged high plateau of the reservation. They were beyond the limits of normal government control where Navajo life moved at a pace and manner unique unto itself. The seductive silence of the region was broken by the road noise of their car as they made their way to Tuba City and north toward Page. They, and an occasional soaring red-tailed hawk looking for an easy meal, constituted the sole activity in this vast, frosted land awakening to a cerulean autumn sky.

They drove on in the empty, majestic landscape of gray and brown solitude spotted with juniper and sage. The terrain, reminiscent of the landscape in their native Afghanistan, took Nazari back to the night he and his younger sister escaped the Russians. He was eight when the Russians bombed the mosque in their village and ground troops swept the zone, killing everyone in the village, including his grandparents, parents, and older brothers. They'd fled by hiding in the rubble of the mosque. Barefoot with no coats, they waited until dark before starting toward the next village. A mile and a half into their journey, they again hid as a Russian armored convoy approached. Scared, tired, cold, and hungry, they spent the remainder of the night huddled together in a ravine half a mile off the road. At daybreak, a Mujahedin soldier found them. Weapon slung over his shoulder, the soldier carried his sister and held his hand, taking them to the base. Nazari remembered the fear in his sister's eyes as she cried when the soldier handed her to a comrade and left to find them a hot meal.

"You're safe now," the first soldier told them, returning with rice cakes and water.

Through the end of the war with Russia, Nazari stayed with the Mujahedin, who stayed on to fight the Taliban and the Americans. Then, he returned to his village.

Cresting a rise in the road, a mud-spattered older red pickup approached. Its driver, an aged Native American, whose long silver braid hung from under his straw cowboy hat, stared straight ahead, never acknowledging their car as they passed by.

"We go to jihad, not because we want to fight," Nazari whispered. "We're compelled for the sake of Islam and serve a mission greater than ourselves. Allah has chosen us to carry the fight to the crusaders, Jews, and infidels."

He exuded a quiet confidence his comrades tried to emulate as they struggled to stay their anxiety. Dawn came, and with it the call to prayer. Selecting a random dirt road, they traveled beyond the highway's line of sight, stopped, waited, and prayed the *Dhuhr*. Remembering Allah and seeking His guidance, they concluded with the traditional, *"Al-Salamu alaykum wa rahmatu Allah wa barakatu."*—Peace and Allah's mercy and blessings be upon you, uttered twice, once to the left and once to the right.

10

Eller

0730 hrs. EDT Washington D.C.
Saturday, October 26

At seven-thirty on a Saturday morning in Washington D.C., politicians, bureaucrats, and most civil servants were gone for the weekend. The rail system attack had brought David Eller, special assistant to the Chairman of the Joint Chiefs of Staff at the Pentagon, and his team to work, perhaps for the duration of the weekend. Pulled into intelligence and counterintelligence in the last president's first term, his team had free rein to cross departmental boundaries and access any data to predict international terrorism's next move.

No fewer than fifteen of David Eller's white papers had landed on the president's desk, unedited. Bright, hardworking, dedicated to a fault, he and his team were America's best information technology hope in the war on terrorism. He'd tracked bin Laden and had him in his sights three times. Unfortunately, others failed to pull the trigger.

Following September 11, 2001, Eller had been tasked to look beyond the devastation and decipher bin Laden's message—his long-term goals. This morning, he and his team hoped to sort out the *why*, hoping it might narrow the field of the *who*. Tenacity paid off. For these cowards, time would be limited.

In the time it took to put an end to bin Laden, Al Qaeda became the bad apple spoiling the whole bunch. Proving feasibility, they demonstrated how a world power could be engaged in long-term battle on the terms of a minor assailant capable of gaining notoriety, public support, and financial backing. It gave birth to many bastard children, not the least of which was ISIS.

At the request of the Secretary of Homeland Security, David assembled a "shopping list" of potential soft targets, including several key power plants; the ports in New York, Los Angeles, and Houston; large city airports; major amusement and theme parks; and events drawing large crowds like auto races and college football games.

His response to the secretary's late Thursday afternoon call concerning the ongoing unrest throughout the Middle East resulted in the secretary's Friday-morning news conference warning: "The national security threat level continues to be high risk. Our intelligence community believes international terrorists have entered a new operational period. The terrorist attacks Tuesday in Paris, Wednesday in Quezon City, the Philippines, and yesterday in Munich, were strikes on societal infrastructure. While we have no credible information with respect to specific targets, the potential use of weapons of mass destruction cannot be discounted. The decision to continue the high-risk security level is based on phone and data transmissions intercepted by the intelligence agencies who monitor these activities."

David was troubled by the developing news of trains being derailed or marooned across the western half of the country, the action intended to prolong the delivery of transcontinental goods and increase their cost. He also recalled the testimony of Major General Robert Isom, special liaison to the CIA, to the subcommittee briefing of the Senate Armed Services Committee earlier in the week. In his summary of the former USSR nuclear arsenal, the general told them most of the arsenal remained in Georgia, Chechnya, and Siberia. Among those items of concern, however, were twelve "suitcase" bombs—nuclear devices named for their small size. General Isom explained his intelligence indicated the bombs had been converted from uranium to plutonium, reducing their weight by more than one hundred pounds, while retaining destructive capability two-thirds that of the bomb dropped on Hiroshima. They fit in a traditional steamer trunk and weighed upwards of two hundred fifty pounds. Two were unaccounted for.

Closing his news conference, the secretary said, "We must consider that we live in an open society. While it has its benefits, this puts us at greater risk for those bent on doing us harm. People should not change or disrupt plans over the weekend, but vigilance at large public events or other locations where crowds gather is our best deterrent against possible terrorist aggression. If you see something, say something. We will not be deterred by cowardice."

The secretary did not voice the fears he shared with David Eller.

The United States was next, and next could be measured in hours, not days or weeks.

With game-time temperature expected in the mid-thirties and wind gusts of twenty-five miles per hour, Ann Arbor, Michigan was awash in maize and azure blue with an occasional showing of crimson and silver. Campus excitement was contagious, building all week for this encounter with their biggest rival. The bands, the colors, and the pageantry were on full display for the lead game on ESPN's tripleheader national lineup.

Zahi Mansour and his party meandered past the front desk. He had waited until 0620 to check out of this modest Detroit hotel. The night clerk, a new employee just arrived from Haiti three weeks ago, wanted as little contact as possible with the clientele. Should she be asked questions in the days to come, Mansour knew she would confuse the issue.

His team member had inserted a twenty-four-hour loop on the lone surveillance camera in the lobby. Activity nonexistent. Five days earlier, he'd paid cash in advance for a room with two double beds. He checked the final bill. No calls, minibar, or other ancillary charges. No evidence of his two colleagues.

Ten days ago, the two pilots had flown from Istanbul to Mexico City and on to Montreal. At a safe house in Toronto, they spent their time studying drone launch operations and prayer. They had prepared, practiced, revised, and practiced again. Successful completion of any strategic operation required planning, timing, and execution, every detail considered.

The day before yesterday, Mansour had met them in Windsor, Ontario. Providing valid passports and driver's licenses, he presented his and their documents and his well-used, pre-paid Ambassador Bridge Reward Card to the Canadian official before driving across the bridge and into Detroit. Yesterday, they'd inspected the launch site, tested the high pressure, lightweight, plastic canisters, installed them on the drone wings and performed in-depth maintenance checks. He had texted his coordinator with their status.

This morning, after months of training and preparation, they were headed to launch one hundred and eighty miles north. Mansour and the pilots reviewed the plan one final time as they studied their maps, recalculated their distances, and reviewed the latest weather conditions, including wind speeds and directions. Stopping in Standish for gas, they made the trip to the south side of Loud Dam Pond in the Huron National Forest in two hours and forty-five minutes. Pulling off State Road 65, they stopped behind two box trucks. Greeted by five men from the trucks, the eight men unloaded the 20 by 28 by 4-foot, half-ton Searchers and readied them for takeoff. Today would be a day people remembered, a day when preparation met opportunity. Today would change the course of nations.

The first pilot used his hand-held controller to launch his aircraft into the wind, the 47-horsepower piston engine powering it thirteen hundred feet skyward in less than a quarter of a mile. Two minutes later, its companion joined. Their bluish and off-white underbellies made them invisible from the ground on this clear day. Anyone not witnessing the event was unaware it had taken place. Soaring to 2,600 feet and turning east, the lead drone was soon over Lake Huron's Saginaw Bay. Its companion, three minutes and three-quarters of a mile to the west, mirrored the path of its predecessor. They would modulate between 2,100 and 2,800 feet and stay off Detroit Metro Airport radar throughout the duration of their mission.

The rhythmic vibrations of their engines returned them over land east of Bay City. Cruising at 110 miles per hour, their computer navigated southern paths, keeping above dairy farms and cash crops of soybeans, corn, and wheat, expecting to make their target in ninety minutes.

Coach White's defensive line, averaging six feet eight inches in height and 322 pounds, the "big uglies" as they called themselves, had finished breakfast, watched some game film, done their stretching exercises, and gone to the locker room for pregame taping of ankles and knees.

It gave Paul White, their position coach, the only thirty-minute break he'd have until after the game. Grabbing his cellphone, he called his old Army buddy in San Antonio whose son was in Ann Arbor on a recruiting trip. "Bobby Joe? Bobby Joe Crutcher? Hey! Paul White. This has gotta be quick. Last time I talked to you, you were boardin' that C-130 Hercules, haulin' outta Kabul and back to Texas. How the hell are ya?"

"Damn you, you Mississippi mud rat, how the hell are ya? Whatcha been up to? Ya ever find the football team ya always wanted to coach? Reckon if ya did, you'd be coachin' 'em up, not callin' me."

"Matter of fact, it's part of why I'm callin'. I'm the D-line coach here at Michigan, and I spent a good bit of time yesterday afternoon with Billy Joe," Coach White said.

"I'll be . . . Put him on the airplane yesterday, no idea you were there. Damn long way from home. Momma's not too keen on him going there. She won't git ta see him play every Saturday 'cept on TV."

"Didn't tell him you and I go way back. I could tell he's got a lot of his old man in him. Damn good work ethic. I'll pass it on to the other coaches. We need kids like him here. Finding a kid with good football skills is one thing, finding one who has 'em and strong character's somthin' else. Can't measure heart lookin' at film! It sure as hell makes a difference in the weight room, which translates to the fourth quarter when you gotta have a stop or need two yards to punch it in. If he's anything like you, he's a kid I'd climb in a foxhole with! You've fed him a little 'grow pup'; he's got good size. We'll put meat on those bones and make him into a hell of a football player."

"Michigan . . . ya got to the big time after all. Bet it's a little nippy on your Mississippi ass in the middle of winter. Ya like shovelin' snow?" Crutcher laughed.

"No! And the wife's on me pretty hard to find something closer to home. You? Billy Joe said you're still kicking through the woods with nothing but your Bowie knife."

"Yeah, well, there're a lot of crazies out there, Al Qaeda, the North Koreans. The damn Jews and Arabs pissin' in each other's canteens. Hell, a neighbor's kid gets on the internet, next thing you know he's killing everybody at the movie house or the school. Can't be too careful. Something stupid happens, I want me and mine to have a place to go and a way to survive till all the shit settles. Who knows, a few days, a few weeks, a year or two? Don't want to be a statistic because a bonehead idiot gets up in the morning, has a bowl of stupid fer breakfast and does something dumb! Don't have all the answers, wanna be as prepared as we can. If we've got thirty minutes warning, we'll be out and on our way. Our place's self-sustainable for six months or more depending on the weather."

"Don't disagree, never have," White commiserated. "It's been a little tougher doing what I do, moving from team to team. I hear you. Listen, gotta get 'em dressed and out on the field to get loose. Then back to the locker room for one last chat 'em up to make sure these guys are ready for the Buckeyes. Need to run, I'll be up in the press box. Look for Billy Joe behind our bench and along the sideline. We'll talk after the game. Wish us luck."

11

Honeybees

0645 hrs. MDT Mackay, Idaho
Saturday, October 26

The snow, dropping at a rate of a foot an hour, severely curtailed the Escalade's progress. Two hundred yards ahead of them, Don and Mike watched a mother elk and her calf cross the road, move into the heavily forested tree line on the other side, and disappear. Don brought Mike up to speed regarding the numbers and locations of rail displacements, then got back on the phone with John Tilden, using the SUV's Wi-Fi connection and speaking through the Escalade's booming audio system.

"Don, Captain Tucker in Sandpoint called. They destroyed the south end bridge abutments and two trestles in the middle of the lake. He walked the vicinity, found a bundle of eight sticks of dynamite, and secured the zone. He took a bunch of pictures of how it was positioned and put together. He's deactivated it, dusted it for fingerprints, and is on his way to us."

"Let's meet him, and your guys can send it to Salt Lake and the Feds this afternoon," Mike suggested.

"You're a good man and a good friend but you're a civilian. I can't ask you to take that chance. Besides, if we do, you won't get to Texas till tomorrow," Don protested.

Mike's eyes widened as he fixed them on Don. "I may be a civilian, but I'm an American civilian, and America was attacked. Like everybody else, I want to do whatever I can to catch these guys. We're in this together."

"You sure you're okay with this?"

"It's going to be a long, complex case, and a break like this could help. Let's go."

"John, we'll head his way. Touch base with our forensics guys. We may need them this morning," Don said.

"Not sure where you are. I'm guessing three, three and a half hours southeast of him," Tilden replied. "He's headed south. I'll have him meet you at the coffee shop next to the Farm, Feed and Seed on Highway 95, south of Grangeville. I'll text you his mobile number."

"If this is the lone dud, out of three or four hundred or whatever the total number, it's pretty tight quality control. Why'd it fail? Was it the fuse, the timer, what? Coordination of the entire effort, the explosion in Texas—this much destruction—required a small army," Don mused.

"These are smart guys. Sandpoint's a mistake, and I'm betting we find more along the way; we always do. Lots of people means lots of opportunity for miscues. We need to buckle down, follow the evidence to catch 'em. I want to be there when we do," Mike said between gulps of coffee. "With luck, we can find a lot number or other means of identifying the explosives. How do you generate so much destructive power distributed over such a wide expanse in weather like this? How big an army did it take? My money is on a single fabrication site and transporting them to distribution centers. Last night's conversations are still a bit fuzzy for both of us. Remember talking about honeybees?" Mike asked.

"Honeybees? What do they have to do with anything?"

Shifting his weight behind the wheel, he looked at his friend. "Our foundation got involved with honeybees because a third of what we eat is dependent on pollinators—bees, butterflies, wasps, and their kind. A few years back, it looked like we might lose a high percentage of our honeybee population. They're fascinating little creatures and more capable than you might think. Everyone's heard of drug-sniffing dogs. They're good, but it turns out honeybees do a better job. They've also been trained to find explosives."

Closing his eyes and rubbing his forehead, Don responded, "Don't know what's worse—the pounding in my head from the scotch or from all this destruction. You thought Paris was a new level. After this, those guys look like pikers. I doubt these guys will be as easy to find."

"If my hard-drinking days weren't already behind me, this would do it," Mike said. "This much scotch and this little sleep—haven't had a combination like this since high school. The night we won the football state championship. Next morning, no lecture from Dad. He started me at daybreak. I dug post holes by hand till sundown. Lesson learned."

"Listen," Don said, his voice tense. "All this destruction's taken place between midnight and three this morning. What's the count, forty-odd derailments here in Idaho? And the other states. This is massive. They had staging units. Let's say the entire effort was coordinated from Boise. You couldn't run from there to Sandpoint with all those stops and back to Boise. From there to Blackfoot and on to Dubois with fifteen or twenty stops and back to Boise. Do the same from Boise to Salt Lake and back all in one or two days or even a week. The distances are too great. Hardware store timers max out at seven days, so unless they used expensive timers or GPS detonators, they had to get it all done in a week."

"Or," Mike countered, looking over at him, "they daisy-chain it all. Store it at stations along the way and have runners plant the explosives between depots and move on."

"Makes sense," Don said.

"We do lots of modeling to determine where to look when a client's been hacked. We can identify the cities with the highest probability of having been dynamite storage depots. From there we can look for public storage units and abandoned warehouses, places where boxes can be stored without calling attention. The foundation has funded more than a little work on honeybees. I'll call our researchers and see what it'll take to train the bees and fly them here. If we can identify the cities and locate the staging zones, maybe we find fingerprints, get a composite sketch of one or two people, a license plate number. Just another suggestion from that same old civilian."

"Slow down, civilian," Don interjected. "It's a good idea. I'll need to generate the paperwork before we can buy the bees."

"They'll be my gift to the Idaho State Police Department. If it works—the sooner, the better. It's an olfactory function. They've gotta sniff the explosive. Time is not our friend."

"You're sure they have a better success rate than dogs?" Don asked.

"I'll show you the published studies in the scientific journals. My concern is tricking them to work in the snow," Mike assured him.

"Okay, call your guys. You work on where we should start. We'll do the same and compare notes. How many teams do you want to start with?

"Let's look at the map in your conference room. I'll talk to the bee guys. I'm betting on six or eight to start. If I remember, the bees can be trained in four to six hours. They put them in little plastic holders. A positive response is sticking out their tongues. I saw a demonstration last year in Florida. Today's Saturday. I bet we can have 'em in Boise by tomorrow afternoon, ready to go Monday morning. Work for you?"

"You're on. If your beekeeper guy can show our guys what to do, we'd be better served with just uniforms at a self-storage unit asking to look around. It's liable to take a week to ten days to complete this. Can your beekeepers keep them warm, healthy, and fed?" Don asked as the snow intensified.

"Good question. They'll bring whatever is needed to keep them going. They'll train your officers, bring extra bees, and stay in Boise to answer any questions, go to a site, or replace bees as needed. If this works, we've got lots of other states to work."

Focused on the road, his mind racing, Mike made the first of three calls.

"Hey, Jack." He paused to question his word choice. "I know you're busy, but have you heard about the other train derailments? Agnew wasn't a freak accident but the beginning of an all-out attack."

"What are you saying?" Jack answered. "What other track derailments? Unless it's happened within a three-mile radius of where I'm standing, I've got no clue."

"Overnight, every state west and north of you experienced hundreds of track displacements. A train got dropped into a lake here in Idaho. There are stranded Amtrak passengers all over the region, and they're trying to work out how to rescue them off the trains. Union Pacific and BNSF are focused on recovering their marooned engineers, equipment, and loads. The Feds aren't sure if it's impacted the Midwest or east coast yet. Transcontinental rail traffic is a mess."

Jack took a deep breath as he contemplated this new information. "Damn. Lotta deaths or mostly equipment? Since they've stopped all the trains, reckon the flights will follow?"

"So far, it's equipment. No flight announcement, but I'd imagine you're right. If so, it may mess with my Texas plans. Told you I'm fishing with a friend. He's Deputy Director of the Idaho State Police. He's trying to get his arms around this here in Idaho and the surrounding states. We're headed back to Boise with a side trip to retrieve a dud explosive bundle. Snowin' to beat the band. Hope to be back by one. If the planes haven't been grounded, I should be at your house by 9:30 your time tonight."

"Believe me, you'll be a sight for sore eyes. Come to the folks' house. It'll be good for Nanaw; you and I are all she's got right now. It's begun to sink in. For her and my folks, the pain is unbearable. Nanaw's saying she has no reason to live, and Dad's worked all these years to build a strong future for Sammy Joe and me and our kids. Now, everyone's gone." He paused briefly. "The head Bexar County fire guy liked your idea and brought in three bulldozers, an excavator, two front-end loaders, and three dump trucks. Had over sixty loads by 4:30 this morning and began pushing. It works. Like you said: dirt soaks the oil. More dirt, no oxygen, and bingo, the fire's out!"

"Great. Maybe it'll be out in a few days."

"Or sooner, we hope. Brought in generators and lights and going to run till it's out. Hopefully, late tomorrow afternoon," Jack said. "Got a project for you. Carlos Valdez's wife, Maria, was on her way back from her sisters' laundry in Pearsall with the team's jerseys when she was run off the road five miles west of the rail crossing. Told me it was a new, dark blue Toyota Camry with a green license plate with a white number six and the letter T in the middle. She's sure of the make because her sister has the same car. She didn't recognize the driver or the car. Doesn't think either are local. It may not be the kind of stuff your computers can track, but it may have been the guy who derailed the train."

"I'll have our guys look at it this morning. Make sure tha—" The call dropped. "Damn mountains," Mike groused as he glanced over at Don, who smiled and shrugged.

12

May Allah Be Pleased

0745 hrs. PDT Los Angeles, California
Saturday, October 26

Working non-stop for the last thirty-six hours, Niousha Rostami could feel the stress knotting her neck and shoulder muscles. In the passenger seat of a car in front of the Stingray Hotel in suburban Los Angeles, she sat for a moment, eyes closed, taking deep purposeful breaths as she flashed back to Ana Shehadi's house when they were high school seniors.

Inseparable from the third grade, they'd been in Ana's room as she relayed her father's challenge for her and her cousin Jamal to study in America and Europe and develop a plan to reestablish Persia as the leader of the Middle East. Ana had wanted to please her father and talked him into giving Niousha a role—long ago, yet it seemed like yesterday. Would Allah be pleased? Would Ana's and her efforts be recognized and open doors for women in the new Persia?

In March, she and her team had begun identifying major east-west rail routes. At each stop, they took dozens of digital photographs, made note of hotels, public storage units, and fast-food locations. By June, target location schedules, overnight accommodations, and storage locations were finalized. In August she was on the road, often with a U-Haul trailer, renting public storage units and placing file boxes full of four, six, and eight stick bundles of TNT brought from Los Angeles in each.

In the past six months, she'd also been to Washington D.C., New York, Detroit, Ann Arbor, Dover, Houston, and Page. She and her team leaders reviewed plans and made sure every resource needed was in place. She had received status updates from every team leader over the last four hours. All was on schedule. She prayed for Allah's guidance and that, when the sun set, he would be pleased.

Acting on an anonymous tip, the Coast Guard, DEA, and Houston Police boarded the *Rio Chartrus* out of Caracas, Venezuela, docked at the adjacent berth to the *Martina Southampton*. Their search uncovered 1,500 kilos of heroin with a street value in the hundreds of millions of dollars while massive thirty-story cranes off-loaded the last of 159 ammonium nitrate containers from the *Martina Southampton*. The containers, many double-decked, were loaded onto Port Terminal Railroad Association flat cars to be added to trains for destinations throughout the country.

On trailers stationed on the loading dock, cranes placed five of the remaining six containers awaiting their tractors and transport to their final destinations. A single ammonium nitrate container remained in the hold of the *Martina Southampton*.

13

Moving Parts

1045 hrs. EDT New York City, New York
Saturday, October 26

Jim and Ole Mae Bergsten had been up since their customary six in the morning. After breakfast, Jim had filled the auxiliary tank on the back of his flatbed truck with gas and had driven it and an ice chest full of cold, bottled water to the men working the fire break. Ole Mae had turned the volume up on the television in the living room and was busy in her kitchen, baking a coffee cake and an apple pie for the meeting she would host later today with several couples, the ranking DPS, and fire officers as they tried to determine those who had perished.

"Good morning, and welcome to this special news bulletin from *CBS News*. I'm Celest Velasco in New York. Overnight, thousands of rail bridges, overpasses, and trestles were destroyed across the western third of the country. At this time, it does not appear the eastern seaboard has been impacted.

"The White House is calling this a terrorist attack but has yet to determine those responsible. The president was awakened this morning at 6:00 a.m. and apprised of the attack. Already moved to a safe location because of the assassination attempt, she is scheduled to return to the White House later today. For more on that, here is White House correspondent, Carson Harper."

Standing in front of the J. Edgar Hoover Building, Harper began his report: "Celest, at a news conference this morning, FBI Director Ferguson Townsend stated the attempt on the president's life, the derailment and fire which destroyed the town of Agnew, Texas, yesterday, and the overnight destruction to our rail system are related acts of terrorism representing an increased level of devastation previously unknown to this country. He compared them to Tuesday's attack on the power grid in Paris, saying these attacks are not the work of one or two people targeting a specific location. Instead, they're designed to impact entire nations. In each case, these efforts required extensive planning, significant use of sophisticated technology, substantial funding, and, in the case of last night's attack, many, many people.

"He warned that, as officials continue to search, the number of outages is bound to increase. Union Pacific and BNSF, our nation's two largest rail carriers, appear to have suffered the heaviest damage. UP has called crews in from their yards in North Platte, Nebraska, North Little Rock, Arkansas, and Rochelle, Illinois, to assist their crews in Roseville, California, and Hinkle, Oregon. The remoteness of several affected areas and the possibility of additional snow could delay the start of repairs, pushing them back until spring next year. The National Weather Service predicts an increased probability of another snowstorm in the higher elevations of Idaho and Montana, moving southeast starting Monday. Celest, back to you."

"Carson, thanks." Celeste turned her gaze back to the camera. "Los Angeles' heavily used Alameda Corridor, the 20-mile-long freight rail system connecting the ports of Los Angeles and Long Beach to the major rail system near downtown, suffered extensive damage in the attacks. Much of it is below-grade, double-track main line. In more than sixty instances, the walls of the ten-mile-long Mid-Corridor Trench that's thirty-three feet deep and fifty feet wide were smashed. For a report on this, we take you there with CBS correspondent, Allyson Ulam."

Standing beside El Segundo Boulevard, yellow crime scene tape and one end of a train overpass crashed onto the highway behind her, Allyson spoke, "Thank you, Celest. It's eerie standing here this morning. No traffic. The silence is deafening, and the smell like following the deliberate demolition of an old high rise. The Port of Los Angeles and the Port of Long Beach serve as major automobile receiving centers for the Asian automotive industry and the primary ports of entry for most goods entering this country from Asia and the Pacific Rim.

"Until last night, the Alameda Corridor was among the most efficient cargo distribution centers in the world. Unfortunately, the overnight attacks destroyed much of it, and the junction where Amtrak and the Metrolink passenger train lines cross the Corridor freight trackage has been rendered inoperable. Authorities tell me it will be at least a year before this interchange can be functional again.

"Most of the twenty-nine vehicular traffic bridges and two freight rail crossings for east and westbound streets spanning the fifty-foot-wide Mid-Corridor Trench between State Route 91 and 25th Street have received heavy damage and are impassable. The Corridor was built to improve access to the San Pedro Bay port cluster, which handles almost 70% of the American West Coast containerized traffic. Last night's extensive damage will favor shifts toward the Port of New York/New Jersey and the Port of Savannah, the Port of Houston, and Lázaro Cárdenas on Mexico's Pacific Coast. An NTSB official told me reconstruction costs will likely be in the billions, while the economic impact will start in the trillions. Celest."

"Thank you, Allyson."

Celest continued her broadcast as a video of a train hauling oil, automobiles, and containers was shown on the screen. "The nation's economy relies on our rail system to serve a wide variety of shippers in all industries. The industry transports over 1.2 billion tons—totaling 40% of the nation's trade goods every year. Unlike other modes of transportation, US railroads own and maintain their rights of way and are responsible for improving their infrastructure and expanding capacity as needed. The industry has invested an estimated fifty billion dollars in the past ten years to maintain and expand track, yards, and terminals. They've also invested in new technology and newer, more fuel-efficient locomotives to reduce greenhouse emissions while reducing the cost of transporting the nation's goods."

"Joining me now from Washington is Dr. Brent Middleton, a transportation expert with the Brookings Institute. Dr. Middleton, can you tell us what the economic impact of these attacks might be?"

"The final estimated cost of the work stoppage at the Port in Los Angeles back in 2002 was put at forty-five billion dollars. The walkout lasted 10 days, impacting incoming goods at the port. Here, California and the western states are cut off from the rest of the nation. The economic impact will be overwhelming."

"Excuse me, Dr. Middleton. This just in from KRQE, our CBS affiliate in Albuquerque. Joining us live, reporter Doug Segura."

"Thank you, Celest," Segura said as the image cut to him. "New Mexico State Police report an explosive device consisting of eight sticks of TNT bound together with twine, a detonator, and timing device have been recovered along Union Pacific's Sunset Route east of the southwestern town of Deming. An FBI forensic team from Albuquerque is enroute. Apparently, this explosive bundle is like one found earlier this morning in northern Idaho.

"The discovery of this second bundle begs the question of how many others have yet to be discovered. More importantly, how many may go undiscovered? If they didn't explode, why not? And might they in the future? Even after the rail lines are rebuilt, how safe will they be?

"From Albuquerque, Doug Segura, back to you."

"Thank you, Doug," Celest said as the camera cut to a split screen with her and Dr. Middleton at his home.

"We're back now with Dr. Brent Middleton with information on the projected economic impact."

"Yes, thank you. We export over twelve million tons of coal from the Powder River Basin in Wyoming and Montana to South Korea, Japan, India, China, and dozens of other countries annually. The current selling price is thirteen dollars per ton with a projected delivery cost of PRB coal at seventy-seven dollars per ton. As of this morning, activity is at a standstill. This is one example of the thousands of products dependent upon rail for their transportation. Until the rail issues can be resolved, it will be impossible to estimate the overall economic impact, but it's safe to say it will be in the trillions of dollars."

"Thank you, Dr. Middleton."

Looking directly into the camera, Celest Velasco continued, "The Office of Homeland Security has established a telephone hotline for anyone who may have seen or heard anything or might have additional information regarding those responsible for this attack." She read aloud the phone number to call, then said, "We'll broadcast it across the bottom of the screen for the remainder of the day.

"We're told the president will address the nation at 12:30 eastern standard time, 11:30 central today. We, of course, will bring it to you in its entirety, starting at 12:15. Following the address, we'll be bringing you CBS's NCAA College Football doubleheader, beginning with the Georgia-Florida State game from Tallahassee, followed by the Oregon-Washington State game from Autzen Stadium in Eugene. Stay tuned to this CBS station for continuing coverage of these events. This has been a *CBS News* Special Report. I'm Celest Velasco in New York, returning you to your regularly scheduled programming."

Still in her apron, Ole Mae washed her flour sifter, rolling pin, and mixing bowl and set them to dry on her clean countertop. The pie in the oven; the coffee cake ready to bake, she cleared off her table, counted her chairs and the number of expected guests to ensure everyone would have a seat, set out a new tablecloth, and dusted the family picture that hung on the wall at the end of the room.

Thirty minutes before kickoff, both teams' pre-game calisthenics drills complete, the players were back in their locker rooms. The Wolverines could sense it. They owed Ohio State for four straight losses, and today they intended to pay in full. In the press box, work moved at a rapid pace. Michigan's radio play-by-play broadcasters reviewed statistics and proposed "what if" scenarios: *If Iowa loses to Wisconsin . . . a Michigan win today and a loss by Michigan State at the hands of . . .*

Inside Revelli Hall, the anticipation, tension, and excitement were palpable, everyone longing to soak it up and savor it forever. For the seniors, it was their last shot at Ohio State. Time to let the hundred-thousand fans and everyone in a five-block radius of the stadium know the Michigan Marching Band was on its way! From Revelli, the drumline led to Hoover, left on Green to the Crisler Arena parking lot full of tailgaters. Stopping, they played *The Victors*. Before entering the tunnel into the stadium, they played *Let's Go Blue* and, again, *The Victors*. Once in the tunnel, they were joined by the dance team preparing to take the field with their signature block-style M.

He appeared out of nowhere, a man in a workman's uniform, ski mask, and rubber gloves, pointing his gun at her in her own kitchen.

A thousand thoughts had run through Callie Kelly's head as she pulled into the driveway of her upper-middle-class home in Inglewood, California. Returning from a successful shopping trip, she'd been too engrossed in her own world to take notice of the white-panel van parked across the street. She'd found the gift she knew would make her seven year old, Jenny, happy, and the plates, hats, napkins, and birthday party favors were what she'd hoped.

She would bake the cake, finish the arrangements, and this morning at 11:30, nine little girls would arrive for the party. After putting the cake in the oven, she'd finished setting her party table. She wanted the cake frosted before her fifth grader, Joy, and her friend came home to help with any last-minute details. Emily, Callie's best friend, had taken Jenny and her own daughter to their softball game.

But in a calm Middle Eastern accent, the strange man in the ski mask asked for the keys to her husband's Beechcraft Baron B55 airplane, and suddenly she knew there would be no party. He was asking questions. When had it last flown? Did she know of any problems? Was it still in Hangar 31 at the Municipal Airport in Hawthorne?

Heart wedged in her throat, she feared that her fifth-grade helpers might walk in and surprise this terrible person and something awful would happen. Promptly moving to the desk in the corner of the kitchen, she opened the middle drawer and handed him a key ring just as the girls bounced through the front door.

Bringing the girls home, Emily stopped in the driveway. Wanting to check for any last-minute items, she followed the girls inside. The girls called out as they opened the door. There was no response as they bolted upstairs to Jenny's room. Emily moved to the kitchen. Rounding the corner, she shrieked, a sound she'd never made before. There on the floor in a pool of blood lay Callie, Joy, and her friend. Gathering the younger ones, she took them back out to the car where she called 911 and her husband.

Moments later, a black and white with two uniformed police officers pulled in front of the house to find her still in her car in the driveway. As one of the officers redirected those coming to the party, Emily told the second officer what had happened. As backup arrived, officers entered the home, evaluated the scene, and called Dispatch, requesting the Homicide Division. Smelling the now burnt cake, they took it out of the oven, placed it on the counter, and turned off the oven.

Canvassing the neighborhood, a patrolman found an older neighbor who thought he had seen a white repair truck with writing on the side panels. He wasn't sure. They rarely were.

Through additional canvassing of the neighbors, the police established that a white service van had been in the neighborhood earlier in the day. No one had noticed anything out of the ordinary, and investigators were unable to determine if more than one person had been involved. No physical evidence. No witnesses.

The detectives talked to Emily and the two girls. It had been a routine day. The girls had won their softball game, all the while excited about Jenny's party.

Bob, Jenny's father, arrived. He found Jenny and comforted her. They took a few minutes together as father and daughter to regain their composure. He then turned to the detectives to learn what had happened. The officers explained the events and findings from their preliminary investigation. Canvassing the neighbors had revealed little information.

Bob asked if they had talked to the older woman across the street, one house over. Mrs. Walter. She was home and often kept a watchful eye on the street. Deaf, she turned her hearing aids off in the middle of the day and wouldn't answer the door if not expecting a guest. He would call from his house phone. She would see the TTY apparatus on her telephone, and they could go over and talk with her.

The detectives asked Bob the routine questions: *What kind of business was he in? Was anything missing? Did his wife work outside the home? Did he or his wife have any enemies? Did they own their home? Did they owe any money to anyone? Where did they bank? Was either of them involved in any extramarital affairs? How long had they been married? Hobbies? Oh, they own an airplane. What kind? Where was it hangared? When was it last flown?*

To the officers, it didn't make sense. No signs of forced entry. Nothing missing. Maybe Mr. and Mrs. Kelly weren't as squeaky clean as they'd first appeared.

A detective called the Municipal Airport in Hawthorne to tell them uniformed officers would arrive in the next few minutes. The officers checked on the older Beechcraft Baron B55 in Hangar 31. They reviewed the flight logs and talked to airport personnel. Seldom used in the last three months, the plane had been limited to weekends, mostly day trips. Mr. Kelly was the pilot, his outings typical of a flying enthusiast: sightseeing, taking friends up for a few hours, and flying to San Francisco for the weekend and to wine country. He was a nice guy, good to his wife and kids. Airport personnel would call if they noticed any strange activity.

A female detective continued to work with the girls and Emily. After talking to them, she suggested they go upstairs and check if everything was all right then collect a few of Jenny's things so she and her father could stay the night at the Richardsons'.

Later, a detective certified in American Sign Language, and four members of the crime scene investigation team moved in. The backdoor lock had been picked. No fingerprints. The perpetrator had waited in the kitchen, fired three shots, one to the back of each victim's head, retrieved the shell casings, and left the way he, or she, came in. Nothing appeared to be missing. Callie's purse, money, and credit cards appeared to all be intact. Maybe drugs, a mistress, or gambling debt, but it was no random killing.

The detective communicated with Mrs. Walters in ASL. Yes, she had seen a white van with a red and blue name, 3-T something Plumbing, and an Inglewood address parked in front of her house for forty-five minutes.

The company, 3-T BREECO Plumbing Services and Supply, off Western Avenue, had reported the theft of a service vehicle Thursday morning.

Tomorrow they would go to work on background checks, bank accounts, credit card expenditures, and work environment. She was enthusiastically involved with her girls' academic and extracurricular activities, including sports and music; he taught adult Sunday school and was involved in the neighborhood watch program and his girls' activities.

Still, there must be a reason, and the investigators would stay with the case until they found it.

"And welcome to Dover International Speedway! If you're new to the sport, it can be a little confusing. Hang in there, though, it's a great ride and a lot of fun. The Xfinity Series Chase Champion will be determined at the completion of ten races among sixteen drivers. Today's race, the fourth of seven playoff races," John Bates said as he opened the ESPN broadcast of the day's NASCAR race.

"A perfect day for racing, folks. The winner today will have a clear shot at the championship. This is among NASCAR's premier venues. Far enough north it's not too hot to run in the middle of summer and close enough to the coast to enjoy these beautiful days this late in the season. This track started out as Dover Downs International Speedway, a dual-purpose track for horse racing and motorsports. NASCAR first ran here in 1969, with "The King," Richard Petty, finishing first to win the Mason-Dixon 300. Paving the track with concrete was another milestone, improving conditions and safety in '95," Bates continued, ever mindful of balancing information for the veteran race enthusiast and the novice.

"We've got a good car. Randy and his team worked hard, and we should do well today," Peter Wilkins, former driver and now owner of his own two-car team, told Natalie Williams, the ESPN on-track reporter, as the drivers prepared for the start of the race.

"Our plan is to be aggressive. To win, you gotta race hard from the get-go. We're gonna do what we always do. Be the fastest in practice, the fastest in qualifying, and the fastest all day."

"Thanks for the time, Peter, and good luck," she replied. "John, back to you."

"Thanks, Natalie. We're just minutes from the start. Next week it's Kansas City, followed by Fort Worth, and on to Homestead-Miami Speedway for the finish. We'll come right back after these messages . . ."

"The pace car brings 'em down to a clean, live start, and we're racing!" Bates barked in his now-famous race-start call.

"Eleven cautions last year—how many will we see today? Davy Anderson in the 89 grabs the early lead, and we're set for four hundred miles of racing on a great, clear, fall day. Trouble at the top of turn one. Ernie Garcia in the green and white 78! Oh, oh! He got a little too high, too far into the corner, and up on the wall!" Bates shouted. "The yellow caution flag's out. So, two laps in, and we have our first victim of the day. Ernie Garcia's day is done. An old racing adage: yellow begets yellow. Man, I hope it's not the case today."

14

Snow

0830 hrs. MDT Mackay, Idaho
Saturday, October 26

Well into their journey, visibility nil, the cold outside was dangerous, monotonous, and mute. Tree boughs, underbrush, outcrops of rock, and the roadway were all blanketed in white. Coming into an open valley from a mountain pass, the snow switched from having fallen straight and steady to blowing in a horizontal blur driven by a punishing, blizzard-like wind. Mike leaned forward, arched his back, stretched, yawned, and downed another swallow of coffee, settling back in as the Escalade forged its way through the storm. His last call was to his college roommate, Zia colleague, and best friend.

"Frog? Sorry to wake you so early. I need your help."

"Normally, I would gretch at you for the early hour, but I'm already up and at 'em, working on a Brooklyn Medicare fraud case," Frog responded before his voice lost its characteristic energy. "Mike, I heard about Agnew. Man, I'm sorry. Can you get down there today? Go. Do what you need to do. Take some time. You've more than earned it. I promise we won't change the company locks while you're gone."

"Thanks, Frog. Right now, I wish you would." Mike chuckled. "I thought I'd been through it after losing Toby, Sally, Jessie, my folks. Now, I don't know. It sure isn't getting any easier with practice. These last few hours haven't been any fun. Don't know, maybe you and I throw in the towel, go to Hawaii, and become beach bums," he concluded with a laugh, though it didn't hold much mirth. "Don and I are headed back to Boise from fishing. I hope to get home by tonight if they don't shut down the airways."

"Knew you'd booked some serious time on the Paris project and didn't want to wake you in case you hadn't heard," Frog said. "Waitin' till seven your time to call. Was it as bad as it sounds? Losing friends and neighbors is one thing—tell me none of yours got bit by this? You've got cousins, aunts and uncles, and your grandmother there, right?"

"Yeah. Grandma, an aunt, uncle, and my cousin Jack survived. We lost sixteen. Jack's wife and four kids, his brother Sammy Joe, and his family. And my other aunt, Connie, and her clan, including her mother and father-in-law. By Jack's count, maybe fifteen farmers, a few wives with small children, and ten to fifteen retired couples are all that's left from a population of a thousand."

"That more than sucks. I'm sorry."

"Just hope they don't ground the planes."

A silence lingered between them for a moment before Frog broke it. "What's going on?" he asked. "You mentioned you needed some help."

Mike's phone, an incoming call, interrupted them. "Hold on, Frog. It's Jack. Call you back."

"They found Emma! She's alive!" the words tumbled out of Jack as Mike answered. "In the panic to escape the gym, she fell or got knocked to the ground under the bleachers. She broke her arm and suffered a concussion, but it's what saved her. EMTs found her unconscious when they came through looking for survivors. She's the lone gym survivor. Houston's Life Flight's on their way. They'll take her to Texas Children's."

"No way! That's the best medicine Nanaw and your folks could get. Can you ride with her?" Mike asked.

"There won't be room. I've got a reservation for the last flight out of San Antonio. I'll be there by ten. She's in a coma. They won't wake her till she's in the hospital and they've checked her for possible traumatic damage from the shockwaves. Told me it'll be months before they know what, if any, long-term impact there might be. Thank the Lord she's alive. Your idea of pushing dirt made the difference. Once they could start through town, they looked at the remaining portion of the wall. She was under a section of the foldaway bleachers. They said she would have died of dehydration and exposure if they hadn't found her when they did."

"That's the best news I've heard since any of this started. Anything I can do?"

"Not right now, I'll let you know. Mike, there is a God, and He saved Emma.

Ask Him to be with her as she recovers."

"You know I will."

"We'll be in Houston at least three or four days. Folks are still expecting you. Any changes, call Dad." Jack became more difficult to hear as the sound of helicopter blades filtered into the background. "Life Flight's landing, gotta run. Talk to you later," he yelled.

"Hey. If they found one of my kids, I'd yell through the phone, too." Don smiled as Mike hung up the phone. "That's super. It really is. Hope she's gonna be okay."

They talked for a few minutes before Mike returned the call to Frog, bringing him current news, including the discovery of Emma.

"Only one in the building smart enough to get under cover when the roof fell in," Frog quipped. "Seriously, with all she's been through, sure hope she doesn't have any lasting complications. Besides, you've already admitted you're getting too old to go rock climbing with me. I'm banking on her being my new partner, or a ballerina we could watch in our old age."

"Yeah, or an astronaut, or professional basketball player," Mike countered.

The snow remained unrelenting, the wipers clearing the way. Mike took a deep breath as he and Frog reviewed the national train disaster and the number of outages state by state. "Everything's at a standstill. Federal Railroad Administration's stopped trains nationwide. All told, we've counted three hundred and thirty-one separate targets in a snowstorm in the middle of the night. The number's going to grow this morning now that investigators can see what they're doing," Mike lamented.

"No idea if they used electronic or mechanical timers, or a combination. If they're mechanical, most have a maximum span of seven days. Whoever did this has had a busy week. Five hundred targets across a third of the entire country in a few days took serious planning and a small army," Frog said.

"Yeah. Was it a hub and wheel distribution, a daisy, or something else?" Mike asked.

"So, all you want me to do is tell you how they did it. Did they steal the explosive all at once, make the bundles over time and distribute to a holding unit or public storage, or send out their teams and cover all the regions in less than a week with timers set to go off at the same time? Did they start from Denver and move west or on the West Coast and move east? Ouch!"

Crash! The phone died.

A minute passed before Mike's phone rang, "Sorry. Jake wanted me to let him out. I tripped, spilled coffee down my shirt, and broke the cup when I got up. Give me a sec to clean this up," Frog said, the sound of his fumbling filtering through the background. "Where was I? Oh, yeah, is it over, or will there be additional attacks in the next twenty-four, forty-eight hours out to two weeks? Can I devise a plausible plan which allows you to retrace their steps and find a fingerprint, a description, a clue to catch these dudes? That about cover it?"

"Pretty much." Mike laughed for the first time in what seemed like forever. "In your spare time, tell us who and where they are. Finish before you have breakfast, and we'll have them in jail before I get to Agnew this evening. We're on our way to retrieve an undetonated bundle. I'll text you the phone number for a guy named John Tilden, who works for Don. He's plugged into Union Pacific, BNSF, the New Mexico state police and state cops for all the states north and west of there. He'll feed you names, locations, and numbers for all the states as they come in.

"Remember my trip to Florida last spring? Told you how those guys used honeybees to find all sorts of things, including explosives? I've called. The bees will be here tomorrow. We need to hit it as soon as possible. If they housed explosives in storage units and distributed them days before detonation, we might be able to identify their location, which in turn might lead to a name or some other clue. If other materials are stored in the space after the explosives, it'll diminish the bees' ability to identify the locations. If this works, we'll use 'em in all the other states. You've gotta build a map."

"And you've gotta hope to trick those little critters into thinking all that snow is blooming flowers. Like my chances better than yours." Frog chuckled.

"I'm not taking your bet. Appreciate your help. I'll text you Tilden's number, and Don will let him know you're calling. Driving in the middle of a friggin' blizzard. It'll be a long morning getting back."

"Safe trip. I'll see what the numbers say and have a preliminary map for you." Frog paused on the other end, voice taking a more serious edge. "Hey, Mike? I'm sorry for your loss, buddy."

Mike took a breath. "Thanks, Frog. I'll talk to you soon."

Don arched his eyebrows as Mike hung up. "Frog?" he asked, having ended his own call with Tilden.

Finally, after what seemed like an eternity, the sun was beginning to beat back the darkness. Approaching yet another incline and heading into a pass, they hit a patch of black ice. Fishtailing, Mike turned into the curve, the lower boughs of a large Douglas fir scraping the paint on his side of the Escalade as they passed. In an instant they were head down on the highway embankment.

"Man, that was close. You okay?" Mike asked, frustrated and suddenly exhausted.

"Good. Scattered my laptop and phone on the floorboard, but I'm okay. You?"

"Glad that's all we scattered," Mike answered, breathless as his heartbeat thundered in his ears. "Considered putting on my chains before we left your place. I knew if this happened, we might be stuck for three days before someone came along. Thought it was all new snow, and if we stayed in the middle of the road at a decent speed, we'd be okay."

"If we'd put the chains on then, we'd have worked in the Quonset hut on a nice flat, dry concrete slap. Instead, we're out here in a freezing blizzard wondering what it's going to take to get back on the road and putting chains on in this never ending cold," Don said as they opened their doors, put on their coats, and surveyed their circumstances.

A chain, a come-along, the tree they'd averted, and a lot of physical exertion got the Escalade out of the ravine and back on the highway. Another twenty minutes later, Don was hot and sweaty despite the cold, but the chains were on, and he and Mike were again under way. After exchanging stories of similar experiences from their pasts, Don added, "We're supposed to be older and wiser now."

"One out of two—not bad if we're playing baseball," Mike quipped. "I know we haven't been traveling the Santa Monica Freeway, but if you look ahead about three miles, I think that's an Idaho Transportation Department snowplow. It's the first vehicle we've seen since starting this trek." Mocking his friend, he continued, "Mr. Police Officer, Sir, I know it's against the law, and I could go to jail, but if it's all right with you, I'm driving in the plowed lane."

"Whatever it takes to get us home safe and sound. I'm just along for the ride," Don replied.

Driving on the freshly plowed road, the tension in Mike's neck and shoulders eased. "Nice to get out of 'pathfinder' mode,'" he said, pushing his speed up to forty.

"Before we were so rudely interrupted, you were going to tell me about Frog," Don said.

"Yeah, my college roommate and best friend. He's the brightest guy I know—a quick, innovative mind. The first person I hired when I started Zia. Met him the first day of class freshman year at Stanford. I entered as a second semester freshman with eighteen hours of advanced credit. He came in with twenty-seven, almost a sophomore before he'd even attended his first class. I knew this guy was at a different level. Exceptional musicians see patterns in music and can tell where, when, and why a melody will go before it does. Frog's like that with math."

For a moment, Mike was lost in a wash of fond memories. "Blew out my knee, second game freshman year. Ended my football career but not my need to stay in good physical shape. Frog and I spent many hours climbing rock faces in the San Gabriel Mountains, working in one computer lab or another, and bending elbows at one of our favorite watering holes. He was a nerd's nerd but had been a wrestler in high school and had incredible upper body strength. At five ten, I had him by eight inches. At times on the rock face, he has the advantage; other times, I do. Along the way, I shortened Phillip Randolph O'Grady to P-H-R-O-G, Frog. He wasn't too keen on it at first. Now it's how he refers to himself. To everyone else, he's Phillip." He broke from his reverie, coming back to the current issue. "He'll do a Bayesian analysis. It's a statistical procedure used to estimate parameters of an underlying distribution based on observed patterns. The more data John feeds him, the higher the probability he'll have on knowing explosive storage locations."

Between calls with John Tilden, his director in Boston, and his wife and kids to assure them he was well and homeward bound, Don stayed busy. For Mike, the monotony of a sea of white, the continuing blizzard, his pounding headache from too much scotch, the loss of his family, the inability to get to Texas and do something about it, the repairs now needed for his new SUV, the Paris attack, the nation-wide derailment, and the looming possibility of more trouble made his head swim. Perhaps as a respite, the day he met Maggie popped into his head . . .

Six months ago, the first weekend in May, he hosted the wedding reception for his cousin David Mutschler and Rebecca Loddy, at the Golden Gate Yacht club. He'd spotted her from across the room in a simple but elegant, long-sleeved black dress, and he was about to introduce himself when a familiar voice spoke up.

"Mike, let me introduce you to my best friend, Maggie Barrington," Becca Loddy's oldest sister, April, said. "She and her string quartet provided the pre-ceremony, wedding, and early reception music. Maggie, this is Mike Paxton. Mike is David's cousin and the one responsible for this beautiful setting."

"Nice to meet you, Mike." She smiled, extending her hand. "The setting, the weather, and the couple made for a perfect wedding."

"And the music. Very well done—the crown of the event," Mike said, taking her hand. "And thank you for not including Johann Pachelbel's "Canon." Nice tune, but way overplayed." He returned her smile.

"Agreed, on both counts." She laughed. "Do you enjoy classical music? Have you attended any symphonies?"

Glancing over at Don, Mike came close to laughing out loud, remembering how this tall, attractive woman with shoulder-length auburn hair and green eyes, who carried herself with poise and grace, had captured the attention of every man in the room.

"I have and enjoy them immensely." He smiled. "You've got an exceptionally talented group; do you have a busy schedule?

"No, this is a one off. We all have regular jobs," she replied. "How do you know April?"

"I met her when Becca and David were planning their wedding. How about you?"

"I've known her since junior high. Now, she's my CPA." Maggie smiled a captivating smile that held his interest and made it hard to look away.

They talked music, classical, jazz, R&B, '60s rock, folk; he was as conversant with the artists her younger sisters listened to as with the latest electronic technology the music was played on. Their game progressed for half an hour, each trying to see if they could make the other take the last bite of the cookie.

Finally, Mike broke the pattern. "Are you hungry? Would you like to get a lite bite and maybe a drink?"

She smiled. Then, she nodded.

"How did you get here?" he asked.

"I came with the viola player. Give me a moment; I'll check and see if he can take my cello home."

"How do you know the valet, and how did he know to pull up your car even before you gave him your ticket? Is he your cousin, too?" she teased a few minutes later.

"It's not my first time visiting, and there are some advantages to being six foot six." With that, Mike laughed as he slipped the valet a twenty before he slid behind the wheel.

"Nice car. What made you choose a Maserati?"

"I like the way it looks, and with the standard transmission, it keeps me on my toes with the hills here in town."

Always a good listener, Mike gained considerable insight by paying attention to a person's diction and speech patterns and watching their body language. Allowing them to take the conversation in the direction of their choosing, he learned what people valued by their chosen topics. Describing a person as tall, smart, or involved in civic activities gave him insight into what was important to the speaker. It wasn't by chance that, when asked of his background, the questioner found themselves talking more of issues important to them, learning nothing of him. It was a skill that had paid handsome dividends in his line of work. Potential clients weren't always forthright when showing interest in wanting to engage his services.

After a glass of wine, despite her quiet demeanor, Maggie shared her day job: principal cellist for the San Francisco Symphony. Mike learned she led an intense, busy life, averaging seventeen engagements per month with concerts, rehearsals, recitals, special concerts, presentations, celebrations, events, and her faculty position with the San Francisco Conservatory of Music. Add her personal practice time; her commitment to helping the children at UCSF Benioff Children's Hospital write, play, and record their own songs; and her efforts reintroducing music to the primary grades of the public schools, and her schedule could become difficult to manage.

He attended her concert the night following the wedding. They again went to dinner, and he learned of her double major, with degrees in accounting and music, as well as her master's in music performance. She explained that the complexity of studying for and passing her CPA exam while playing for the symphony and while developing and maintaining music programs for hospitalized, chronically sick children and kids in lower elementary school had her struggling to find enough time.

"Why accounting?" he asked.

Her father, the long-time University of California San Francisco Provost, supported her musical aspirations but understood how hard it might be to find work. He wanted her to have a fallback option.

Mike never let on that he'd immediately recognized Maggie. As a long-time San Francisco Symphony season ticket holder with two row C orchestra seats, he had first noticed her two years prior when she assumed the principal cellist chair. Sitting to the conductor's immediate right, closest to the audience, she had been directly in front of him. His work schedule and travel between San Francisco and Boise had prevented him from more than a casual appreciation of her.

It had been a decade since the loss of Sally, Jessie, and his parents. He had not looked at another woman since the tragedy. Till Maggie, no interest. After their second dinner, he'd found ways to see her at least twice a month. Her positive, upbeat attitude, smile, energy, and genuine zest for life made her a pleasure to be with. She was equally at home with school kids, with her music, and in the corporate boardroom, seeking support for the symphony. In blue jeans and a tank top or dressed to the nines in a black dress with pearls, she could be elegantly simple or simply elegant. And when they were alone, laughing, talking, having a good time, she could give him an alluring look that spoke directly to his id.

Between phone calls, Don looked over at his silent friend, concerned the stress, tension, and loss of family might have sent him into depression. He was pleased to see a smile on Mike's face. Hours of endless white stretched ahead of them.

15

Watching From Afar

1730 hrs. CET Vienna, Austria
Saturday, October 26

Enthroned atop three floors of a historic building on *Kirchengasse*, five blocks west of the *Naturhistorisches Museum Wien* in Vienna's *Museums Quartier* District, Asha's corporate offices reflected an international asset management organization with holdings approaching 380 billion dollars. Managing partner Parsa Shehadi's office occupied the corner of the top floor with floor-to-ceiling windows, which provided extensive views in two directions and rivaled those of any of his clients. His mahogany desk, leather chairs, original artwork, and Persian rugs reflected his heritage and Western work history.

Now fifty-five, with graying hair, a short nose, broad jaw, and wide eyes magnified behind steel-rimmed glasses, Parsa, the eldest son of the eldest son of Yamani Shehadi was the clear leader of his generation. Schooled at Harvard and the HEC School of Management in Paris and fluent in Arabic, English, French, and Chinese, he'd learned the importance of building a strong network of friends, associates, and friends of friends. With the blessing of his father and uncles, he had handpicked the senior management of Asha—all devout Shi'ite followers of the Qur'an.

Today, he had given everyone the afternoon off and brought in an expansive catered spread of dates, olives, figs, apricots, other fruits, hummus, various bean and cheese dishes, and fish, and three big-screen HD television sets for the principals of

TLS, his cousins Jamal Shehadi and Anosha Shehadi Saleh, and for Anosha's husband Omar to monitor the news from the American, European, and Middle Eastern perspectives.

"Jamal, today is your day. Congratulations," Parsa offered as they waited for Ana.

"Not congrats to me. Congrats to us *all*. A team effort all the way," Jamal replied, having helped himself to some hummus and cheese.

"I can't remember when you weren't working on it. How long's it been?" Parsa asked.

"I was thirteen when my father and two brothers were killed in southern Lebanon trying to halt Israel's efforts to extend their northern border. It destroyed my world, and I vowed to inflict as much pain as possible on the Jewish nation for my loss. Uncle Rami was kind. He brought mother and me to live with him. It took a little give and take from us both at first, his house being more organized, disciplined, and regimented than what I was used to. I was a hate-filled, angry, bitter, bulletproof teenage boy. He was a respected, international banker with a very pretty, extremely bright, highly compliant daughter. Looking back, he would ask me a question, and I would ramble and vent and tell him how unfair the world was. He would listen patiently and ask another question."

He paused. "This is quite a spread; everything I've tried is good." Jamal walked with his plate of figs, dates, and cheese to the window and admired the view.

"Sounds familiar. Uncle Rami was good at that," Parsa replied, joining him at the window.

"He gave me homework assignments to study Israel's government, banking systems, military, economics, and infrastructure. The US was everywhere, and I realized making any impact on Israel required the removal of America, however briefly, from the equation. It struck me that a major blow to America would have to be so massive it would not allow them to come to the immediate aid of their puppet. For Israel to be impacted in any meaningful way, the relationship with their neighbors would have to change permanently. The task seemed insurmountable. He told me to study *you*," Jamal said.

"Me? I'd transferred to Singapore to help establish Goldman Sachs' Shenzhen, China, office. What did he expect you to learn from *me*?" Parsa frowned, walking back toward the sofa to refill his plate.

"You opened my eyes to finance and how, with enough money, anything's possible. I watched our banker uncles. All successful, tied to other people's money.

You use other people's money differently. You have a downside but a much higher upside. I realized I couldn't work hard enough or invest fast enough to make the money necessary to affect the change I desperately wanted.

"Uncle Rami dared me to develop a plan to achieve my goals. Told me I needed to be conversant in every phase of the plan and understand its logistics, economic implications, and long-term political outcomes. Challenged me to devise and implement a mechanism to raise several billion dollars and, above all, to design a plan that in no way implicated the family."

"You were thirteen, and he had you developing business plans?" Parsa asked. "No wonder you're so focused and driven. He never let you be a kid. All work and no play makes Jack . . ." Parsa trailed off.

"Whenever I broached the need for at least tacit support from the Arab nations, he would smile, tell me to focus on the tasks in front of me, and assure me our cousins, the Antars, were already working on it."

Omar, now joining them at the window, exclaimed, "This is great! The corner windows give you a magnificent view of the city. What's that?" He pointed to a building in the north.

Parsa answered, "The Hofburg, the official residence of the president of Austria. Originally it was the Imperial Palace of the Habsburg Dynasty. Just past that is the Spanish Riding School, and beyond that, Stephansdom, the mother church of the Roman Catholic Archdiocese of Vienna and the Danube Canal. You guys really ought to come for a few days and visit the city. The architecture is incredible. There's a lot of history here."

An hour before sunset, the late afternoon shadows lengthening into early evening, the trio at the window watched the city transition from the activities of a busy day to the inner rhythm set by twilight. Parsa, Jamal, and Omar each dealt with the anticipation of the *Hujum* in their own way. Omar, dealing with his foreboding sense of darkness, was concerned for Ana, hoping she would return while there was lingering daylight. Jamal, much more talkative than normal, appreciated Parsa's apparent interest in the early stages of *Hujum's* development. And Parsa, who continued to engage Jamal, knowing it would keep him calm, was confident the ensuing events would go as planned and the Stygian darkness would lead to the fulfillment of their grandfather's vision. He looked forward to the dawn of the new era.

A moment passed silently before Parsa queried, "Did you have your *Hujum* well-fleshed out by the time you got to the Energetic Materials Research and Training

Center at the New Mexico Institute of Mining and Technology? That was genius." Parsa ran his hand through his gray hair, returning to his conversation with Jamal.

"Hardly. I went there between my junior and senior years at USC. Knew I'd need explosives, and they were on the cutting edge of technology. Since Ana isn't here, I'll tell you the story. I'd gotten a job cleaning EMRTC offices. I'd been there all summer, frustrated about not getting specific data when my supervisor came to me and said, 'Tony'—Tony Duran was the name I used—'start with the director's office—all the admin areas—and pay special attention to the conference room. They're having a big pow-wow with the Washington-types tomorrow morning and want it to look good. Carlos will do the rest. You focus on the areas the suits will see.' I unlocked the director's door, flipped on the light, and walked to the wastepaper basket beside his big mahogany desk. As I bent to pick up the plastic trash liner, I heard a rustling sound and turned to see what caused it. To my surprise, there was the director, sitting up on his couch, putting on his shirt. He stood and pulled up his trousers. A woman lay motionless on the couch, her hands shielding her face, the lone covered part of her. He grabbed his shoes and said, 'Yes, well, I must be leaving.' And he was gone."

Omar laughed. "Horny bastard."

Parsa, recognizing this as Jamal's way of dealing with the imminent start of the *Hujum*, smiled as he continued. "I recognized her as the director's executive secretary, looked at her and asked, '*¿Cuánto tiempo has estado durmiendo con él?*'—How long have you been sleeping with him? She answered in English, sitting up as she found her bra and put it on. 'Two years. His wife doesn't know, and neither does my boyfriend.' Scared his wife would find out and it would cost her the job, she didn't seem the least bit embarrassed or inhibited as I leaned back on the director's desk and watched her get dressed. Great body, I might add.

"'What do you want? What can I do?' she asked. 'If my boyfriend finds out, he'll tell my parents and leave me. My father will beat me and turn me out on the street.' And I'm looking at this pretty young thing and thinking I just won the lottery." Jamal laughed. "'I have no place to go. I'll be a disgrace to my family. I don't have any money. I'll do whatever you want. Please don't tell anybody! Please,' she pleaded as she walked over and touched my arm. 'Is there anything I can do for you personally?'

"I'm not believing this. Not in my wildest dreams. 'Three things,' I told her. 'The passwords to your and your boss's word processors. The keys to the top-secret file cabinets, and, to keep you honest, sex with me.' She asked me what I meant by keeping her honest. That was funny. She didn't quibble about giving me total access to their top-secret data and plans, essentially becoming a traitor to her country, or the sex. She was hung up on what would 'keep her honest.'"

By this time, Omar was snickering and Parsa nodding approvingly as the story unfolded.

"'It's simple,' I told her. 'If you tell your boss or anyone what you have given me, I'll tell all those you mentioned, my boss, the university president, and the local paper. Your boss will lose his job and won't be able to find another,' I said."

Omar laughed out loud. "You'd just created your own sex slave."

Jamal looked over at him and smiled. "I told her, 'And you'll be lucky too if you're not raped by every guy you know before you can get out of town. Now get dressed, give me the passwords, yours and his. And show me where the file cabinet keys are. If I come to look for them and they're missing, I'll go to your boss. As for the sex, I'll be in touch. If it's good, we may do it again. If not, it may be a deal killer. Comb your hair and get out of here. I've got a suite to clean,' I said."

"I can't believe you didn't take her, right there on the spot." Omar laughed.

"I'd figured out where the information I needed was, but not how to get it. It was locked in a metal cabinet. I didn't want to force my way in and cause an institution-wide alert. Remember, those were the pre-personal computer, internet days. Dedicated word processors were all the rage. File storage was a serious improvement over tape storage, and I'd watched this super-efficient secretary and figured she had every speech and letter, his dentist's info, his kids' birthdays—everything about him and the lab—on her machine. I'd tried and failed to locate her password. Walking in on them accelerated the process.

"I needed to know where the technology was going, and as our targets evolved, what weapon would help achieve our goals as efficiently and effectively as possible. I had to match the explosive to the target and both to a workable delivery system. TNT, TATP, RDX, PETN, HMX, EPX-1, at that stage of my education, was nothing more than alphabet soup. Overnight I learned TNT doesn't explode spontaneously and is very easy and convenient to handle; RDX, the explosive agent in C-4, is 18% more powerful than TNT. Ammonium nitrate is weak but when combined with fuel oil, its explosive power is almost that of TNT. The PETN-coated crystals in EPX-1 give it one of the highest detonation velocities of all plastic explosives. CL-20 is widely superior to conventional high-energy propellants and explosives. It shaved years off the development of the *Hujum*."

"Why'd you stay after you got the materials you wanted?" Omar asked.

"I'd missed the start of fall semester by two weeks, the volume was much greater than I'd imagined, and I wanted to make sure I had it all."

"So, you took the semester off and just played with the girl." Omar laughed. "She must have been busy between her boyfriend, her boss, and you."

"I used the time to focus on what it would take for America to concentrate on its own needs and began focusing on their infrastructure, supply lines, and communications. Going to school in California in those days, I realized drugs were everywhere. It struck me that, if done intelligently, laundering illicit drug money could be extraordinarily lucrative. I roughed out a basic plan and shared it with Uncle Rami. In typical banker fashion, he asked a thousand questions. I answered them, and he asked a thousand more. It was the first of many, many iterations and a great precursor to what developed into the final plan. I started my senior year spring semester and graduated end of summer. Glad Ana's not here, she wouldn't have appreciated my story. Speaking of Ana, she's coming in from Hanoi. When do we expect her?"

"It's a sixteen-and-a-half-hour flight," Parsa answered. "She left yesterday afternoon at 4:30, her time. Time changes and all, she should be here in less than an hour. Get some more to eat. It's going to be a long night."

"Good morning, ladies and gentlemen, and welcome to today's game between the Buckeyes of Ohio State University and the Wolverines of the University of Michigan, here in Ann Arbor. I'm Brad Swinton, here with my colleagues—Larry Stanhope, here in the booth and Jimmy Tachick and Ellen Newman on the sidelines. We'll be bringing you today's action. Of course, we'll keep you apprised of the news regarding the destruction of the rail lines, and *ABC News* will break in with any new developments."

"Brad, it's sobering to think anyone could be so displeased with the United States they'd carry out a terrorist attack with such destruction, disrupting so many lives. The economic impact will be even more massive," Stanhope interjected. "My thoughts and prayers go out to that little town in Texas. We're in uncharted territory. Our focus is on one athlete or another, but compared to a national emergency, does it matter? What we do, you and I? It's not medical research saving lives—we're not protecting our country—but at times like this, maybe it is important. People need a pastime, a means to take them away from their trials and tribulations. And after last night, we all have those. So, if we can give the people of

Michigan and Ohio a couple hours of enjoyment, and our colleagues can do the same for other regions of the country, it's what we need to do."

"Brad, Larry, if I may," Ellen Newman broke in. "I grew up in a small town in the Oklahoma panhandle and know what life was like in Agnew. Generations of hard-working people whose families worked the land. They focused on the weather and the price of their crops and hoped that their football team could win on Friday nights. I hope for the best for them but know they have some difficult times ahead."

"Thank you, Ellen, for helping us keep our priorities straight," Brad said.

"Two great college football teams, Brad. Both ranked in the top ten. A lot riding on the outcome. OSU won it all last year and has many players back. Michigan knows if they execute, they can win. You might have Alabama-LSU, Texas-Oklahoma, even USC-Notre Dame, but no rivalry's any bigger than this. Michigan-Ohio State in the Big House. Over 107,000 spectators here. This is the best of the Big-10. Many argue it's the best football in the nation. The raw emotion, the bands, the flag bearers, the dancers, the cheerleaders, and generations of fans make college football a unique experience. For sheer spectacle and tradition, this is as good as it gets," Stanhope concluded.

"Here comes the Michigan Marching Band, high-stepping at 220 beats per minute in their traditional block-M and playing the *M Fanfare,* followed by one of the most recognized school fight songs in the country, *The Victors*. *Varsity* and the *National Anthem* are next. Gotta love the sights, sounds, and pageantry of college football," Swinton said, the excitement in his voice palpable.

Ana greeted Omar with a smile and a hug and joined him, Parsa, and Jamal in Parsa's office. Having slept only a few hours on the plane, she was tired but excited for what was about to transpire. "Parsa, I've always loved your office; you've done a great job tastefully mixing eastern and western cultures. And the food, my, are you expecting to feed an army?" She smiled and set her overnight bag and briefcase at the door. "Why all the televisions?"

Their adrenaline levels soared as the hour approached, now mere minutes before four o'clock in the afternoon, six hours ahead of American's eastern standard time, the full *Hujum*, the attack, on the verge of unfolding. If all went as planned, the United States would look back on September 11, 2001, as a mere prelude to the atrocity about to envelop them and all they hold dear.

"Just want to ensure we see the news from multiple perspectives," Parsa answered.

Tested, modified, and tested again, the plan had undergone a feasibility study, including acquisition of all necessary materials, logistics training, funding, and security. Burnished and brought to operational status over the past three years, it was the most comprehensive attack ever between two nations not engaged in declared war. The primary goal: disrupt America's infrastructure, forcing them to focus on their own needs. Secondarily, undermine American sovereignty, and prove they can be hit any place, any time, and their government cannot protect them.

"Parsa, got a minute?" Ana asked, leaning forward and rubbing her arms as she stood at his office windows overlooking the Viennese rooftops and the evening rush hour.

"You fly all night from Hanoi, bring me another four billion dollars, our collective adrenaline levels sky high as we witness the manifestation of the full *Hujum,* and what, I don't have a few minutes for you? Did I forget your favorite food?" he kidded, waving his arm around his posh corner office.

Looking at her, he thought how she had grown to exceed even her father's highest hopes. An attractive woman of forty-one, her poise and professional demeanor belied the way in which she executed her TLS responsibilities, always ahead of international banking regulations, law enforcement, and cybersecurity. At another level, she had opened the eyes of her uncles, her younger female cousins now being groomed for leadership positions at Asha and TLS. Such roles had been unimaginable for women when she was a girl.

Strong and capable, he questioned how she would handle the aftermath of her efforts. Would the emotional impact of the death and destruction of all those families cause her to make a mistake with the plan or TLS?

"You've got a serious look on your face. What's wrong?" he asked as they turned away from the others and looked out at the setting sun. "Are you okay? Is it your mother?"

"No, no, nothing like that," Ana protested, apprehensive and consumed with anxiety. "After today, our lives will change forever. The process has already begun. It's been five years; the last three have been the most intense of my life. It's true for Jamal and Omar, even Niousha. We couldn't have picked a better person to finalize the scope, identify the targets, or work through the logistics. She's done a magnificent job building layers of protection for you and our fathers." She paused, taking a moment to meet his gaze, before reminding him, "None of us can be implicated in any way. Recruiting the right people is crucial. We must be careful not to leave any tracks, physical or digital. We've worked it, reworked it, and worked it again and again. Now, as it should be, *Inshallah*, Allah alone will receive the credit."

"Our fathers, their brothers, and the Antars have reviewed the plan and are pleased with the three of you," Parsa affirmed. "They're confident Allah will be served, and the Arab nations, led by Persia, will be repositioned in a new world order. Israel will be forced to accept its subservient role in Palestine. As you say, the culmination of a plan three generations in the making has begun," he said, permitting himself a slight smile.

Frowning with concern, Ana voiced, "I'm his daughter. I've spent my life dedicated to serving Allah and trying to make Father proud of what I do and how I do it. I'm ever mindful he had no son. I'm not complaining. I wanted my life to have meaning, and TLS, Asha, and this plan are indeed meaningful. Expanding TLS revenues while developing this plan and its safeguards has been a challenge. Father's pleased with Jamal and Omar and is proud of me." Her voice slowed, took on a somber yet aware tone. "Still, culture, traditions, and old habits die hard. He is more open with them than me. It's not punitive. I'm a woman. For him, it's not my place to know all. I've done my job; TLS is performing better than any of us expected. The funds we provide exceed what any of us could have imagined. You have invested well, and it's why we're here now and not five, ten, or twenty years from now."

Facing Parsa, she stared at and through him and continued, "You are my cousin, the first of our generation. You've been the closest thing to a big brother I could ever want. You taught me how to roller blade, to play soccer. You encouraged me to pursue my education when father pushed me toward international law. You've been there for me, supportive and kind. When Jamal's father died, and he and his mother moved in with us, you helped him. And now that Omar and I are married, you continue to provide guidance and support. I will always be grateful."

"What is it? What's worrying you?" he asked, the sun now all but gone.

"We're hours away from a new world order. We have the funding, you've worked hard to ensure infrastructure construction, and new projects will be completed in record time. The Antars have worked to ensure a united Arab front. Is now the right time? I mean, with the political upheaval in America, North Korea, China, Ukraine, the ongoing regional fighting in the Middle East? With Europe and America inundated with migrants, will this result in global cataclysm?" she asked, sounding matter of fact.

Parsa's gray hair contradicted a youthful smile. Thirty years of professional asset management all for the moment he would be freed to return to a world he loved best. "Good questions. The short answer is yes, the perfect time." He told her how the impending global recession and lack of leadership in the west would leave a void Russia, China, and the Middle East would be delighted to fill. How NATO's role had diminished, following the end of the Cold War, the creation of the European Union, and serious efforts toward a global economy. And how China's state-supported capitalism had surpassed Japan as the leader of Asian trade. And how Russia's annexation of parts of Ukraine, military support of rogue regimes, exportation of energy for political gain (coupled with cyber-meddling in America and other countries) had allowed the Russian government to gain international favor and discredit democracy in the eyes of the Russian people.

"Now's the time to push for a more united Middle Eastern front. America has serious internal infrastructure issues. Europe's mired in economic mistrust. Israel's cries will go unheeded, and the collective Middle Eastern nations, with the support of Russia and China, will win the day. The time first envisioned by our fathers to reestablish Persia as the true leader of the Middle East with a respected seat at the table of world leaders is upon us."

16

Niousha

1130 hrs. EDT Ann Arbor, Michigan
Saturday, October 26

"The team captains head to midfield," Brad Swinton said, voice raising in excitement. "An appealing note, Larry: Jerrod Guyer, Michigan's All-American cornerback, will be meeting his cousin, Desmond Oradell, the four-year starter, and consensus All Big 10 free safety when the captains meet. Jerrod told us yesterday he's looked forward to this meeting since he was six years old. Along with Desmond's older brother and younger sister, they lived with their grandmother growing up. He said that, regardless of who wins, they'll all eat dinner together tonight with Grandma. Way more to this game and all who are part of it than any of us can ever appreciate. It is part of the fabric of what makes this country special.

"Ohio State has won the toss and has elected to receive," Brad continued. "The wind will be an issue. Calm one minute and gusts to twenty and twenty-five miles an hour the next. Michigan will defend the north goal. Owen tees it up, and we're underway."

Omar Haz, Niousha's top Los Angeles cell lieutenant, had reserved a first-floor single room on the backside of a Whittier hotel away from the street for two nights. That morning, he, Niousha, Mahmud Khan, also a senior team member, and the two pilots had huddled in the tiny room.

Niousha smiled at the news she read on her phone. Of the 4,174 original targets, national news reports identified over twenty-two hundred and acknowledged they expected more. It had taken months of planning and work to compile the timers, igniters, and other supplies and to prepare the packets and deliver the bombs to the weigh stations. She had heard from Detroit, Dover, Houston, and Phoenix—all on track. *Today all glory to Allah,* she thought.

Weekday evenings throughout the spring, she and her team had driven to the smaller airports in the region. Their goal was to identify facilities with an abundance of private planes, the closer to Los Angeles International Airport, the better. They identified four airplanes. As September approached, they selected two, developed plans to gain access to them, and determined how and when they would affix the underwing canisters. Their plan included aircraft disposal following completion of the mission. Mahmud assured her the canisters, equipment, and necessary tools needed were checked, rechecked, and loaded into her and Haz's vehicles.

The pilots arrived from Mexico via San Diego on Thursday afternoon. Each considered his selection a great honor and a chance to bring glory to Allah. After studying their maps and listening to the weather channel for the latest wind conditions, Niousha reviewed the plan with them one last time. She would contact Ann Arbor and coordinate synchronization of their approach to the Coliseum with the Big House.

They worked through airport departure times, potential holding patterns in case of delays, elevations, and how long they could be in the air without causing unnecessary alarm on LAX radar. Leaving from separate airports south of the Coliseum, they would make visual contact over Montebello and fly the remainder of the trip together. Approaching the USC campus, they would reduce speed, open their canisters, and lower their altitude to 150 feet, clearing the east end of the Coliseum as low as possible. Their first pass would cover both benches and sidelines with their respective inside wing tips. One would circle to the left, the other to the right, and make a second, third, and fourth pass over the stadium farther apart, covering more ground and increasing exposure. As they approached the west end zone the last time, they would leave the canisters open and bear to the north over the campus, continuing in a low arc to the south.

"At the completion of the mission, fly to the Compton airfield, taxi to the Union 76 aviation fueling station, and leave your aircraft on the tarmac in front of the hangar to the south of the station," Niousha explained. She produced two eight-stick TNT bundles with attached timers and detonators from a pasteboard box. “Bundles like these destroyed the railroad overpasses across the city and much of the western part of America earlier this morning.” Showing them how to set the timers, she handed a bundle to each. “Set the timer on your charge for six minutes,” she told the first pilot, “four before disembarking,” she indicated to the second. Looking at both pilots, she instructed, “Walk to the hangar where we’ll be waiting for you. We’ll take you to San Diego. From there you’ll both cross into Tijuana. Arrangements have been made to fly you to Mexico City.” Pointing to the taller pilot, she said, “You will fly to Frankfurt and on to Istanbul.” Turning to the other man, she said, “You’ll go to Caracas then Paris and on to Cairo. You’ll meet in Tehran on Wednesday.”

Standing, they raised their open hands to shoulder level, and proclaimed, “*Allahu Akbar.*” God is great. Crossing their right arms over their left and across their chests, they listened while Haz read the first chapter of the Qur’an and other supplications. Bowing toward Mecca, their hands on their knees, they repeated three times, “Glory be to Allah, the greatest.”

Emergency Services Chief Uribe had spoken with Carlos and Maria Valdez and Jim Bergsten the previous night. This morning they, Jack’s neighbors, Brent and Jo Everett, Maria’s sister Mary, and her husband from Pearsall sat around the elder Bergsten’s dining room table. Chief Uribe and Lieutenant Jim Griffin, ranking Texas Department of Public Safety officer, joined them. Mary and Maria had spent the previous hour hand-drawing a street map of the town on a large piece of butcher paper. Mrs. Bergsten had made coffee, an apple pie, and a coffee cake.

Over the next hour and a half, they created a list of those who had perished, and those who were missing, Maria entering them in a spreadsheet on her laptop. The Bergsten’s confirmed whose parents, aunts, uncles, brothers, and sisters had come to town, intending to attend the big game.

Using the railroad tracks as the divider, Carlos and DPS Sgt. Ralph Nelson had ridden north while Brent rode with Officer Hector Cruz and worked south of the tracks. They spent two hours checking every farm, barn, and outbuilding in the area. Brent and Hector found the charred remains of Odie Johnson and his wife face down in their yard; they’d apparently tried to get to their car to escape.

Calls to family, friends, and neighbors verified those who had come to town, including several members and coaches of surrounding towns’ football teams, and the two families spending the night in San Antonio gave them their best official estimate: 886 dead, 31 unaccounted for. The previous year's census listed Agnew's population at 873.

The town site fires were extinguished late Friday, and the grounds were now sufficiently cooled for an initial area walk-through by fire investigators. Finding Emma, the only known pep rally survivor, was a joyous occasion. One hundred eighty-three bodies exclusive of those in the gym were recovered. Almost all were burned beyond recognition and identified based on ownership of the homes where they were found and the relative size of their skeletal remains, the larger being assumed to be the male. Seven bodies would need additional study and were to be sent to the forensic laboratory in San Antonio. No one was found in nine of the eleven homes closest to the fire's epicenter, presumably because explosions had vaporized the bodies.

17

The List

0730 hrs. PDT Los Angeles, California
Saturday, October 26

The plan's framework had been approved and in place for a decade, its operational development ongoing for the past five years. Niousha Rostami, tasked with coordination of the entire plan, held an undergraduate degree in chemical engineering from Cal State Fullerton, an MBA from Cambridge, and a law degree from Harvard. She was organized and experienced in large-scale construction logistics, corporate strategic planning, and operations.

She had access to sleeper cells in New York City, Houston, Oakland, and Los Angeles, where members had been in place gathering intelligence on potential targets for the Attack on America for several years. Each cell was responsible for a specific plan component. They had checked and rechecked every detail, knowing the comprehensive nature of the attack, its intended purpose, and the consequences should any element fail. Cell members included those with hands-on knowledge of international trading, aeronautics, rail and shipping industries, finance, software development, and cybersecurity.

Two months ago, a cell member misdirected a boxcar loaded with dynamite from its original destination to a siding near the Port of Los Angeles. Members of the Los Angeles cell rented storage lockers, and with three pickups, handcarts, and dollies, unloaded the boxcar the evening of the drop. They now possessed TNT, fuses, timers, igniters, and eighteen tons of trinitrotoluene.

Working four-hour shifts six evenings a week, they broke the shipment into 4,600 four-, six-, eight-, and ten-stick bundles with fuses and igniters packed in file boxes. They established distribution centers with 20% of the bundles stored in Spokane, Salt Lake City, Denver, and Tucson while the remainder stayed with them in Los Angeles.

Unbeknownst to her supervisors, Azadeh Ebadi, a quiet, amicable, efficient admitting clerk at the Los Angeles Veteran Administration Hospital and member of the Los Angeles team, had worked for the past three years identifying patients whose height, weight, and picture could easily be mistaken for someone with similar features. Hospital admission files provided considerable personal information: name, address, telephone, date of birth, employer, relatives' names, social security number, medical records number, and insurance information. As an admissions clerk, Azadeh could access these medical records and approach patients to ask specific questions under the guise of needing the information for the records. She learned long ago that a smile, pleasant demeanor, white coat, and display of genuine interest could elicit patient information.

Azadeh profiled individuals in four categories: first—Middle Eastern men and women with certain facial features and in their late-twenties to mid-thirties; second—men of Middle Eastern heritage in the same age range, who were well-employed homeowners living in Southern California no farther north than Fresno; third—dark-haired women five foot six to five foot eight inches tall, one hundred twenty-five to one hundred thirty-five pounds, twenty-eight to thirty-five years of age; fourth—men with specific training, knowledge, or experience, such as ex-soldiers who worked as engineers, schedulers, or maintenance men in the railroad industry or servicemen with experience with ordinance. Minor scrapes with law enforcement were not disqualifying factors.

Trained in military ordinance with civilian experience, Ivan Marshall fit the last profile group. Azadeh had befriended him, buying him coffee in the cafeteria, and being a sympathetic listener of all his complaints, from his struggles to set an appointment to how his advice about how they should expand Metrolink to ease his trips to the hospital. A liver disorder had him feeling twenty years older than he was. He had come home from his tour in Afghanistan hoping to improve his life. He always ended their conversations saying his life was as good as he had ever expected.

The fourth of seven born to a single, crackhead mother, he found that school had not been much more to him than a place to go before football practice. He had been named Greater Los Angeles, second team defensive end. His poor academic record meant junior college before any hope of playing for a Division I school.

Ivan had gone to junior college in Mesa, Arizona, and found a lot of players bigger, stronger, and faster than he was. After his freshman year, he stayed home and worked with his cousin delivering furniture. Laid off after four months, he enlisted in the army and wound up at Camp Dwyer Marine Base in Helmand River Valley, Afghanistan. Ordinance is not the most transferable of civilian occupations. Ivan had talked to another cousin who worked for Los Angeles County and was able to put him in touch with a construction company building roads. Ivan had also worked for a year at the Anaconda Copper Mine in Montana. It had been good work—they needed him year-round—but the winter was too cold. He got by smokin' dope and even dealing a little when needed to make ends meet. He supported his needs, stayed with one or another of his sisters or at a shelter. For the last four years, he'd rented a room and helped his younger brother Vince when he could. It was hand to mouth.

The alcohol, drugs, and a general reckless lifestyle had led to liver and kidney damage. When it got bad, he sought help at the Los Angeles VA Hospital. Over the last four years, he had two short inpatient stays, and for the last ten months, regular outpatient visits at the clinic.

Vince Porter, Ivan's brother, enlisted in the army the day after high school graduation. Had it not been for JROTC, he would have quit school after the ninth grade. Good at the drill and the marching, he shined his shoes, polished his brass, and was recognized as the top cadet during inspections. He too had been trained in ordinance and lost three fingers on his left hand trying to defuse a landmine in South Korea. When he got home, he married. He and his wife Shanice had four babies in five years.

Vince worked in the switching yard for Union Pacific in Colton, building trains. In a hurry one night, a misstep off a covered hopper pulled him under the coupling, costing him his left leg below the knee. Union Pacific paid him over two-hundred thousand dollars as a lump-sum settlement for lifetime disability. They worked with him to ensure he would invest the money, receive additional training and job skills, and find lasting employment. Instead of using it as Union Pacific had hoped, because he'd never had access to such a lump sum, he shared the money with Ivan and his sisters, and they blew it on cars, clothes, liquor, and drugs. When he returned to Union Pacific, they showed him the door.

Finding and keeping steady work proved hard. Vince and his old high school buddies spent more and more time at the bar and less and less time at home. Having had too much to drink, he and a friend decided to take all the bourbon at the corner liquor store and help themselves to the cash register. It cost him six months in County and made finding work even harder. In the end, he moved out, or more correctly, Shanice ran him out. He worked when he could as a day laborer, an hour, a morning, or a day at a time. Neither he nor Ivan had anything positive to say regarding the rail industry.

Ivan and Vince could easily disappear for two or three weeks at a time without much notice, making them excellent candidates for Azadeh.

She kept her information in a spreadsheet on her computer among hundreds of files she moved through in her regular work activities. Last week's efforts would change the brothers forever.

18

Retrieving the Bundle

0845 hrs. MDT Mackay, Idaho
Saturday, October 26

"Mike, there's the Farm, Feed and Seed. Captain Tucker's car is next door at the diner," Don said.

"I can't ever remember looking forward to meeting a policeman. I hope this place has something good to eat," Mike said around a yawn as they parked next to the patrol car.

They entered the nearly deserted eatery.

Captain Tucker rose from his seat in the back and approached them, a big smile on his face. "Good to see you, Don, and this must be Mike, your Texas fishin' buddy," he said, extending his hand.

"Good to see you, Frank. You're right on both counts. He is from Texas, and he's a heck of a fisherman."

"They always say things are bigger in Texas, so I'm gonna blame this blizzard on you." Frank laughed. "I've got to admit, I can't remember a storm like it. My dad always used to talk about the blizzard of '69. Snowed for nearly six weeks and dropped sixty-seven inches. He said the official accumulation in Sandpoint was eighty-two inches with twelve-foot drifts covering parts of town. Hope this thing lets up soon."

"You'll get no argument from me," Don said. "I've been in some serious storms but none bigger. If we don't keep going, we'll have to follow a snowplow home."

"What can I get you boys this morning?" the gray-haired waitress in a pale-yellow uniform asked.

"Is it too late for breakfast?" Frank asked. "If not, I'll take a short stack, two eggs over easy, a sausage patty, small OJ, and some more coffee."

Don smiled up at her. "He's just a growing boy. You ought to see what he eats for lunch. I'll have an egg sunny side up and biscuits and gravy. And some of your hot coffee."

"You, hon?" she asked, looking at Mike.

"Glad this isn't a contest. I'll have a two-egg cheese omelet and a glass of orange juice. Oh, can we fill our thermos with hot coffee before we go?"

Over their meal, Frank described the massive destruction and the scene of the submerged engines and cars of the train. "These guys knew what they were doing. They are going to have to remove the old bridge abutments and start from scratch for the rebuild." They talked for half an hour, Frank answering all their questions. "Oh, I told Tilden to tell the forensic boys to see if they can cast a right boot print and a second right heel print. Might be two different guys. I've left them well-marked and built a cover over them, so they won't get lost as the snow continues.

"I imagine they wore gloves but didn't want to spoil the opportunity for fingerprints, so I put padding in the box before I clipped the wires and set it in there," Frank said as he handed the cardboard box containing the TNT bundle to Don.

"We found this one adjacent to several that exploded. Who knows how many others didn't go off but might in the future?" Don mused as they again faced the oncoming snow.

Mike continued to hold out hope that he could still get to Texas.

19

A Family Affair

1030 hrs. PDT Los Angeles, California
Saturday, October 26

With festivities in full swing, the Trojan band pre-game show finished, both teams on the field ready to go. Ninety-five thousand tickets sold by late Thursday; game time attendance exceeded 110,000. With both teams still undefeated, the game had national implications. After an extended period of mediocrity, winning college football was back in Southern California. The Hollywood types, the moneyed alum, and the power people were all in attendance for this one.

In the television production truck outside the stadium, producers considered the possibility of an overtime game in Michigan. They worked through the possible options of ending in regulation, one overtime or two, a news brief from New York, national ads, and local station breaks. If it went to a second overtime, they would stay with the game for the national audience and start the game on the coast for the PAC 10 audience. All the options had been relayed to the officiating crew, both coaches, and the USC band coordinator. Soundmen and cameramen had run their final technical checks.

The crowd rose as the Trojan Band played the national anthem. Team captains met for the coin toss. USC would receive, Notre Dame would defend the west endzone. The USC public address announcer detailed each team's starting lineup.

The producer told the umpire on the field to hold for two and a half more minutes. For sportscaster Floyd Trujillo in the booth, it was like riding a bicycle; he could stretch it or squeeze it. He'd done it a thousand times, and the television audience still considered him the best in the business.

Hawthorne Airport buzzed with activity. Weekend pilots out in full force, activity surrounded every plane at the field. The telephone rang off the hook. People filing flight plans, checking weather conditions, an inquiry for flying lessons, another asking where they could go skydiving. Was there a commercial helicopter available for a one-time use? Did anyone have the name of an aerial photographer for beachfront property?

Ten minutes after the plane cleared the tower heading east, the air traffic controller realized Bob Kelly's airplane had taken off. The pilot had checked with the tower, followed every procedure, and handled the aircraft in a professional manner, but he hadn't filed a flight plan.

A controller called the number the police officers had given and told the detectives they would send a security guard to Hangar 31. They would copy the license number of any vehicle and copy the tower conversation for the police. They promised to watch for the plane and call as soon as it approached the tower requesting permission to land.

The detectives told them not to investigate the hangar. A patrol car had been dispatched and should arrive in a matter of minutes.

"*Morning, Asian Princess, Topper60 and the Sidney Wayne here to help you in.*"

"*Morning, Asian Princess, Bull 1-A, with the Alice.*"

"*And top of the day to you as well, Asian Princess, Purple Taco, and the Miss Fancy at your service.*"

"*Morning, guys, happy to have you.*" The harbor pilot continued, "*Let's go with 7–7.77 as the radio channel. Topper60, swing about and we'll connect,*" as the *Asian Princess* and *Sidney Wayne* began to attach their respective 9 ½-inch diameter, braided Kevlar lines.

Topper, captain of the big 30-80 class tug *Sidney Wayne,* had looked forward to this day for the past six months. He and two M-Fender, twin-screw push tugs, the *Alice* and *Miss Fancy,* met the 780-foot-long, 115-foot-wide, Liberian-registered freighter, *Asian Princess,* two miles east of the Shell refinery in the Houston Ship

Channel to connect to the ship and, under the direction of the on-board harbor pilot, help her to her assigned berth.

Ninety minutes and fourteen miles later, they approached the *Asian Princess's* assigned berth. Lining either side of the channel were warehouses and storage tanks for products ranging from petroleum byproducts to molasses. Traveling at eight knots, it was time to slow the ship and set it in place in front of a giant grain silo. Across from their berth, a massive container ship refueled for its return voyage across the Atlantic.

"*Topper60, half ahead, transverse*," the pilot called over the radio.

"*Half ahead*," came the reply from the pilothouse as he reversed the direction of his propellers, acting as a brake. The tug shuddered and bucked like a raw bronco coming out of a rodeo gate. "*Five-point-four and backing*." The meter registering the load on the *Princess's* line showed 47 tons. The big ship slowed to six knots.

Closer to their destination, the *Alice* and *Miss Fancy* rode alongside, dragging back on their lines, continuing to slow the big ship, and preventing it from rocking and damaging other ships already moored to the dock. Twenty minutes later, the ship was at two knots, the berth a hundred yards ahead. The pilot banked on his and the tugboat captain's intuitive knowledge and collective years of experience to bring the ship in safely. Closer to the berth, the commands came more rapidly.

"*Topper60, take me on down*."

"*Roger, taking you down*."

"*Easy, Bull 1-A, easy*," as *Alice* pushed hard amidships.

"*Thirty percent Purple Taco*," as *Miss Fancy* swung around to the bow.

"*Easy, Bull*."

"*Topper60, stronger, stronger*."

It happened imperceptibly. The huge ship slid through the water with no sound of metal straining, work by the three tug crews brisk and calm. Pressed at ninety degrees to the ship, the *Alice* and *Miss Fancy* held it against the dock until the lines were connected on shore.

"*Stop, Topper60. In position*."

"*Thanks, boys. Good job*."

Tow rope retrieved, the *Asian Princess* secured, and paperwork completed, Topper, his first mate, deckhand, engineer, and their special guest, Topper's daughter, headed to their next assignment, the disembarking of one of the world's largest ships, the Very Large Crude Carrier, the *Nordic Spirit*.

20

Falling Like Rain

1330 hrs. EDT Ann Arbor, Michigan
Saturday, October 26

The lead drone slowed over a preponderance of nurseries and greenhouses west of Detroit, allowing its companion to draw near. Together, receiving their final course corrections, they initiated their descent.

"Well, Brad, you couldn't have asked for a better game, score tied twenty-eight all. In a game with a little of everything, it's not going to be easy selecting the Players of the Game for each team. Let's see how it turns out."

"A picture-perfect afternoon, thirty-seven degrees, clear skies, the wind has settled, now the slightest hint of a breeze out of the south at five miles an hour. What a great day, what an exciting football game. Forty-one seconds remaining in regulation, Michigan third and six on the Ohio State twenty-two-yard line. Right now, this is the play of the game. Michigan must make a first down, or they'll have to try a field goal. Time management becomes critical. If they don't make it, they're out of timeouts and can't stop the clock."

"You're right, Brad, the kicking game has been sporadic. If they don't pick up the first, they'll have to consider going for it on fourth down!"

"Saunders brings 'em to the line. Here's the snap. It's play action, he rolls to his right, he's got a man open. It's Williams!"

At that moment, the drones descended on the stadium. From either end zone at slow speeds, passing no more than a hundred feet from the ground, they released a fine mist, covering everyone to the eightieth row in the stands.

Williams, Buckeye free-safety Oradell, and the back-judge slumped to the ground. The ball fell to the turf.

"What's going on?" Larry Stanhope shouted.

"We're under attack!" Brad yelled. "Drones are flying over the stadium. They've sprayed something on the field and the stands. People have collapsed. From our vantage point, it's impossible to tell their condition. If they're unconscious or worse. Here they come again!"

Peter Jacobson, the Michigan place kicker practicing on the sideline, bent to retrieve the ball before collapsing on top of it.

A man with his ten-year-old grandson who was returning to their seats tumbled down the stadium stairs, his body landing on a family of four, already dead.

Facing the band, baton at the ready, the gloveless Michigan drum major called the band to attention, ready to play *The Victor* yet again. Then she clutched her chest and fell onto the first-row clarinet and flute players. Excited clarinet players in the first row moved to her aid and inhaled more of the falling mist.

A mother sitting thirty-one rows above the tunnel and south end zone turned to attend to her two- and four-year-old children. Seeing them slump, she started to scream, before stumbling dead on top of them.

Three blocks north of the stadium, four ten-year-old friends playing flag football in the street and two barking dogs restrained to their backyard by the chain-linked fence all fell silent.

Leaving their nozzles open as they cleared the stadium, the drones widened their orbits and returned for a third pass.

"Carl, we need help in here!" Brad yelled at his producer. "An incredible catastrophe! The drones keep coming, over and over spewing death and destruction. Nothing anyone can do. Nowhere to escape! Panic has embraced the stadium."

Turning away from the field, Swinton walked to the back of the press box, trying to catch his breath and comprehend what he had witnessed. "Ladies and gentlemen, excuse me a moment, this is the worst thing I've ever seen. It's dreadful."

Panic gripped the stadium as row after row, the scene repeated itself. The announcer called for calm, asking the crowd to make their way to the exits as university officials, campus security, Ann Arbor City Police, students, faculty, alumni, and tens of thousands of fans died on the scene. People surged for the exits, trampling victims on the ground.

"Dear God, here they come again!"

Leaving their nozzles open as they cleared the stadium, the drones returned a fourth time, covering all in and around the stadium with the mist from the canisters.

Outside the stadium, everywhere: death and destruction.

The ESPN producer yelled into his headset: "Camera 31, follow the silver drone. 22, stay with the blue one. 22? 22! Raymond? Do you read me? Can anyone stay with the blue drone?"

Lifting from their final pass, the silver drone moved north, gained altitude, turned northeast across campus, and with another hard right dove kamikaze-style into the sixth floor of the Michigan Health System's main hospital. The blue drone, canisters wide open, passed again over the parking lots with their dead and dying tailgaters, turned north, and plowed into St. Joseph Mercy Hospital. Ten pounds of CL-20 explosive packed in the nose of each drone destroyed portions of three floors of each hospital.

"Station 31! Station 31! Ambulance 6. Michigan Stadium south entrance. We are under an aerial attack! REPEAT! We are under attack! Bring protective gear, including gas masks," the EMT screamed into his ambulance radio, having watched the drones' first pass.

"... Brad, we're going to hold it right here and not go to the West Coast. This is unbelievable," his producer said.

"Bobby, turn your camera on Brad. Brad, are you okay? Deep breaths, take a minute, collect yourself. Treat this as a reporter. Describe what you see, stay calm, and don't panic the viewers. I'm on with New York. They're scrambling. Help is on the way. Stay calm, coming to you on my count ... three, two, *one*."

Brad rubbed his hand over the front of his hair, adjusted his headset, took a deep breath, and turned to face the camera. "Ladies and gentlemen, this is what we're piecing together," he said, his voice taking on the serious, yet controlled tone of a newscaster. "Two large drones, one approaching from either end zone, made several passes at low altitudes and slow speeds over the stadium, spraying what appears to be a toxic agent or knock-out gas. A replay camera shows canisters attached to their wings spraying a mist on everyone in the stadium. Whatever it is, it has impacted everyone in sight, players, officials, coaches, cheerleaders. Most of the fans in the stands lie motionless. From here, we have no way of knowing their health status." As his mind began to process what played out before him, Brad continued, "We're inside the press box and the air, I guess it hasn't gotten to us yet. Stadium officials have shut off the air in here and the temperature's already rising. We send you now to our studios in New York."

Sitting at the light, windows rolled up, his steering wheel and even his cheeks vibrating, all Mel Simmons could think about was the bass from the sound system in the Ford Explorer next to him. At thirty-one, he didn't consider himself old, but it had been years since he'd heard so much noise rolling down the street. *How can the driver stay in their vehicle without suffering permanent hearing loss?* he wondered.

Wanting to buy a present for his coworker Pedro's new baby and give it to him at shift change, he hated running late. Mel had worked for Union Pacific for eight years, and the three-to-eleven shift at Port Terminal Railroad Association, PTRA, for the last four years. The Port's busy schedule kept him engaged, his work pace brisk. Seldom working weekends, he and Russell Hammaker, his partner, agreed to help their coworkers. One needed to attend to his mother's broken hip in Baton Rouge. The other's wife had been diagnosed with cervical cancer Thursday. It hit them hard. A good crew, they looked out for one another.

The light finally turned green. Subconsciously thankful to be rid of the rolling noise machine, his mind shifted to the Texas A&M-Clemson football game and on to the baby gifts for Pedro. Oblivious to the black Honda Accord sliding in behind the Explorer as they followed him into the Wal-Mart parking lot, Mel knew Pedro was anxious to get home to his new baby and could not believe his luck in finding a vacant slot, four rows back, straight out from the main doors. As he pulled in, unbuckled his seatbelt, and slid out, the now silent Explorer, one row back, rolled to a stop. A figure in dark clothing stepped out from the passenger's side of the Accord. It crouched down. A metallic object flashed in the sun. Keys in hand to lock his car, Mel was determined to get in and out and not be late to work.

That was his last thought as the 9mm round ripped off the top half of his ear on its path into his brain.

Slipping back into the passenger seat, the sedan and Explorer rolled to the end of the row. The Explorer turned left, skipped a row, and made its way to where it entered. The Accord turned right, moved to the rear of the lot and back into traffic, moving through the intersection as the Explorer pulled back onto the street, one not acknowledging the other.

"How unfortunate. Had the car where we wanted. Bill Morrison's the best. Worked all night to set the suspension. Runnin' good out there. Sorry for Bobby Ray and the whole team," Earl Tucker, owner of the green and white 97 car, told Natalie Williams from pit row, their day now over.

"Thanks, Natalie," John Bates said as he continued to call the race. "Ernie Bowerman tries to go wide on the outside again. He doesn't have enough car to pass Alex Corliss for the lead. There's battle for third between Roy Coyle and Donnie Dunn as they go at it again down the back straightaway. After being as high as third, Ronnie Courtney and his 96 red and white car start all the way at the back of the pack, the penalty for pit speeding. There's the green light, the lead is two full seconds, with seventy-one laps to go. We've been rewarded with a magnificent race. One more round of pit stops. It doesn't look like anyone's going to catch Corliss. He's been brilliant today."

The intensity of the race kept the entire arena fixated lap after lap. No one noticed the modified IAI Searcher II drones until they were on top of the Speedway, canisters open, spraying their poison. Just moments after Ann Arbor, tens of thousands of Americans enjoying a family outing died. As in Michigan, the flying distributors of death reduced their speed and elevation, cleared the grandstands by no more than twenty feet, left the canisters open and, spraying as they pulled up, turned and made a second, third and fourth pass before heading in a direct path toward Washington, D.C.

Within eight minutes, two F-16 fighter jets dispatched from Joint Base Andrews had the drones on their tracking devices as they crossed the eastern shore of the Chesapeake Bay. Neither unmanned aerial vehicle responded to multiple electronic communication tries. Instead, they separated, one staying the course due east toward D.C., the other veering to the north and the heart of Baltimore. A squeeze of the trigger and an AIM-9 Sidewinder short-range air-to-air missile eliminated the D.C.-bound drone over open water.

The second regained its top speed at the outskirts of Baltimore and crossed Loop 695 over Pomphrey and Lansdowne. It continued to fly at an elevation of approximately two hundred feet, forcing the F-16 to postpone its destruction order. Continuing north over US-95, it experienced a mechanical difficulty, cleared the right field wall of Camden Yard, crossed Eutaw Street, and crashed into the second story of the historic Baltimore and Ohio Railroad Warehouse, the longest building on the East Coast. The explosion carried across the fifty-one-foot-wide structure and into the second external wall. The integrity of the old walls breached and the structure collapsed in upon itself.

With over 80,000 determined DOA and at least 30,000 injured, trying to establish order from mass confusion was daunting. Ann Arbor first responders, police, firefighters, emergency medical personnel, and volunteers from within the crowd tried to help evacuate the stadium and keep any ambulatory calm as many neared hysteria at the loss of family and friends. A spokesman for the Fire Department spoke over the stadium PA system, trying to curtail the panic. His constant requests for calm included instructions to breathe through a handkerchief or Kleenex.

"If you need medical assistance, move to the exits where paramedics stationed outside the stadium will assist you. For those able to return to your cars, do so and go home. Don't touch the exterior of your vehicles. If you can walk, you can drive. Once inside your car, you are out of immediate danger. Leave your windows rolled up and do not turn on your air conditioner. Please show your fellow fans courtesy and patience as you exit the stadium parking lots. As you reach your homes, put on gloves, use a cloth, don't touch your clothes directly. Take off all your clothes, including your shoes and socks. Place them in a plastic bag, leave it outdoors. Take a shower and wash your hands, face and hair with large amounts of soap and water. If your eyes burn or your vision's blurred, rinse your eyes with plain water for ten to fifteen minutes. Shelter in place until further notice. Listen to your radio or local TV for further instructions. Wipe down your car seats with a 50% Clorox solution. Rinse with clear water and repeat. Leave your car windows down. If you must use your vehicle, wear long sleeves, cover your face, head, and hands. Be careful and stay calm."

First responders worked in protective clothing, including gas masks, gloves, and shoe covers. Starting at the uppermost expanses of the stadium, they worked row by row, evacuating those still breathing to a parade of buses and the VA Hospital. Many died in transit. Others were evaluated and triaged to other inpatient facilities or outpatient clinics, or they were sent home. Succumbing to a rumor of Ebola, one hospital put themselves on drive-by, not wanting to risk the health of their other patients. The scene was frantic, demanding, and exhausting for all frontline workers.

The governor activated the National Guard, Michigan State Police, and county officials. Law enforcement personnel from the entire region arrived at the scene. The coordination of crowd control, emergency rescue, transport of casualties, efforts to calm the survivors and those in the surrounding neighborhoods was all-consuming.

The offices of the mayor and the Washtenaw County District Judge were beehives of activity as county health officials worked to identify available hospital beds. Hospitals throughout the state prepared to accept as many patients as possible. Officials from Ohio, Indiana, and Illinois offered help. Pulmonary and cardiovascular specialists came from Indianapolis.

The clear sense of urgency was met with an equal sense of focused determination.

Two battle-hardened veterans of the Afghani-American conflict waited atop the University of Southern California's Jefferson Exit Parking Plaza at the corner of Jefferson Boulevard and Figueroa Street, American-made FIM-92 Stinger shoulder-mounted, surface-to-air missile launchers at their sides. A Los Angeles cell member waited in the van on the ground floor. A second cell member had taken the elevator out of service, a pistol at his side for any civilian who climbed the stairs looking for his car. They watched as the planes, their cannisters open from their first Coliseum approach, left a swath of kids, pets, pedestrians, mail carriers, and young mothers with baby strollers victim to the toxic agent.

The Cessna and Beechcraft approached the stadium, moved across and peeled back for their final pass. As the planes again advanced toward the Coliseum, they brought their weapons to their shoulders. Flying in tandem, the planes cleared the western end of the stadium, pivoted around the Jefferson Exit Parking Plaza in a 270-degree arc, a mile and three quarters away, and swung south toward Compton. The stingers launched at two and a half times the speed of sound and in less than four seconds, found their mark. Detritus scattered over a fifteen-block region. Two separate homes took the brunt of the wreckage as what was left of the fuselage of the Cessna ripped through the roof of one and an engine and most of what had been the cockpit of the Beechcraft slammed into the bedroom of another.

Carrying their launch tubes by their reusable grip stocks, the shooters took the elevator to the first floor and the waiting van. Pulling to the corner, it turned right on Figueroa, left on Exposition Boulevard, made the light at Flower Street and again at Grand Avenue. Turning left, it accelerated and entered the 110 Pasadena Freeway.

They would drive straight through to a safe house in Oakland. In four months, the shooters would find passage on a freighter bound for the Philippines. From there, they would go to Indonesia and back home to Qatar.

"This is Charles Wortman in New York with breaking news. A third attack, like those in Michigan and Delaware, has occurred at the start of the Notre Dame USC football game in Los Angeles. This time, the attackers used single engine airplanes. We take you now to our colleague and ABC Sports announcer Floyd Trujillo at the Coliseum. Floyd."

"Thank you, Charles. We'd just learned of the terrible attack in Ann Arbor when two, low-flying planes approached us here at Memorial Coliseum. They drew down on the stadium from the west and made a single pass over the stadium at a low speed and altitude. They bore to the south, circled the stadium and, as in Ann Arbor, made a second, third and fourth pass, turning a glorious Southern California day into a toxic, unexpected disaster. As they left the stadium, they were destroyed by what I can only guess were surface-to-air missiles. Their wreckage landed in residential neighborhoods.

"Those few who've survived the opening flyovers are in a panic. The field and stands are strewn with bodies, players, coaches, and several of our own colleagues, cameramen, sound men, sideline reporters, all set to bring you today's game. Survivors are making their way to the exits, many falling to the ground as they go. Just an incredible tragedy."

The television screen showed two single-engine aircraft approaching the Coliseum. "Here's a video as the planes made their second pass over the Coliseum. Look how close they come to the peristyle as they leave the stadium. To this observer, the pilots were very experienced and intent on delivering whatever agent they were spraying. And here, on the third pass, the registration numbers of both aircraft are in plain sight. One of our cameramen stayed with the planes as they left the stadium, making a long, low arc two miles north of us. Watch now, they'd started south when the missiles hit them. We have no knowledge of the fate of the pilots or possible damage to people on the ground where those planes crashed. Or if the agent they sprayed here will affect those neighborhoods.

"Emergency calls have gone out to all area hospitals, though it's not clear how or even *if* they can respond to all these victims. I'm sure our dilemma is similar to the one in Ann Arbor, where tens of thousands of people have been impacted.

"We're okay here because we're in the press box, but the death and devastation outside is beyond description. Charles, I've been reporting major sports events for more than three decades. I have no other words for this. Reporting from the Memorial Coliseum in Los Angeles, California, I'm Floyd Trujillo. Back to you, Charles."

"Thank you, Floyd. Good luck and stay safe."

21

The Pentagon

1430 hrs. EDT Washington, D.C.
Saturday, October 26

Inside the Briefing Room at the Pentagon, the press secretary answered questions from members of the press corps. The ceiling-mounted video camera depicted her standing in front of the right lectern, the oval emblem with the footprint of the Pentagon attached to the center wood, the backlit panel behind her flanked by dark blue curtains. "Ladies and gentlemen, the Secretary of Homeland Security."

"Good morning, America. As you all know, within the last ninety minutes our nation has been attacked using chemical weapons of mass destruction. In Ann Arbor, Michigan and Dover, Delaware, unmanned aerial vehicles, also known as drones, attacked the crowds at the University of Michigan—Ohio State football game and the NASCAR races in Dover, killing what we believe to be 150,000 people and injuring thousands more. A similar attack was carried out by low-flying aircraft at the University of Southern California—Notre Dame football game in Los Angeles, where an additional 75,000 people died. These attacks, combined with yesterday's attempt on the president's life, train derailment, fire and destruction of Agnew, Texas, and the overnight demolition of thousands of miles of our nation's railroads, stranding passengers in isolated locations, prove our nation is under an ongoing attack by an unknown entity threatening the peace of the world.

"We are not certain of the perpetrators or if more attacks are yet to come. Earlier today, I ordered the Federal Railroad Administration to halt our national rail system, including freight, Amtrak, commuter, and light rail nationwide. As a result of these most recent acts, effective immediately, I'm ordering the cancellation of all domestic air traffic, cruise ship departures, athletic events of all types and at all levels, including all remaining NCAA and high school football games, tomorrow's NFL schedule, and MLS soccer until further notice. I am advising everyone to stay away from all public gathering locations, including shopping malls, movie theaters, festivals, and concerts.

"The number of American lives lost in these vicious attacks is approaching the combined total of US soldiers lost in World War II and Vietnam. This is the most comprehensive terrorist attack suffered by any nation since 9/11. As I said, the perpetrators of these acts are unknown at this time, but we believe they are one or more of the larger Middle Eastern terrorist groups, or one or a combination of the international drug cartels. We are working with our counterintelligence colleagues around the world to identify those responsible. Our military is on high alert, as are all state and local emergency response teams.

"I urge you to stay calm, shelter in place, and stay tuned to your local and national radio and television stations for additional updates and further information. The president is safe. She has been moved to an undisclosed location and will address the nation at 7 p.m. Eastern Daylight Time this evening.

"Thank you, no questions at this time, and may God bless America."

22

Port Houston

1430 hrs. CDT Houston, Texas
Saturday, October 26

Russell Hammaker walked into the Port Houston's PTRA Operations Center at 2:40 p.m., anxious to talk to the current shift—Pedro and Robert. As devastating as the track destruction was, it paled in comparison to the tragedies in Ann Arbor, Dover, and Los Angeles. He was sure they knew more than what the media was reporting. Pedro seemed especially glad to see him. Russ knew what it was to have a new baby at home. *Three weeks of no sleep, and he won't be quite as anxious to go home,* he mused.

"Russ," Pedro implored, "my nephew's a junior mechanical engineering major at USC. Plays trombone in the Trojan band. His mother is at my house. Came to help with the baby and watch the game. She and my wife are beside themselves trying to see if the boy's okay. Don't know where Mel is, but now that you're here, I'm gone."

"Understand, my man. Go. I hope your nephew is okay. Hug everybody at your house. Now git," Russ said.

Robert told Russ the track destruction was worse than reported because of the attack locations and the massive amounts of resources and labor it would take to rebuild. "Working flat out, preliminary estimates are twenty-eight months to reestablish a primary route. These guys picked specific, strategic targets. It'll be years and a ton of money before we're back to yesterday's status," Robert said. "You've got six trims, outbounds, scheduled to leave late afternoon. The bowl's full, no worries. Five en-routes scheduled for arrival, the second's the Agnew replacement. It rerouted through Hearn and is due in 1810. Should be business as usual."

"Mel should be along in a few minutes. I've got this. Go on home," Russ countered.

The afternoon passed, and at ten minutes to 3 there was still no word from Mel. Concerned, Russ decided to wait five more minutes to call Mel's wife and check on him. Even sick, Mel always called in. The workload was no big deal, he could do it in his sleep. *So out of character not to call, the guy's a lifer. Like trains, he does his best to be on schedule,* he thought.

Alone in the control room, Russell settled in and turned on the radio, 740 KTRH, news/talk radio, expecting a good overview of the national news and Washington's strategy. In a few minutes, he would call his buddy in Tucson on the UP-tie line. In the thick of it, he would know what was going on.

"Breaking news," the radio blared, "Pasadena Police are reporting a shooting in the parking lot of the Wal-Mart Supercenter in the 1100 block of South Shaver. One man dead in what appears to be a gangland-style execution or a professional hit." Sittingin his chair, Russell turned up the radio. "The victim, identified as Mel Simmons, was leaving his car when he was killed by a bullet fired by a lone gunman. Witnesses say two men in a black or dark blue, late model Toyota or Nissan followed Mr. Simmons into the parking lot. As Simmons exited his vehicle, a man in dark clothing got out of his car and shot him once in the head. The shooter got back in the car and drove away. Police have indicated the possible involvement of drugs or other extenuating circumstances. Anyone with any information regarding this case is asked to call the Pasadena Police Department or Crime Stoppers at 713-222-TIPS. We'll do traffic and weather together and send you back to ABC News and the latest developments of yet another attack with the release of chemical weapons in Los Angeles, right after these messages . . ."

Stunned, Russell couldn't believe what he had heard. He would call Julie, Mel's wife, but for now, he needed time to pull himself together. This happened to other people in other cities, not to coworkers and friends here in Houston. He sat there for three or four minutes, his mind spinning as he debated his next steps.

Without warning, the office door burst open. Three dark-complexioned men in full body armor with AK47's rushed in, yelling, "On the floor! *On the floor!* Head down! Arms above your head! Hands flat on the floor!"

Flung back into reality, he did as he was told. *Who are these people? What do they want? No money, it couldn't be a robbery. Can't steal a train*, Russell thought.

An intruder stood beside him, even with his ribcage, two feet away. A second, by his outstretched hands. He was not sure of the third. Unexpectedly, the man above him brought the heel of his boot down full force on the back of his left hand. The man to his side kicked him. He wanted to scream from the blow to his hand, but the kick to his chest had taken his breath away. He rolled over, writhing in pain.

"Your friend is not coming to work. I killed him. Do not worry, he did not see it coming. We followed him from his house," the man standing in front of his outstretched hands told him. "Today is your lucky day. Had he come straight to work and you second, I would have killed you. You will help destroy this port. You will suffer. If you pay attention, do as you are told, you will live. It is your choice. We have business to do. Do not cooperate and I will cut off your fingers, starting with your thumbs and forefingers on both hands. Continue to disobey and you'll join your friend before the sun sets.

"Get up!" the same voice commanded. "We used this morning's drug bust to hijack five PTRA switch engines. We have outfitted all the ammonium nitrate containers with fuse systems, electronic timing devices and detonators mixed in fuel oil. You have two and three car deliveries to make to two hundred locations. Inform security at each plant the drops are standard. Any questions, tell them you are sorry for failing to inform them earlier. It will take two hours for the switch engines to deliver and position their containers. Pull yourself together, you have work to do."

23

Mapping the Destruction

1245 hrs. MDT Boise, Idaho
Saturday, October 26

John smiled as Don and Mike walked into the State Police Headquarters conference room. "Welcome back. Heck of a way to start your weekend. Sorry to take you away from the river."

"Not a problem," Don responded. "Talked to the new FBI Special Agent-in-Charge. He's sending an agent over for our bundle. They'll fly it to Salt Lake this morning. We caught a real break finding it. Told him our forensic guys were on the scene. Your idea of the big map and pushpins is good. It's one thing to say it, another to see it graphically. You've been a busy boy," he concluded approvingly.

"Guess you heard what happened in Michigan, Delaware, and California. Man, this is war. Our issues are massive but at least we're not dealing with the huge numbers of dead and dying."

"It's beyond awful," Don agreed with a shake of his head. "We've been working on it on the way in. The resources, money, materials, and manpower of this were enormous. They had to have had governmental involvement. Who else has the resources, not to mention the expertise, to execute an attack of this magnitude?" He paused and gestured to the other man in the room. "John, this is my hunting and fishing buddy, Mike Paxton. It's his friend Phillip you've been relaying locations to all morning."

"Nice to meet you, Mike. Don tells me when you fish, there's nothing left in the lake," he smiled. "Phillip's quite a character. I'm looking forward to what he's found. Hope he's made some sense out of this."

"Nice to meet you, too, John. I wish it were under more favorable circumstances. What I know about fly fishing I learned from Don. He's kind enough to leave a few little ones behind for us beginners." He gave Don a pat on the shoulder before turning back to John. "You're right, Phillip comes at things a little differently, but I appreciate your helping him. I'll call, let's see what he has."

Walking them to the map, John said, "This was one well-coordinated undertaking. Moving north to south, here's where we are. We're hearing they targeted anything above grade. It reads like a travelogue across the state. More than thirty cities with a lot of destruction along the way. We've activated every officer on the force. We've paired officers with the UP and BNSF work crews, trying to identify sites, marking them as crime scenes and ensuring public safety as much as possible."

"The director is in contact with Homeland Security and FBI," Don interjected. "And we've enlisted the help of every county and municipal law enforcement agency in the state. Director selected Howard Booth to coordinate with the state and federal boys. Wants me to have overall control from here at headquarters. Told him I'd call once I got in. He's talked to the governor. Planes and trains are all grounded. He's not sure how or when he'll return from Boston. He wants me to be with the governor at his news conference in an hour."

"Need to go home for your uniform?" John asked.

"Nah, Nancy can bring one and my razor. I need to stay with you and come up to speed."

"Local people are double-checking. If they find anything, we've instructed them to tape off the region and wait for the bomb squad," John offered. "When we have enough manpower, we asked them to stay on site. So far, no other undetonated explosives have been found. Homeland Security believes it's an attempt to block all east-west rail traffic. I've fed reports from all the western states to Phillip. We haven't heard anything from the plains or the East Coast."

"Good job, John. I'm impressed."

"Thanks. I've had help. Very glad you're here."

Holding out an index finger, Mike looked at the others. "Phil, I'm here in the State Police Headquarters conference room in Boise with John and Don. Got you on speaker. What do you have for us?"

"Morning, everybody," Frog's voice crackled through the speaker. "Let me start by saying I'm sorry we have to meet under these conditions. Still, I appreciate the opportunity to work on this. John, thank you for the data feeds. The more you provide, the more confidence we'll have in what we're trying to accomplish.

"Mike asked me to use our statistical tools to determine how they positioned explosives over such a large expanse in a period of a week or less. I started where they did, with the premise their objective was to do as much damage to the country's east-west rail-carrying capacity as possible.

"If the premise is correct, a look at the rail system's nationwide tracks shows seven of what I'm calling cross checks. Points where UP and BNSF share tracks or where their tracks come into proximity. Working from these in all directions, it becomes easier to see how they might have used them as regional hubs and distributed from there.

"I'll spare you the math. Our assessment indicates the explosives emanated from five sources across the west: Spokane, Salt Lake City, Denver, Tucson, and Los Angeles. Using these as major depositories, they found storage units in towns along the rail lines and used them like weigh stations for the Pony Express, daisy-chaining the bundles from station to station. Let's look at Idaho. Figuring they don't want to backtrack, John's data indicates Bonners Ferry and Post Falls could cover the northern portion of the state, while Payette, Mountain Home, Shoshone, and Pocatello account for the west and central. McCammon will take you to Preston, south and into Utah. Whoever came out of Montana from Butte, Divide, Dillon, and Lima could continue to Dubois and Idaho Falls back to Pocatello for the eastern side. Mike, you wanted a road map to look for storage units. I looked at the terrain and the distance from as close to the tracks as I think they could drive, added how long it would take to walk to the target, added ten minutes to set the explosives and the time to walk back. Working from these locations, doing twenty-five to thirty sites per day, we can account for all of John's sites.

"This is where I am after six hours and the data provided. John or Don, if you'll keep feeding me data as you find it and tell your counterparts in the other states to continue as well, we can refine this and tighten it up." He paused briefly, then asked, "Mike, any more from me?"

24

Up In Smoke

1400 hrs. CDT Houston, Texas
Saturday, October 26

Producers at Houston's NBC affiliate, KPRC, Channel 2, wanted a nice human-interest piece and had worked the story for the past ten days. They taped interviews of the third generation Baytown native, who'd followed his father and grandfather to work at the massive ExxonMobil complex and retired after forty-two years. His sons and grandchildren had broken with tradition and gone to work on the ship channel. His older son piloted tankers and other ships into and out of the channel, while his younger son and grandson were tugboat captains. Today the tugboat captain's daughter, who this week received her Merchant Marine Credential issued by the Coast Guard, and her Transportation Worker Identification Credential issued by the Department of Homeland Security, would make her maiden voyage as a tugboat captain.

The interviews would run prior to the live feed of the Very Large Crude Carrier, *Nordic Spirit,* as it disembarked from the Shell refinery and began its voyage to Japan with the pilot at the helm and his brother, nephew, and niece captaining the tugs responsible for taking her out to sea. They had a cameraman and reporter on the *Nordic Spirit*, a cameraman on the *Sidney Wayne* with her new captain, and one across the channel at Texas Terminal LP to document the event.

The reporter turned to his driver and cameraman as the Channel 2 van slowed, entering the public parking lot. "I've been here fifteen years, and this is my first time seeing Barbours Cut," he said. "We have two hours to do our post-Panama Canal expansion update before the *Nordic Spirit* shot. Let's set up over there for background footage of those working cranes. Then we'll do a closeup with specifics."

"The Ship Channel's fifty-two miles long and among the biggest economic engines in the state. Most of Houston is unaware of it even when they go over the 610 Bridge," his cameraman replied. "If you live on the north or west sides of the city, it doesn't cross your mind."

"It's hard to appreciate how big this is. We're thirty miles from 610, and the Bayport Container Terminal's five miles further as the crow flies. Stop a minute, and let's watch this. I bet that baby holds ten to fifteen thousand containers," the reporter said matter-of-factly.

In front of them, a row of thirty-story-tall, 1,500-ton cranes extended across enormous post Panamax vessels twenty-two containers wide, latching onto thirty-ton containers, hoisting and whisking them from the ship onto waiting trucks, train flatcars or stacked on the yard. Effortlessly, the behemoths repeated the process, container after container, every ninety seconds. Containers were everywhere, on trucks, trains, in warehouses. A patchwork of green, yellow, red, and blue containers began to form on the yard in a seven-by-six array, eight high, joining any number of like stacks as over a quarter of a million containers, 70% of the containers in the Gulf of Mexico, passed through Houston.

"This is well-choreographed chaos," the reporter noted. "Imagine the computer it must take to unload all these containers. Fifteen thousand per ship times thousands of ships. What's in this container? Where does this one go? On a truck, a train, or in a warehouse? How do they keep it straight?"

"They didn't take every container off. How do you reload to ensure proper weight and balance? Where do the new ones go so they're not in the way of the ones destined for the next port?" the cameraman asked.

They completed their assignment and headed to Texas Terminal LP. "Look at that ship. Cops all over the place. Why all the crime scene tape? Back at the station, remind me and we'll check it out," the reporter said. "Can you see the name of the ship?"

"*Rio Chartrus*. Got a picture on my phone. Do you like doing these human-interest stories?"

"Yeah, they're a break from the monotony of domestic violence, drug deals, lost loads on the freeways, and hurricanes. Besides, it's pretty cool to see one family moving a mega ship out to sea."

Midafternoon, hot, bright, and blue, the *Nordic Spirit*, a Belize flagged, Norwegian-owned 310,000 ton Very Large Crude Carrier completed on-boarding a full load at the Shell refinery and initiated the uncoupling process. The *Patty Bess* tugboat nosed into the ship's starboard bow and tied on. The *Sidney Wayne,* its new captain in the pilothouse, latched to the stern behind 191 feet of line. The *Alice,* with Topper at the helm, waited amidships as the *Nordic Spirit* continued to uncouple, men readying the release of the moorings from their cleats.

Eruptions! One hundred eight simultaneous eruptions, akin to the blast from an awakening volcano. Shock waves killed longshoremen, warehousemen, crane operators, children playing in nearby neighborhoods, even passing motorists. The enormous boom burst forth and was heard throughout the greater Houston metropolitan area and in communities a hundred miles away. The detonations rocked the entire Ship Channel as sirens from the Emergency Command Center screamed.

Residents of Pasadena, La Porte, Galena Park, North Shore, Bayport, Seabrook, Baytown, Houston, Galveston, and Texas City, people whose lives had been intertwined with the petrochemical industry for generations, knew this time it was different. This time it was not a plant; this time, the whole earth moved. Homes and businesses within a half mile to either side of the Ship Channel were shaken off their foundations, windows blown out, ceilings collapsed, metal outbuildings crumpled like tin foil.

Windows shattered in downtown Houston and as far as Conroe 40 miles to the north. People in Louisiana, 250 miles away, experienced the shockwaves. For the second time in twelve hours, the seismograph in Albuquerque registered a disturbance to the southeast. Massive amounts of fire for fifty miles.

Ships docked in port broke their moorings and sustained substantial damage when they rammed each other or slammed back into the dock. Fire raced up the lines of the *Nordic Spirit* and into her tanks before exploding. The middle of the ship, wholly gutted, sank in twelve minutes. Taking the three tugboats with her, she marooned all ships between herself and the turning basin at the upper end.

The cameraman at Texas Terminal, blown thirty-five feet in the air, died before hitting the ground. His camera, jammed in the on position, continued its live feed back to the station. At once, more than 1.6 million barrels of oil, unleashed and on fire! Oil-laden water, the width of the channel, half a mile long and expanding, ablaze, burned unabated into the upper San Jacinto Bay. The spill, seven times larger than the 1989 Exxon Valdez incident on Bligh Reef in Alaska, and a third the size of the Deepwater Horizon disaster, complicated the immediacy of the attack and increased its environmental impact many-fold.

Petrochemical complexes, several the size of the downtown of a city of 50,000 people, collapsed upon themselves, ablaze. Doors, windows, and roofs of businesses and homes in communities on both sides of the channel were blown away. Most of the closer homes were blown off their foundations. An inferno! The heat and odor were overwhelming.

Immense pillars of heavy, black smoke rose into the sky, covering the sun for twenty miles. Fire! Fire exploding three and four stories high, half-mile on a side, drank from twenty, forty and forty-eight-inch pipes of flammable petrochemicals. Melted and twisted metal, heat, and residual smoke rendered the entire site a war zone. Air fouled with ethyl benzene, sulfur, acrylonitrile, olefins, ethylene, and nitric oxide choked and burned the eyes of the first responders as, in vain, they tried to establish order.

At Barbours Cut, the container in the hold of the *Martina Southampton* exploded, ripping an immense gash in the ship. Shrapnel penetrated the hull of the *Rio Chartrus* as both vessels sank. The six tractor-trailer containers on the loading dock detonated, incapacitating all eight of the massive high-capacity loading cranes. Shipping containers strewn in every direction across eighty acres rendered the container complex inoperable.

Everything along the Ship Channel was aflame. In all, two hundred fires. The list, a who's who in oil and gas. A huge mushroom shaped cloud from the ExxonMobil plant billowed 1,500 feet into the air, the shockwave knocking the local ABC affiliate's helicopter flying overhead out of the sky. At the massive Shell complex, the sheer power of the first explosion triggered a domino effect throughout the plant as cracking plants and cooling towers erupted with such force, pipes and tanks of flammable liquids ripped open.

The ChevronTexaco conflagration was so immediate and intense, the entire weekend shift died instantly. The service and technical staff on the yard vaporized. The engineering technicians in the control room were thrown about like rag dolls before the structure collapsed upon them.

The scene of fire, explosion, destruction, and devastation repeated, again and again, as waves crashed ashore at the height of a Category 3 hurricane. ExxonMobil, Phillips Petroleum, Lyondell-Citgo Refining, Occidental, Great Lakes Carbon Corporation, all in ruins. The list continued with Monsanto, Marathon Oil, service companies, blending companies, terminals and storage, cooling tower support people. In Freeport, the Dow Union Carbide complex also burned.

The explosions were so massive and intense, the safety and firefighting equipment on hand within the refineries and plants disintegrated. The air tasted of refinery chemicals, smoke, and fire. Houston Fire Department and their Hazardous Materials Unit, and Pasadena and Deer Park Fire Departments responded, trying to determine how best to defeat this monster they now faced. Even with the fire boats, it was clear in the immediacy of the moment that the fire outstripped the capacity of the entire region. The situation could only be likened to the Kuwaiti oilfield fires started by Iraq following Desert Storm.

At DuPont's La Porte processing plant, the hydrofluoric acid storage drum ruptured, and 50,000 pounds of hydrogen fluoride gas escaped, killing thousands and putting the 650,000 people within a ten-mile radius of the complex at risk. Conditions worsened further when explosions from containers in tractor-trailer configurations positioned alongside the Kinder Morgan Terminal in Galena Park caused several chlorine storage tank walls to collapse, releasing a dense, yellowish gas cloud that killed hundreds. Thousands more suffered from pulmonary edema, violent coughing and sneezing, nausea and vomiting, eyes tearing and nose and throat irritation, and other complications as the cloud rose.

Area firefighters, who had dealt with the Phillips explosions of '89, '99 and 2000, the Nova Chemical fire in '06, and the BP explosions of '05 and '16, possessed considerable experience with smaller issues and trained for refinery explosions on an ongoing basis. Still, nothing could have prepared them for this.

The FBI found three volunteer local television cameramen, who boarded HPD helicopters and flew to access the extent of the damage. To the old timers, it brought back distant memories of Texas City, 1947, and the loss of 600 lives.

The FBI met with representatives from the Port Houston Authority, Houston Fire Department, company executives, and their maintenance and safety officers to determine what was still at risk. Were additional explosions possible? What could be saved? Could they establish a priority list to keep the public safe and yet preserve what was salvageable?

Port Authority personnel and the Coast Guard would work through the night to capture as much of the fuel as possible while still in the confines of the Ship Channel. If it escaped, it could foul Galveston Bay and do untold damage to the estuaries, wetlands, and the fishing and shrimping industries of the Gulf of Mexico.

They were not trying to save a single refining operation, but to salvage an industry, a part of the national capability. This was war.

Towering black columns of smoke served as grim beacons summoning firefighters, state troopers, and law enforcement officers from neighboring communities as they poured in to assist with search and rescue, traffic control and the restoration of order. Firefighting equipment from all over southeast Texas responded to the need. Sadly, it was much too little, way too late.

Surges of injured patients consumed the considerable medical capabilities of the region. Those with burns triaged to Galveston and John Sealy Hospital with its history of treating offshore, oil-related burns and other injuries. Those with severe pulmonary compromise were sent to the Texas Medical Center and their major acute care hospitals. Texas Children's Hospital received many children. The emergency room at Pasadena Bay Shore Hospital converted into a massive clinic for smoke inhalation and heat exhaustion. The Harris County hospitals, Ben Taub and LBJ General, treated the endless supply of emergent acute patients.

The thick curtain of black smoke moved ever westward, engulfing downtown Houston, Bellaire, and Katy, fifty miles west, before dissipating.

In San Antonio, 170 miles away, many noted the beautiful yellow, golden, and orange sunset.

25

Martyrs

1630 hrs. MDT Page, Arizona
Saturday, October 26

The sun approached the western horizon in the opalescent northern Arizona sky. The air was cool in this remote region, and the inch and a half of new snow from the night before still pristine. Pulling off Highway 98 onto the dirt road leading to Betay Summit, twenty-five miles south of Page, Nazari, Javadi, and Mahta traveled four miles in absolute isolation before coming to a stop.

An owl, a motionless silhouette atop a power pole forty yards away, watched them. His eyes faced front, giving him stereoscopic vision. Feathers surrounding his uneven ears helped focus sound waves, allowing his brain to process the time difference and determine the distance to his mark when he dove toward his unsuspecting kill. Swift and silent as he stepped off the pole and into the air, the owl glided toward Nazari, who was using his jacket to clear an eight-by eight-foot expanse of the pristine snow from in front of the SUV. Closing to within two feet of his head, the owl let out a loud screech, raising the hair on the back of Nazari's neck. Then it flapped its wings and disappeared into the horizon.

The moment passed in silence as the men exchanged glances, a consensus reached; the mission would succeed. Allah would be served.

Spreading their *namazliks* in the clearing, they paused, turned toward Mecca, bowed and prayed Salat al-Zuhr. *"O Allah! we beseech You for help and seek Your protection and believe in You and rely on You and extol You and are thankful to You and are not ungrateful to You and we declare ourselves clear of and forsake him who disobeys You. O Allah! You do we serve and to You do we pray and prostrate ourselves, and to You do we obey, and Your mercy do we hope for, and Your punishment do we fear, for Your punishment overtakes the unbelievers."*

In the silence of the late afternoon of this vast country, they had again demonstrated their strong, quiet faith, wishing for a swift and successful end to the struggle they believed had been forced upon them.

Replacing their woven goat-hair prayer rugs, they worked in silence. Javadi opened the back of the SUV and the smaller suitcase from the storage unit, removing a 9mm Glock, two Soviet AKM's with 30-round magazines, and three bullet-proof vests. Each with extensive firearms experience, they checked their weapons. If any weapons survived and were later traced, they came from the police department property room in Atlanta, Georgia.

Nazari drove, Mahta sitting beside him, holding both AKMs. Javadi in the back had trained for this day for two months and now, as he checked and rechecked his 9mm, the day had come. He prayed Allah would find him a faithful servant.

Twenty minutes after the Beechcraft Baron left Hawthorne Municipal Airport, the Marin Oil Tanking and Terminal corporate jet with a single passenger cleared the tower. Two hours and twenty minutes later, close to exhaustion, reflecting on the events of the past nineteen hours, Niousha was back home in Oakland. She poured a glass of merlot and stepped out onto her patio. It had been a long, arduous journey. She loved the serenity, the view of the lake and park. One more: *At last, the end! the last mission. Complicated, yet straightforward in its simplicity,* she reminded herself. Unwilling to relax, she was prepared for everything, even escape. *They have the element of surprise. They're professionals going against civilians. They're in the parking lot by now. No better men for the job. Allah will be glorified; the plane will come; they'll be whisked across the border and on their way home before the water traverses the canyon.*

Ernie Ramminger was not happy. A week from today would be his last day, and then mandatory retirement. *I can do this job the same in three weeks, three months, or three years. Damn pencil-pushing bean counters decide when you turn sixty-five, your brain turns to mush,* he thought. An Army sergeant major with thirty years of service and seventeen as a Senior Operator at Glen Canyon Dam, his finances and benefits were secure. He struggled when others tried to limit his options.

On the other hand, he was three weeks from a chance to complete his collection of horned North American wildlife. He had won one of New Mexico's fourteen out-of-state licenses in their lottery and would be hunting Rocky Mountain Bighorn sheep in the Rio Grande Gorge south of Taos. As a lifelong hunter, he'd led his battalion pistol teams to championships in both the Southeast Asian and Middle Eastern theaters, winning personal championships along the way.

Pulling into the parking lot of Glen Canyon Dam's Visitor Center fifteen minutes before closing, Nazari and his team noted the National Park Service vehicles and private cars of the staff and volunteers clustered together off to the left. A large group of senior citizens clambered onto a tour bus, and a smaller cadre of more nimble aged folks made their way into two vans with *First Baptist Church, Grand Junction, Colorado* painted on the side. The remaining cars with license plates from across the country would soon be claimed as the day's final tour concluded. Nazari and his colleagues waited while the bus and vans loaded and left, and three other couples exited.

Ramminger tried to distinguish between speakers as the voices approached well past the last visitors' tour. One he knew well, the other he did not recognize. The familiar voice, Park Ranger Ray Mathews, was answering questions in a succinct, measured tone, out of character for his friend whom in jest he referred to as "motormouth." Instinctively, he grasped his briefcase with its vintage .357 Magnum brought in today to show the maintenance man. He placed the firearm on the floor between his feet as they approached.

Ray, who was pushing a hand cart, and a man wearing a flak jacket and carrying an assault rifle entered the Sound Generator room filled with computer screens, dials, pressure gauges and flow meters. Pointing his weapon at Ramminger, Nazari demanded, "Where are the engineer and maintenance man?"

"Engineer's out on inspection, should be back within the next few minutes. Maintenance man's gone to the workshop for his ladder and three new fluorescent bulbs to change the fixture in the gallery elevator lobby," he answered in an even monotone.

As he spoke, they heard an aluminum ladder being expanded and the maintenance man climbing the steps. Stepping through the door, Nazari fired a single shot. The bullet struck the base of his brain, exiting through his left eye as the maintenance man fell four feet to the floor, knocking over the ladder and breaking the bulbs. Reentering the room, Nazari turned toward Ramminger, who shot him in the left groin.

The impact threw Nazari to the ground, crying out. The pain was excruciating as he reached out, trying to regain control of his weapon before Ray wrestled it away.

"What's going on? Was that gunfire? What's happening? Who's that?" the engineer gasped, running into the room.

"Slow down. One thing at a time," Ray said. "Three of them came in as we were closing the gift shop. Put everyone on the floor and this one told me to bring the box and him to Ernie. Asked how much concrete between here and the outer wall. Our maximum power generation, a handful of questions along those lines. He killed Kenny."

"Is this guy gonna live?"

"If we do and help comes soon," Ramminger replied. Turning to the Ray, he asked, "Is your brother-in-law working this afternoon? Call him and tell him to bring the cavalry. No need to be heroes, but if we don't stop these guys, lots of people will die, and our country could take a hell of a hit—more than it already has. Doubt the bomb's been armed. Bet his instructions were to kill us, then arm it with enough lead time to be several miles away when it detonated. Let's lock it in the storeroom. It's got a steel door and door frame. If we don't make it out, they won't find it and if they do, doubt they have the firepower to blow the door."

"Wayne? It's Ray," he said to the Page chief of police. "Three terrorists tried to blow the dam. Two are in the gift shop with six civilians, and Ellen and Gail. The third forced me to wheel what I'm guessing is a Cold War era atomic bomb to the control room. The bastard killed Kenny. Shot him off his ladder. Ernie had his .357 with him and shot the son of a bitch in the hip. We've got his gun. We're in the control room. All three of these guys are wearing flak jackets. Bring the cavalry and the EMTs. We're locking the bomb in the maintenance storage room. Gotta go. Hurry!"

They bound the terrorist's hands together above his head with duct tape, secured his wounded leg to the leg of one desk, and, moving a second desk, secured his outstretched hands to its leg. "Sam, stay here and watch him. If he moves, kick him in the groin. Ray, help me move this," Ramminger instructed.

Locked away, they taped the key to the underside of the workbench, which held a large vise. "Are you more comfortable with his rifle or my .357?" Ramminger asked Ray.

"His rifle. Damn, never killed anything bigger than a cockroach. I don't know if I can do this. I might be good for one shot. Not two. Remind me, where's the safety?"

"You can. You want to wound him, not kill him; he's wearing a flak jacket, shoot him in the leg. Point it at him and squeeze the trigger. It'll fire more rounds than you can count."

"Two more in the gift shop, right? Sam, help me set this guy on the floor of the elevator and prop him up. Put paper clips in his mouth and tape it shut. He won't be able to talk intelligibly. We'll all take the elevator to the basement and leave him sitting on the floor. Sam, hold the elevator for three minutes. Ray, you go up the south stairs. I'll go up the north. Top of the stairs, open the door and listen for the elevator. When the bell rings and the doors open, those guys will be expecting their buddy. When they don't see him, they'll come to the elevator. Shoot the guy closest to you. You'll have a clear shot. His focus will be on his comrade. Shoot him in the ass. Are we good? Let's roll."

Three distended minutes passed in silence, Ray sweating profusely. The door ajar as he pressed his back against the wall, he gripped his weapon.

The elevator bell sounded, and the doors opened. Mahta glanced toward it, not seeing his friend. "Hashem?" Hearing a muffled groan, he sprinted to the open elevator yelling over his shoulder, "He's down!"

Shots rang out. Mahta, hit in the right hip, fell, his body trembling. Hearing a metallic object hit the ground, Javadi turned to face his assailant; the room exploding with the sound of bullets from his automatic weapon as he fell, spraying bullets across the ceiling, his right knee shattered from behind.

"Sorry, Ernie. I thought I could do it. He was right in front of me, standing still. I dropped the gun trying to take the safety off. Glad you backed me up."

"He's out of commission, and you've got his gun. That's all that matters."

In mild shock, the older couples in the gift shop found nearby seating.

"Ladies and gentlemen, the Page police will be arriving any minute. Do any of you have any medical training? Ellen, Sam's downstairs. Retrieve him and bring the first aid kit. Where's Gail? Ray, help me with these guys," Ernie said.

Page Police Chief Wayne Emery, fifteen officers, and both ambulances arrived and were met at the door by Ray. While the police secured the premises and began interviewing everyone, the EMTs addressed the wounded and tried to calm the visitors.

"How bad are they?"

"Doubt any of them will ever walk again, Chief. The one shot in the left groin appears to have lost most of his pelvis. He's lost a lot of blood and unless we get him to surgery soon, we can't help him. I've called the hospital and put them on alert. The other hip I can't tell. And the leg, if I were a betting man, I'd say he's going to lose his leg above the knee," the senior EMT replied. "Call Flagstaff and tell 'em to send the helicopter. These wounds are way out of our league."

"I'm sending two officers with you for security and will have two more meet you at the hospital. Tell them to keep a lid on this till I get there. No need to cause a panic in town," the chief said.

After calling the Arizona Department of Public Safety, the Flagstaff Medical Center and the Phoenix FBI, the chief took Ray, Sam, Ernie, and his sergeant to the administrator's office.

"Start at the beginning and tell us everything."

Mission aborted.

The Cessna 172 Skyhawk pilot messaged his emergency contact, seeing several police cars and two ambulances as he flew over the parking lot of Glen Canyon Dam's Visitor Center at forty-seven hundred feet. He headed to Goodyear Airport in Phoenix to refuel for his return to Los Angeles.

26

Emma

1930 hrs. EDT Ann Arbor, Michigan
Saturday, October 26

By 7:30, eight and a half hours after the assault on the stadium, the government officials and the citizens of Ann Arbor had come to grips with the enormity of the attack and were addressing the issues. The mayor and county judge provided frequent updates on the local television and radio stations. They urged calm, requesting all to shelter in place, reminding everyone that the secretary of Homeland Security had suspended all train and air travel.

They provided updates regarding identification of loved ones lost in and around the stadium, as well as a hotline number to call for information regarding those transported to hospitals. They reviewed the proper procedure for disposal of contaminated clothing, reiterating the danger of coming into direct contact with the bottoms of their shoes or any surface with a viable agent.

If people had driven to the game, they were advised to wash their cars with chlorine bleach. Asking for calm, patience, and support for first responders, they explained the real possibility of a new public health risk from the overwhelming number of bodies. For this reason, they asked people to consider cremation. If a viable option, operators were standing by to help.

Critically ill patients consumed the first responders, emergency rooms and hospitals. Authorities asked the thousands suffering with broken bones, sprains, abrasions, and contusions incurred escaping the stadium to wait one day before seeking treatment. The mechanism of how and when cars left in the area could be retrieved was also frequently relayed, as were safety precautions for those who feared they had contacted the deadly agent.

University, Ann Arbor, and East Lansing police provided traffic control and cordoned off the four-block section around Michigan Stadium. Their increased presence offered a sense of calm and curtailed any attempts of looting in the area.

The atrocity consumed the medical capabilities of Ann Arbor and the entire state. Loss of the city's two largest hospitals and the relocation of their patients compounded the circumstances. Addressing even the temporary needs of over 30,000 patients was impossible. No drill or exercise could have prepared the healthcare system for devastation on this scale.

Officials in Ohio sent additional medical equipment, personnel, and National Guard personnel. The Guard coordinated transportation needs throughout both states and worked with state health departments, while county coroners' offices established temporary morgues.

Identifying and removing the bodies was both tedious and exhausting for the 300 Guardsmen fitted with the Quick2000 gas masks, protective overalls, rubber gloves, and shoe covers flown in from Fort Knox. Having exhausted their supply of body bags, the Guard took advantage of the cool weather to use plastic trash bags, duct tape, and ID tags. As sections of stadium parking lots were cleared and decontaminated, they laid victims in rows of fifty behind signs of the first letter of their last name, knowing several days would pass before relatives could come to the stadium for positive identification and final arrangements.

The numbers were staggering as the death toll approached 85,000: 79,000 from the stadium, another 4,714 from the four-block zone around the stadium, 156 from the impact of the single engine plane into St Joseph's and 92 at University Medical Center. In all, more than twice the number lost in the Korean War.

Stadium lights were on throughout the night. Starting at the stadium and moving outward in a meticulous circular fashion, Public Works sprayed the air with a half-percent chloride solution in the hopes of pulling any remaining agent out of the air and neutralizing or denaturing any residual.

Throughout the night and early morning hours, the Department of Motor Vehicles and Ann Arbor Police began the task of decontaminating and relocating unclaimed cars in university lots and on neighborhood streets. Wanting to clear the vicinity and keep people away from ground zero, they filled university lots away from the stadium and moved the overflow to public school stadium lots, contacting the owners' families.

The university established a relief zone across campus where workers received updates, hot coffee, sandwiches, and personal protective equipment. In all, a work force of 3,000 was mobilized to complete this painstaking work.

The last vestiges of sunlight cast long shadows on Andrus Park as Mike looked out his office window. The afternoon was spent at the State Police Headquarters with Don where they debriefed the governor, secured the unexploded bundle transfer to the FBI, and prepared for Monday's statewide honeybee canvas. Exhausted, he intended to make some notes and a few phone calls and go home. The snowstorm had pummeled the region and moved eastward, leaving a clear sky, tens of thousands of blinking stars, and the promise of a cold night.

"Mike. Want to give you an update on Emma. She's awake and asking a thousand questions," Jack exclaimed when Mike answered the phone for what felt like the hundredth time that day.

"Wow! That's great. What a blessing. Did they call or are you in Houston?" Mike asked. "What's going on there? Can you even breathe?

"I'm with Emma in Houston. The Ship Channel explosions happened as I was driving into town. It's all over the radio. Nobody knows what's going on, is it over, what's been bombed, will the city be next, all kinds of rumors, something about a chlorine or some kind of gas leak. The city's in a panic, ambulances are streaming into all the hospitals here in the Texas Medical Center. Don't think they know yet how bad it is.

"Broke windows all over town, including some here at the hospital. But we're okay. When they grounded the flights right after we talked this morning, I got in my Dad's pickup and, five hours later, I'm holding Emma's hand in the ICU saying a little prayer when she opens her eyes, smiles, and says, 'Hi, Daddy, where am I? What happened?'" Jack said softly, choking back tears as he looked out the window from the hallway outside the ICU. "The doctors, a social worker, and the chaplain all want to give her two days to recover before we tell her what happened in town and to our family."

"That's smart, as much as she's been through and has ahead of her," Mike concurred.

"Doctors said she was lucky to fall where she did, but her lungs have suffered permanent damage from the scorched air she inhaled, and she faces a long, uphill battle," Jack continued. His voice was heavy with exhaustion but undercut with a twinge of hope that Mike was glad to hear. "They got her stabilized and rehydrated and have run more tests than I can count but they say her brain, eyes, ears, and tummy are all clear and are hopeful there won't be any other lasting effects from the shockwave. Also said only 10% of people who wake up from a coma ever fully recover, but it looks like she's well on her way.

"Her lung damage, especially her right upper lobe, will mean she can't exert herself too much so she'll never run track or play basketball. But regular exercise, like walking, riding her bike, will be good for her. She'll also have to watch what she eats. No junk food, fried foods, excess salt, soda or caffeine. Still, a small price to pay for having her back."

"Sounds like a good diet for all of us. Can she still ride her horse?"

"Funny, that's the first thing she asked the doctor. We'll have to see. No dust. So, the cats and the dog are probably out and maybe she can ride if she doesn't go in the barn."

"Nice that her horse is her biggest concern," Mike mused. "No matter what happens from here on, we've all won the jackpot. She's alive and well. So much loss, so many challenges for all of us. But we can focus on her. Considering what she's been through, sounds like she's got a remarkable life ahead of her. A lot more things she *can* do than can't. She's not out of the woods yet, but this is great news. This has got to help your folks and Grandma."

"I was talking to Mom. She wants you and as many of the Mutschlers as can to meet us in San Antonio for Thanksgiving. After what's happened, she really wants to celebrate family."

"Count me in. Any time, any place. Speaking of seeing family, there's nothing I can do till they open the skies and start flying again. Whenever that is, I'm headed your way. How long will you be in Houston?" Mike asked.

"If she does as good as the doctors think, we'll go home on Tuesday. We'll come back for check-ups every six weeks and if she's okay, they'll push it out to twice a year."

"Don't rush—and make sure she's okay."

"Oh, yeah," Jack continued, "Dad said they brought in an excavator, two front-end loaders and another dozer and hope to have the fire out by morning. Excavator started digging right there on the Gin yard. Made sense, it's as close to the fire as you can get, and when it's over you can put the dirt back. Trucks started dropping their loads on either side of the track. With the short distance, and the extra dozer and loaders, it's made a noticeable difference. If we'd started on this when it first happened, we'd be close to done by now."

"Don't go there. Best you guys built the firebreak and kept it contained," Mike said. "Got some news for you. Maria's statement on that rogue car may yet provide a lead. We found a new dark blue Camry with a Colorado license plate 026-TXN, rented by a guy from Fresno, California at 7:40 yesterday morning at San Antonio International and returned at 2:36 in the afternoon. The mileage fits. Did Maria get even a glimpse of the driver? Male, female, young, old, dark hair? Anything?"

"She said she didn't recognize him, so it must have been a guy. I'll check to see if she has any more. I knew you guys were good but that's impressive," Jack said.

"Only if it pans out, and we catch 'em. I passed the information to the FBI in San Antonio. We'll see what comes of it. They're gonna want to talk to her," Mike responded. "Small steps, big issues, we're going to get through this. Talk to you in the morning. Give Emma a hug. Y'all are in my prayers."

27

Taking Stock

1730 hrs. MDT Boise, Idaho
Saturday, October 26

The call from Jack and the good news about Emma buoyed Mike's spirits and gave him hope. Taking a deep breath, exhaustion was about to overcome him as he remembered how tired he'd felt yesterday while catching his last fish. He also understood that the combination of last night's four-hour nap, the morning's horrific hangover, an eight-hour drive in a blizzard, and working straight through until now hadn't helped.

Standing, he stretched his six-foot, six-inch frame to its fullest, walked around his desk to the middle of his office, and laid on the rug where he did five minutes of stretching, exercise, and a yoga breathing technique. Back at his window, he gazed at the southwestern sky and the Milky Way. It always gave him peace and great comfort. After today, even more.

Walking to the conference table in the corner of his office, he made quick notes of Frog's progress with the possible explosive depots, his conversations with the Florida beekeepers, follow-ups with the FBI regarding the unexploded bundle, and Maria's possible intel for the San Antonio FBI office. He was just getting to his travel plans for Texas when his phone rang.

"Doctor Paxton?"

Answering, he saw a dark-haired woman in her mid-fifties calling on a video call. "Yes."

"Do you have a few minutes to speak with FBI Director Ferguson Townsend?"

"Yes, of course." He sighed and sat back in his swivel chair.

"Please hold."

At the center of the table sat a 110-year-old Fukien Tea Bonsai tree, a gift from Frog when Mike had decided to establish the second Zia office in Boise. A sister tree was on the conference table in his office in San Francisco. Sally had given it to him as a wedding present, saying, "May this tree be a symbol of strength and beauty no matter the obstacles in our path." Frog found the nursery, talked to the arborist and, when presenting this tree to him, said, "No matter the circumstance, look to the perseverance of this tree to survive and thrive." Mike had nicknamed the San Francisco tree Hither, this one Yon.

"Doctor Paxton, Ferguson Townsend," a balding, bespectacled, and serious-looking black man of forty-eight said in a deep, bass voice. "I'm sure you're still trying to come to grips with what's happened today."

"Come to grips and hope beyond hope it doesn't continue tomorrow, or ever," Mike replied.

"Doctor Paxton, we use your Zia Securities systems here at the FBI, because we believe it's the best cybersecurity option in the world. I'll cut right to the chase. The president would like you to consider heading a Special Task Force for Cybersecurity to help us find these people and bring them to justice."

"Thank you, Director. I appreciate your confidence. The timing and coordination of today's attack has internet communication written all over it. They must've left footprints, and it's those footprints we must find and follow to catch them." Mike stood and covered his mouth before yawning. "Excuse me, Director, it's been a long day."

"Not a problem, I bet we see a lot of those before this is over. We're in a global cyberwar against people who steal military, industrial and intellectual property for their own gain. They've no moral compass and are involved in undermining our national cultural beliefs, infrastructure, and societal underpinnings. We need to bring the full force of our national resources to bear against this enemy, and we believe your software capabilities can enhance our efforts. I know what I'm asking is monumental, to put your life on hold until we find these guys, but you'll have absolute program authority and unlimited access to all our IT resources, to me, and the vice president. You'll meet with the president. You may need time to think this through. Is there any information I can provide or questions I can answer? Bottom line, will you consider such an undertaking?"

Mike sat back in his swivel chair, closed his eyes, and thought. Then, looking directly into the camera, he said, "Oddly enough, I've been working on this since last night when I heard of the Agnew fire on the national news. Grew up there. Lost most of my family in the explosions and fire."

"I'm terribly sorry. Did any of them survive?"

"Thank you, yes. My ninety-six-year-old grandmother, an aunt and uncle, one cousin and his daughter. We lost sixteen."

Mike described his day, the steps they'd already taken to begin identifying possible explosive depot storage sites, and his desire to use honeybees to validate them. "As for your offer, I have a few logistical questions. I'm a businessman and don't handle bureaucracy and red tape well. I'll need your assurance my efforts and energy can be focused on the task at hand, and I can leave all the bureaucratic machinations, politics, media circuses, and other nonsense to you. I'd prefer if you alone are aware we're involved. If we need access, clearances, whatever, to complete our work, I'll come to you. I will not go through channels, put it out for bid, fill it out in triplicate, or whatever. We do, however, appreciate accountability and will document everything we do."

"Keep me in the loop. You'll have my personal cell phone and 24/7 access," Townsend assured him.

"Our guys are all handpicked. They've been in the trenches for years and are good at what they do. They're what's kept this company at the forefront of the international cybersecurity market. We also have people who work with us I don't know and don't need to. These guys are a dynamic group unto themselves. A trusted and loyal friend of mine has earned their trust and worked with them for years. They can go places and find information you and I can't imagine. I pay them with specific pieces of computing equipment, the latest versions of technical software, or cold hard cash. Whatever it takes. Few are Americans, and they're the best in the world at what they do.

"If you're serious about finding those who attacked us today, this resource can expedite the search. They do what they do at a tempo set by themselves. They'll not ask for or wait on the legal system. Subpoenas, search warrants, Interpol, you guys, they don't care. They're confident you don't have anyone on your staff who understands what they're doing or can catch them. I'll provide the information they uncover and its current location, and I will leave it to you to determine how to translate it into the legal system. Strong possibility a large part of the data will come from outside of the US."

"Doctor Paxton, that is, in fact, part of why I called. We trust your company and are aware of your international resources and contacts. I see now why you said you would prefer that very few know of your involvement. For both our sakes, I assure you great pains will be taken to see that is the case. We need your help."

"It's taken over two decades to build Zia. I'm willing to help, but not at the expense of sacrificing my business. We must care for the needs of our clients. Taking this on will require additional resources. They won't be cheap."

Townsend laughed. "We're the federal government. Our checks won't bounce."

"Let's hope not," Mike chuckled. "Director, it's been an arduous week. Thank you for your confidence in our company and trust in me. What you're asking is a huge responsibility that will impact me, my company, and many of my most trusted employees. Let me sleep on it. Can I call you tomorrow, say 2 p.m. your time?

For the first time all day, Director Townsend realized he had missed his oldest daughter's violin recital. An involved father and family man, Ferguson was proud of his two daughters—his violinist and his swimmer. Three years apart, the girls were buddies. He knew they had already had dinner but called home to see how everyone was holding up and to let his wife know not to expect him for at least another hour. If the president wanted the senior staff briefed in the morning, the possibility of an all-nighter of preparation loomed large.

As he reran his conversation with Mike Paxton in his head, Ferguson wasn't confident Paxton would take the job and wondered who he might turn to next. His phone rang, jarring him back to reality.

"Director, Caden Vickers, do you have a minute? I think you'll want to hear this."

"Hey, Caden, what d'you got?" Ferguson asked, recognizing the voice of the SAIC of the FBI's Detroit office.

"Standish is a community of 1,500 people north and west of Ann Arbor. Cub Scouts from Pack 129 camped out on the shore of Cranberry Lake last night, three adult leaders, eleven Cubs, and the twin 16-year-old, Eagle Scout sons of the scout master. The adults and Cubs went on a hike, leaving the older boys with instructions to have lunch ready upon their return. The boys heard a commotion a hundred yards to their east and set out to see if anyone needed help. As they approached, they saw two box trucks, a Toyota 4Runner, and a Ford Explorer parked on the side of the road and eight men working to unload what appeared to be two large gliders.

"Smart enough to keep their distance, their heads down, their eyes open and their mouths shut, they used their cellphones to videotape the launch of two drones used in the Ann Arbor attack. The kids weren't the best videographers we've ever used, but they got something we could work with. As of thirty-five minutes ago, we've matched their video with video recovered from fans in the stands and television coverage of the attack in Ann Arbor and are confident we have the make and model numbers of the Israel Aerospace Industries Searcher Unmanned Aerial Vehicles. Older model drones. We'll be able to track where they're from. In addition to footage of the assembly, we have a view of the ground operators and their handheld line-of-sight controllers used for launch. We're still studying the footage. We believe once airborne, ground control switched them to a satellite link for the attacks. The kids got head shots of all eight terrorists, audio, and vehicle license plate numbers.

"The boys stayed put until the vehicles moved away, then made it back to camp. Dad gave them what-for for missing their lunch deadline. When they got home, and Mom brought Dad current on the events at the stadium, Dad called us and, at our invitation, brought them here to our offices in Detroit. We've spent several hours with them, fed 'em dinner. They're spending the night courtesy of the taxpayers."

"This is great, Caden. Thanks. Send me a copy of the video, and we'll have the team here look at it as well. It's nice to have something concrete to work with."

Sitting at his desk in the J. Edgar Hoover Building, Ferguson looked at the names on his list: Robert Van Horn, Ann Arbor, check; Larry Belton, Los Angeles, check; Brent Conrad, Dover, check; Matt Ratliff, Houston, check; John Springer, Phoenix, check; Morgan McBride, Salt Lake, check; Ron Stewart, Baltimore, check; Mike Paxton, Boise, check; Julie Cummings, Albuquerque, check. His last call, often local, Pennsylvania Avenue, tonight to a bunker in Montana.

"Madam President, I'd like to say we believe they've done all they're going to do, but I can't. We don't know who they are, and we have no idea when they'll stop. We're treating each event as an independent crime scene," Ferguson stated without enthusiasm. "These are smart, well-organized professionals. They're not going to be easy to apprehend."

"I know, Ferguson, but they are human, and humans make mistakes. This may be one of the most difficult tasks we've ever undertaken. Still, I have immense confidence in you and your team, Homeland, and the Pentagon, and I believe we'll sort out this awful mess and find them."

"Thank you, Madam President. I'll leave you with three positive notes. I've spoken with Michael Paxton. David Eller says he's the best we have and puts him in the top echelon worldwide. Paxton told me he'd let me know tomorrow."

"Great! Would a call from me help? I'd be glad to talk with him," the president said.

"Maybe. FYI, he was raised in Agnew and lost sixteen family members yesterday."

She sighed, the sound weighted by her exhaustion. "Please give him my condolences."

"I will. Second, the destruction of the Glen Canyon Dam was averted because of the quick action of the staff, namely Ernie Ramminger. He shot the terrorists. Without him, we would have lost the dam.

"And last, thanks to some Boy Scouts on a campout, we have video footage of what we believe to be the launching of the drones used in Michigan. I'll send you the contact information for Ramminger, and the scouts. I'm sure they'd appreciate a word from you, and I will let you know Paxton's decision tomorrow."

"They may be smart people, but we've already got tangible evidence to work with. We've a long, long way to go," the president said. "I pray this attack is over. It's been the first of what will be many long, hard days. I'd like to say go home and get some sleep, but I need you to do a briefing for the vice president, the Cabinet, Joint Chiefs, Attorney General, and a few others in the morning in the Situation Room. I'm sorry to do this to you, but it's important to start everyone on the same page. I'll talk to them at 0900. Thank you, Ferguson. I've got to get ready to address the country."

28

Montana

2000 hrs. MDT Helena, Montana
Saturday, October 26

"Ladies and gentlemen, the president of the United States."

Dressed in a charcoal gray suit and a white silk blouse with simple, diamond stud earrings, the president looked polished without appearing overdone. Her customary composure was on full display. The lights and television camera focused on her head and shoulders as she sat behind a desk in studio one of a television station in Helena, Montana, American flags to her right and left behind her.

"My fellow Americans, yesterday and throughout the day today, those who would do us harm carried out a complex scheme, attacking the foundation of our country. Taking advantage of our free and open society, they have forever altered our way of life. In the history of mankind, no nation has ever suffered so great a single day loss at the hands of others. Today, life ended for more than a quarter of a million Americans. As I speak to you, tens of thousands continue to struggle for breath.

"Americans, as diverse as our country itself, the rich, the poor, people of all races, creeds, colors and kinds, those who make this country great, part of our past, present, and future, were lost when cowards unleashed weapons of mass destruction on football games and auto racing. The generational fabric of our country enjoying their lives together, supporting their favorites and passing their passion on to their families and friends now gone, as are families on vacation, train men and longshoremen, working to make a better life for their families, innocent young children playing in playgrounds and streets when their homes were set ablaze and reduced to rubble.

"Our allies and adversaries alike have voiced unequivocal condemnation of these acts and the people who perpetrated them. Acts of war, depredation, even terrorism have been with us since the dawn of civilization, but the scale of these cruel, callous, and unprovoked attacks set them apart as among the most heinous of all time.

"Those responsible for this barrage are afraid to speak of their desires. They are unwilling to work within the boundaries of international law, too weak to seek consensus among the world's leaders. These henchmen are unwilling to accept responsibility for their actions.

"We have and will continue to pay the price. This was a major assault on our best and brightest. The future of our nation depends on our young people. Our next generation of doctors and lawyers, teachers and scientists, businessmen and philosophers, musicians and artists, craftsmen, and farmers have suffered a great loss. Entire families have been lost. Fine universities have suffered in unimaginable ways. Research programs, musical scores, training programs, art, and cultural events in development or ongoing have been damaged or lost.

"What was attacked was our way of life. Our democratic society allows us to live where we want and do what we want. We raise our families with every expectation they can exceed our highest hopes.

"This wasn't a localized indiscriminate shelling, a bus, a plane, shopping mall, subway station, concert hall, night club, or school. It was a well-planned, well-financed attack on a nation and its people. For terrorist pilots, gunmen, and suicide bombers of bygone attacks, the ante has been upped an order of magnitude. This attack sends a powerful message: state-sponsored attackers or terrorists allowed to acquire military-grade weapons are not playing by the rules. They do not believe anyone will have the intestinal fortitude to respond."

Looking directly into the camera, she paused and spoke directly to the terrorists. "To those who perpetrated this attack on America, my message to you is clear: we have the finest investigative tools known to man. We have unparalleled data gathering, storage and analytical capability. We will work together tirelessly, county with county, agency with agency, federal, state and city, to bring you to a fitting end."

Pausing to let that message sink in, the television camera pulled back and she continued.

"This attack on America impaired our economy and pushed the world toward an economic recession. The attack on our oil and gas production and processing and our petrochemical industry will make thousands of the products we use every day hard, if not impossible, to get. The attack damaged our ability to feed our nation by destroying a primary way by which we move food and other goods across our great land.

"This assault attempted to use a nuclear weapon to destroy the Glen Canyon Dam, among the largest manmade structures on the face of the earth. The quick action of the staff disarmed the terrorists and saved the lives of six people taken hostage. In so doing, they saved the ecosystem of the Grand Canyon, Lake Mead and Hoover Dam. Had these heroes not been successful, the hydroelectric power generated by those two facilities could have been lost, causing major damage to the western power grid and leaving the western third of our nation without power.

"We're a great nation, filled with remarkable people. These acts cannot take away the fabric of our country. They cannot dim the beacon of freedom and opportunity that draws citizens from around the world to our shores. As a nation dedicated to the ideals of freedom, opportunity, and the right of all to be what they can be, we might not embrace our neighbor's legal actions yet will fight to the death defending their right to those actions. The cowards who perpetrated these terrorist acts cannot diminish the strength of our resolve.

"These acts intended to cause chaos, civil instability, and withdrawal, will not. In Ann Arbor and Dover, Los Angeles, Page, Agnew, and Houston, people saw those in need and moved to help. They gave blood, provided nourishment, brought comfort, shelter, and caring. Our emergency response plans through FEMA and the Red Cross are already at work with local rescue efforts, helping the injured and those providing their care.

"Tomorrow, this nation will fill the pews of its churches, synagogues, temples, and mosques to pray for strength and guidance. Afterward, we'll roll up our sleeves and get to work.

"Our military is strong and ready. Our security systems will redouble our efforts to determine what has happened, how it happened, and resolve it will not happen again. Our government agencies at the local, state and federal levels will continue to function without interruption. Our financial institutions will open on Tuesday, ready to do business and help repair and strengthen our national infrastructure, our rail, petrochemical, agricultural, and utilities sectors.

"The cowards who devised this plan tried to destroy our nation and what it stands for. To the contrary, what they have accomplished is to bring international condemnation and global unification to find those responsible and bring them to justice. Every member nation of the United Nations, except Afghanistan and North Korea, has sent their condolences for our losses and has pledged support to root out this evil and put a stop, once and for all, to international terrorism. The nations of this world cannot and *will* not tolerate the use of weapons of mass destruction. On behalf of the American people, I thank the many world leaders who have reached out to us.

"Speaking with those leaders over the past few hours, I assure you this band of outlaws will find they have no place to hide. We have rooted them from their caves and tents. Now we will flush them out of their remote hiding places or their urban penthouse apartments, wherever they may be, and bring them to justice. Together with the civilized nations of this world, we'll go mile-by-mile, acre-by-acre, and rock-by-rock until they're found, no compromise, no negotiation.

"It's no longer an issue of security here in the United States. The world's no longer safe. And it cannot be until these terrorists and evildoers are stopped. It may take many years to unravel all the tentacles of this terrorist network and stamp them out. Tonight, we, here and now, redouble our commitment to this task and will not stop until it's done.

"No one has yet claimed responsibility for these abysmal atrocities. The magnitude of these attacks, their national scope, and their brazen fashion suggest those responsible may have crossed traditional ideological boundaries for the expertise required. Terroristic attacks on civilian soft targets where people are going on with their day-to-day routines is a strategy of the weak. It also reflects the total disregard these cowards have for the rule of law.

"To those who have suffered loss of family and friends, we, a knowing and caring nation, feel your pain and share your loss. Though we are a nation of many cultures, we are a country of neighbors and friends who support each other and come together as one nation under God. What these dealers of doom do not and cannot understand is the thousands upon thousands of acts of kindness shown to those who have suffered. Many have lost all they have or ever hope to have and yet they share what there is with friends, neighbors, and people they've never met. It's the fabric of our country, aid and support pouring into those in need. We will survive. We will rebuild. We will emerge a stronger nation.

"On Monday, I shall ask Congress to designate next Sunday as a National Day of Remembrance in acknowledgement of those who lost their lives and all whose lives have been forever changed. It will help us to focus on the task ahead, fighting terrorism, intolerance, and hatred, against those who would kill innocent men, women, and children to force their will upon others.

"The search has already begun. They cannot rest. There is no impunity for mass murder or crimes against humanity, no mitigating circumstances. The events of today have touched all Americans from every walk of life. Terrorist attacks can shake the underpinnings of our largest industries but cannot obstruct the foundation of America. These acts can shatter steel rails across our country but cannot blemish the steel of American resolve. As with December 7, 1941, and September 11, 2001, none of us will forget this day. I ask for your vigilance and alertness as we move forward, united with our neighbors, friends, and allies to defend freedom and all that is good and just in our world.

"Stay alert, talk to your children, reassure them theirs is a great country full of extraordinary people, and they are, and will be, safe. We will bring those who did this to a fitting end.

"Our nation was founded on religious freedom, the freedom to worship our God as each of us sees fit. We call our God by many names: El Shaddai, Brahman, Yahweh, Jehovah, Tao, Allah, Lord God Almighty, and more. Our Native Americans, those here first, know Him by yet another name, and I close tonight with a quote from an unknown speaker addressing the National Congress of American Indians in the mid-1960s:

'In early days, we were close to nature. We judged time, weather conditions, and many things by the elements—the good earth, the blue sky, the flying of geese, and the changing winds. We looked to these for guidance and answers. Our prayers and thanksgiving were said to the four winds—to the East, from whence the new day was born, to the South, which sent the warm breeze which gave a feeling of comfort, to the West, which ended the day and brought rest, and to the North, the Mother of winter whose sharp air awakened a time of preparation for the long days ahead. We lived by God's hand through nature and evaluated the changing winds to tell us or warn us of what was ahead.

'Today we are again evaluating the changing winds. May we be strong in spirit and equal to our Fathers of another day in reading the signs accurately and interpreting them wisely. May Wah-Kon-Tah, the Great Spirit, look down upon us, guide us, inspire us, and give us courage and wisdom. Above all, may He look down upon us and be pleased.'

"Hug your children. May God bless you and this great nation. Good night."

29

The Miasma of Uncertainty

Watching

0600 hrs. CET Vienna, Austria

Sunday, October 27

Post Attack, Day 1

Exhaustion had overtaken Ana as she slept on the couch in Parsa's office, while he, Jamal, and Omar monitored the *Hujum.* "The Attack on America continues," the American newscaster said as he began what would normally be the lead story for the Saturday night local news in Washington, D.C. "Fortunately, this time their efforts were thwarted by quick action. At a news conference in Phoenix, an FBI spokesperson said three armed men wearing flak jackets stormed the Carl Hayden Visitor Center at Glen Canyon Dam at the northern entrance to the Grand Canyon as the center closed. They took thirteen people hostage, six visitors and seven employees, forcing the civilians to lay on the floor and killing an employee. The terrorists compelled Park Ranger Ray Wilson to transport what authorities believe is a post-World War II-era Russian made, 'suitcase atomic bomb' on a two-wheeled hand cart to the operations control center deep within the dam. There, the gunmen shot and killed Kenneth Salters, the maintenance man on duty. Plant operator Ernie Ramminger, a decorated Army veteran and seventeen-year employee at the dam, shot the gunman. He and Wilson were then able to disarm the terrorist and call the Page, Arizona police. With the help of the plant engineer, they took the remaining terrorists by surprise, wounding both as the police arrived. All three terrorists are in custody and receiving medical attention. No other hostages were harmed. The bomb squad's working to secure the bomb.

"Had the attack been successful, authorities say it would have produced major damage to Glen Canyon Dam and the Grand Canyon. It's possible Hoover Dam may have also been impacted. The loss of the hydroelectric power generated by the two facilities would have resulted in a major, long-term shutdown of our nation's western electrical grid. The loss of water would've had an immediate and long-term impact on how we as a nation feed ourselves, and a catastrophic impact on Las Vegas, Phoenix, Los Angeles, San Diego, and all of Southern California. The FBI has heralded Ernie Ramminger and his two coworkers as heroes.

"Repeating, three terrorists attempted to blow up Glen Canyon Dam with what appears to be a Russian-made atomic device. The attack failed. Even so, we have suffered the greatest loss of life on our own soil since Gettysburg and have endured the most devastating thirty-six-hour period in the history of mankind. Our lives, as Americans, have been changed forever.

"Join us tomorrow morning at 9 a.m. Eastern Time when we bring you a special report, 'Soft Targets—Attack on America.' We'll update you on today's latest developments and take an in-depth look at how we Americans are vulnerable to the actions of terrorist groups because of our free and open society."

"Damn!" Omar remarked, "I wanted that one. It would have made a ghost town of Las Vegas, destroyed the economies of Nevada and Arizona, played serious havoc with the western electrical grid, demolished a multibillion-dollar fruit and vegetable industry, and, in combination with their inability to move coal, shuttered at least half of the electrical generation capacity of the western states."

"Don't beat yourself up," Parsa said. "Their infrastructure took a serious hit. I too wish Glen Canyon had succeeded. Still, you should be proud, your *Hujum* achieved its primary objectives. Listen, they'll pursue the atomic bomb and Russian angles first, then chase the flood of information we'll provide on social media about the drug cartels. It wasn't a total loss."

"Yes and no. We planned, ran every option. The percentage of success for Glen Canyon as designed was 98.6%. Those were three experienced, dedicated soldiers," Omar countered.

"We're not beating ourselves up," Jamal interjected. "We're frustrated. What should have been the easiest, failed. Now I must rectify the problem and nullify a potential link. The American television reporter didn't name him, but he said Nazari died on their helicopter en route to the hospital. Javadi and Mahta are seasoned professionals. They'll remain silent until released from the hospital. I'll speak with my contact in Colombia. They have inmates in the Federal Correctional

Institution in Phoenix. If Javadi and Mahta are released into the general population, they'll be executed in the yard. If held in the prison infirmary, their food will be poisoned. Either way they will die before the sun sets on their first day in the Phoenix FCI. Unfortunate. They are good men. We'll monitor America's investigation, but all they'll find is two nameless inmates killed by drug cartel hitmen already serving life sentences for multiple murder convictions."

"I am sorry for the loss of the mission and the personnel. We'll expand on your use of Colombian inmates to fan the fire of illicit drug involvement in the attack on social media," Parsa said. "Even in death, they will be of service to Allah."

Omar helped Ana up from the couch. They joined the others at the window, watching the first rays of light chase the darkness, the outline of the city coming into view. All at once, everything became distinguishable, and day was upon them. The majesty of the morning belied the cataclysm of what had transpired a few short hours earlier. On the television behind them, the American reporter stared at the camera. ". . . the loss of so many lives, as the president said in her address to the nation, a greater single day loss than any other in the history of mankind. The massive destruction of our petrochemical industry and our rail system seem to be the result of meticulous planning, an enormous logistics undertaking. This effort took potentially hundreds of people, extensive time, effort, and money. Those who planned and carried out these attacks are without a doubt the cruelest, most barbaric, evil people the world has seen since the atrocities of World War II."

FBI Director Ferguson Townsend, his senior assistants, three Watch Team Duty Officers, their communications assistants, and intelligence analysts worked through the night. Together, they prepared a modified version of the PDB—the president's daily brief—containing the latest summary of yesterday's attacks, including videotape and before and after photographs. He opened the meeting of the vice president, the majority and minority leaders of the House and Senate, cabinet members, the attorney general, the national security advisor, the White House chief of staff, high-ranking representatives from homeland security, the FBI, CIA, FEMA, the state and justice departments, and the Joint Chiefs of Staff, in the Situation Room in the basement of the West Wing of the White House. A three-ring binder sat in front of each of the thirty seats at the conference table. Chairs lining the walls increased the room's capacity to seventy-five, all with binders. Large television monitors, depicting graphic scenes from each impacted location, hung on the long walls of the rectangular room and behind and above Townsend's head as he stood, prepared to address the group.

A slender figure, Ferguson got to his feet, stiffly, unsteadily, numbness invading his leg. Thankful for his rubber-soled shoes and gripping his cane, an artifact from a near fatal automobile accident five months earlier, he faced his audience, knowing he had two hours to recite the lurid details of the previous day's disasters. "Welcome and thank you for coming. I hate to have drug you out so early this morning. Each of you has been invited by the president or handpicked by your secretary or director," he told them, his signature bass voice commanding their attention. "The president has been moved to a secure location and will be joining us via video conference at 0900. At this moment she's talking to our NATO allies and other heads of state. Between now and then, I'll bring you current on where we are with yesterday's attacks and correct any misinformation being portrayed by the media. Her top priority is finding those responsible and bringing them to justice.

"She wants Homeland Security to coordinate this effort. The secretary has asked me to establish the infrastructure for our plan of action. We'll have time for questions before the president speaks to us. If you have additional questions, see me afterwards."

Ferguson laid out a detailed plan, breaking the investigation into its several component parts, assigning field offices, information hubs, and roles for the Pentagon, CDC, FEMA, and ATEC, the Army Test and Evaluation Command, at Aberdeen Proving Ground.

"Cybersecurity and the use of the internet will be coordinated through our offices here in Washington," Ferguson continued, not knowing Mike Paxton's decision. "One last note before we move on. David, please stand. Ladies and gentlemen, this is Dr. David Eller. He'll be providing all IT support. David and his team played an essential role in the tracking and eventual capture of Osama bin Laden. We've included his contact information in your packets. Before you leave today, I want each of you to provide him with the names and contact information of your in-house IT lead. David has resources and can find information you can't yet imagine you'll need or have interest in. Don't hesitate to call on him. The president wants me to emphasize we're all in this together. We'll share our knowledge; there'll be no information silos! She is serious about this.

"DOJ will be involved every step of the way. We'll do these probes by the book. When we find these guys, she wants no possibility of any legal issue standing in the way of swift, clean convictions. She wants the full weight of our national resources brought to bear on this.

"Let's start. We have a lot of ground to cover in a short time," Ferguson said firmly. "Look at the packet in front of you, it's current as of two hours. At the outset, let me say this attack was the most well-designed, organized, funded, and executed terrorist assault ever carried out worldwide. These terrorists are both smart and brutal, demonstrating a degree of sophistication never seen before. Their use of weapons of mass destruction is about more than killing. They intended to send a message: no one else is merciless enough to retaliate in kind.

"There have been no calls on social media or any other communication claiming credit for these heinous acts. We don't know if this is the result of a single organization or a consortium. Was it carried out by a known terrorist group or groups, or by, or in conjunction with a drug cartel? Is this the first of many or a single all-out attack? Will there be additional attacks today, tomorrow, next week? Will it be expanded to our allies and other countries?" Ferguson paused to let his audience contemplate the magnitude of yesterday's violence and the difficulty of the task before them.

The commanding voice continued, "In the hierarchy of horror, this is the first time both chemical and nuclear weapons were attempted to be deployed in tandem against a population. The CDC is working to determine if a biological agent was also used. These acts have been condemned by every nation as the entire world stands in awe of the carnage, annihilation and devastation resulting from this attack. Later today, the UN will convene and pass a resolution vowing to find those responsible and try them in The Hague for crimes against humanity.

"Let's look at what we know and what we don't know, beginning with who they are, where they are, and their mission. Are they homegrown terrorists or a foreign fanatic group? How did they enter the country? *How* did they depart, or did they? Was the attack self-contained by an external group or supported by members of embedded cells of like-minded people?" Ferguson's expression reflected some irritation.

"We cannot discount the possibility this was done by a drug cartel or a combination of cartels. We've recently hit them hard, taking away their profits. Drugs are a commodity market. If you're losing money, you won't stay in business. It's possible this entire attack is in response to this effort. Have they partnered with a Middle Eastern terrorist group or groups providing money and other resources?

"How and why did they choose their targets?" he asked rhetorically. "Their attack targeted our transportation, energy, and petrochemical infrastructure and required months if not years of planning, practice, and coordination. The costs associated with personnel, supplies and execution were substantial. How was it funded, and who funded it? Was there direct or tacit state support by a foreign government faction? Why haven't they taken responsibility? Is this attack a diversion for another action?" Ferguson asked, making eye contact with everyone at the table in turn as he spoke without notes but limped, pacing back and forth in front of them.

"The allover death toll stands at 258,632 and climbing. We expect it to rise as much as fifteen to eighteen percent throughout the week. Yesterday's attack resulted in the largest single day loss of life in recorded history. Add the elderly and children, those chronically ill, in need of mechanical respirators and other medical devices compromised by the loss of power, it will be months before we have a final number. It's safe to say it'll exceed a quarter of our nation's cumulative war dead of 1.3 million."

Ferguson paused to catch his breath, drink from his water bottle, and let all this sink in. "Let's look at each site so you're working with the most current information. We'll take them in chronological order." Stepping to the large television monitor behind him, he projected a short video of Friday's fire in Agnew, Texas. "The Agnew attack was our nation's worst rail accident in history and remains an active crime scene. Last year's census counted 873 residents of Agnew, and 886 are confirmed dead, 31 missing—exceeding the population due to a local gathering in the area. They hope to have the fire extinguished later today."

For the next ninety minutes, he brought the group current with detailed information on each crime scene, projecting slides of each location, drawing comparisons where appropriate and pointing out unique differences. Of the 376 Amtrak passengers stranded in mid-journey, all but twenty-two had been taken off the trains to safety. Those twenty-two would be recovered via helicopter this morning. Recovery of the engineers and crews would be complete by late that evening, but securing equipment and cargo was another story. Page 14 of their packets listed the destruction site totals by state. Current count, 1,842. The anticipated final total in the 3,000-4,000 range.

The loss of life, as bad as it was, could have been much worse. The strength of the chemical toxin had been calculated as strong enough to kill less than 100% of the people it contacted. This was not an act of kindness, but one designed to inflict as much fear and distrust as possible. The terrorists knew it took many more resources to care for the ill than it did to bury the dead.

"A word about CL-20. Found in the nose of each of the drones, it's the highest energy and density compound known among organic chemicals. It's a newer generation compound, developed by our own Navy for use as an explosive and rocket fuel. Ironically, a significant amount of CL-20 research has been done on the Michigan campus. We've no idea how the attackers acquired it, or their awareness of the work done on campus. Or if it played a role in the selection of this stadium and university as a target."

Pausing again, his pace slowed but the intensity in his voice remained undeterred. "More than 1.2 billion tons, 40% of the nation's goods every year, are moved by rail. The Ports of Los Angeles/Long Beach and Houston have effectively been marooned, accessible by neither truck nor train."

The screen showed a short video of Port Houston, tankers offloading crude oil, and containers being loaded onto the decks of large ships, followed by scenes of mountains of billowing black smoke and the hull of the *Nordic Spirit* protruding from the water as it lay crosswise in the channel. "The Houston Ship Channel is the second largest petrochemical complex in the world. In all, over 180 plants were targeted. The explosions and fires have rendered the entire fifty-two-mile-long complex crippled and the nation at risk. Discharge of hydrogen fluoride gas has killed 9,000 and counting. Release of massive amounts of chlorine gas has put another 650,000 people at risk, causing 400 deaths and an estimated half-million people seeking medical attention for upper airway swelling and obstruction, violent coughing, nausea, and vomiting. Air quality issues have brought the city to a standstill with major portions of the metropolitan region under shelter-in-place orders, further complicating recovery and hampering efforts to bring these fires under control."

Ferguson stopped, took a deep breath, closed his eyes, and leaned heavily on his cane. Exhausted, he inhaled, held it, let it out slowly, and gathered himself before continuing.

"What we know: The terrorists wanted to destroy America's oil, gas, and petrochemical industrial capability. We postulate they used ammonium nitrate. The same technology used in the Oklahoma City bombings. It's low tech, but effective. We're checking possible sources of the material, including the hijacking of an incoming train."

As another video showed on the screen of acres and acres of twisted tanks, housings, and pipes ablaze, he continued, "Our petrochemical industry has been crippled, impacting thousands of products used in the manufacturing of goods we use daily. Our country consumes 800 million gallons of gas a day. More than 10% is produced along the Ship Channel. The short-term frustration and inconvenience felt in the northeast by the hack and subsequent closure of the Colonial Gas Pipeline will be compounded a thousand times over before this is done. This will send oil prices soaring and will cause another recession here and worldwide. Our military's ability to protect our interests around the world and domestically has been dealt a devastating blow. How long will it take for the port to reopen? How long for the refineries, chemical and petrochemical plants to come back into production is anybody's guess.

"I want to take a moment and look at the loss of the ports of Houston and Long Beach/Los Angeles as a reflection of how these people think and what we're up against," he said, limping to the conference table and again taking a drink of water. "Together, Port Houston and the ports of Long Beach/Los Angeles provide over six million jobs throughout the country with an annual economic value exceeding a trillion dollars. The designers of these attacks knew the destruction of these ports would cause worldwide recession.

"Finally, Glen Canyon Dam." The scene on the screen shifted to a video of an aerial view of Lake Powell, the visitors center, and the full view of the dam from the western side. "What we know: their intended device has been recovered and is a USSR Cold War-era bomb. General Isom's assessment at last week's Senate Armed Services Committee was correct.

"We're fortunate this attack was averted. If not, hundreds of civilians on Lake Powell and in the Grand Canyon would have been lost. If the waters of Lake Powell had caused a tsunami in Lake Mead, enough to cause even the slightest structural defect in Hoover Dam, the water and electricity they provide could have been lost. Had it happened, more than twenty-seven million people, one in every eight Americans, would have been driven from their homes.

"Portions of our country's infrastructure are in tatters. Had they been successful at Glen Canyon, it would have been an order of magnitude worse. Many, many unknowns. Yesterday's events forever changed the lives of generations, their history, their present, and their future. Obviously, this is the president's number one priority and I quote: 'There must be tons of physical evidence to find and evaluate. Use local and state resources. They'll know the terrain better than anyone. We will have total cooperation at every level, with no silos of any kind.'

"She expects a progress report every morning. Send your findings to Homeland no later than 1630 hours every day. I'll take whatever questions you might have before we take a few minutes' break and are back in our seats by 0850 for the president."

The regional head of the Office of Homeland Security opened the meeting in the fourth-floor conference room at Houston's City Hall and turned it over to FBI Special Agent Langdon Bates, who stated, "The FBI will be in charge of the sharing of information through open communication and cooperation." Eleven federal agencies, thirteen local police departments, five county agencies and officials from the Harris County Office of Emergency Response, the Red Cross, and Texas Department of Public Safety were all there. Harris County Emergency Management would coordinate support and assistance logistics. As the meeting adjourned, Agent Bates stressed the importance of public safety, assistance, and environmental protection, saying, "Those of you who'll be working security at the sites need to ensure safety and security for the bomb technicians and forensic chemists collecting samples. You may be called on to assist with the arduous task of collecting evidence. All evidence must be documented on site, establishing the chain of custody. Leo, please come here. Ladies and gentlemen, this is Harris County Sheriff Leo Sanchez. When you have potential evidence, call Leo's Office." Turning to the whiteboard behind him, he wrote Leo's name and phone number in big block letters. "His people will be responsible for transportation to Ellington Field. Our offices have worked all night, putting together a scheme to store the evidence in a logical manner.

"The importance of doing good old-fashioned police work, collecting and logging evidence, talking to everyone possible, cannot be overemphasized," Bates continued. "With this much destruction at so many sites, somebody had to have seen something, a shift worker, a security guard, a store clerk, kids out running around, a couple parked in a dark corner. It's up to us to find those people and put this puzzle together. We've cordoned off the entire region and broken it into manageable portions, assigning them to the people with the most familiarity to those neighborhoods. I appreciate you'll have a lot of specific settings and crises. I ask you to put those people in touch with the proper agencies and stay focused on collecting evidence and talking to people. You all have your assignments. Report it all; the most insignificant issue could be the key that cracks the case. We'll collate it and send it back to each of you. Collectively, the security and investigative teams on the ground today will exceed a thousand people."

He squared his shoulders as he scanned the faces of those in attendance. "Let's plan to meet here again tomorrow morning at six. Thank you for what you've done and what you'll do today. Let's roll!"

From Ann Arbor, Coach White called his old Army buddy. "Bobby Joe? Paul. I identified Billy Joe's body. The medical examiner said it was quick, he didn't suffer. They say cremation . . ."

"No, his Mamma wants a funeral, whenever we can. I'll trust you'll keep in touch. God, this sucks . . ."

"Bobby Joe, I can't tell you how sorry I am."

"Damn, this's hard. He was a good kid. Worked hard. Loved his Mama. Did what I asked. Ain't right. Shit, he was just a kid. Who are those bastards? Chicken shits. Flyin' drones, dumping nerve gas on thousands while they hide in a bunker, half a world away! Thought we were as ready as could be, never expected this. Even wiped out a whole damn town south of here. Tipped over a train full of crude, burned everybody in the gym for a pep rally. Sneaky Arab, Muslim bastards! Should've kicked their asses and taken over back when we were there. Damn politicians! Start a war, declare victory, get re-elected. Peddle their power, get rich. Let the other guy's kid do the fighting and get killed, lose a leg, get his head screwed up. Comes home, gets no help, and hurts himself or other people. But their kid? Hell no. Keep him home safe. Send him to a fancy ass private school, make him a lawyer to cheat the working man outta what's his. Should never re-elect nobody! They're all a bunch of crooks, only wanna get rich. Government of the people and for the people, my ass!

"Sorry for the rant. Lost my boy for no good reason. Paul, your clan okay? Sorry, didn't even ask. You got two little girls, right? Everybody okay? Tell me they didn't, any of 'em, get caught up in any of this shit."

"We're okay, Bobby Joe. Live nine miles from campus, not in any danger. Half a dozen of the kids' good friends were at the game. Two of 'em died; four are in serious condition at Cincinnati Children's. My girls are undone. Everything's canceled. All those little girls have been over to our house a lot. Junior high kids, giggles, sleepovers. It's hit 'em pretty hard. Thanks for asking."

"I'm sorry, I really am. This'll color their lives forever."

"It beats the worst firefight we were ever in," White said. "Nothing I could do. It's gonna take forever for the university, the town to recover from this. The school president is dead. Board members of both schools have closed them for at least a week. It's a zoo. Canada's sending body bags. Everybody's trying to help . . ."

"Both clean," the head of fingerprinting at the FBI's primary fingerprint identification complex in Clarksburg, West Virginia, told her supervisor, handing him copies of fingerprints from a right thumb and forefinger as he approached her workstation. "Maybe the explosive fell over after he'd positioned it, he took off his gloves and repositioned it without thinking, expecting it wouldn't matter after it exploded. Glad I got a chance to work on this, but I trained Teresa Martinez and she's as good as we have. She heads the program in Albuquerque and could've done it and saved time."

"You're right, but for all the news media and the public relations concerns, we're better off having done it here," the supervisor said. "I'll check them against our files; send them to all fifty states, and Interpol. Unless this guy has spent his entire life as a monk in Tibet, we're going to ID him. Thanks for coming in. You and I trust your staff, but on this one, the director will be glad the 'A team' was on it. Appreciate it. For both our sakes, I'll go over it one more time before I tell the director we've got a clean finding. Man, I hope we're lucky and find these guys. Don't want to chase more people through more caves half a world away."

"I don't care where we find them; just hope it's soon."

30

Into the Fray

1200 hrs. MDT Boise, Idaho
Sunday, October 27
Post Attack, Day 1

Finishing the first of his freshly made blueberry muffins with a swallow of hot coffee, Mike Paxton moved from the island in his kitchen to the living room and a view out the picture window of his house in Eagle, a small community just north and west of Boise. The number given to him last night was answered with a recognizable deep bass voice.

"Mr. Director, Mike Paxton. Just before you called last night, my cousin in Agnew called with promising news about his daughter. The only survivor of the fire, she was in the gymnasium when the roof collapsed. She fell under the bleachers, breaking her arm and being knocked unconscious. In a coma when found, she was medevac'd to Texas Children's Hospital in Houston. When we spoke, he was excited by the progress she'd made. Sadly, overnight she's had a serious relapse, is in critical condition, and faces an uphill battle to survive.

"I'll be honest with you. I was leaning against taking your offer when we spoke, but now, the fight to find these guys can't be any more demanding than the one she's facing. With all the trauma, destruction, and tragedy of yesterday, no one's paid a higher price than me. I assure you no one is more motivated. We've got some details to work through, Mr. Director, but if your offer still stands, I accept. For Emma, and for everyone else these assholes have hurt. Let's take 'em down."

"Dr. Paxton, you've made my day. Thank you, and I'm sorry to hear about your niece," Director Townsend said.

Picking up the discussion at hand, Mike started. "You've got, what, fifty plus field offices plus your resources there in DC? If I'm going to oversee this, I've got to know what they're working on, what they think they want to work on, what they're thinking and *why* they're thinking it. Director, I'm a big team player. I won't deal with hidden agendas, egos, information silos, or petty politics. Those are deal breakers for me. As I take this on, I'll shoot straight with you and expect you to do the same. Those are my terms. This is serious business. We'll give it a full court press, no holidays, no nine to five, just gut busting effort. We don't play games, suffer fools, or take prisoners," Mike stated.

"I promise, you'll have the full support of the FBI, Congress, and the president. We're committed to catching these guys, and we want you on our team. You have my personal assurance you'll have what you need, and others will work through the red tape."

"I'll need access to your Carnivore 'sniffer' software program to covertly search for emails and other computer messages. And your team of software engineers in Quantico who upgrade it."

"You'll have both by 1430 your time today, but how do you know Carnivore?"

"It's what we do. We know what you, the Russians, the Chinese, Japan, EU countries have and what's on your drawing boards. It's how we stay ahead of the pack. Oh, and one last item, I'm sure you guys have data and data processing, which will be helpful in the beginning when we're looking at the macro-level. We'll need access to a person who knows what you've got and where it is."

"Do you, by chance, know David Eller? He's special assistant to the Chairman of the Joint Chiefs of Staff at the Pentagon. He worked at the Justice Department, got pulled into intelligence and counterintelligence. Along the way, he was given free rein to cross any departmental boundaries and access any data to make sense out of the project he's been assigned. He'll be a good resource and can find any information you need."

"David Eller, Harvard law, clerked for Justice Scalia? That David Eller?"

"He's the one."

"A year ahead of me in grad school at MIT. We shared a couple of classes and bent an elbow or two in some of Boston's seedier bars. He set a high bar for the rest of us. He's a good man. It'll be good to reconnect. Director, I hope you don't expect any quick fix, any sudden *Eureka* moments. These are smart, cunning guys. This'll be a long slog of collecting bits of information, trying to find a common thread, and a bit of luck. In our business, the single dominant characteristic in any search is dogged persistence. We're looking for electronic footprints of people we don't know, in places we've not been, left there by smart guys who took great pains to cover them up. I promise to keep you in the loop every step of the way. When we learn it, you'll learn it. No mindless reports."

"I can live with that," Townsend said.

Mike stood, stretched, and walked across the room to his window. "Two issues. First, I spent a good portion of yesterday trying to determine how you set explosives to destroy thousands of bridge abutments and rail over a third of our country in less than a week. We've got ideas concerning staging and the logistics of how this could be done. When we spoke last night, I told you of our plans to use honeybees to identify potential places where TNT bundles were stored. All air travel's been suspended."

"I remember. Impressed you'd moved so quickly, not only in identifying potential depots, but in finding a way to validate them," Ferguson interrupted. "You said honeybees can be trained to smell the residue?"

"Correct. I need your help bringing trained honeybees from Florida here to Boise, today if possible. For the bees, it's olfactory. The more time goes by, the more difficult it will be to validate the location. We've been collecting data in Idaho, Washington, and Montana. If this works over the next few days in Idaho, we'll want to expand the search to all the other states. Maybe we can talk to people who remember the person who rented the space."

"Point taken. Get me the details. I'll get you your bees. Do you need FBI agents to accompany the bees?"

"Thanks, but no, Idaho State Police are already on board. Second, a friend of my cousin was run off the road minutes before the train derailed in Agnew. She got a make, model, color, and a partial license number and was sure it wasn't a local car or driver. My guys worked on it, and we believe it to be a Colorado-licensed rental out of the San Antonio airport leased to a person from Fresno, California. We tapped into the rental car system. The departure, return times and mileage all coincide. I gave the rental company, car, and lessee's name to FBI Special Agent Stephen Delacroix in San Antonio. You might want to touch base with him.

"You and I have a lot of details to work through. We have responsibilities to our clients we won't compromise. And, as I said, we don't work for free. I'm honored and eager to take this on. Let's start by you calling me Mike; no one who knows me calls me doctor."

"Okay, Mike, I speak for the president and all of us in the federal government when I say I'm sorry for your loss. I truly am. Do you need time to work through issues in Texas?"

"If the attack's over, and I can get there this week, I'll be okay. Small town, big fire, few survivors. My grandma and uncle have lost their life's work. But life goes on in the agriculture world. Crazy as this sounds, my cousin and I have sixty new heifers to vaccinate."

"Hopefully yesterday was not a prelude, and they've done all they're going to do. I spoke with David Eller. He concedes since we don't know who they are, it's hard to predict their future behavior. Still, he's leaning toward yesterday being all there's going to be. I want a week before I have any confidence they're finished. If you need to get to Texas before flights resume, let me know. Again, my condolences."

"Thanks. I will. We'll follow the evidence and let it lead us where it will, not bend the evidence to prove a theory," Mike replied. "If we weren't the primary target and this attack is part of a greater conflict, I hope our politicians understand fighting an idea is like dancing in a quagmire. Since Korea, not one of the armed conflicts we've been in has had a clear objective or a reasonable exit strategy. Let's see where the evidence leads us. Unless there is direct or tacit indication of state involvement, and we expand our response beyond those responsible for this, I hope the sons and daughters of the president and leaders of Congress are in the first platoon of ground forces deployed when orders are approved and signed. Sorry, didn't mean to get political on you."

"I agree with you. I've served under two presidents, one from each party. This one is singularly focused on finding who did this and bringing them to justice."

"Director, give me your email address. I'll send you the details for the bees and a list of my key people who'll need clearances and access to yours and other department people."

"Will do. The president will be pleased. Thanks, Mike."

"Thank you, Mr. Director. Tell the president I'm honored to be part of this effort and will give it my all."

"Just got off the phone with FBI Director Ferguson Townsend. I've agreed to head the federal IT effort to catch these guys," an exhausted Mike said, opening a Zoom call with Frog and Steve Nottrott, his chief financial officer, as he sank back in his office chair.

"No shit. Congratulations! I think," Steve said as he laughed.

"You'll go to no end not to climb with me. Congrats, Mike. I'm not surprised and glad they recognize quality when they see it," Frog said.

"Thanks, guys, but it's not me, it's us. Steve, I told him we won't compromise our duties to our clients, and this effort will require more manpower. We'll need to add people and coordinate with the Washington IT types and the FBI field offices. It will take a good bit of my time and Phil's and our key people. I'll look to you for a larger admin role. Look back eighteen months, see what's on our plate, estimate our expected natural growth and include a bump from the French. Let's talk budget and budgeting process tomorrow morning.

"Phil, you're already up to your neck in this. The Florida honeybee guys will be here this afternoon, and we expect to start at first light tomorrow morning. Stay with John Tilden and your database but start thinking of expanding your map to include the entire western third of the country. In your spare time, check out drones, nerve gas, how you destroy major ports, and where and how you find the expertise and enough explosives to derail three thousand miles of train tracks. Oh, and how one would steal a Cold War-era Russian 'suitcase' bomb. The Director knows we have international resources. Be thinking of ways our contacts can help and how much you think it will cost. Steve and I will need to put together a working budget. Get some rest, gents. We'll talk in the morning."

31

Global Impact

1500 hrs. CDT Houston, Texas
Tuesday, October 29
Post Attack, Day 3

Dawn, on the otherwise crisp, clear fall Houston morning, broke with a dark purple ball rising from the east. City and company structural engineer investigators surveyed cracking plants, fractionators, distillation units, condensers, reactors, heaters, cooling towers, and storage tanks, all destroyed or so damaged they would have to be demolished.

City and county officials issued mandatory evacuation orders for a four-mile-wide swath either side of the Ship Channel as huge plumes of billowing black smoke continued to rise in the morning sky. Six hundred thousand people found themselves out of their homes with no idea when they would be able to return. The incredible heat and petroleum-thickened air, impregnated with sulfur, nitrogen oxide, benzene, dense clouds of soot, liquid particulate, uncombusted oil components, aerosols, and other gasses made staying in the vicinity untenable. With over ninety-six hundred known dead, at least 890 missing, and more than five thousand either hospitalized or being treated outpatient, officials continued their search for those affected by the release of the hydrogen-fluoride and chlorine gasses.

Houston-based international oil-well firefighting companies, Boots and Coots, Blowouts and Wild Well Control, and Port Fire Boats worked to quench flames fed by hydrocarbons while Houston Fire Department pumper trucks worked the others. The object with any fire was to eliminate the fuel or abolish the oxygen.

The challenge: the abundance of both, like trying to smother an open caldera during the eruption of a volcano. After considerable preparation, they attacked ExxonMobil's Baytown Refinery. Using equipment from the fire boats, six HFD, three Baytown pumper trucks, and eight ladders to flood the site, they ignited four nitroglycerin charges at once, thirty feet above ground, removing the available oxygen for a moment and snuffing the fire. Flooding the zone with water for several minutes, they covered the fuel source with foam and watched to ensure it did not reignite. One down, more than a hundred to go.

Forensic chemists from the FBI, ATF, Harris County Sheriff's office and Houston Police Department expanded the tedious process of explosive residue collection as more sites were cleared for evaluation.

Jack sat in the easy chair in Emma's hospital room while she napped. She'd had a full day, two breathing treatments, physical therapy, visits from several doctors, and talks with her dad about what had happened at home. She was worn out. Tomorrow they would meet with a social worker and a chaplain. An exhausted Jack was pleased with her progress, both physically and emotionally. Picking up the remote, he turned on the national news.

"The events in the United States over the weekend have industrialized nations around the world reeling. The common concern: 'If it can happen there, what's the risk of a similar event happening in our country?' The world's financial institutions have reacted as expected. Our stock markets, closed today, are expected to reopen tomorrow. China's Shanghai Composite dropped more than 30%. Japan's NIKKEI 225 Index is off 1,468 points or 43%. The German Stock Index, DAX, ended at its lowest point since unification. Panic over recession, depression, and collapse is rampant," the CNN anchor said.

"Let's look at oil, iron, and food to try to appreciate the short- and longer-term impact of this attack. The global oil glut, expected to continue well into next year and beyond, has been upended. Oil's key for manufacturing, transportation, and agriculture. Houston has three of the nation's top ten refineries. All now inoperable. How fast they recover will be key as Iran now stands to make substantial gains in market share.

"Steel will see a sharp decline in global production. A slower economy and construction downturn will continue in China. International steel production will experience serious complications with American coal unable to move from its source in Montana to the west coast for shipment to Asia. Analysts expect the metal's price to double from current levels.

"Expect to see increased prices at the grocery store due to hikes in transportation and fuel costs as many of our fruits and vegetables are transported from Imperial Valley in Southern California or imported from Mexico and Central and South America. The price for beef, pork, mutton, and fish will see seasonal variations with a slight bump upward for transportation. Wheat, corn, and soybean production is centered in the Great Plains states and will have to be trucked to market."

For the first time in days, Jack thought about something other than his immediate here and now. *What's going to happen to Agnew? Where's Emma going to go to school? Maybe we'll move. Not many left to work the farms. The Ship Channel attack will impact the state's economy. How's that going to impact maintaining my equipment? Stop it! Just watch the news.*

"We invite you to tune in tonight for a special report on the economic impact of this attack. The massive loss of life combined with the many states and millions of people without water or power has changed the course of our country's history forever. The economy, ours and the world's, has many asking if this event has moved us past a theoretical tripwire of debt to GDP? Where will the money to move forward come from? The EU, not likely, with Brexit alongside the struggle of several smaller counties. Japan's economy has been stagnant for a decade. China? Hardly. Their dependence on Russian and Middle Eastern oil and American coal makes them a doubtful option. The Middle East? They have the oil, and the money. No simple answer," CNN news anchor Gloria Douglas continued. "The special report starts tonight at 9 p.m. Eastern Time. Be sure and join us as we look at the economic realities of the future."

That's ten o'clock, local time. If I'm not asleep, I'll watch, Jack thought.

"For the latest on our nation's oil refining and petrochemical capability, we take you to Elizabeth Barron in Houston. Elizabeth."

"Thank you, Gloria."

The remote cameraman focused on Elizabeth, wearing a yellow fire-retardant slicker borrowed from the Houston Fire Department and standing in front of the M/V Sam Houston, the ninety-five-foot Port Houston's public tour vessel. "Around us, overturned trucks, twisted metal, and wreckage is everywhere. Much of it still smoldering. The scale of this disaster is only now becoming clear. These bombs changed this city in an instant, ripping apart lives and reducing major portions of the ship channel to rubble. Across the city, shockwaves from the explosions smashed windows, destroyed buildings. The explosions were heard as far away as Beaumont. People experienced what they believed was an earthquake fifty miles away. Authorities have evacuated people in a four-mile swath on either side of the fifty-two-mile-long Channel. More than half a million people are displaced, not expecting to return to their homes for at least a week. Every part of the city is experiencing major power and water outages. With the lingering effects of the enormous chlorine gas leak, you can imagine the mayhem these people are facing. The massive search for the missing continues both in the water and on land. Divers and the Coast Guard are expected to finish today, four days after the explosions. Unfortunately, it has turned from rescue to recovery."

The television screen, showing a video taken as a helicopter traversed the Channel, displayed unimaginable destruction and devastation, continuing fire and smoke. Black smoke boiling up obliterated the sun as Elizabeth continued her report.

"The Houston Ship Channel is home to a 20-billion-dollar petrochemical complex; it plays an essential role in improving the lives of all Americans. 60% of our country's aviation fuel and 30% of our gasoline is produced here. Three of America's largest refineries have been lost. These facilities processed 15 million gallons of crude oil per day. Gasoline, diesel, jet fuel, heating oil, propane, butane, and kerosene, a few of the products produced.

"To many of us, these are numbers, big numbers, but just numbers. What do they mean except that it will cost more to fill our cars? Maybe more than you realize. Products which will now be in short supply include plastics, solvents, lubricants, paints, dyes, asphalt, insulation, anti-freeze, pharmaceuticals, insecticides, detergents, cosmetics, and hair spray. Everyday plastic pellets leave the port for foreign plants, where they are transformed into plastic wrap, trash bags, packaging, disposable diapers, car parts and thousands of other everyday products. 80% of the nation's polyethylene exports move through the port," she reported.

"Elizabeth, as you say, the price at the pump will go up," Gloria interjected. "As will the price of jet fuel, so plane ticket prices will increase. For those of us in the northeast, the price of heating oil this winter is liable to double. We hope the effects of El Niño will be mild for winter. These are a just few of the ways our world has changed."

"So true, Gloria," Elizabeth agreed. "Many of the thousands of miles of oil pipelines crisscrossing our country come to Houston. Valves as far away as a hundred and fifty miles have been turned off to help starve the fires. Authorities feared it might take thirty days or more to bring all the fires under control. Earlier today, a spokesman for Harris County Emergency Management reported they're now hopeful the remaining fires can be out sooner, warning the massive storage tank fires may be the last to be extinguished. He credits the remarkable cooperation of the firefighters, who've fought these fires around the clock, and the assistance of plant managers, who've provided invaluable information regarding physical layouts and sources of the fuel."

"Excuse me, Elizabeth, I hate to interrupt. We have breaking news in Paris. We're back to you as soon as possible. Two Israeli men in custody have confessed to this mornings' killing of the Gaza Minister of Agriculture and one of his administrative aids outside the Russian Embassy in Paris. We take you now to Paris and Charles Bell, our reporter onsite."

Wind gusted as the reporter wrestled with an umbrella and squinted into the camera in front of the Paris Police Headquarters at Place Louis Lépine. "Yes, Gloria," Charles said. "It rained all night. This morning is overcast and foreboding. Gaza Minister of Agriculture Rashid Awad was anxious to attend his meeting with the Russian Consul to finalize details of a new trade agreement increasing building supplies. Gaza City is in desperate need of materials to help with reconstruction, following the latest Israeli bombardments. Israel has long opposed allowing building materials into the region for fear of construction of tunnels into Israel for suicide and lone wolf attacks on Israeli public and religious shrines. Without materials, nothing can be done to clear the rubble and destruction. Awad knew he'd be paying a premium, but community morale and public health are both in decline, and he was intent on showing progress. Despite substantial foreign aid from the international community, high unemployment and the lack of government services, education, and healthcare have kept the standard of living for the entire Gaza Strip among the lowest in the world among industrialized nations.

"At 8:30 this morning, Awad's driver pulled into the driveway and opened the door for him when shots rang out. Two gunmen approached from opposite directions and opened fire within several feet of their target. Awad was struck twice in the back and once in the face. He died at the scene. One aide was also killed, another is in surgery at the University Hospital of Bordeaux. Russian and French security forces apprehended the shooters and took them into custody."

Charles staggered as a wind blast ripped away his umbrella. Regaining his composure, he continued, "Authorities believe the suspects are part of a growing militant sect inside Israel bent on reclaiming the Gaza Strip for Israel. Both men have been under intense interrogation here at police headquarters. It's not clear if either are members of the group or disciples of the organization's ideals. The French president expressed his deepest regret for the attacks and assured the people of Gaza these assailants and all involved will be brought to justice.

"A spokesman for the Israeli Embassy said Israel hopes investigators will determine whether the assailants have ties to any larger organizations. They're calling on the French government to do all in its power to protect their citizens, the diplomatic corps, and tourists from around the world from any further terrorist attacks.

"Last month, two Pakistanis assassinated Fauzi Abuelaish, perhaps the most influential member of the Hamas leadership. A week later, Mahmoud Nassar, a respected international businessman, was killed when a gunman hiding behind a hedge ambushed him as he left a meeting with the Minister of Agriculture. Now, this same minister has died. Last week, a senior aide to the Palestinian Prime Minister was found dead in his hotel room the morning of his scheduled meeting with Gaza City Mayor Itamar El-Amin. El-Amin was killed this past Friday. His senior aide is still hospitalized, facing additional surgeries and a long recovery.

"Today's assassination was the second in as many days. Yesterday, Gaza's Prime Minister and three of his cabinet members were killed as they prepared to board a flight to Damascus. These recent attacks are an indication of the growing unrest in Gaza, because of the rampant corruption and fraud plaguing the country. Awad's assassination brings to fourteen the number of high-ranking officials and business leaders who have been wounded or killed in the past two months. Back to you, Gloria."

"Thank you, Charles. Get in out of the wind. We're back now with Elizabeth Barron in Houston. Elizabeth, we're looking at live images of the disaster and, like you, are beginning to get a sense of the devastation as the smoke continues to boil unimpeded. Many of the injured fell victim to falling glass crashing from office buildings. Elizabeth, can you give us a sense of what it was like?"

"Yes, much of it was a matter of luck, where you were when disaster struck. If you were downtown, shattered glass was everywhere. People died, others suffered severe injuries, others walked away unscathed."

Gloria interjected, "What's the city, the state, even the nation going to do when a port supporting one and a half million jobs in Texas, and over three million nationwide, goes dormant? The economic activity of the port accounts for more than 20% of Texas' total gross domestic product and more than $800 billion across the nation. It's a huge loss."

"The city has suffered one disaster after another," Elizabeth responded. "The loss of so many lives, displacement of thousands of families, loss of most of the petrochemical industry, a major blow to the oil and gas industry, and loss of the Port has brought this city to its knees. Each year, more than 250 million tons of cargo move through the Port of Houston, carried by more than 8,300 vessels and 220,000 barges. The port leads the nation in foreign and total waterborne tonnage. It's first in import and export tonnage and total vessel transits. And it's the country's largest container port, handling well over half the breakbulk cargo of all Gulf Coast ports.

"It is way too soon to guess how they will respond. I have no idea what's going to happen to those who suffered the complete destruction of their homes and businesses. The Red Cross, FEMA, local churches, and schools have come together to meet the needs of people who have lost everything, their homes, their cars, in many cases, their families, and their health. Our nation faces an economic freefall from the destruction of its petrochemical industry and loss of more than 30% of its oil-refining capability."

The cameraman focused on Elizabeth before panning the city skyline, blotted out by the billowing clouds of black smoke. "Saturday's explosions produced craters twenty feet deep, obliterating everything within a 150-yard radius of their epicenter and sending fireballs one to two thousand feet into the sky. More than 1700 homes and businesses near the plants either collapsed or had a combination of doors, windows and roofs blown off."

As she spoke, the screen showed a series of images, including the bent and twisted aftermath of the ExxonMobil refinery and the massive cranes now inoperable at Barbours Cut. "A chief component of fertilizer, millions of tons of ammonium nitrate are produced each year. With additives, it can be used as a blasting agent. The bomb that demolished half of the nine-story Alfred P. Murrah Federal Building in Oklahoma City consisted of 1500 pounds of ammonium nitrate. Each unit in this attack contained 70,000 pounds of explosive, making them fifty to sixty times larger. Detonation of double-decked containers at the Shell Chemical, LyondellBasell, and Valero plants, and others, were over one hundred times more powerful than the Oklahoma City bomb.

"Moving a hundred properly labeled containers going to routine destinations through this or any other large port would not be difficult. Authorities had no concern with the arrival of the cargo aboard the *Martina Southampton*. As with every attack associated with the monstrous event, this was a well-designed act, requiring careful, accurate planning and precise execution. They knew where best to position the explosives to achieve maximum destruction."

"Elizabeth, are authorities there looking to see if there is a possible link between the terrorists and the owners of the *Martina Southampton*, or if the ship was collateral damage? Is the FBI trying to determine the legitimacy of the original manufacturer's orders? Is it common to send such a large volume on a single ship?" Gloria asked.

"We're told the ship's Bills of Lading appear to be in order and the size of the order is not uncommon. An FBI spokesman told me they are looking into any connections to the *Martina Southampton*. After 9/11, officials recognized the vulnerability of the port and its importance to the nation and have spent a lot of time and money improving security. Inspectors and customs agents are everywhere and can inspect whatever, whenever they want. Bureaucracy compounds the problem since 85% of the facilities are privately owned, and while the companies cooperate through a mutual assistance association, each plant's security measures and what they entail are considered confidential. The 52-mile Channel, stretching from near downtown Houston to the Gulf of Mexico, has no master plan.

"Lost in all this is the threat of the oil spills from the *Martina Southampton, Rio Chartrus,* and *Nordic Spirit* on the fishing industry in Galveston Bay and the entire coastline of Texas. This is still a developing story and an ongoing investigation. We'll continue to follow it and update you as we learn more. Gloria, back to you."

"Elizabeth, thank you. Elizabeth Barron speaking to us from Houston. Layered on the tragedies in Ann Arbor, Dover, and Los Angeles are the critically ill fighting for their lives. Patients from Ann Arbor are in every available acute care hospital in Michigan, northern Ohio, Chicago, Evanston, and Indianapolis. Two companies, which manufacture mechanical respirators, have provided over a thousand each out of their new inventory. The Army and the VA Hospital System have provided another 650. Hospitals in Florida and New York have sent respirators.

"Without their help, many more would have died. As we came on the air, a spokesman from the Washtenaw County Judge's office told me they are dealing with 3,287 critical patients, and 86% of those survived the attack. Many other survivors are sick but expected to recover. Thousands have also been treated for broken bones, the result of being trampled by others trying to escape the stadium. Dover and Los Angeles are experiencing similar conditions.

"Moments ago, an NTSB spokesman reported the current rail destruction count stands at 3,817. Inspections continue throughout the nation. Thus far, the eastern seaboard has been spared. We know two bundles did not detonate. It brings to question, how many more will be found, or more frightening, how many won't? With all this snow, it may be well into next summer before we have confidence that all have been accounted for.

"As hard as the rail carriers have worked to identify additional track destruction, they've worked even harder to recover the Amtrak passengers, and the engineers and crews on equipment now marooned between rail outages. They continue to identify and evaluate cargo requirements and limitations, and secure engines and equipment for hundreds of trains and tens of thousands of cars. It's a monumental task.

"NTSB, Union Pacific, and BNSF met this morning to determine how to patch together a shared transcontinental line. Equipment from other rail lines has arrived or is on its way and will work around the clock to provide a functional track. Although the nation's supplies are substantial, additional rails and ties will be needed to replace all those destroyed in the attack. It's estimated that, even at full capacity, it will be over four years before the lines are back to pre-attack levels. Severe weather this winter will slow the process. Now, we'll send you to your local stations and be back at the top of the hour . . ."

I've been at the center of two national news stories today. That's two too many, Jack thought as Emma began to stir.

Getting out of the shower, then brushing his teeth before bed, Parsa noticed when his phone lit up with Omar's number—an incoming call. "Watched an American newscaster doing a piece on the global economic impact of the *Hujum*. They expect the cost of iron to double. We should've bought building supplies before construction costs escalated!"

"Relax, Omar. I saw it. We've been gathering the steel, concrete, lumber, and building supplies for the last two years and have amassed enough to complete the major infrastructure projects, the airports, desalination plants, the port, schools, and hospitals. Most is warehoused in Indonesia. The heavy equipment, bulldozers, excavators, cranes, and all are on the loading docks in China, ready to go. America will be paying the exorbitant prices, not us."

In the months since their introduction, Maggie had grown accustomed to glancing out at Mike when the curtain rose at the start of her performances. She looked forward to their dinners following her concerts. When they met, she had noticed he wasn't the typical symphony groupie, the pompous patron, the hanger on, the wannabe struggling artist. No, far from it. The sparkle in his eye and his infectious gusto for life captured her attention. She had never encountered anyone like him and smiled, a little surprised when she recognized something astir in herself. She'd jumped at the chance when Mike asked if she would like to accompany him to Texas to meet the president. They had flown to San Antonio and driven on to his Uncle Jim's house, where they met Jack's parents and his grandmother. They hoped Jack and Emma might be home by the middle of next week. After lunch, Mike took Maggie on the cook's tour of his parents', brothers', and his aunt and uncle's homes, and the remnants of Agnew. For all the loss, Maggie gained an appreciation of Mike's early life.

Seated at the center of the field on the fifty-yard line, facing the stands and the press box at the Karnes City High School football field, with the remaining Agnew families, senators, congressmen, the secretaries of the interior and homeland security, the Texas Governor, Lieutenant Governor, and Karnes City Mayor and city council, Mike turned to Maggie and remarked, "More political types here than survivors."

The president addressed the thirty-four-hundred people assembled: "Ladies and gentlemen, the tremendous loss of life, jobs, and property in our nation three days ago is beyond measure. Countless lives lost, industries, ports, and cities devastated. None more so than here in south Texas, where the entire community of Agnew was destroyed. Not a single building was spared. Fire snatched what was active and sacred, full of joy and life, the sense of home, roots, and legacy, hurled it screaming into the sky on glowing red embers and tumbling mountains of black smoke, cast it on the winds, scattering it across the countryside, at last allowing it to settle as shattered lives, broken dreams, and blackened ash.

"Yet in this close-knit farming community, survivors, despite their devastating loss, provided food and drinks for the firefighters, police, and other rescue personnel. Tragedy didn't hit families. It consumed neighbors, friends, and generations of people who have lived, worked, played, and prayed together for decades. This morning I had the opportunity to meet with the surviving families of this senseless crime. They continue to meet one another with handshakes and hugs. The grieving process has begun and will continue for many years, but their spirit is undaunted. Their resilience and strength are examples to us all."

She went on to talk about the support the federal government would provide to the region, the EPA studies to ensure the safety of the Edwards Aquifer, low-interest loans for reconstruction of the grain elevators and the cotton gin, and other support from FEMA and the Department of Agriculture. From there, she talked about the support being provided in Dover, Ann Arbor, Houston, and Los Angeles.

Following her remarks, she met Mike for a few minutes in private, thanking him for taking on the cybersecurity task, assuring him he would not face any bureaucratic encumbrances, and giving him her heartfelt condolences for his loss.

"Thank you, Madam President, for your assurances, kind words, and the opportunity to lead this effort. As I told Director Townsend, these are smart people, but people make mistakes. It won't happen overnight, but we'll find them," Mike replied, permitting himself a slight smile.

32

One Foot in Front of the Other

0700 hrs. PDT San Jose, California
Wednesday, October 30
Post Attack, Day 4

The crisp, cold wind whipped against his face as Frog and his Weimaraner, Jake, entered Piedmont Park. Midway through their five-mile run, his phone played the opening stanza from *Jaws*, Mike's distinctive ring. It gave him an excuse to find a park bench and sit down. "What's going on?"

"You sound out of breath. What are you doing? Are you okay?"

"Doing great. Jake's trying to run my legs off. It's good. Want to be in shape when we take on those overhanging basalt walls of Jailhouse Rock in two weeks. You're not gonna bail on me, are you?"

"Maggie and I are at Jack's house. Brought her to Texas for the president's talk yesterday afternoon in Karnes City. We'll be back home late tonight. You and I are getting too old for this rock-climbing gig, but no, unless this attack eats us both alive, I'll be at your door Friday evening, and we'll be climbing Saturday morning. Changing the subject, thanks again for your help with the bees."

"No problem. I thought bees only wanted to find nectar, make honey and more bees. You've turned them into multitaskers."

"Your analysis helped find eight locations in Idaho, seven in Washington, and twelve in Montana. Can you expand what you've done to the other nine states? The credit goes to the bees, but your map was the key. Twenty-seven for twenty-seven. You're battin' a thousand. The Giants need you."

"Love my Giants, still no thanks. No way I'm steppin' in the batter's box, facing a ninety-nine mile an hour fastball. Too old, too much travel. Besides, when we played road games, you'd have to come feed Jake and take him for a walk," Frog said, chuckling. "You're calling to see if I can expand it? Already have. It's driven off the numbers, and numbers don't see state borders. Since we talked last, Tilden and his guys have fed me 3,209 data points. I'm ten minutes from home. I sent you a printable copy of my findings right before Jake took me for this run. Print it. I'll share my desktop. Call you in ten."

"I'm sure Jack's got a printer. I'm betting Jake beats you to your front door."

On the television in Frog's den, "Breaking news," the CNN anchor said from her studio desk. "Two Middle Eastern men identified as Defendant 1 and Defendant 2, anonymous because they had refused to speak since being taken into custody at the Glen Canyon Dam Carl Hayden Visitor Center last Saturday, were found dead in the infirmary at the Federal Correctional Institution in Phoenix this morning. Inmates Yordan Chirinos and Aledmys Gutiérrez, both serving life sentences for multiple murders in connection with drug trafficking, have been charged. This and more when we return . . ."

"Crap," Frog muttered, staring at the screen.

"Got a few minutes?" Frog asked, having settled in front of his laptop.

"Looking at your printout. Talk to me," Mike replied, leaning back in Jack's desk chair, ready to take notes on his ever-present yellow pad.

"Most Pacific Rim goods pass through California or Washington ports. Remember Saturday and our rail line cross-country links conversation?" Frog offered.

"I remember."

Sitting at his desk in the nook off his kitchen with a large glass of ice water next to his laptop and Mike on the video call, Frog held court. "Using those crossing routes, here's what the data's telling me . . ."

For the next thirty minutes, he rattled off the names of cities and towns across the western United States. Locations the data indicated served as explosive depots and overnight stays: Klamath Falls, Hinkle, Huntington, and Bend, Oregon; Las

Vegas, Carlin, Reno, and Battle Mountain, Nevada; Ogden and Mounds, Utah. Recognizable and unknown names of towns in Montana, Wyoming, Colorado, Arizona, and New Mexico.

"A long list, yet considering the region, maybe not. Don't know if it's all inclusive or even correct. It's what the data points show. More data, better predictions," Frog continued. "I looked, and every location has a public rental storage unit, even Ash Fork, Arizona. Fewer than five hundred people there, but they've got public storage and a hotel. These guys did their field work. There were hard calls based on volume and expediency, amount of destruction vs. remoteness and ease of access. 'If we do this one, we can't do those four.' This took a ton of preparation," Frog stated.

"They rented lockers to serve as depots, daisy chained it. Amassing all the materials, timers, igniters, and a team of ten to assemble the bundles, it was a forty-five to ninety-day project start to finish. Depending on the geography, ten to twenty sites per team per day. Average fifteen per day, six days, maybe seven, 105 sites per week, per team, max. Inexpensive, mechanical timers give you a week, at best. We know of 3,700 sites; bet it tops out between there and four thousand. Forty to forty-five teams of two, eighty to ninety soldiers and 240-plus hotel rooms and storage units."

Staring at his printout, Mike nodded his agreement. "Their ordinance teams started each morning with a pickup or panel truckload from the storage locker and worked a section of track for however long it took to set them. When the track and highway run parallel, maybe half a mile to one side or the other, they made good progress. For less accessible targets, they walked the explosives in and hiked back out. No reports of dolly or cart marks. With only a week, they had some long days. Following day, they repeat the process. Busy boys."

Continuing, he added, "I'm betting they worked in two-man teams. By the time they loaded their vehicles, found their sites, and set the charges, half their days must have been sixteen to eighteen hours long. This time of year, having enough daylight would've also been an issue. A single guy couldn't do it. The weight and number of trips would be prohibitive. They spent the night in the town of their next arsenal. Don't believe Friday was a full workday. It all hit Saturday, chances of being remembered the day before is a lot better than two or more days earlier. Did they depend on local or paid help, a guy with a grudge against the railroad? Otherwise, you've got to import a lot of hatred toward this country."

Picking up from there, Frog said, "Even with forty to forty-five two-man crews, they'd have to hustle. Look for pickup and van rentals in LA, Portland, Reno, Vegas, Salt Lake, Pocatello, Denver, Tucson, Phoenix, Albuquerque, and El Paso. Eight or nine days prior to the attack with returns anywhere from the day before to a few days after, but not to the location of origin. Imagine the car rentals detail all their vehicles upon return. Still, you might put your bees to the test there, as well. With luck, might be able to find one and use the mileage, start to finish, a good check on the path they took.

"Your friend Eller has more manpower than we do. It's a long shot, but can he check one-way flights from Los Angeles, San Francisco, Oakland, Portland, or Seattle to any of these other cities? Do the names on the tickets match names on the truck rentals? Do any match those on the storage lockers or the hotel rooms of the towns where these guys stayed? Zia can check if any of the hotel reservations in these cities came from the same IP address. As smart as these guys appear, good chance they used an onion router. Bet they walked in and paid cash. It's worth a look. Crank up your bees and cops, let's see if we can discover how they did this, if not *who*."

"Told the FBI Director you're good," Mike replied with a chuckle laced with hope. "Here you've got it done before he asks. I'll have him talk to the state cops in each state and coordinate getting the bees to them. Hopefully, we'll know a lot more this time next week than we do today."

"Mike," came Ferguson's now familiar bass voice over the speaker phone. "We caught our guy. Manual Cassados, a San Salvadorian graduate student, is in custody. We'll arraign him tomorrow on attempted murder of the president of the United States."

"Wow, that was quick. So can I expect you'll have this whole Attack on America wrapped up by this time next week?" Mike laughed, smiling at Maggie.

"We can only hope," came the pragmatic reply. "Surveillance cameras, canvassing the neighborhood, the tip of a partial license plate, and positive identification by the White House employee he approached, routine police work did in our failed assassin. We believe he acted alone. The brightest kid in his village, he was the first to come to this country, first to go to college, first to go to graduate school. Local drug interests tried to exploit the parents, they and his younger sister fled, where they got ensnared in the immigration mess on the border in Texas. The fourteen-year-old daughter was sent to Wisconsin where she was raped and held in isolation for eight months before giving birth to a baby girl, then sent back to San Salvador. The parents were held in separate facilities, one in Texas, the other in New Mexico, before being deported. The drug cartel killed them all upon their return. Cassados pledged revenge. Can you sweep his phone, personal and school computers to make sure nothing was there we overlooked, no others involved?" Ferguson asked.

"Sure."

"Oh, underneath all the mess and tangle in Agnew, we found a box truck we believe was filled with ammonium nitrate. It triggered the derailment, crashing the train. We were able to recover the vehicle identification number. Turns out the truck had been stolen from a greater San Antonio fresh vegetable vendor after hours Wednesday night," Ferguson said.

"There are a lot of public storage units between San Antonio and Agnew. We can train some bees and check some of the more likely ones for ammonium nitrate if you think it's worth it," Mike replied. "Speaking of bees, you know we're twenty-seven for twenty-seven for the sites in Idaho and Washington and Montana. Remember last week, I told you if it worked, we'd expand to the other states? Phillip now has more than three thousand data points from all the western states. If you'll call your guys, or the state police in each state, tell them what we're doing, and give the contact information to our Florida bee guys, they can take it from there and have trained bees on-site, ready to go tomorrow."

"Will do."

Located in the heart of the Xinyi district, the R Hotel and Conference Center Taipei served as the cornerstone of Singapore's world-famous nightlife. The old man's generous tip to the bell captain had generated prompt and discreet service and a claim ticket.

Satisfied, the old man found a seat in the lobby by the window, opened his copy of today's *London Times,* and smiled as he read the story on page A15:

> Barcelona: Fifteen members of a family, including a sleeping mother and her 8 day-old baby, were killed yesterday, leaving the city in shock as authorities launched a massive manhunt for whoever is responsible.
>
> The shooting took place in the lavish apartment of businessman Geraldo Lucero on *Paseo de Garcia,* a prominent Barcelona neighborhood. The dead include

eight adults and six children ranging in age from thirteen years to the newborn.

Authorities believe this was a professional killing and the shooter or shooters are at large and should be considered armed and dangerous. They have not found any apparent motive, and nothing appears to be missing from the home. Mr. Lucero was in the shipping business, having taken over from his father a little over a decade ago.

All the victims have been identified as members of the Lucero family, Mr. Lucero, his parents, wife, their adult children, and grandchildren. According to a neighbor, they had gathered to celebrate the 50th wedding anniversary of the parents.

A spokesman for the police said, 'There may have been more than one shooter, possibly even three.' She urged neighbors to take precautions and advised all area residents to stay inside and lock their doors for the next few days, declaring a matter of public safety.

TLS works on trust. Violate it and there are drastic consequences, he thought as he waited for his contact.

Dressed in business attire, her purse at her side, the attractive 32-year-old TLS operative entered the R Hotel lobby, thinking it an odd place for the transaction. On second thought, it was as open, diverse, and public as any. Midday—a safe setting for both parties.

Surveying the lobby, she spotted the distinguished-looking mature man seated alone by the window, reading the *London Times*. "Mister Liu?"

Turning in her direction and looking up, he smiled. "How may I help you?"

"The answer is the old woman's shoes are black," she replied stoically.

"Correct. Did you drive or come by car?"

"By taxi."

He handed her the claim. "Give it to the bell captain. He'll have his men load three suitcases for you. I've tipped him well, there should be no need for anything from you. I'm sure you'll find all to your liking," he said as he walked away.

Her Uber driver stopped at the side entrance of the National Bank of China, where the assistant bank manager and three associates helped unload the suitcases and bring them to two waiting tellers in a room off the main lobby. She watched the tellers break the seals on the suitcases and count bundle after bundle of Singapore dollars. After twenty minutes, they whispered to their manager.

"I agree with your count, 2.3 million US," the assistant manager told her. "Do you have the accounts where you want it deposited? Are there any special instructions?"

She handed an envelope to him. "All you need is here. Please review it before I go so I may answer any questions," she replied.

The envelope contained the numbered accounts for the deposit, the names of twenty-seven students, their school tuition, payment dates, and electronic fund transfer information. Five at Princeton, four Stanford, seven MIT, five Cal Poly, and six Caltech. Total expenses: $2,225,700, USD. "Leave forty-five thousand dollars in the account. The rest is your fee. I'll return Tuesday evening."

33

Counting the Cost

0730 hrs. PDT San Francisco, California
Saturday, November 3
Post Attack, Day 7

"Director?" Mike answered his phone, looking out his living room window at a rare, crisp San Francisco morning. He hoped for the start of a productive day. "Hey. Don't say I haven't shared with you. Sent you the same wet storm we enjoyed in Boise last week. Weatherman says you guys are buried. It's Saturday. Do feds work weekends, too?" He chuckled.

"Eleven inches and still falling," came the deep bass laugh. "Considering trading my car for a dog sled, but my girls would make pets out of the dogs. Should have worked from home, enjoyed a picturesque day, and when it stopped, gone out and built a snowman. They've closed the schools for at least the first three days this week. Looking out my window and the lone sign of life is the guy driving the snowplow."

"I'll send my instructions for the construction of an igloo." Mike paused, tone turning serious. "What's happening?"

"Talked with the head of the CDC. In addition to VX, these bastards included live virus for equine encephalomyelitis. It's called Triple E. Sleeping sickness for horses. It's not prevalent in horses and less so in humans. Like malaria, it's a virus transmitted via infected female mosquitoes. The VX spray included high concentrations of the Triple E virus."

"No way!" Mike exclaimed.

"Didn't see it at first because many of the symptoms are similar—cough, diarrhea, headache, eye pain, nausea, abdominal pain, even loss of consciousness and paralysis. With all their patients and the sense of urgency, providers were treating with tunnel vision. As people returned to the clinics with neck stiffness, tremors, disorientation, seizures, and generalized edema, doctors began to understand something else was going on. Additional blood testing found the infection. It can affect anyone. Healthy adults recover within two weeks, with symptoms going away in another week. Fatality rates vary but can be as high as 75%. Permanent neurological problems, including brain damage, are possible. Only 10% of all patients ever fully recover."

"Thought mosquitoes transmitted it."

"The mosquito vector is the normal transmission method in nature. In this case, as people inhaled, it transmitted to their bloodstream through their lungs. CDC says this type of transmission hasn't been reported. They predict between 20,500 and 34,000 children will suffer severe brain damage for the rest of their lives, however long it might be. These are cruel bastards."

After a moment, Mike answered, "So, they weren't content to kill three hundred thousand people, they want to impact thousands of families for generations. You're right, they are barbarous. You want to come at me, kill me, okay, come try. But to impair the lives of thousands of children and destroy the lives of their parents and caregivers, man, these suckers are sick."

"No argument here," Ferguson commiserated. "CDC's working on the specific strain and hopes to identify where it came from. As bad as this is, it may be just the break we've needed. The world of virologists and people who understand this stuff can't be that big. At least the needle we're looking for is in a smaller haystack. Expect to hear from the CDC. They need your help."

"Look forward to the call," Mike said, kissing any rock-climbing goodbye.

"Oh yeah, one more thing. That bomb you frivolously carried around in the back of your SUV last week?" Ferguson continued, sounding amazed at his audacity.

"You got the analysis back? Let me guess: all made in this country, nothing special or unique, plain vanilla, right off any shelf?" Mike interrupted, trying to move on.

"Pretty much." Ferguson laughed. "We're honing in on the shelf. Our guys have looked at both the bundle you guys found and the one from New Mexico. The lone difference was in the timers, both inexpensive, available at any local hardware store. Our technicians found the crimp in the paper wrapping at both ends of each dynamite stick was the standard 6-fold machine crimp instead of a 4-fold hand wrap.

"There is a single dynamite manufacturer in America. Every stick has an identifying label on its waxed-paper wrapper giving the brand name and explosive strength. Made in Missouri, they're all from the same production lot. Here is where we need your help," Ferguson said. "The manufacturer's not a distributor. They ship to several vendors who repackage and sell it under their own labels. This production lot left the plant but didn't get to the vendors. It makes sense from the terrorists' point of view. To do the billions of dollars' worth of damage over such a large region took an immense amount of explosive. To steal it in another country, transport and smuggle it into the US is more complex and riskier than stealing it here and moving it. Either way, you still must break it into bundles. We need you to determine how one might steal an entire boxcar of dynamite and move it without being detected.

"Manufacturer's been cooperative. They've documented safety procedures and processes. We have their records of every step of the process from procurement of raw materials to finished product, documentation including the date and time when this specific lot was made. They took our field agents out to their bomb-proof test site and demonstrated the explosiveness of the bundles, showing them how the attackers positioned the bombs to maximize the power. They reiterated that whoever positioned the bombs was well-trained and professional in their approach."

"With the lot number, can they tell us who they sold it to, and we track it from there?" Mike asked.

"You're trying to make it too easy. It was ordered by a distributor in Pennsylvania whose clients include coal mines in West Virginia, North Dakota, and Wyoming. The manufacturer and vendor are checking their records. Five Class I freight lines service Missouri. Three have no record of the shipment."

"Let me guess, the other two are BNSF and UP. And they're consumed with their own issues and can't say for sure if they shipped it," Mike said, then promised, "We'll find it."

"There you go, volunteering before I even ask. I'll save you the rest of the report since neither of us are chemists and won't appreciate all the hoops it took. The blasting caps appear to have come from either Switzerland or India. Should know for sure in a day or two. Last thing they looked at was the fuse. It's the same one used in mining, quarrying, and road construction projects."

"I'm familiar with fuse cords," Mike interjected. "My brother and I stole one from a highway construction site when we were in junior high. Took it apart. He came close to losing a finger, and I didn't sit for a week when Dad got through with me. Pulled a lot of fourth grade stunts growing up."

"You deserved it and more," Townsend's bass voice rumbled with laughter. "So, you remember pulling the fuse apart and all the different colored strands. The lab did a good job of characterizing their structural characteristics and the fuse powder. Again, more chemistry than either of us know or want to. Suffice it to say, the fuses came from outside the US.

"Faulty fuses are frequent culprits when bombs don't explode. After lengths of fuse have been cut, the exposed powder absorbs moisture and may fail to burn. The snowstorm might have played a role in the one you found. These fuses were crimped into the blasting caps. If the powder was damp, it may have fizzled, or if the fuse contacted oil or grease, it could've made the powder non-flammable. Bet we find a few other 'duds' still in the field."

"You're right. Now go home. With luck it'll stop snowing by the time you arrive, and you and your girls can build that snowman," Mike said, returning to Frog's latest report.

Although the operational complexities of TLS demanded constant communication, Jamal, Ana, and Omar met together off site once each quarter, to check progress against their goals and ensure their money laundering efforts aligned with the greater objectives of their elders and Asha, Parsa's wealth management organization. They met all over the world, seldom in the same place. A week after the attack, they felt it important to include Parsa and review the *Hujum*.

The day's drizzling rain and sleet continued into the evening, finally giving way to high cirrus clouds, and allowing the cold to penetrate the city. Paris's unending blackness matched the hard realities of death, destruction, and the sober certainty of lives changed forever from the events half a world away. The soft underbelly of the world's largest military and economic power lay exposed for all the world to see without a shot being fired or a stock being traded.

Paris, Ana's favorite city. *The Riviere Nadia* seemed empty from the outside, but upon entering, amazed them with its crowds. The staff, attentive but respectful of their privacy, allowed them to relax as they were shown to a small, private room off the main dining area.

Introducing himself, the waiter suggested several off-menu items, took their orders, complimented them on their French, and departed. Their conversation consisted of a mixture of Farsi, Arabic, French, and English.

"To us, it's the *Hujum*, the Attack. For them, it's war," Parsa mused as he picked up the centerpiece on the table and looked underneath. "Their president has already given the perfunctory 'thoughts and prayers and track down the international terrorists and bring them to justice' speech. Congratulations, you three. Your *Hujum* achieved its objectives."

"What are you doing, checking for bugs?" Jamal asked, only half-joking.

"In your business or mine, you can never be too careful," Parsa said.

"The plan consumed us these last few months. Knowing how distracted we've been, I'm thankful TLS has performed as well as it has. We've all played a role. Ours, to raise the capital and develop and carry out a plan eliminating American interference to Gazania self-rule," Jamal replied, seated to Parsa's right. "You've grown the funds, identified the infrastructural needs, and overseen architectural and construction support for their completion. Much has been done, much remains to do."

"True. But a second step's not possible without the first having been taken. You three deserve congratulations of the highest order," Parsa countered.

"I knew the numbers, but didn't think of them as families, women, or children," Ana responded, choking back her emotions. She sat across from Parsa, the weight of her burden visible in her expression. "The whole town in Texas, four generations, gone. The families watching American football." Her voice wavered. "Maybe it was all a mistake. We thought we'd planned for every contingency, but we didn't anticipate the release of gas in Houston! It's odd. Since the attack on Agnew, I've had a sense of abandonment. It's as if I died at the death of the children in that gymnasium. I've had a sense of worthlessness. How could Allah demand such a price? I've done my father's bidding, have succeeded beyond all expectations. Why would Allah punish me now? If I bear a child, will He take him from me?"

"Don't go there, Ana. You're exhausted. You've worked on this for three years and done more than anyone could have asked. Certainly beyond your father's highest expectation. You've served Allah well," Parsa said, reaching across the table to hold her hand. "Your father's a brilliant, world-class banker. Good bankers are smart; they know how to make money in good times and in bad. You've learned at his feet, and you know banking better than most. He has helped his brothers, my father and Uncle Ahem in California through difficult periods. He had the vision to see how Marin Oil Tanking and Terminals shipping and warehousing facilities could benefit other users. As you three were beginning to build TLS, he came to me and laid out how Asha should be structured and funded. He knew there was too much international pressure for there to ever be a physical dismantling of Israel. A political solution would require great sums of money and the coming together of the Middle East, Shi'ite and Sunni, to address the common issue of Israel. Both were possible, he told me, and together the four of us would play significant roles in seeing such a great day come. Last Saturday was that day."

"My father holds yours in the highest regard," Ana said. "I had no idea he helped him. He told us our task was difficult but simple to measure, saying the task of our cousins, the Antars, was built on integrity and trust, and much more difficult to quantify."

"He was right. We've had the financial wherewithal for this for the past two years," Parsa agreed. "We needed to wait until the Antars were convinced of the cooperation and support from the Sunnis. Grandfather's mantra was correct: 'We're Persians, we're Muslims, we are not Arabs.' We could have done this without them. Still, their support compounds Israel's plight tenfold."

As the waiter cleared their table and served Noon Chai, Kashmiri tea with salt, topped with pistachios and almonds, Ana handed him five hundred euros and told him to keep the change. He smiled and thanked her, closing the door as he left.

Leaning forward, Jamal spoke in slow, deliberate tones, pointing out that while there was no way to anticipate the scout camping trip and the young men with their cellphones, the one day the Glen Canyon operations manager would bring his gun to work, or the gas release in Houston, the plan had met its objectives.

"We achieved our expectations," Jamal concluded. "Allah has been served! Look at the successes. We attacked from the sky, resulting in indiscriminate loss of life. They didn't see it coming and will forever live with the fear death can fall from the sky at any time. The psychological seeds of living with drones have been planted, well-watered, and can be expected to bear fruit for years to come. Their transcontinental transportation system and their petroleum and petrochemical industries are in shambles. Global recession is imminent."

"Stop there," Parsa, protested, "and each of you consider what the impact of this will have on TLS. Omar, let's start with you."

"I doubt it will have any impact on demand in the US. It may compound our efforts to remove money from the country. I don't see any issues with production or worldwide sales," Omar said.

"I agree," Jamal said. "If anything, it should loosen moving money out of the country. Now they have more pressing problems."

"I seldom deal with any Americans or Israelis, so it won't affect my world," Ana added.

"So, give yourselves credit. You achieved your objectives with no negative impact on your own business. Not easily achieved in any business transaction," Parsa smiled, pointing his index finger at each of them.

"Jamal, your points are well taken, but let's not kid ourselves. No one and no plan is perfect," Omar countered. "The entire world's looking for those responsible. We've taken great pains to build in safeguards, layers between us and those who carried out the plan. I'm not so conceited as to think we didn't make a mistake. We're bright people who studied and worked and refined and burnished the plan many times over. However, the depth of the United States government's resources cannot be underestimated! They'll not stop till they bring someone to task."

"It doesn't hurt that they pride themselves on a free press, or their ample supply of morally bankrupt reporters seeking self-aggrandizement as they file fake drug cartels news reports on social media. Or that those reports are now being picked up and broadcast by the major news outlets," Parsa interjected. "Remember, the morning after the *Hujum,* we began releasing the first of more than two million blogs, forums, tweets and other social media outlets blaming the attack on Mexican and South American drug cartels, with a few nods to the Russians and their new nerve gas and their atomic suitcase bombs. We'll plant seeds of suspicion and support both right and left-wing conspiracy theorists." Laughing quietly, he said, "We've even got a series of blogs supporting a Russian/Chinese Communist plot to overthrow Western capitalism that feeds the right wing. The more time and energy they spend checking each of them out, the colder any clues we might have left become. Do we have any information on the guy who tried to kill their president?"

"Talked to Nandi this morning. She's trying to sort it out. Right now, we have no idea, except that it didn't come from us," Ana added. "No matter, it will add to the uncertainty."

"What went wrong? Glenn Canyon," Omar asked. "Three quality soldiers lost with nothing to show for their forfeiture. Did we leave unintended clues? It's been seven days, a week, the FBI and Homeland Security are still ramping up their efforts. Are there ways they can track our operatives? Should we pull the longstanding California and New York cells? Are they, or we, more at risk by leaving them in place or would moving them bring unwanted attention? Something that will need to be monitored closely and resolved as we move forward."

Omar continued, "We weren't totally self-contained. It should have been our own pilot who took the engineers from Houston to Mexico. The US Army-trained demolitions man, his brother, and others, provided uniformity and a clear military influence. Jamal, you've forgotten more about explosives than they will ever know. I hope we don't pay for them in unexpected ways."

"Your misgivings are well-documented," Jamal responded. "We debated this issue as much as any in the plan. Better they find a countryman involved in an incidental role with no direct contact to us than one more involved."

"Maybe. What needs to be improved, you ask? I would never do this again without using 100% of our own people." Omar frowned, swallowing the last of his tea.

"Hold on, boys," Parsa warned, holding open palms up to each of them. "We all know this was a one-time event. There will never be another."

The attentive waiter opened the door and was again waved off by Jamal, who leaned into the table and, looking into Ana's eyes, asked, "What have you heard from the uncles?"

Impatient, annoyed, and sleep-deprived, Ana rubbed her arms and looked at her plate, her tone growing sharp. "I can plan and design, refine and plan again, but nothing I can do will assuage the feelings I have for the children and families, those innocent children," she replied icily. "To answer your question, I've heard the highest praise," she whispered. "May Allah forgive me, the memories of all the children will forever be with me." Not believing anyone could free her of her heavy heart, she feared unhappiness could become a habit. "Niousha acquitted herself well and has gained favor in the eyes of many. I knew she would and I'm proud of her. Like us, she has dedicated her life to this cause. Unlike us, she has no one and is destined to live alone. I hope she'll be given more responsibility. We could double our workforce if you would allow more women to participate. Look at their contribution to TLS. They earned credibility in your grad school study group . . . and have more than paid dividends," she trailed off.

A controlled Jamal let the moment pass. In a voice as cold as snow, he spoke. "Omar?"

"Like Ana, the gravity of it has hit me harder than I imagined. I understand why all those people had to die and the rationale for the locations," Omar said with more than a twinge of apprehension. "If it were only facilities and infrastructure, American morale wouldn't have been shaken and they would have responded to the cries of their Israeli puppet. Answering your question, those who task us with this mission are most pleased."

Parsa prided himself on his self-discipline, not merely the outward appearance of composure, but the cold calm he forced upon his deepest fears in times of crisis.

"Enough!" he said, demanding everyone's attention. "You've all been under enormous pressure. Nothing like this has ever been attempted, much less successfully carried out. The Uncles realized the risks involved not only for you, but for the entire family. If you had failed, it would have meant death to you and the downfall of the entire Shehadi/Antar effort. Three generations of work, ending in disgrace. They went over the plan with a fine-tooth comb. They were pleased with the plan and the layers of insulation you built into it. If they had not been confident in its success, we would all not be here talking tonight. We can never let our guard down. America and the world have been put on notice to extract some form of justice. We're a long way from being able to relax. We'll monitor their every move, but for tonight, let us take a moment to acknowledge a job well done and look toward the future."

"Speaking of what's on the horizon, my friends," Omar said, grinning from ear to ear. "On a much lighter note, Ana and I have news for you. We're having a baby. Found out for sure three weeks ago, but we wanted to wait until now to tell you."

"No way!" Jamal exclaimed. Surprised by his own exuberance, he ducked his head and lowered his voice. "Boy, girl, do you know? When's it due? Have you told her parents? Congratulations! Of course, I'll be the best uncle of all time. I'll spoil 'em rotten."

"I'll try to answer at least a few of your questions," Ana replied, warming to the thought. "We just want a healthy baby. The baby's sex will be a surprise. I'm doing better than before I got pregnant. I'm not a spring chicken and wondered how I'd do with this. Chances of complications are way higher than if I'd done this twenty years ago.

"Best guess, baby will come on June 23rd. Be fun if she'll wait two days and come on your birthday. It doesn't matter, though, so long as she's healthy. We told my parents, and my father wants a boy. He also wants us to move next door to him. Neither's going to happen any time soon.

"And of course, we want you to be part of the baby's life. Omar wants you to keep her till she sleeps through the night and is potty trained. He wants a boy. Don't know why, I have no experience of how any baby feels, but she feels like a little girl. I'm going to refer to the baby as 'baby' or 'her.' We're having a baby, not an 'it.'" She smiled.

34

Ivan

1930 hrs. PDT Los Angeles, California
Tuesday, November 5
Post Attack, Day 10

It took the FBI's Clarksburg primary fingerprint identification laboratory two days to identify and match the fingerprints to the unexploded bundle found in New Mexico. Another three to find Ivan Joseph Marshall. A resident of Chino, California, a suburb of Los Angeles, Marshall had served in the Army during Desert Storm and had led an undistinguished life since. He lived in a once modest, now run-down neighborhood.

They initially planned to wait and see if he would lead to other co-conspirators. After four days, it was clear he was a simple foot soldier with little or no idea beyond the immediate role he played. They talked to his job supervisor and the manager of his apartment. Working on a construction roofing crew, he'd disappeared for six days prior to the attack, before reappearing and begging for his job back. Living in the same apartment for the last four years, he paid his rent, ofttimes late but paid. Quiet. Getting to work was his challenge, not getting it done or getting along.

He was a bit player, at best.

They decided to arrest him.

After working as a roofer each day that week, Ivan walked to the corner store for cigarettes and beer. He returned home, about to open his first-floor apartment door, when a white van pulled up beside him. Three men leapt out, pointed their guns at him and, yelling, forced him against the van, hands over his head, feet spread apart, beer and cigarettes spilling to the ground. They searched and cuffed him, arrested him, read him his rights, shoved him into the van, and sped away. In less than thirty seconds, the Federal Bureau of Investigation had taken suspected Attack on America terrorist Ivan Joseph Marshall into custody.

IRS agent Elliot Robinson paced back and forth in front of Marshall, who sat at the table in a stark, gray windowless interrogation room on the eighteenth floor of the FBI headquarters in the 11000 block of Wilshire Boulevard. "Ivan, you paid $2,400 in cash for a car last week. You haven't filed your taxes for the last four years, and we don't see where you got the money to buy it. You don't have a steady job. We believe you either got it from dealing drugs, laundering drug money, or robbery. Unless we hear a real good story, you'll go to jail. Add time for delinquent taxes and tax evasion, and you're not looking too good. You go to the VA for liver treatments. Ivan, I can promise you the prison guards don't send you to the infirmary for preventive care. You ain't bleeding, you ain't going."

"I don't have the car no more. Gave it to my sister."

"Nice of you to be so charitable. Mind telling us why?"

"She's helped me out and needed a car. Her boy gots cancer. She needs a ride ta git him ta da doctor. Why's that so bad?"

"Brotherly love's good, Ivan. Where'd you get the money?"

"Don't 'member," Ivan protested.

"Too bad. By the way, have you ever been to Silver City, New Mexico?" Robinson asked.

"Don't know where that is."

"Ivan, you seem to be having real trouble with your memory. Now here's the deal," FBI special agent Sam Dove explained. "Listen careful and decide how you want this to go down. If you continue to have memory problems, you'll take a fall, and it's going to go hard on you. If, on the other hand, your memory improves, we might be able to help you out in a real way. We're going to turn the page and give you a fresh start. If you lie to us one more time, you'll go to jail for the rest of your life, for crimes against humanity as a co-conspirator in the Attack on America."

Sitting directly across from Marshall, eyes wide open, IRS agent Robinson studied Ivan's downcast, pensive face while the pace of Dove's questions quickened. "We found your fingerprints on a bundle of eight sticks of dynamite under the east end of a Union Pacific train bridge crossing the Mimbres River near Deming, New

Mexico. We showed your picture to the manager of the Silver City Red Roof Inn. He remembered you and another man, because no one ever came to his motel and paid for another person's room in advance. The woman who did gave him an envelope for you and fifty dollars for his trouble. Why do we call you Ivan Marshall when you registered at the hotel as Oscar Brown?" Agent Dove asked.

Pacing back and forth in front of Ivan, Dove's voice increased in intensity and volume. "If you tell us a real convincing story, it proves true, and because of the story, we're able to find other people involved with last weekend's attack that killed lots of people, we might be able to help you face income tax charges for the money you used to buy the car with a little help to foreign terrorists. Otherwise, the full weight of the Department of Justice will land on you. You'll be tried and convicted as a participant in the largest terrorist attack in the history of our country. Unless they sentence you to death. Tell me Ivan, you wanna die in the chair or by injection?"

"I don't believe you're a bad guy, Ivan," Agent Robinson said more calmly. "You've never wanted to kill anybody, but this is way bigger than you. Once we found your fingerprint, we got a search warrant and searched your apartment. Guess what we found? Hair from your brush. We matched it to hair we found in a storage locker in Tucson. Funny, they're a perfect DNA match. You used the storage locker for TNT. Ivan, I hope you can swim, because the crap you're in is a bottomless pit, and you're miles from shore. You'll be convicted. Your one chance of not facing the question Agent Dove asked is total cooperation. They won't give you a choice! Dead is dead. If you help us, we may be able to keep you alive."

"We're going to give you a few minutes to get your thoughts together, then you're gonna tell us a story to help us out. Remember, the more you help us, the more we can help you. Lots of times the little details turn out to be the best part, remember all the parts of the story, because we're going to be here all night," Robinson added, rising from his chair as he and Dove left the room.

Ivan sat alone in the interrogation room for thirty minutes until the two agents returned.

Robinson asked, "Well, Ivan, what's it going to be? Do you have a story to tell us, or should Special Agent Dove take you to central booking?"

"You got a bathroom 'round here? I gotta go."

"Not what I asked. Ivan, we can take care of your personal needs in a little bit. Now is the time to decide if you'll help yourself or be tried and convicted of the most heinous crime in the history of the United States, and even your mama will be ashamed to claim you."

"I'll tell ya all I know. Ain't much, but right now I gotta go."

"Much is a relative term, why don't you tell us everything, and we'll decide if it's helpful? Let's start, and if we like what we hear, we'll show you to the restroom," Dove remarked.

"Okay, okay, but I gotta go soon."

"Start talking," Dove demanded.

"Couple weeks ago, I'm comin' outta West LA VA Hospital over on Sawtelle when a dude come ta me, give me a cigarette and offer me a beer. Says, 'Sit on da bench right there.' Dude opens his cooler, hands me a Bud. Says me and Vince—Vince, he's my little brother—could both see five Gs in a week if we completed a job. Cash money. Drivin', ordnance, nobody git hurt, only UP. Me and Vince, we don't like railroads, 'specially UP.

"Was we interested? If so, meet him right here 9:30 tomorrow mornin' and bring work gloves. If we's late, the deal's off. Next mornin', dude come by jus' like he say. We git in his ride, 405 to I-10, head east. He don't say nothin'. So, me and Vince, we's cool. Ride thirty minutes and he pulls into Mickey D's, and we goes in. Set in a booth, acts us what we wants fir breakfast.

"Deal's simple. Wants us ta drive ta Albuquerque. 'Long the way, set ordnance ta take out certain bridges and overpasses. Goal's ta cause as much damage ta the railroad as possible. Dude keep sayin' ain't nobody gonna git hurt. Only causin' problems for UP, cost 'em money, lotsa money. Told me I'd been picked 'cause my Army training and work I'd done fa' Anaconda Copper. Was clear ta me, dude knew lot 'bout me. Name, what I done in da Army, knows Vince name, know I's goin' ta VA. Didn't know jack 'bout this dude. Axed 'em his name, told me it make no never mind, 'sides we's gitting paid cash. Still, one thang bother me, maybe see me at ta VA, but how he know 'bout Vince?

"If we was gonna do the deal, we'd leave right then. Didn't trust this dude, I mean, dude walks up and starts talking. Much as me and Vince likes ta stick it ta UP for way they done 'im. Still, notin' bout this dude. Right now, a lotta air and a ride 'cross town. Could be a deal, guys got no cred. Dude can tell I'm still thinkin'. Looks at me and says, 'call your sister. Tell her to go look in her mailbox. Envelope there witch your name on it and a thousand dollars in hundred-dollar bills. Tell her she can keep half, other half's yours.' Called her and like the man say, there the money. Told her me and Vince be gone 'bout a week, not ta say notin' ta nobody till we's back." He shifted uncomfortably. "Man, I gotta go. Where's the head?"

"Okay, Ivan. One more thing, what did the dude look like? White, black, Asian, tall, short, fat, old, describe him," Agent Dove said icily.

"I'll tell ya, I will. But I gotsta go!"

"You're doing pretty good. Follow me," Robinson said as he headed for the door.

The windowless media relations room at the Port Houston Authority contained forty chairs and a podium set upon a small stage. A stationary camera in the back and a handheld in the front of the room were live streaming to the major networks, CNN, and Telemundo. In her prepared remarks, the spokesperson announced the tapered re-opening of the Ship Channel below Barbours Cut in twenty-seven to thirty weeks.

Reporters learned seven new replacement cranes were on order at a cost exceeding thirty-three million dollars each. The Gulf side of the cofferdam around the *Nordic Spirit* was completed yesterday with the remaining sides to be finished tomorrow. An onsite inspection would allow a repair/salvage plan to determine if the hull could be repaired to refloat and tow it to dry dock. The hydrocarbons would be separated as the water and remaining oil from the ship's hold were removed. Recovery efforts of escaped oil continued, and the EPA was pleased the cofferdam had halted any additional damage.

The cofferdam surrounding the *Martina Southampton* and *Rio Chartrus* was completed Sunday afternoon, the water pumped out, and work was expected to start the following day. Both were total salvage efforts, and their hulls would be cut into pieces and removed. This process could take 90 to 120 days.

"We continue to work with the Corps of Engineers, Coast Guard, and EPA to ensure as little oil as possible reaches Galveston Bay and the Gulf. Skimmers and other oil collection means have been in constant use since the attack. Workers and volunteers have picked tar balls out of the sand all along Galveston Bay since the day following the explosions," the spokesperson said. "It's disheartening to the volunteers as they work to clean a site only to have the night's incoming tides wash more ashore," she said earnestly as she looked at the audience. "We've been pleased with the small number of birds impacted. As expected, we've had several. It's been much lighter than anticipated and less than other spills we've experienced.

"A total of sixty-six ships were docked or waiting to leave the port, fifty-one waiting to enter when the channel was attacked. Three hundred and eighty-one tugs and barge movements were ongoing at the time, as well. Of the sixty-six in port, nine ships have now been classified as total losses, thirty-eight will require refurbishment, amounting to multi-millions of dollars per vessel, the remaining nineteen are expected to return to active use within the next six months. Over a hundred barges and their cargo have been identified and scheduled for removal from the bottom of the channel in the coming weeks."

In San Francisco, Mike answered Steve Nottrott's call on the first ring. "Good timing, Steve."

"Mike, I've negotiated a lot of government contracts in my career but never anything like this. They've completed background checks on all the names you submitted. Everyone's approved. They've granted online access to all of the sites on our list, agreed to pay for any hardware needed during the course of the contract, and conceded that none of us know the cost of Frog's people, so they accepted our proposed initial funding level of three million dollars a month to be reevaluated every six months. They also gave us a 12% cushion on new hire salaries, and increased your base rate by 14%, acknowledging you're effectively on call 24/7. No invoicing. Direct deposit, first of every month. Everything we asked for and more. You sign off and we're good to go."

"Good. Maybe we should've asked for more." Mike laughed. "It's funny, sometimes they'll beat you up over a misplaced comma, but when they need something, they can move fast and there's no haggling over work or cost. I'm sure we'll earn every penny. You've read the fine print, right? So, fax it if they need a real signature. If an electronic one will do, you've got that. If I need to verbally agree, I'll call Director Townsend."

"Electronic works for them. Done."

"Excellent, Steve. Thanks."

"Okay, Ivan, so far it's a story of a guy you don't know, and we can't verify." Agent Dove paced back and forth in front of his beleaguered suspect. "We're going to need a lot more details and facts we can check. You better step it up, or it's going to be a long time before you see the sunshine again."

"Yeah, well me and Vince figure we'll take a flyer, got the time, need the green. So, acts him how we gonna do it. Dude puts two cellphones on the table and tells us to give 'im ours. Says he'll put 'em in my sister's mailbox. Say take six days. Expenses be paid. We's each gonna see five G's cash when we gits back, and if all our targets destroyed, we both git ten K bonus. If we don't complete the job, or if more than three targets survive, we don't see nuthin'. Say their guy be watchin' the whole way.

"Told him we's in. Don't make no sense. How we gonna git there, when'd we know what targets was, where we gonna git the dynamite?

"Dude reaches in his pocket, pulls out a key and says, 'Look out the window, see the mailbox? Look two spaces to the left, the tan Ford pickup? It's your ride'. Hands me envelope with Tucson address and eighty-five dollars in cash. Say me and Vince ta drive ta Tucson and check in the Comfort Inn off I-10, west ta city. Room already paid fir in name of Oscar Brown. Clerk will give me envelope with a Tucson address fir a storage locker, code ta access the place, key fir the unit, a road map with target numbers and miles from number to number on it and enough cash ta pay for dinner, breakfast, and gas ta git ta next location. Say ta set charges ta take out each target ta the max. Says to set the timers to go off at 0240 hours Saturday. Next mornin', we was ta go ta the Public Storage place and load all the dynamite. We'd be settin' it all day. Say we'd need to leave by seven in the morning if we's gonna git all done each day. Sum them targets was easy, others not. Told us ta wear gloves at storage places an take lock when we's done loadin'. We could keep 'em or throw 'em away, no matter, jis not leave 'em."

"What did you do with them?" Agent Dove asked.

"Me and Vince still got 'em. Vince trades 'em for smokes mostly. Anyway, we starts ta leave and he stop us, opens his briefcase, puts our cellphones in and hands us both a Western Union cashier's check already made out ta our names for five hundred each. Says, 'call it a good faith gesture.' Puts 'em checks in these stamped envelopes and hands us two pens and tells us to address the envelopes however we want. Say, not to call out on the cellphones. Says he'd be talkin' ta us each day. Takes out a pad, looks at me and say 'Show me how you set ordnance to git the most out of each blast.' Is he jivin', testin' me, or what? But the money's been paid. I walks 'im through ordnance straight outta my Army AIT course. What ta look fur, how ta maximize the blast. How ta use wheres ya at, I mean if ya got rocky ground, if you's got water, all it. Army trains ya real good. Done it long as I have, ya don't forget.

"'Member,' he say, 'if ya stopped by anyone, a local wantin' ta help, cop, whoever, act dumb. Ya don't know nut'in 'bout nut'in. Don't be smarter'n the other guy. When ya talk, don't tell 'em nothin they doesn't know or needs ta know. Don't say nut'in if ya doesn't haf ta. Be nice, smile, don't ever lose control.' Seemed kinda funny. Dude ain't from round here. We knows jis growin' up. Say we cain't drink no beer on the trip. Be plenty time and money when we done. Mailed 'em envelopes, got the truck, headed ta Tucson. Took nine hours.

"In da Tucson storage locker 6:30 nex' mornin. Prepaid storage, jis like he say, entrance code, key in envelope hotel clerk give me. Side locker, boxes of pre-assembled 'plosives, electronic detonators, mechanical timers. UP line run mos' long side I-10 from Tucson ta Santa Teresa, New Mexico. There be sum bridges, spans, crossovers, and overpasses ta make trains' route level as can be. At da map numbers, we gits off da interstate, drives ta da tracks. Sum targets gots pitchers, others jis da number. We's sits da 'plosives so's ta cause maximum damage ta the rail bed. Each bundle come wit timing device set off in days, hours and minutes. Dos jis what 'structions say.

"We git ta Las Cruses, map sin's us north to Clovis and works the BNSF double track from there to Vaughn, Fort Sumner, Mountainair, Belen, and on into Albuquerque. Easy stretch. Track run parallel south side of highway 84 elevated fifteen, twenty feet above grade, we's cross and run besides, outta sight of the traffic and set charges whole way. Easiest, fastest part of whole trip. Done the most damage. Albuquerque west ta Grants and Gallup with more stops there than we's do 'long I-10.

"All together, we done probly hundred fifty, hundred seventy-five targets. We done 'bout twenty, twenty-five a day. Most we done in one day's twenty-eight near coal mines west of Albuquerque. Glad Vince was with me, he done most da driving. Was surprised on Sundee when da radio say more'n three thousand across da country. Musta been a buncha dudes working. Drove from Albuquerque ta Barstow Sunday and on ta LA next day. Left the truck and cellphone in the VA parking lot and caught the bus home. True ta his word, five G's in an envelope next day when I checked the mailbox."

"Ivan, do you still have the envelope?" Dove asks.

"Yeah, keep the money in it. Now's see why didn't git the other ten."

Agent Dove stopped pacing and looked at Ivan. "What's Vince's phone number and address? Is he home now? We'll need to talk to him and see if your stories match. Still have your map? Can you describe the guy to an artist?"

35

Rome

1930 hrs. CET Rome, Italy
Thursday, December 5
Post Attack, Day 40

A highly vetted subset of the Antar and Shehadi families would meet for a day and a half, twice a year in high-end hotels in historic international cities. This time, the *Grand Hotel de la Minerve* in the center of Rome, a two-minute walk from the Pantheon. They had arrived mid-day yesterday, twenty-eight in number—sons, selected grandsons, and a few great grandsons of Sayyad Antar and Yamani Shehadi. Clerics and bankers who carried the vision of ensuring the safety and security of the two families to the fourth generation.

Last night, they had heard from Amir Antar of how the Arab nations had come together and provided the collaboration they had hoped. Next, Parsa Shehadi reported TLS financials had again exceeded projections and those funds, invested by Asha, now totaled more than enough to pay for all anticipated improvements in Gaza, the Golan Heights, and the West Bank. This morning the group waited with great anticipation to hear a firsthand account of the *Hujum*. By all counts the "Uncles," as the third generation referred to the second, were pleased. The operation had gone well, security was tight, and the next phase well underway.

The sun would not begin its morning ascent for another twenty minutes. Jamal, in a reflective mood, sat at a table in the rooftop garden restaurant, enjoying the solitude before his presentation. Looking southwest across the Tiber, he could make out the fruit and vegetable vendors bringing in their seasonal produce as they prepared for another day at the century's old *Mercato San Cosimato* in Trastevere's open market. He smiled, remembering his first visit to the shops, selling everything from books, to pasta, fish, and meat, spring break of his first year at the London School of Business. TLS meant the Three-Legged Stool to Omar, Ana, and him, ever a reminder of their solid base and interdependence upon each other. To the Uncles, it was The Lasting Solution. Either way, he marveled at how it had grown beyond their wildest dreams. Their accomplishments and completion of this initiative changed the world's power equilibrium.

A handful of British colonists had energized their countrymen, revolted, won their freedom, and set in motion the dismantling of what was then the world's largest empire. Even fewer dedicated themselves to the successful overthrow of Russia's czars. Now, here they were, a dozen, repositioning the Middle East and the global economy.

The American and Russian revolutions started small and found success, in part, because talented people filled key positions in the effort. The case here, as well. His first day at the London School of Business came into his head.

Passing George IV pub on Portugal Street, he spotted a man his age, an inch shorter, and fifteen pounds heavier. "Hey, I'm Jamal, want to go to the park and pass a while?" he asked, a smile on his face and a well-used soccer ball under his arm.

Jumping to his feet and shaking an outstretched hand, the other said, "I'm Omar, and that's the best offer I've had all day. I start class here on Monday and must admit I'm not sure of my bearings. I'm good with the lecture hall, the reference library, and the closest coffee house. You?"

"A bit better off, got here last week and have been to London several times. Your first time in London?"

"Yeah. Help me with your accent. You've spent time in America. Your English is good, American, not British."

Jamal laughed. "You, too. Seems you have spent considerable time in the States. You're not a native. Middle East? Let me start again, Jamal Shehadi, from Tyre. Did my undergraduate work at Stanford and an MBA at Pennsylvania's Wharton School of Business. You?'

"Omar Saleh, Tehran, by way of Princeton and Yale."

They fell into an easy exchange, passing the ball to each other and off the side of a brick building for the next half hour. Each noticed the other's quiet self-confidence and direct way of answering questions in a measured manner without being terse or offering more than was asked. Jamal spent considerable time in his youth playing soccer in the streets and parks of his neighborhood and by local standards was considered among the better players, but recognized Omar would win if they ever engaged in a real game.

"You're pretty good. Did you play on an organized team?" he asked.

"When I moved to New Jersey, friends and I played in an intramural league," Omar responded.

"They say these courses are pretty tough. Let's see how it goes, and maybe we can pull together a group and play as time permits. Interested?" Jamal asked.

"Count me in. You want to catch a bite to eat?"

For the next hour and a half, they sat in a booth looking out on the street in the Starbucks on High Holborn, down the street from the school. Omar had done his undergraduate work in chemical engineering and computer science. From there, law school, then focusing on international business.

"Jamal Shehadi, from Tyre, Lebanon. Ever been to Tehran? Do you happen to have two uncles named Antar who are clerics there?"

"I wondered how long it would take you to figure it out." Jamal laughed. "They're high on you and gave me strict instructions to find you. They hope we will do well together. We seem to have started off on the right foot. They have plans for us."

They'd been at the new student mixer thirty minutes when an older, distinguished, British-looking man with a wireless headset stood and began to speak.

"Hello and welcome to the opening for the Fall semester of the London Business School's Master's in Finance. I'm Dean Thurgood Alston. Let me begin by telling you a little bit of yourselves . . ." He talked of their backgrounds, expanding global economies and the opportunities before them, the rigors of the course work and the benefits of study groups. "We suggest you make your group as diverse as possible. You'll know your group best, and they will introduce you to others.

"Form a group to augment your existing skill set. Good luck."

Together Jamal and Omar circulated among the others, Omar taking the lead. They found three girls and another man. The six of them sat around a table at Balaji's Pot, a spot specializing in fresh, fiery-hot vegetarian fare in the tradition of South India. "Let me introduce myself, I'm Omar Saleh. Let's go around the table and each tell who you are, where you're from, the school you attended, your interests, your strength for the group, and what you hope to do when you graduate. I'll start by saying we used a similar study group approach in law school and when each group member works their assignment in earnest, the process can be effective. This promises to be an intense twenty-

two months, and at $85,000 per year, one we need to maximize. Again, my name is Omar, I'm from Tehran, Iran, Princeton undergraduate in engineering and Yale Law. I've worked for Precision Deliveries Logistics, a privately held supply chain management and consulting firm in Chicago, for four years. My interest is business operations. I bring both logistic and legal perspectives to what we study."

Turning to his right, the short, pretty girl with jet black hair smiled. "I'm Nayomi Tsumagari, from Osaka, Japan, a math major with strong analytical skills and a work history as a senior financial officer for an international distribution management group."

"Hi, I'm Chesa Castillo, from the Philippines with a degree from the University of Melbourne in marketing and management, and eight years with an international trading company headquartered in Singapore," she said confidently. "My strength's in identifying markets and designing efficient ways to bring products to them. I'm looking forward to working with you."

"Joaquin Ortez-Pino, from Mexico City. Graduated from Cal Tech, with a degree in computer science and information technology. I have an MBA from McGill University in Montreal, Canada and have worked as a senior analyst for the US Immigration and Customs Enforcement Agency for five years." Making brief eye contact with each girl, he said, "I've talked to these guys and hope you can kick a soccer ball, at least a little. All work and no exercise isn't very healthy." He laughed. "Oh, my family owns a fleet of ships sailing from Guaymas, Sonora, Mexico. Upon completion of this program, I'll work for them."

"My name is Nandi Zola, from Cape Town, South Africa," the tall, attractive, black girl said. "Did my undergraduate work in computer science and information systems at the University of New South Wales in Australia. I completed an advanced degree in cybersecurity from Oxford. I've worked here in London for Scotland Yard in their cybercrime division for the past six years and know my way around the city better than the rest of you combined. And Joaquin, don't worry about us, and don't leave your game at home. As they say, we'll be kicking and running while looking stunning," she finished, garnering a laugh from everyone.

"And I'm Jamal Shehadi, from Tyre, Lebanon, graduated from Stanford in electrical engineering, hold an MBA from Wharton School of Business at the University of Pennsylvania, and I'm a CPA. I've worked in the acquisitions division of National Petroleum Company in Amman, Jordan for three years. I will join an asset management firm after graduation."

Immersed into the life of fully engaged, serious graduate students, they fell into a regular rhythm: class, study, paper, project, presentation. As older students with graduate degrees and work experience, they stayed focused on good applications and concepts, and let go of the theories and ideas which sounded good in the classroom but have no basis in the workplace. They found themselves different enough, dedicated enough, and intelligent enough to work well together, appreciating each other's idiosyncrasies. A strong bond grew within the group. The six cared for each other, appreciated the cultural differences among them, and realized they were building lifetime relationships.

Walking back from the corner market with food for the evening meal one night, Jamal looked at Omar. "Did you know Nandi's Muslim? Except for Joaquin, we all are."

"You think our study group came together by chance?" Omar questioned. "Your uncles wanted you to meet me. They'd schooled me for three months on you and your cousin. By the way, when are you going to invite her down from Oxford? I hear she's smarter than you and much nicer. Apparently, she's done well. She's opened the eyes of her uncles regarding the capability of women and how they can play a significant role in achieving the greater good."

"You're right, and you're right," Jamal responded. "She's smart as they come, and she has opened some eyes."

"Back to the point, the uncles want us to use our time here wisely, develop networks, and make friends. Our class includes fifty-eight Muslims, and they've done background checks on them all. Many are devout, others, most from places distant to the Middle East, are faithful believers with much less distinction between Sunnis and Shi'ites. They handpicked our study group. Even Joaquin, he's not Muslim, not anything. Like you, his father and brothers died when he was young, caught in a crossfire over a turf war between drug dealers. He's ingenious and creative, has family in America and Mexico who own a shipping line. He can be an important asset.

"Your father was there at the beginning, helping to conceptualize and operationalize Hezbollah. Now the uncles have invested in you to be a major part of the new and ongoing leadership for many years to come. It's why they sent you to school in America and now here. You're being groomed to play an important role in the long-term success of the families Antar and Shehadi. The hope is Hezbollah and Hamas can work together in Gaza. If they can, by extension, the Sunnis and Shi'ites can, when they focus on their common goals instead of their differences. They envision an economic isolation

of Israel via the emergence of a strengthened Gaza and West Bank surrounded by a solid Arab trading block. Anosha and I are here to help you. They hope we meld as a group and each member of the study group will be an extension of the effort."

"Ana. Call her Ana. I'll see if she can come next weekend."

Omar, Ana, and her father, Rami approached Jamal at the rooftop garden restaurant as the sun began to fill the sky with shades of orange and pink and the peeling patina of the city's terracotta-colored buildings began to warm at the start of a new day. It was time for *Fajr*, morning prayer. Finding their bearings, they joined Jamal, spread their rugs, bowed, and prayed twice alone, twice together, sincere, religious believers, desperate to do the will of Allah. Rising, they folded their prayer rugs and started to join the others.

Jamal cleared his throat, drawing their attention. "I'll share the summary of the plan. We failed at Glen Canyon. Still, the *Hujum* has been an overwhelming success. The devastation, the loss of life, the impact on the global economy, the international outcry against terrorism and magnitude of the global effort to find those responsible weighs on us all," he said, looking straight ahead as he and his companions walked toward the elevator.

"You had a contingency for every eventuality and executed the plan to the fullest. Rest assured, the uncles are pleased," Rami replied.

The elevator's descent to the second floor was swift, their walk over the beige-carpeted hallway to the conference room much slower. "Papa, how is it with you? Mother, she is well?" Ana asked. "I'm sorry we didn't have time to speak last evening."

"All is well, sweet girl. Your mother sends her blessings. She's doing well, slowing a little as, I fear, we all are. She's a good woman. I'm blessed and proud of your progress and the work you're doing. I am pleased, as are your uncles. I've looked forward to this meeting. From all indications, the plan worked as designed, maybe even better. Indeed, Allah is pleased."

"*Salamo Alaykom*," Peace be Upon You, Ahem and his son Ardashir murmured as they passed in the hall, hurrying to the meeting.

"And to you," Rami replied gently.

As his younger brother and his son moved on, Rami halted, looked at his daughter and said with concern, "I fear your cousin, Ardashir, has embraced American ways too much. I hope I'm wrong."

"Father, I cannot speak of him as my sole contact is Uncle Ahem, and it's seldom. As for us, all we do is a team effort. We worked hard on each phase, the targets, the timing, those selected to carry it out. Niousha's work was exceptional. You'll hear from Jamal. She was magnificent. And Parsa has helped keep us grounded. We work hard every day to bring funds to the cause. He works on the world's stage through diverse clients and governments. His investments continue to multiply, and the international network he has built is strong and will serve well for generations.

"Next month we anticipate exceeding our projected target of 2.6 billion," Ana whispered as she walked with her father, behind her cousin and husband. "Joaquin has been creative, moving increasing amounts of money out of America via tunnels, trains, trucks, and container ships. For large cash volumes or when DEA shows special interest in Arizona tunnels, or California border crossings, he concentrates the funds in a container, and loads it on a family ship departing Los Angeles for Mexico or Houston bound for Grand Cayman. Either way, the money's out of the country and in a friendly bank within thirty-six hours of arriving in the American port. He has proven to be every bit the champion you predicted many years ago."

"I spoke with Joaquin two months ago. He wanted a business expansion loan," Rami interjected. "It's a competitive industry. As you would expect, when we visited, he presented a solid business plan with strong letters of support from regional agencies, provisional governments, and rock-solid corporate financials. He's the complete businessman, yet Parsa's fingerprints were behind it. The fleet expansion will establish a strong foothold in Africa and southeast Asia, helping him and TLS. Of course, we gave him the money at the 'family' rate."

"Thank you for helping him. I'm pleased you considered him worth the risk," Ana said, squeezing her father's hand. "Speaking of risk, or lack thereof, Hawala and the Black-Market Peso Exchange continue to be important in the US. Thank you for helping with proper currencies when we have a tight time frame."

"You're welcome, dear one, I taught you well, measured risk for substantial gain is well worth taking when the safety net is in place. I'll always have you covered, as will your uncles. Your stellar record has earned their trust. You'll hear more today. We, too, have been busy. The Russians and Chinese are on board. We were amazed when Saudi signed off. We're all aware, agreeing in principle and putting yourself at risk are a long distance apart. Still, they can't be invested if they don't agree."

"*Ya'teek el 'afye*"—May God give you health, Jalil and his oldest son offered as they overtook the quartet in the hallway.

"*Mashallah,*" Allah be praised, Rami replied.

Nodding his head toward his older brother, "Your uncle Jalil flies to Moscow tonight. He meets in the Kremlin tomorrow morning, from there to Beijing, and on to Jakarta. Through intermediaries, we have funded five new war planes from Russia and three from France for Indonesia. You know, these planes are destined to Gaza for their new air force. For their cooperation, through a separate set of intermediaries, we have contributed five hundred million dollars to their soldier's welfare program and worked with the government to relax home mortgage regulations and extend their loans to thirty years for their soldiers. Design and construction documents are complete for the major projects. China will announce the signing of another infrastructure improvements contract at a joint news conference with Hamas in Gaza City next week. Egypt and Saudi hope to have the pipeline completed in eighteen months."

"Omar, the Antars continue to impress. They've pulled the Egyptians and Jordanians into a working agreement. The corruption in Gaza, and, to a lesser extent, in the West Bank has been eliminated. Unfortunately, this did not come without targeted bloodshed. Even the United Nations has noticed the improvement and has quickened the pace of support and funds to rebuild from this last Israeli bombing."

Rami continued, "Of course, this has happened because of the money. You, Jamal, and Ana were right from the start. I knew you would do well. I did not grasp the size of the worldwide drug market. You have exceeded all our highest expectations. Even at my advancing age, having worked in international finance my entire career, I'm amazed what people will do if the money's right. Russia has always been a self-serving prostitute. They'll do anything if it will give them an advantage. And a warm water port has been their dream for over two hundred years. More surprising is how our Arabian colleagues have decided to put their serious differences aside to focus on the common enemy, Israel. When the money issue drops out of the equation, everybody wants in. Gaza's moving forward. Jordan has surprised me with their role in the West Bank. They're aware of where it can lead when we provide the funds. Last Thursday I met with their assistant secretary of agriculture. He asked if I'd be open to discussions regarding the Golan Heights. I told him I welcome the opportunity. This is two years earlier than we hoped we could broach the subject with them.

"Finish your tea, Ana, we don't want to keep the others waiting. Forgive me for not asking before, Nayomi, Chesa, Nandi, they are all doing well?"

"Yes, Father, well. We would not be where we are without them." She smiled as Omar opened the door to the conference room.

The room accommodated the group comfortably, chairs arranged in concentric semicircles facing two large screens. Amir Antar stood before the handpicked group and motioned to Jalil Shehadi. "Come, my brother, stand with me. Our fathers witnessed the wrenching aftermath of World Wars I and II, and the harsh reality of the desires of colonial Europe and Russia. They learned the importance of living in service to Allah and vowed to survive and prosper.

"Today is a great day, *Masha'Allah*, what *Allah* wanted has happened. My brothers, let us pray:

O Allah, how perfect You are, and praise be to You.
Blessed is Your name, and exalted is Your majesty.
There is no God but You.
We are ever aware of the blessings you bestow upon us,
we acknowledge and give thanks to you who is master of all worlds,
who cares for us, wakes us from sleep, provides our physical needs, gives us a new day, each day, so we may do your will.
We thank you for your servants, Jamal, Omar and Anosha;
We pray now for their protection and safety.
For the work they do and will do in your service.
We ask for your continued blessing on them,
That they may find favor in your eyes and be pleasing to you.
In the name of the Most Merciful One
We praise you, sustainer of all worlds.
You alone do we worship, and whose aid we seek.
Continue to show us the straight way.

"We're blessed by Allah, our strength and our guide, who has led us to this day. A day we have looked to for many years," Amir concluded.

Jalil stepped forward, "All here have played an important role in this achievement. The necessary funds have been raised, as have the resources to move this process forward. Those assets have been applied so nations can work together for a common goal. Still others have worked to build relationships and trust, finding paths for the Arab nations to look beyond their own deep-seated differences, righteous intransigencies, and complicity, and acknowledge that achievement of common goals leads to greater prosperity for all. We're one step closer to positioning Israel in a subservient role, ensuring lasting economic superiority over them.

"America has been rendered ineffective as they focus on rebuilding their infrastructure. When they emerge from their reconstruction, they'll understand Russia and China have tilted the political balance in favor of the Arab world, and they have neither a seat at the negotiating table, nor a military role. Let us now move to the heart of our morning's discussion. Jamal, please come and share the summary of the *Hujum.* Parsa will follow him with the next steps moving forward for economic revitalization, first in Gaza, then the West Bank, and Golan Heights."

Jamal, appearing ten years younger than his age, stood before them, erect and calm. "Thank you, Uncle Amir. Anytime you undertake a major action like this, you learn. We've learned to never underestimate the Americans. They have been a great help since the action in fabricating stories, spreading them, and getting millions to believe the Colombian drug lords were the culprits. Fake news is great. We've joined in the fun, having spread hundreds of stories regarding the evils of drugs and the pettiness of those who deal them. The FBI and Homeland will see through this soon enough. In the meantime, we buy time, and those existing clues and evidence grow cold. Now to the real story . . ."

36

Social Media

2230 hrs. EST Washington, D.C.
Friday, December 7
Post Attack, Day 42

Mike's phone rang, showing his cousin Jack's number. "Hey, what's going on?"

"Couple of things. Got a minute?"

"Sure, sitting at the United gate in Washington, about to board the redeye back to San Francisco. What's up?"

"Politicians and bureaucrats! Right after the accident, they descended on us like locusts. 'So sorry for your loss, anything you need, let me know.' When the lights and cameras disappeared, so did they. We can't get the state to talk to the feds, and the EPA isn't talking to anyone. Have no idea if they're going to condemn or let us rebuild."

"I wish that weren't the case. I'll see if I can find someone to help," Mike concurred.

"Thanks. We're all coping as best we can. It's one thing to say everything was lost in the fire, but when reality sinks in, you realize for the older farmers, everything means wills, notes, handshake agreements, understandings; they have no place to turn. Now, in-laws, ex-in-laws, crooks, hucksters, and Big Oil have surfaced with lots of claims and demands. People who moved away generations ago are making it hard on those of us who still call this home . . ." His voice trailed off. "Our San Antonio attorney doesn't do any of this and old man Hettler and the few remaining farmers don't have the money to pay for a long-drawn-out legal fight. God knows they've suffered enough." Jack paused to take a breath.

"How can I help?" Mike asked.

"Can we arrange to funnel all this legal mumbo-jumbo through one entity? Talked to Bob Schneider, a CPA in Dallas. Said he'll help keep it straight and pay some of the expenses. Remember Schmitt's kids? He's kept in touch with them and will see what they can do. Aunt Connie's kids, Sam and David, were the last of the Müller bloodline. Mom thinks Nanaw has a copy of their Will. I'll get her to look for it."

"I've got a friend with one of the big law firms in Houston. I'll check with him," Mike promised.

"I'm not asking for a *gratis* arrangement. I'll pay and am sure you will, too. Just trying to simplify it and make sure the surviving family farms, and those farms now in the hands of second, third and fourth generation absentee landowners, aren't taken advantage of."

Jack's sincerity reminded Mike of his own father. Before he boarded his flight, he said, "Let me do my homework and see what we need. Like you, I want to keep the home folks whole. Changing the subject, I talked to Nanaw yesterday. She sounded tired and old, not good."

"You're right. She and Mom aren't doing well. And Dad, stiff upper lip and all, won't admit his world's shattered. I think of you a lot. Despite losing Sally, Jessie and your folks, you survived and prospered following the loss of your world. That's big. You must know a thing or two."

"I don't pretend to have all the answers. Bottom line, it's the hardest thing I've ever done, it never goes away, and it forced me to rediscover myself. It doesn't make sense, and there are no simple, neat answers. If you keep silent, it hurts more. The mental pain's much harder than the physical. Jack, I'm here for you, but you've got to be there for Nanaw and your folks. If your dad swallows it, it'll kill him.

"What helped me was to learn something new. Sailing was it for me. Taught myself from scratch. Get Carlos or somebody to watch the cattle. I'll pay for Nanaw's, Toby's, the Müller's, and my place for custom cutting to gather the crops. Nanaw and your dad will push back, but don't take no for an answer. Come to San Francisco next week. It'll give us a chance to talk. We've all lost a lot. Everybody we love. It hurts. Thanksgiving was good, but way too short. We'll do whatever we want." He paused briefly. "Grandma and Bob Mutschler have a special relationship. Bob and his tribe would like time with her. Come now. Stay through Christmas and New Year's. Trust me, the holidays are rugged. Let's get through them together," Mike finished.

"*The Washington Post* reported this morning a consortium of Colombian and Mexican drug cartels are behind the massive attack on our country on October 25th. Lead reporter John Maddeaux joins us via video link," CBS anchor Mary Ann Holland said. "Thank you, Mr. Maddeaux, for being with us."

"Thank you for having me," Maddeaux replied, smiling as he sat in a chair in what appeared to be his living room.

"How did you break this story? What led you to look at drug cartels instead of toward the well-known terrorist groups?" the anchor asked.

"Several items. The attempt on the president's life: Manuel Cassados was recruited, provided technical support, and paid by South American interests. Second, the United States is the world's largest cocaine market. In the last several years, the Colombian drug lords have ceded the market to the Mexicans. Efforts by the DEA, IRS, FBI, and others have made it expensive to deal drugs here. The risks of arrest, extradition, seizure of assets, money laundering disruptions, leading to loss of revenue and opportunities in other markets, made the US market much less desirable. The Colombians moved to Europe, China, and even Australia where risks are lower and profits higher.

"Today's Colombian drug lords learned many lessons from their forefathers. Gone are the days of open warfare with authorities, flashy cars, and private compounds with their own security forces. They're much lower profile, choosing to live in anonymity in upper middle-class neighborhoods. They've found partners specializing in sophisticated money laundering methods and others able to create strong, diverse, international investment portfolios of legitimate businesses," Maddeaux said.

"Fine, but how did you tie it all back to the Attack on America?" Holland interrupted.

"Revenge and greed. Two of the oldest characteristics of man," Maddeaux said with a smile. "When the Mexicans took over the US market, they looked for other cocaine suppliers. Today's Colombian cocaine production exceeds 1,500 metric tons per year. Bolivia, Peru, and Afghanistan are also well-established producers. The Mexicans pit the suppliers against one another, looking for quality, price, and supply chain logistics. The Colombians lost."

Maddeaux continued, "The drug business is the nimblest profession in the world, able to adapt to changing conditions much quicker than governments or enforcement agencies. The attempt on the president's life and the anonymous tip leading to the drug bust on the *Rio Chartrus* at the Houston Ship Channel came from the Colombians. They wanted to send a serious message to the Mexicans, while inflicting major damage on the US. They hoped to force us to focus on infrastructure reconstruction while buying time to renegotiate their Mexican deal, or barring an agreement, retake the market. Our ongoing investigations indicate the Colombians have substantial in-house expertise and sufficient capital to purchase the materials and knowledge necessary to complete the attack."

"Your story has exploded on social media with over twenty-six million followers on Facebook, Instagram, and Twitter. Have you been in contact with officials from Homeland Security or the FBI?"

"No. It's a developing story and they have way more resources than I do. I'm sure they're looking at it."

"Would you be willing to share your sources if they asked?"

"They haven't," Maddeaux said smugly.

"Thank you, Mr. Maddeaux." Mary Ann Holland then said, "We'll be back with more after these messages."

37

Another Family's Future

0730 hrs. PST San Francisco, California
Saturday, December 22
Post Attack, Day 57

It had been a frantic nine weeks since the attack and Mike's agreement to head the Special Task Force for Cybersecurity. As feared, it consumed him. Air travel constrictions, introductions, security clearances, and Director Townsend's insistence that Mike have a regular Washington presence made him wonder if he'd made the right decision. Frog's well-timed jabs about the aborted rock climb didn't help. After his second trip, he convinced the director that traveling coast to coast wasted his time. Mike sold his new friend on the use of secure, face-to-face, electronic communication.

The first month, he'd squeezed in a gray wolf hunt. It was therapeutic, restorative. He had hunted for hours without a round in the chamber of his rifle, walking or riding a horse through the woods. Being outside allowed him to be engaged in the wilderness. The ebb and flow of the season, the silence in the morning forest as the sun began to rise, the give and take of nature cleared his mind and helped him fit the pieces of this new puzzle together. *They call it fishing, not catching*, Mike reminded himself. The search was in high gear and fourteen to sixteen hours, six plus days a week now the norm. Try as he might, he hadn't found time to fish, and he missed the time with Don. He decided to work from San Francisco with infrequent trips to Idaho and the wilderness to let nature help him sort through the disparate data.

Mike turned the day-to-day administration of Zia over to Steve Nottrott in Boise. The San Francisco Bureau offices had better communication and more support. Still, he needed an outlet, a way to put this aside and recharge his own batteries. He tried meeting Frog in Sausalito, halfway between their houses. Try as they might to talk baseball, rock climbing, even Frog's new girlfriend, the conversation always returned to the Attack and additional issues to explore. It was good for the program but draining rather than restorative on their spirits.

The storm that dropped twelve to fifteen inches of new snow in the higher elevations of the Rockies was reinvigorated crossing the Great Lakes and was now making life miserable for everyone from Virginia to Maine. Dark, dreary, snowing, the evening D.C. rush hour traffic a crawl, Ferguson wouldn't start home for another hour.

Calling San Francisco, he started, "Mike, we've got an update. Got a minute?"

"Sure, what's going on?"

"You and your bees. It's been an intense ten weeks. We've had incredible support from all the State Police departments and with their help we've completed all the sites Phillip gave us. The guy's remarkable. Mike, he was right on the sites over 94% of the time. I bet when he missed, too much time passed or the space re-rented. I have no idea how you guys tricked those bees into thinking it was spring, or warm, or why they shouldn't be huddled together in this endless snow and ice."

"Told you he was good. Thanks, I'll let him know."

"We included a sketch artist with the teams as they moved from site to site. They worked with the rental agents, hotel clerks, or whomever we could find who'd been in direct contact with the renter. Again, and again, they identified a woman, five feet five to five feet seven inches tall, one hundred to one hundred and fifteen pounds, late thirties. In all but two cases, she covered her head and wore a veil," Ferguson said. "Here's the interesting part. The images are similar. We have the makings of a reliable image to identify our mystery operative. Probably not the major domo. Still, she's a mid to upper-level player."

"Congratulations. People are easier to find when you have an idea of what they look like. Can you track the payment methodology? Did they use the same credit card for the rentals?" Mike offered.

"You want to make it easy? Oh, no. She paid in cash, well-worn tens and twenties. Gave the same or similar story at each location, moving into town, would need the storage unit for three to four weeks. To the storage unit leasing agents, she was businesslike. Her English was good, not her first language but good. When she rented a hotel room, she was shy, timid, with a strong Middle Eastern accent. Before checking out of the hotel, she would make a future reservation in the name of a man whom she referred to as her brother or cousin and pay for it in cash. She would leave an envelope with her 'brother's' name and pay the clerk fifty dollars to make sure he got the envelope when he checked in," Ferguson concluded.

"Mid-level isn't top echelon, but it's closer than anyone we've found so far," Mike replied.

"My turn. You asked us to investigate Manual Cossados's computers. Five months ago, he used a university computer in the library to do basic research on sarin, cyanide, and phosgene. Unable to find a supplier for any of them, he searched for coronavirus, anthrax, botulism, equine encephalomyelitis, and a few other toxins. He found botulism in Venezuela, anthrax in southern Turkey, and coronavirus in Georgia. There is every indication he acted alone. We found no contact between him and any of the major drug cartels, or any suggestion he was in touch with any radical group.

"Speaking of drug cartels, we continue to look. So far, we've found no individual outreach or communication between them to suggest they were in any way involved with the Attack. The murder of the Glen Canyon terrorist by known drug hitmen is still a mystery. I don't believe in coincidences. We'll sort it out. We're continuing our efforts into any connection between the supplier of the drugs found on the *Rio Chartrus* and the owners or operators of the ship. We're also looking at the *Martina Southampton* and possible relationships with one of the oldest ammonium nitrate producers in Estonia, or a link between the drugs and the ammonium nitrate."

"You've been busy. Keep me posted."

"This is fabulous. What a remarkable hall. It must be a joy to play here. You've been a most gracious hostess, and I can imagine how busy you are with all your performances and the practice you do. We appreciate your time," Ole Mae Bergsten said. She rose from a center seat of a VIP suite with help from her nine-year-old granddaughter as Maggie completed their private tour of the Davies Symphony Hall on Van Ness Avenue in San Francisco.

"You could fit the entire town of Agnew in here three times," ninety-six-year-old Gretchen Bergsten whispered from her wheelchair at the top step of the suite.

"I can't thank you enough. You're so knowledgeable about the music, orchestration, acoustics, the building, everything. Your parents must be proud of you." She smiled at Maggie. "I played the piano when I was young and taught my girls. I can't imagine how wonderful a piece would sound in a place like this."

"It's my pleasure, ladies. Thank you all for coming. It's a labor of love. I love this place and enjoy showing it off." Maggie guided the elder Ms. Bergsten's wheelchair, her daughter-in-law following on her walker, and great-granddaughter toward the elevator and lunch. "Emma? If your great-grandma keeps teaching you and you practice every day, you could come and play here. Would you like that?"

Ducking her head and smiling, Emma said, "Gotta get my arm out of this dumb cast first. But yes, very much."

"Michael has our schedule. Let's look for a concert or two you might enjoy."

"She tires easily. If we could find an afternoon performance, I'm sure she would love it," said the younger Mrs. Bergsten.

Over soup and salad, Maggie learned Mike's grandfather, Homer, had lied about his age and served in the Army during World War I at just sixteen. When he returned home, his mother gave him all the money he'd sent her during the war. He bought young steers in the spring and sold them in the fall. At the end of his third successful year, an elderly, newly widowed family friend offered to give him her general store and gas station if he would split the profits for the next three years and not sell or change the name of the store. He parlayed it into a bulk fuel plant, delivering bulk diesel and gas to farms throughout the region. He expanded the general store to include hardware, lumber, and farm implements.

He started a farm insurance business. Over the years, he bought farms when they became available. His first wife died of pneumonia. With Gretchen, his youngest sister's best friend, he raised a boy and two girls. He lived long enough to see the discovery of oil on three of his farms. Homer died when Michael was eight.

While Maggie took the Bergsten ladies on the Symphony Hall tour and to lunch, Mike and Bob Mutschler took Jack and his father, Jim, to Bob's office. Bob sat on the corner of his desk, Jim and Jack on the couch. Mike stood by the window facing the bay.

"Mike, I want to thank you for suggesting we come here for the holidays. It's been good for Grandma and us all to get away and appreciate there is still much good in this world. You, Maggie, Bob and Barbara have been great hosts, and I can see what keeps you from coming home any more than you do," Jack said. "When it's nice here, it's nice. But I can't imagine it ever being as hot here as it is at home. You must be a little cold most of the time."

Jim Bergsten stood, joining Mike at the window. "Bob, thank you, too. You're not a Bergsten by birth, but Dad watched Mike's dad pull pigweed out of his young cotton by hand, knew he was a hard worker and a good match for my sister. He was right. Mother has always considered you part of the family. You and your clan epitomize what Mom and Dad wanted for us all. You've done very well, but Jack's right. Too cold, too much of the time. And way too many people," said the old farmer as he smiled.

Joining the others, Bob spoke. "Mike and I share your loss. We don't wake every morning to the devastation, but Agnew's part of who we are. We know your pain. Allow me to walk you through a few ideas to help us move forward." From there he reminded them of Homer's basic premise: people must eat and being part of the production process ensures work. "We try to keep an eye out for companies that succeed and those that don't. For example, had Santa Fe Railroad understood they were in the transportation business rather than the train business, there would be Santa Fe trucking and Santa Fe airlines instead of Burlington Northern/Santa Fe Railroad."

Mike picked up from there, presenting the formation of the Homer and Gretchen Bergsten Family Trust. He explained that he and Bob would make substantial contributions to the trust. The Trust would expand the bulk fuel plant and increase delivery of diesel and gas to a greater number of farms. It would acquire the better farms around Agnew where children have moved on, allowing Jim and Jack to find good, young area farmers to work the land with an option to buy. The Trust would acquire the leases of the oil wells on the land they purchased and buy the better producing wells. Their plan included wind and solar energy production in west Texas, Oklahoma, and New Mexico. Finally, they would increase cattle production, initiate a feeder pig operation, and explore production of products required for the plant-based and cell-produced veggie burgers.

Tag-teaming the presentation, Bob asked, "Are you beginning to see a pattern here? We're in the energy and agricultural businesses. We'll produce it and process it. If we grow grapes, we'll have a winery. If we raise cattle, chickens, or pigs, we'll process them, thereby providing employment opportunities for the region.

"Sadly, we don't have a lot of the next generation left. The Müllers are gone. Jack, you and Mike have lost your families. My boys are grown, chasing dreams of their own. Homer wasn't afraid of hard work, nor are any of his kids. The idea's not to build a family dynasty. We want to serve the region by diversifying. Kids are leaving the farm in droves, in part because startup costs to farm are exorbitant. Many have grown up on the farm, know the hardships and aren't willing to put their family's future in the ground each spring and hope they make a crop. But for those that do, we could set them up to farm with an option to buy. We could provide scholarships and training for the kids in the county and help them find work. Those interested in livestock, oil, and energy can stay in the region and have meaningful careers. The trust could dovetail with Mike's foundation as we seek to make life better for all."

Jim listened, hands folded as he stared out at the bay. "It's been said I'm in the autumn of my life and have no business making long-term plans. But I've got Mom's genes, which gives me another quarter of a century. I like what you're saying. It keeps us true to Dad's vision, expands our footprint, and protects us from becoming the agricultural equivalent of the Santa Fe Railroad. The land has been good to us, and it was here long before us and will continue long after we're gone. How we protect it for generations to come will be our legacy."

Over the next hour, they outlined plans for Jim to oversee farming and ranching interests and Jack the businesses. Bob would do the accounting. And Mike would look for expansion opportunities once his efforts with the FBI concluded.

38

Puzzle Pieces

0700 hrs. PST San Francisco, California
Friday, January 5
Post Attack, Day 70

"Good morning, Mike. You're up early," Ferguson said, answering the secure line in his office.

"Got a minute? Think you'll enjoy this."

"Walking out the door. Got a briefing with the president in forty minutes. Can I call you right back on my mobile?"

"Great," Mike said, pouring his grandmother a cup of coffee to go with her biscotti as he hung up.

"Mikey, I can't believe I slept so late. It's nine o'clock at home. Can't believe I still haven't gotten used to the time change."

"Nanaw, be glad you did. You're going to the concert tomorrow afternoon, and it will wear you out. You need to bank some good resting time," Mike told her. "Jack and Emma are going to ride the cable cars today. I'll check with Uncle Jim; I think he told me y'all were going to enjoy the sun out on the patio this morning. Maggie will be bringing you some lunch. We'll see what y'all wanna do after that."

He looked down when his phone lit up. "I'll be quick," Mike said, walking into his study. "First, the rail attack. Phillip's analysis provided a roadmap of where to look and proved feasibility of how they did it. When you map all four thousand plus detonations, vast regions are unaccounted for. His work allowed us to find three quarters of the explosive depots. The great start helped us comprehend how these people think and work. It also told us a piece was missing. Either we miscalculated or a basic assumption was wrong. If our assessment worked part of the time, why didn't it work all the time?

"We started with the premise that the terrorists used mechanical timers with a maximum lead time of a week. Now we know they also used GPS detonators, the highest technology and most sophisticated tool in the entire attack, save for their cyber applications. The detonators provided additional distribution time, allowing them access to and success with their remote targets.

"The GPS systems included a master station with a principal receiver, a master transceiver and control stations. The principal receiver set a base time, which was communicated to the control stations through the master transceiver. The night of the attack, the charge stations identified their locations to the master station, which sequenced the actual timing of a thousand explosive charges. Phillip was right 89% of the time. The 11% he missed were sites used weeks earlier. There wasn't a residual scent for the bees to find.

"We started in Idaho and revisited the non-responding storage units. Remember my friend Don Plummer, Idaho State Police Deputy Director? He got a 97% positive response when his team reviewed their security tapes and showed the managers the sketch of our mystery lady. He was also successful in interviewing staff at several motels. We've since completed the same effort in the other eleven states. A 96% or better positive response rate has resulted in a 42% increase in David's list of names. I'm looking at the list as we speak," Mike said, looking at his computer. "I'll send them to you now. Your guys have lots more alibis to check. No idea what connection, if any, there is between these names and the perpetrators. I'm betting none. The people are all solid citizens." Mike asked, "How are we doing on time?"

"Got maybe seven minutes," Ferguson answered from the back seat of his government car.

"Second, don't know by whom but know *how* the dynamite was acquired and assembled. We're working it from both directions. Assembled and distributed from Denver or Salt Lake, moving west and east or assembled and distributed from the west coast moving east. Found where a box car was off loaded on a siding in Los Angeles. I leave it to you how much you tell the president. We haven't asked for permission. Hear what I'm saying?"

"I'll tell her what, not how."

"We scoured the operating systems of BNSF, UP, Amtrak, and CSX Transportation to see if a rail car could be misdirected on purpose. Turns out, when UP brought the Joliet, Illinois Intermodal Terminal online in the summer of 2010, they also did a major upgrade to their operating system," Mike continued. "A piece of software was embedded in a utility, allowing them to track and reroute every car in the entire system. It has laid fallow in the system ever since. UP's upgraded the system twice and has brought the working utility as is both times."

Noticeably picking up his pace, Mike said, "Nine weeks before the attack, the UP system was hacked. An order of dynamite loaded in Carthage, Missouri, destined for Kennecott Utah Copper, west of Salt Lake City, didn't arrive. Instead, when it got to Salt Lake, it transferred to San Bernardino, California. From there it was dropped to a siding not far from the Los Angeles/Long Beach Seaport, where it was off-loaded by hand. The order, deleted from the dispatcher's computer, left UP with no record of the car's whereabouts. Two weeks later, the car was placed back in service, based on a routine order inserted into the local dispatcher's morning rounds.

"The hackers who inserted the software in the operating utility were professional, efficient, and effective. Not imaginative, more mechanical. Their state-of-the-art techniques showed European training or influence. When we found it, we considered them Middle Eastern from subtleties in their programming language. This is where the fun begins," Mike quipped. "We found the IP address of their most recent access to UP, traced it back through alternate secure servers to a proxy in China where they bounced their activity off the system. We didn't expect the Chinese to be supportive of our looking into their systems and didn't ask. Anyway, we did a traffic analysis on a combination of records from several ISPs and cut the proxy service provider out of the loop.

"Eller's guys did yeoman's work on this, by the way. Ground through a trove of data to find these guys. They're working out of Bahrain. It's curious, they didn't use the TOR, the dark net, causing us to question their degree of sophistication, or if they consider themselves clever enough with the proxy to not need it.

"We've narrowed the zone to Manama. No more specific. Yet. They're professionals. There hasn't been any additional traffic. They had a job to do and did it. With no more activity, this is as close as we can come. Because they worked out of Bahrain, we're going to focus our efforts on the Shi'ites and the Middle East. For now, our Western Hemisphere drug cartels are off the hook. These guys are good, but they're human and got a little lazy or overconfident. If they'd worked out of India, Argentina, South Africa, anywhere other than what's likely their own backyard, we wouldn't have narrowed our search as easily. A long way to go, but it's a step."

"Mike, this is great. But I agree, a long, long way to go. Tell your guys and David and his crew, we're proud of them. I've got to run." Ferguson exited the car and showed his badge to the security guard at the gate.

"Peter Booth, Assistant Attorney General for National Security, announced today the government will not seek charges against John Maddeaux, the disgraced *Washington Post* reporter, who first fabricated the report that the Attack on America was initiated by a consortium of Colombian drug cartels. His reports, spread across social media and seen by more than twenty-six million people around the world, misled authorities and the American public into thinking a quick resolution to those behind the worst terrorist attack in human history was at hand.

"He practiced journalistic fraud, creating the illusion of being places and talking to people he had not. Mr. Booth encouraged legitimate news outlets to redouble their efforts to ensure their sources are true and accurate. We'll be back with an update on the school shooting in St. Louis right after these messages . . ."

39

An Unwitting Participant

1330 hrs. CDT Houston, Texas
Wednesday, February 3
Post Attack, Day 99

Houston has no zoning laws. Older residential neighborhoods near downtown often include law, architectural, medical, or other businesses, officing in converted homes. Such was the case for Lone Star Graphics and Visual Communications when two men in business suits entered the office and spoke to the person at the front desk.

"Mr. Roland, two gentlemen from the IRS are here to see you. Can I show them in?" his assistant asked.

"The IRS, ah, sure," he replied. *What do they want?* he wondered as the men walked into his office.

"Mr. Arthur Roland? I'm IRS Special Agent Evan Gibson. This is FBI Special Agent Daniel Miller," Gibson said as both men offered their credentials and Gibson closed Roland's office door. "We have questions for you regarding the flight you made to Brownsville on October 25, last year."

"Here, please be seated, would you like something to drink, coffee, water? I talked to an FBI agent several weeks ago, Agent McGill. How can I help you gentlemen?" Roland stammered.

"No, thank you," came the cold response. "You told Agent McGill you'd planned the trip to Brownsville and Matamoras, Mexico, in large part to log flight hours since you hadn't flown much for a couple of months. Correct?" Miller asked.

"Yes, yes, it's true. I filed a flight plan, made the trip, had lunch, bought my sister-in-law an onyx chess set and board and flew back. I told the agent, even showed him the receipt for the chess set. What seems to be the problem?"

"Are you familiar with the Texas Tomorrow Fund, the prepaid tuition higher education fund?" Gibson asked.

"Yes, I've heard of it."

"Well, Mr. Roland, as of six weeks ago, your four children each have fifty thousand dollars, paid in full accounts in the fund. We've looked at your company's books and don't see the source of those assets. If you made the money, you failed to report it. Unless you produce documentation right now to explain the source of the two hundred thousand dollars to fund those accounts, you'll come with us to Agent Miller's office," Gibson growled.

After several awkward moments, Agent Miller asked, "Mr. Roland, do you have an attorney? If not, you better get one. You're coming with us."

The Federal Bureau of Investigation at One Justice Way in Houston is an unattractive, eight-story concrete structure filled with foreboding interrogation rooms. Distraught, tired, and confused after an hour of intense grilling, Roland was a physical and mental basket case whose hands shook when he sipped his now tepid coffee.

"I can't say anything. She promised if this day ever came and I talked, they'd kill my children. I believe in my heart they'll do it. I don't know who to trust or what to do. Didn't go looking for this, was minding my own business. She came to me and said I would help her, or she would kill me on the spot. I'm just a graphic designer trying to build a life for my family." Roland's eyes narrowed, afraid.

"Get it through your head, Mr. Roland, you better trust us, or you'll spend the rest of your life in a federal prison. You're in way over your head. Start with a story we can verify. If it proves correct, our witness protection program will keep you and yours safe," Agent Miller said, pacing back and forth in front of his sweating, teary-eyed, highly intimidated suspect. "Start at the beginning and tell us a believable story, or I will hold you on suspicion of providing support to a terrorist organization. The obvious problems you have with Agent Gibson and the IRS, and I assure you he has enough to ruin you financially, will seem like a walk in the park compared to what the FBI will do. A conviction for supporting the largest terrorist attack in history is a sure-fire ticket to the death penalty!" Miller exploded.

Unsettled, Roland shook his head, closed his eyes, and took several deep, labored breaths. "It was two months before the trip. Working on my plane when this woman walked up, called me by my full name, and said we needed to talk. She was average height, slight build, dressed in typical Arab attire, with a niqab. Couldn't see her face but her eyes looked as if she was in her mid- to late thirties. She spoke fluent English without any accent. We walked to her car, got in and sat, a gray Honda. It was all so weird. When she drove away, I got her license plate number. And I made sketches of her and how I expected her to look without the niqab. They're all at the office."

Agent Gibson reacted and started to speak when Miller motioned for him to be still.

"She knew my business, my family; my mother-in-law being treated for non-Hodgkin's lymphoma. Mama Nina's a widow and lives with us. She's a legal US citizen, and a citizen of Mexico. She has Medicare but no supplemental or drug coverage.

"My business is beginning to gain traction after four years. It's still on the edge of make or break. I don't have any insurance for myself or my employees. The kids and I are covered as dependents under my wife's policy. She's a third-grade teacher. We were desperate. I'd owned the plane with a friend. When he died in a car wreck, his wife gave me his half. She was afraid to fly. We'd already decided to sell it. Listed it for sale right after the trip. It sold in a month. Even considered selling the business, going back to work for another firm, even selling the house to have the money to pay for Mama Nina's care."

"You seem to have had a turn of fortune. Your business is flush, and your kids' educations are paid," Agent Gibson mused.

"Let him continue," Miller said.

"The woman knew of me and my family. 'We'll pay for your mother-in-law's care and fund your children's education. You'll need to take five people from here to Brownsville on a Saturday. One trip. You'll receive a call the morning of the trip. The plane needs to be gassed and ready to go. Do not speak to the passengers. In Brownsville, take a cab to the corner of Elizabeth Street and International Boulevard. They will leave immediately. You will wait on the corner for seven minutes. Walk to the Brownsville Station, cross into Matamoros, buy an onyx chess set and keep the receipt,' she told me.

"She had a cold, cruel tone I'll never forget. Said I needed to decide. She could bail me out financially, fund my children's college educations in the state prepaid tuition program, pay my mother-in-law's medical bills, and deposit fifty thousand in my business account in three monthly installments, which wouldn't draw any attention from the IRS. The money came with an invoice from me, and I made the appropriate entries into my accounting system. 'Tell me now,' she said, 'are you in or out? If you chose not to, and speak of this conversation to anyone, you and your family will die.'

"What choice did I have? If I refused, she would kill us. I was desperate. We'd worked hard for the past four years. I told her I'd do it. Agent Miller, you have to help me!" Roland cried. "I haven't told any of this to anyone, not even my wife. Told her I'd worked with the hospital to pay off the bills over time. She's unaware of the kids' education funds and the business support. I sold the plane after the trip. She believes the money came from the plane sale. We're not rich. We don't take fancy vacations. We don't drive a new car. Lord, I ride the bus to work most days. We go to Mass every Sunday. I didn't know what to do then; hell, I don't know what to do now. Want to pay my bills and raise my kids. I'd never purposely hurt anybody. Does witness protection work? Will we have to leave Texas? Will my family be safe?"

"We'll want to look at the contributions to your company, check with the Texas Tomorrow people for any information on how and who contributed the money, the same with the hospital. How is it you know it's a niqab and not a burqa?" Agent Gibson asked.

"Our neighbors are from Egypt. Their kids are our kids' age. He's a petroleum engineer, and she's an accountant who dresses in western clothes for work but keeps a traditional home. Our kids are together a lot. Both families believe it's good to learn each other's culture."

"How did you know what day? What time to make the trip?" Miller questioned.

"Got a call from a guy Thursday afternoon saying have the plane fueled and ready to go. Be at the airport at three-thirty Saturday."

"No idea how they got there or how long they'd been there?" Miller asked.

"I didn't have a hangar. The plane was tied to the tarmac. They were there when I filed the flight plan. Talk to the airport security people."

"Let's go back to her. You didn't see her face," Agent Miller asked.

"Not exactly."

"What do you mean, exactly?" Gibson asked.

"When she drove away, she stopped at the corner, no stop sign, no yield, no traffic. It surprised me. As I turned to look, she had removed her niqab and I caught a glimpse of her as she looked for oncoming traffic. She pulled away. Don't know if she removed it because she wasn't accustomed to it, or if she used it to cover her face to make it difficult for me to identify her. I was ten, maybe fifteen yards away and it was brief, a quick glance but I caught her profile. I walked straight to my plane, got my sketch pad, and sketched her."

The agents exchanged glances but kept quiet.

"It's all still pretty unnerving. I needed the money. She didn't ask me to break the law. Flying people to Brownsville isn't illegal. I followed my flight plan. She made clear what would happen if I didn't cooperate. This doesn't happen to guys like me. Anybody willing to pay such a price for a simple trip, it didn't add up. So, I made sure I got her license plate number and sketched her picture." He paused. "Can I stand, maybe get a glass of water, use the restroom?"

"Sure."

He stood and stretched. "No windows, stark walls, not a room I could enjoy easily," he muttered.

Returning, he continued, "The ship channel blew on our way to Brownsville. I was nervous. I focused on getting those guys back on the ground and out of my life."

"Were you afraid they might kill you once you got to Brownsville?"

"It crossed my mind. I prayed a lot. I did the best, most thorough pre-flight check I've ever done. Knew they needed me to take them there, but might kill me, take all my identification, and cut off my hands so I couldn't be identified."

The agents smiled at each other. "You've watched too many movies," Gibson said.

"Coming back, I saw the smoke from Edna. It's halfway home. Turned on the plane's radio. It was chaos. Something bad had happened, and I knew these guys were involved but had no idea what they did. Still don't. I landed before they closed the Houston airports. Average-looking guys. Looked like they worked every day outdoors. Nothing special. Didn't sleep at all Saturday night, not much Sunday. My wife thought I was sick, or just worked up over the attacks.

"Monday morning, got to the office early, closed my door. Spent most of the morning digitizing my sketch and using a commercial software program to compile how she would look full face. I modified it because I'd seen her eyes and the bridge of her nose and got the spacing as close as I could. Changed her nose a little based on how the niqab fell when she faced me. It's not a photograph by any means, still don't imagine it's too far from how she looks."

"Did you sketch any of your passengers?"

"The guy in the seat next to me. I got a good profile of him. His sketch is in the file. Didn't look at the others."

"Call your office. Tell them to put all the sketches and any notes on a thumb drive. And any other notes or material you have and have it ready. I'm sending an agent to pick them up," Miller said. "Are your kids and wife home from school?"

Glancing at his watch, "The three little ones and my wife are. The oldest has baseball practice and will be home by 5:50. Why?"

"We're finished. Call your wife. We'll send an agent to bring your family here. We'll explain it to you all and start the protective custody process. Who bought the plane? There may still be evidence, fingerprints, hair, DNA," Miller said.

"Sold it to a guy named Quackenbush. Peter Quackenbush lives in Sugar Land. His contact information's here on my phone."

"Mr. Roland, obviously, we'll have to verify this story. If it checks out, you may have gone from terrorist to top gun. We'll be taking the money, talking to the bank, the school fund, and the hospital to see if we can determine where it came from or at least how it got to them. We'll work with the bank on the remaining deposits. Any other correspondence, checks or any physical evidence? If so, we'll need it as well. Anything else you want to tell us?" Agent Gibson added.

"Can my kids finish out their school year? Mama Nina's treatments? Will she have to change hospitals?" Roland asked.

"Don't worry, Mr. Roland. This isn't our first rodeo."

Agent Miller brought print copies and Arthur Roland's thumb drive to his bureau chief. "Boss, if they're not the same person, they're close enough to be sisters or at least kissin' cousins. I'd go with his image over the composite sent from the sketch artist," he said, placing the two drawings on the chief's desk.

"I agree. I'll forward your report and Roland's images to the director this afternoon. She's not an unattractive woman. I can see how she could meld into the woodwork. Having an image to work from will help."

40

The Oval Office

1930 hrs. PST San Francisco, California
Thursday, February 4
Post Attack, Day 100

It had been a full court press for more than three months, Mike averaging seventy-plus hour work weeks. Black box data from the drone downed in the Chesapeake helped the team determine the Israeli-built craft had served in a surveillance capacity in Israel's Air Force before being retired and sold to the Republic of Chad. After three years of service, it was purchased by Liberia but never arrived, having been captured by pirates on its journey.

Recovered black boxes from Ann Arbor told similar stories: a stolen drone in North Korea, and one purchased on the black market in Pakistan. While the Ann Arbor and Dover drone launches were controlled locally, the team determined they were flown remotely using signals beamed from a Chinese satellite. Whether the individuals controlling the drones were Chinese, or from elsewhere, was not yet determined.

Frog's mapping led to the honeybees' success in identifying storage units and the realization of the use of GPS timers. The GPS timers indicated a higher degree of sophistication, led to a composite sketch of a suspect, and substantially increased the number of names on David Eller's suspect list.

Having hacked the computer system for the Liberian parent company of the *Martina Southampton,* and the Estonian ammonium nitrate producer, the team determined the Houston shipment to be legitimate. Orders to the producer from the commercial nurseries, custom seed producers and two universities were bogus.

Seriously in need of recharging his own batteries, Mike looked forward to tonight. Dressed in a charcoal gray pinched squares sport coat and open-collared long-sleeve shirt, Mike smiled as he guided Maggie to a reserved table by the window. Dinner in the Embarcadero at twilight, a favorite. With a view of the calming bay, talk was of her upcoming concert, two of her hospital children, how she wished for more time for tennis, and his forgoing gray wolf hunting season.

Maggie knew not to broach the Task Force. He was consumed by the hours, complexity, and weight of responsibility. Looking out at the sailboats returning to the marina, she sighed. "Sailing looks so peaceful and fun."

"I happen to know a sailboat owner with openings on his dance card. Would you care to go?"

"We play tomorrow night and Saturday night, Bach, Salonen, Shostakovich, and I have the Haydn Cello Concerto No. 1 in C major. After that, Sunday would be great, can we do Sunday?"

"I'm on the redeye to Washington tonight for a meeting with political and military bigwigs, then the president tomorrow. Should be back this time tomorrow. I'll pick you up Sunday morning at seven."

The redeye landed at Ronald Reagan Washington National Airport at 0430. He checked into the Key Bridge Marriott, took a short nap, showered, shaved, had coffee and a croissant, and was in Ferguson's office by 0930 EST. Coffee in hand, Mike stared at the wall while seated at the round table in the director's office. He had nothing to do but think as they waited for their 10 a.m. meeting with the Chairman of the Armed Services Committee and the Chairman of the Joint Chiefs, although convinced his time could be better spent working. Ferguson assured Mike this morning's meeting and his two o'clock briefing in the Oval Office would go a long way to assuring the politicians of their progress.

The results of the bees identifying the explosive depot locations, finding a common person had rented most of the spaces, and Ivan Marshall and his brother's confessions counted as successes. Knowing GPS timers were used helped explain how many of the inaccessible targets had been set. Drone makes, models and identification had been known from day one. Work continued to determine how they'd been acquired and transported into and across the country. They had verified drone inflight control had originated from India; commands bounced off a Chinese satellite. But CL-20 and EEE sources, the logistics of the Houston attack, and acquisition of the Russian bomb at Glen Canyon nagged at him. The larger questions of who they were, and their motive kept him up at night.

"Mike, these guys are hiding in plain sight. They've planned this through and are committed to their cause. They're not zealots, seeking recruits, or in it for immediate gain. Do they hate us, or what we represent? Or are we a diversion to their real focus, wanting us sidelined while they achieve their goal? Nothing we've looked at has been left to chance. They're smart, well-organized, and thorough. They've practiced every step, analyzed them and practiced again. We're being played," Ferguson offered.

"We had to look hard, but they fed us Ivan Marshall, his brother, and Arthur Roland. Misdirected, financially strapped, everyday American citizens, who saw a way to do a simple task, destroy property, transport people, no one got hurt, and they were paid handsomely. I doubt they had any idea their actions did anything but support an isolated case of revenge. Connection to a larger plan didn't enter their minds. Simple people sensing isolation, looking to find a way out of their financial dilemma. They figured it was corporate America's loss. The plan's architects incorporated the use of these people as leads we could identify, chase, and catch while they slid further into the shadows," Ferguson added, grabbing his cane, pushing himself up from the table, and limping to the door. "We need to be on our way."

"The sinking of the *Nordic Spirit* was serendipitous and the release of the hydrogen fluoride, I suspect, caught even them by surprise. Then again, they knew production sites at each of the refineries, and where to position the explosives," Mike replied as he stood. "I hate what they stand for, and what they did, but I'm impressed with the professionalism with which they've carried it out. We'll catch them, but it won't be easy."

Ferguson nodded. "Let's go, Senator Booker and General Paulsen want to see where we are and how they can help. They're good guys, Americans first, politicians second."

"Mike, it's good to see you again." The president smiled as she greeted him and Ferguson with firm handshakes, guiding them to one of the white sofas in the Oval Office. "Ferguson tells me you've been fishing, and it's helped you sort some of this out."

"Fishing's a trigger for my imagination," Mike admitted. "When what I'm working on doesn't make sense and I need a little creativity, fishing helps. A good mountain stream and wily old fish moves me out of my methodological rut. Reminds me to look in the bar ditch, travel an overlooked dirt trail, and let what I know, all the pieces, wash over me—no priority, no hierarchy—and see where it leads. The Snake's a great river. Fish it every day for a year and you'll still learn next time out," Mike offered in his hardscrabble, Texan way.

He continued, "Madam President, stop me or shoot holes in what I'm about to say. This is a combination of what we know, and what my gut tells me from dealing with prosaic cyber criminals for the last two and a half decades. Crooks are crooks. We're more than a hundred days in and no one's taken credit, boasted or in any way exercised any ownership of even one part of the attack. There've been no demands, no similar actions against any other country."

Mike's voice gained intensity and speed. "What if this whole attack was planned and carried out to make America focus inward? The perpetrators needed us to be so self-absorbed, we wouldn't respond to activities we'd otherwise object to. Since the attack, we've established regulations to secure air space and the use of drones, begun to rebuild and improve our rail system, and secured the national power grid. Security and expansion improvements for the Houston and Long Beach/Los Angeles ports are forthcoming, and the rebuilding, refurbishing and expansion of our oil refining and petrochemical capabilities is ongoing."

"I don't disagree, and I appreciate the failed destruction of Glen Canyon and by extension, Hoover Dam, as extremely fortunate," the president countered. "But if I were going to cause America to turn inward, I'd have destroyed the water supply to New York City, wrecked the servers on Wall Street, obliterated the Mall in Washington, DC. Focused on infrastructure damage and not the massive killing."

"It's your northeastern mindset," Mike said. "They didn't destroy New York and Washington directly, instead tried to starve you to death, make you walk to work, freeze you from lack of heating oil, and make everything from cosmetics to house paint scarce as hens' teeth. What's changed? How is the world different? Three things: Russia, China, and the Middle East. One, Russia now has warm water ports. Two, China is now a major player in Middle Eastern politics and trade, and three, the Arab states are economically and militarily much stronger . . . and on their way to threatening Israel in every way possible, including long-term resolution for the Palestinians," Mike continued, ticking his points off his fingers. "Look at the bigger picture of the Shi'ite Crescent. Iran is key. Hezbollah controls southern

Lebanon. They've reinforced their relationship with Hamas and, by extension, Gaza. They control Iraq, and with Russia's support, the Syrian regime. They've consolidated and solidified a Persian supremacy of Biblical proportion."

"I have yet to see any cooperation among Arab states," Ferguson said, leaning on his cane as he walked to the window and watching the mounting cumulus clouds float against the crystal blue sky. "Iraq experienced a stable Sunni minority dictatorship through a war with Shi'ite Iran; a war with the U.S., years of sanctions, another war with the U.S., a Shi'ite-dominated government, a Sunni uprising and more political chaos."

"Syria's no better," the president offered with a frown. "Revolt, armed conflict, Sunni versus Shi'ite, Russia-backed support for the government, the U.S. supporting the fight against ISIS. Israel's a thorn in their collective side, still the Sunnis, Shi'ites, Alawites, Kurds, Turks, and Egyptians can't agree. The parties hate each other more than they hate ISIS. No way they would pull together to help the Palestinians."

"Madam President, in the weeks preceding the attack, and for a few following it, there was a systematic cleansing of the key people in the governing class of Gaza. The Gaza City mayor, the Minister of Agriculture, in all, we know thirty-seven people have been assassinated, unknown more at lower levels. The entire government was replaced with professional bureaucrats, many with experience in Iran, Lebanon, and Bahrain. It's still Hamas but more trans-Arab. Corruption disappeared," Mike added after a moment of thought.

The president looked at the director, raised an eyebrow, and mouthed: "He makes sense."

Mike continued, "Look what's been accomplished and what's in the works: a pipeline from Saudi Arabia through Egypt, refineries and petrochemical plants in Gaza, a new port, dry dock, and international airport, two new desalination plants. They're on their way to improving their agriculture to its highest level ever. They're on their way to full employment and have made huge strides in healthcare and education. They wanted us to look away. Plans for any of those projects would have taken years to develop. They had to have been 'shovel ready', as they say, because all this has happened in three-plus months."

"We're starting to see new mining activity in the West Bank," the Ferguson added. "State Department says it's state of the art, highly robotic, much more efficient than the program Israel's running. They'll dominate when they're fully operational. I assure you, Israel isn't happy. The new port will redraw Israel's control over the coastline and their fishing industry. They'll no longer control what comes into or out of Gaza's port, because of the port and the new international airport being built by China. Russia's establishing a military presence. Their influence in the region is new, substantial, and has reduced our influence in the region."

"So, you're beginning to see my point. We can't put bases in the region while Russia's establishing footholds in land, sea, and air," Mike exhaled.

"The previous status quo has been turned on its head," Ferguson declared. "Which begs the question of how did the Palestinians do it? All this costs money, lots of money. Where's it coming from? Have the Arab states decided to put their differences aside and focus on the plight of the Palestinians? Is there direct or indirect State support to the Gaza government? Does this cross the Sunni/Shi'ite boundary? It begs the question, what have Russia and China been doing to gain this increased presence?"

"All good questions," Mike interjected. "And I'm suggesting, as awful as the attacks on us were, they were not the end game—the goal. As I indicated at the outset, the objective of the Attack on America was to have us preoccupied with our own issues so a larger plan, one supporting the Palestinians at the expense of Israel, could be carried out without our interference.

"Madam President, I leave the politics and all that to others. We've looked at money flowing into the region and into the coffers of Hamas. We haven't found any overt state support. Funds from Egypt are expected since Hamas has long standing ties to the Muslim Brotherhood. The post-attack amount has increased, but the sources are not new. It's also coming through banks in Lebanon, Iran, Thailand, even banks here in the U.S. There is private sector foreign investment in several projects. A lot of money is pouring in, but no pattern. We're trying to find common ground between the individuals and entity contributors. Establish who has enough influence to establish a common agenda, and you'll find who attacked us."

"Mike, your fishing trip served you well. Israel has always been surrounded by stronger neighbors. The financial and economic gaps have increased tenfold," the president said, making notes to herself. "It's possible their Arab neighbors will soon compete in every part of Israel's economy, leaving them isolated and bordered by hostile neighbors. The West Bank and Golan Heights are home to an increasing number of Arabs, who own companies hiring Arabs exclusively. The methods Israel employed for years to take control of those lands are now being used against them."

"In the end, it comes back to money and religion. Hard to envisage the riddance of corruption in Hamas was self-initiated. So, where does it leave us?" Ferguson asked. "An entity or entities with both substantial financial resources and the religious capital to persuade the Sunnis and the Shi'ites to stand by until this major transformation is in place. Our intelligence people would know of any Arab-led coalition committed to pulling this off. Russia's the major player. They've brought China in to obfuscate their intentions, but they've got no religious credibility toward major Muslim faction cooperation. There must be a second party. Mike, can you discover who designed all those industrial plants?"

"We're already working on it. We'll discover who they are and how they did it; even find more foot soldiers. But it may be a long time, if ever, before we identify anyone in the inner circle," Mike told him.

41

The Miss Jessie

0730 hrs. PST San Francisco, California
Sunday, February 7
Post Attack, Day 103

Mike knocked on Maggie's door at seven, her favorite Starbucks and a croissant in hand.

"We have reservations at Charlie's 917 for 8:30. Did you bring a sweater and a jacket? Trust me, the wind and water are cold. This is supposed to be an enjoyable experience, not an endurance test."

"Aye, aye, Captain. Packed and ready."

"Great. The real question is, do you want to go for a sailboat ride, or do you want to crew?"

"Crew. You ought to know by now I'm a participant, not an observer."

"Wanted to give you the option," he said with a grin.

After a half hour review of general nautical terms and familiarization with the boat, he was impressed how she embraced the terminology and her innate sense of the how's and why's of sailing into, across, and down wind. She appreciated his patience and quiet assurance, comfortable that on the off chance of a squall he would return them to safety. She smiled to herself, having watched the YouTube videos and studied the sailing vernacular glossaries the previous two days.

Out of the Golden Gate Yacht Club by 8:35, they sailed south under the Bay Bridge, across the bay, north past the Port of Oakland, Alcatraz, and Sausalito. Under the Golden Gate, out into the Pacific, they headed south along the coastline.

They anchored for lunch before turning back. A shift in late afternoon winds added an additional hour to their return into the marina.

A full day on the water, an enjoyable four-course dinner with wine and an after-dinner drink had Maggie's head swimming. Leaning back in her chair, she tipped her head back and closed her eyes. It had been all she had hoped for and more. Great weather. Wishing for a seal or two, she was gifted with more seals, sea lions and porpoises than she could count.

"I can certainly see why you love it so," she almost whispered. "The sea, the sails, and the sun can take you away and let you find serenity."

"I'm glad you enjoyed yourself."

"How long have you been sailing?"

"I taught myself after I lost my family. It helped me through a tough time." Letting out a slight chuckle, he said, "There are only two downsides. One, somehow you always want a bigger and bigger boat. I think I'll stop with this one."

"What's the second?" she asked.

"Finding someone to sail with. I sail alone quite often, but it's more fun when you can enjoy it with others."

"Well, today was wonderful, and I'm more than willing to crew with you anytime." She gave him an inviting smile.

"The night is still young. Would you like to come back by my house for a nightcap?"

Settling on the rug in front of his fireplace, Maggie invited Mike to join her. "Zia? What does it mean? Is it a real name, or did you make it up?"

Taking a pen from his pocket, he drew a circle with four lines coming from each of the four cardinal directions on the back of his notebook. "The Zia symbol was found on a pot at the Zia pueblo in north central New Mexico in the 1800s. It became the state symbol and is on their flag and license plate. Four is a sacred number to the Zia people. It symbolizes the Circle of Life: the four directions, the four times of day, the four stages of life, and the four seasons. The circle binds the four elements of four together. To the Zia, it's the symbol of perfect friendship among united cultures. Sally believed all cultures could embrace cybersecurity as a positive to help keep all people together. I liked her idea of cultural friendship but was not naïve enough to suppose there weren't people out there trying to tilt the scale in their favor. If they did, I wanted us to be prepared to catch them. It also means 'to tremble' in Hebrew. To me, a subtle hint to the unsavory. We fund twelve full college scholarships a year to students from Sandoval County in New Mexico, one for each of the county's twelve pueblos, including Zia."

"I'm curious why you named your boat *Miss Jessie*."

"Would you prefer the long version or the short?"

Warm and a bit drowsy, she stretched out, her head on a throw pillow from the couch. "As much as you're willing to tell." She smiled.

"Dad expected my younger brother Toby and me to one day take over and expand the family operation and made sure we knew how to work. Believed in education with a heavy dose of practical experience and common sense. Find trouble, don't make your grades, don't treat mother with respect, he would wear you out with work, giving you time to think before you said or did anything. Not a lot of rules. But think before you act or talk. You'll live with the consequences. Dad hoped we'd go to A&M or maybe Texas Tech. My senior year, Toby, my cousins, and I won the state football championship, and I got a scholarship to play for Stanford."

"Don't let me change the subject, but how did a Texas cowboy raised herding cows and driving tractors learn classical music?" she mused.

"One question at a time, if you please. Mother taught us how to cook, etiquette, how to set a proper table, and miter your corners when you change your sheets. With no sisters, she taught us how to sew, do laundry, fold clothes, and iron. She also taught us to play piano. I was five when I started. The consummate teacher, she made it all a game, scales, little riffs, all kinds of one or two hand exercises. It was fun. She shared her love of good music. If it was good, she liked it. Chopin, Beethoven, Stravinsky, or Debussy. It didn't matter. Gershwin, the Beatles, Hendrix, or Bacharach. Good music, good musicians. Can't remember not going to the San Antonio Symphony at least two or three times a year. Dad, not much on classical music, but was big on family activities and supporting Mother."

"Your parents sound a lot like mine. We didn't have any brothers. Dad taught us to change a tire, check the oil, mow the grass, and basic plumbing and household wiring," she responded quietly.

"Those lessons didn't hurt either of us. You've seen a piano in both of my houses. I don't practice much, especially lately. I'm not very good, but I enjoy playing. It's relaxing, and it helps me see things from a different perspective." Mike paused, then said, "Blew out my knee freshman year, which finished my football career and allowed me to concentrate on my studies."

"Did you consider returning to Texas to finish school?" Maggie asked.

He shook his head. "No, Texas was home. I intended to return and farm and ranch in Agnew. But I wanted to see the rest of the country. Graduated with a double major of electrical engineering and computer science. I attended grad school at MIT. Seldom ventured to New York, but as a reward to myself for having passed my prelim exams and receiving approval of my dissertation study outline, I took the train into Grand Central for an all-Mahler concert of the Philharmonic featuring his Symphony No. 8 in E-flat major with the Metropolitan Opera. My favorite piece.

"Saw her at intermission at Lincoln Center, our eyes met, and I was smitten. Miss Sarah Ann Duncan of New York City, 'Sally,' she said, shaking my hand. We talked, and she invited me to enjoy the remainder of the concert with her as her uncle, with whom she shared season tickets, hadn't been able to attend.

"Afterwards, I was in New York or she was in Boston at least three weekends a month. We married three and a half years later, the weekend after graduation. Much to the chagrin of her mother, I took her little girl west, borrowed fifty thousand from my father and started Zia. Mr. Duncan could've matched Dad and more. I knew the talent pool of computer nerds was better in Silicon Valley and my uncle, Bob Mutschler, offered free office space in his construction company headquarters building. I decided if I failed and fell on my face, better in front of *my* folks than hers."

"Bob Mutschler? As in Becca and David Mutschler and their wedding? Where we met?"

"Correct. Bob's married to Dad's sister. He's the wisest man I know. My wedding present to the couple was to host their reception, which included your music. Once in San Francisco, Sally made me promise we'd always have symphony season tickets. I used to kid her about where I stood with the other loves of her life, Bach, Beethoven, Mozart, Schubert. All I ever got was a wry smile and a comment about not tempting fate."

"Bright girl, I like her. So, you stinker," Maggie said, sitting up and playfully throwing her pillow at him. "You knew who I was when April introduced us!"

Smiling at her, Mike's mind returned to a time nearing two decades ago. "Those first few years, failure wasn't an option. We poured ourselves into getting Zia off the ground. Sally was as supportive as anyone could be. We lived off her advertising agency salary and commissions. The loan paid for people and equipment. Fast forward three years. It's good to be good, being lucky helps. The embryonic development of the cybersecurity industry, the quality of our product and the timing of the national awareness of its need couldn't have worked any better for us.

"Frog was the first person I hired. He's a genius. He also finds and recruits exceptionally talented people. Many of our staff are the nerd's nerd. They, and Frog's network, have kept us a step and a half ahead of the rest from day one. Zia exploded beyond our wildest expectations and with it, our personal wealth. Sally got pregnant and everyone shared our excitement. From an echocardiogram in Sally's fifth month, we learned our unborn baby girl's heart hadn't developed properly. She would arrive with a congenital heart anomaly. We would have traded it all—the company, the money, the house, the cars, everything—for a healthy little girl."

Maggie watched the transformation of Mike's facial expression as he revisited a long-ago hurtful time in his life. "There was a chance she wouldn't live more than a few days to months and even then, would require several delicate surgeries and a heart transplant," he continued. "Hypoplastic left heart syndrome, HLHS, is characterized by underdevelopment of the left side of the heart, the part that pumps oxygenated blood to the rest of the body. Those two valves hadn't developed and blocked blood flow to the main vessel carrying blood to her body. HLHS only occurs in two or three babies per ten thousand births but when she's yours, your world collapses. At first, we struggled with *why us*, what did we do wrong? We moved on to how we could learn as much as possible, and on to what we could do to help this baby so wanted, so loved even before she'd drawn her first breath?"

Squeezing his hand, Maggie knew Mike was a million miles away. "I was relieved to learn the congenital heart surgery program at the UC San Francisco was a top program. A few well-placed phone calls, and we had a clinical plan in place for birth and treatment. Sally worked with her obstetrician and pediatric cardiologist, learning all she could of treatment plans, surgeries, why they were done in sequence and why it was important for the baby to grow in between each repair. What activities were and were not safe for developing babies and young children. The more we learned, the easier it was to accept if our little Jessica lived beyond a week, she'd have to have surgery with a high probability of a left heart pump until a donor heart for transplant could be located. Sally struggled when she realized our baby's long-term survival was dependent upon the unconscionable loss of another family's toddler.

"Jessica Duncan Paxton was born at 2:47 p.m., July 24th. We were ecstatic, yet terrified. Ashen with cold hands and feet, she lay on her mother's stomach with shallow, rapid breathing. The nurses whisked her away to put her on oxygen and in an incubator.

'She'll be there till she can regulate her own temperature, breathe on her own, and make urine,' a nurse told us. She was three days old when she had her fist surgery. The doctors inserted a tiny pump, no larger than my little finger, and converted her right ventricle to the main pumping chamber, sending blood to both the lungs and the body. It wasn't a long-term solution, but it would keep her alive and buy time in hopes a donor heart could be found. This tiny miracle in the incubator with tubes and lines, monitors and machines everywhere; 'She's tough, a real fighter,' the ICU nurse told us."

"God, it must have been awful," Maggie whispered.

In that moment, he did not hear her. He relived the moment, telling her how he had called his father when Jessie was out of surgery and how her color had changed, and her hands and feet were warm. The doctors had implanted some synthetic graft material that would have to be replaced as her heart grew. *Never expected I'd consider heart surgery for your baby a good problem, but I look forward to the day she'll be bigger and stronger,* he remembered saying.

He talked about how their parents came to support them. How their fathers had bonded with excursions to the wine country, baseball games, and sailing. How Jessie helped fill the void in his mother's heart from the loss of his Marine lieutenant brother from wounds incurred in Iraq. And how he and Sally laughed, saying Jessie's heart was fine, but she might not learn to walk. She was hugged, held, carried, passed from arms to arms and greeted everyone with a smile.

"Months passed with alternating grandparent visits. Then the call came. There was a donor heart. We were ecstatic, of course. Thoughts of the donor family made it bittersweet, but it was the answer to our prayers. She called her parents, and I called mine. My folks would arrive later that night, I'd meet hers at Oakland International Airport the next afternoon. This was Jessica's third cardiothoracic surgery in eleven months. A major operation, the doctors assured us the transplant was less demanding than what she'd already endured. We were concerned, but pleased and confident her quality of life would improve."

Getting to his feet, he walked over and sat on a kitchen stool. "She didn't go to the operating room until 2:30 in the morning. An hour and a half later, we were all in the waiting room. Mom and Dad dozed while Sally and I walked or tried to read. The lights suddenly flickered and then came right back on. I didn't give the power glitch and emergency power generators another thought. Forty minutes later, Dr. Olson came to tell us the emergency generators had performed as designed, but we'd still lost our baby. They tried everything, but she was gone. We were numb. We prayed. We cried. We were so exhausted."

Maggie went to him, rested her head against his chest and held him for several moments. "What an incredible tragedy." She sighed softly. "You poor, beautiful man."

He focused on Maggie. "It took a couple of hours for all the arrangements. No one was hungry, but we knew this was going to be a long hard day, and we would need to eat. The engineer in me kicked in. There were questions for the facilities manager and the bioengineering people. I headed back to the hospital after breakfast. Sally was driving my parents to our house. A kid high on meth, making his getaway after robbing a corner store, hit 'em head on. All three died on impact. The kid walked away unscathed. His parents had money, and the judge gave him six months on the robbery and a probated sentence on the vehicular manslaughter since he was seventeen, and it was his first offense.

"Meeting her parents' flight was by far the most difficult thing I've ever done," Mike recalled softly. "I've shut all this away in a deep recess of my memory. Now, talking to you, it's as if it all happened yesterday. I can't believe I've talked this much. Sally's father, Frog, a fishing buddy, and now you; you're the only people who know this story. Way too much information. I didn't mean to go on like that."

"The magnanimity, love, and tenderness with which you tell the story, you must miss them so. And now you've lost even more in Agnew. I'm sorry. I can't imagine your sadness. If my hug can be strong enough to take away your pain, I'll start now and never stop. You've navigated it all with grace, good humor, resilience, and intellectual curiosity. How do you do it?"

"It doesn't go away. I dug a grave one summer in high school. Most of the markers had the dates of birth and death with a hyphen in between. I learned then it's what you do with the hyphen, the time between, that matters. We will all die. We all have a choice. If you recognize your mortality, seize the day, open your eyes to opportunities, and cherish every moment of the time you have, you can make this world a better place." Impulsively he bent down and kissed her, a gentle meeting of lips and then a second much longer, more passionate kiss.

Gathering himself, he straightened. "Watch it, girl, you may have touched a nerve. It's been a decade since I've even looked at a woman, much less one as pretty and engaging as you. These last few months have been wonderful and, until now, I hadn't considered where this might lead. I'm eleven years your senior, a part-time resident, enjoy what I do for a living, and it pays well. I'm a workaholic, up to my gills chasing terrorists. I'm also committed to funding the work we're doing through Jessie's foundation. Besides, I've become a stodgy old man, who doesn't have sense enough to come in out of the snow when I'm hunting an elk." He looked her in the eyes. "What I'm trying to do is give you an out. I can take you home, and in a little while, see what happens."

"I like what I see," she countered. "April tells me you've been good to Becca and David. David considers you an older brother. He said you've always been there for him and his brothers. As kids in school, they'd come to you when they were in trouble with their dad, and you'd help smooth things out. He gives you a lot of credit for helping them become the men they are today.

"Mr. Loddy, Becca and April's dad, who treats me better than his own daughters, has worked with Mr. Mutschler for years. Remember, he's a plumbing contractor. I took them to lunch last week, because for the first time ever, someone's come into my life who's begun to turn my head around and make me think outside of music and teaching and helping kids. Mr. Mutschler tells me you're wise beyond your years, avuncular and caring, honest to a fault. You're serious about leaving this world a better place than you came into it, and a man of high integrity. He smiled when he told me you've always sailed a boat of your own design. And since you moved to Boise, you adopted a more peripatetic lifestyle, delighting in the natural world. He's glad you enjoy fishing and hunting and being outdoors. I think I can take a chance on you. I'm not looking for a way out. Music's been my life, but it's time to expand my horizons."

Still holding him close, she looked into his blue eyes, deep enough she believed she might drown. "I know this . . . I love your optimism for your foundation, how you've taken all your personal tragedy and turned it into such good. Your perspective has helped expand the kid's music at the hospital. I can only imagine what you're doing with your other projects. I want you in my life, to have you beside me, to help you any way I can." Arms around his neck, she kissed him and led him to the couch.

They kissed for a long time before Mike gently caressed her neck and shoulders. "Are you sure?" he asked.

Smiling, she gave an affirmative nod and a gentle push, resulting in his head resting on the arm of the sofa looking up at her. "I don't want to dishonor Sally's memory, but you shouldn't have to live as an anchorite the rest of your life," she whispered.

42

Beer and Wings

1400 hrs. PDT Los Angeles, California
Wednesday, February 9
Post Attack, Day 104

Arthur Roland's sketch ran on the national evening news and local newscasts multiple times a day for three days. The public response was in the hundreds of thousands.

"Federal Bureau of Investigation. How may I direct your call?"

"Yes, my name is Alya Alhumaivi. My husband is the on-site manager of the Villa Gardens apartments in Maywood," a woman's voice said in broken English. "We recognize the person whose picture you show on the television. Who do I talk to?"

"One moment, please, while I connect you."

Two Los Angeles-based FBI agents sat in the cramped, dark living room of the Villa Gardens manager's apartment. Even with glasses of ice water and the window air conditioner on its maximum setting, everyone in the room was sweating profusely.

"We talked of it for a long time, my wife and me. We saw the sketch once on the television. We did not know if we should say or not. We are from Syria and are not accustomed to dealing with the police. We have submitted all our papers but are not yet citizens of this country. We fear if we get involved, we might be deported. But yes, sir, I know it's a drawing, not a picture and it's been a year, yes, I would say it's Ms. Marsban, Mary Marsban, the lady who lived in apartment number 42," Daksh Alhumaivi, the manager, said.

"We're grateful you contacted us and assure you your involvement will not impact your immigration status. In fact, because of your help, we will do what we can to expedite and complete the process," the lead agent said.

"She rented the apartment here over three years. From the beginning, she would come and go. She'd be gone two or three weeks or be here for a month. Based on how long her mail would stack up, she was away or out of town as much as here. Quiet, shy, modest. Paid her rent in cash. Most of the time she put it in an envelope with her apartment number on it and put it under the office door after hours. I asked her once if she was afraid the money would disappear, and she not be credited with having paid her rent. She smiled, saying she'd worry if it ever happened.

"Didn't bother her neighbors. She could stay in her apartment all day, other times she'd be gone for a long time. I have no idea where she worked or who for, she didn't list it on her application. She got almost no mail." His English was comparable to his wife's.

"Do you remember what kind of car she drove?" an agent asked.

Hearing this, his wife stepped to a two-drawer file cabinet squeezed between the agent's easy chair and the wall. "Let me see if we still have her file," she said. Removing a worn manilla folder, she scanned its contents. "No, I'm sorry, she didn't include either on her application."

"Can I see it, please? Can you make me a copy?" the agent asked.

"Take it. We purge our files after a year on our former renters. I don't know why we still have hers," the manager assured him.

"Oh, when she moved out, I remember she told me she had donated all her furniture to Goodwill. She had already called them for the pickup, and all I had to do was let them in. She smiled and gave me twenty dollars. When the Goodwill truck came, all she had was a bed, a kitchen table, two chairs, and a couch. No television, no phone. I guess she used her cell. It seemed odd . . . she was smart. I would see her carry her computer in from her car. There wasn't much in her apartment. Oh, reminds me, her car was a dark blue Japanese car. Not much help, sorry."

"Every little bit helps. Did she ever go without a face covering?"

"Sometimes. If I came for a maintenance call, or when she walked to her car. It was not uncommon to see her dressed in her full bourka, in a dress with her headgear and veil or in Western-style clothes without any headwear. She dressed well, no shorts, flip flops, or casual clothes. It's why, when you showed me the picture, I could recognize her."

"If you don't mind," his wife ventured timidly, "when she first came to the office to tell me she would leave for two weeks and to save her mail, I greeted her with *Sabah alkhyr, yawm jamil, kayf yumkinuni masaeiduk.* Good morning, it's a beautiful day, how may I help you? She responded in Arabic but told me not to ever speak to her in Arabic again. Maybe she's Persian, more comfortable speaking Farsi. She's conversant in Arabic, but it's not her native tongue. She's not Syrian."

"Thank you both. You've been most helpful," the older agent said. "Here's my card, if you remember anything else, if she ever mentioned a friend, an associate, where she shopped, anything at all, please call me. We will talk to our boss today to see if we can help with your citizenship."

"Not a bad meeting," the lead agent offered as they drove back to the office, the air conditioner on max.

"I'll say. Confirmation of her image, a sample of her handwriting, and verification she's a non-Syrian, non-native Arabic speaker. There's the off chance we might find a fingerprint. It makes fighting the traffic out here worth it." His partner smiled.

The president's grateful voice sounded over the phone, "Ferguson, I had my secretary check with your wife. Your daughter's spring breaks start in three weeks. I've made Camp David available to you and your family for ten days. Take your girls and their best friends, go, enjoy, and most of all, relax. You've more than earned it. I got elected to wear this hat, which will define my presidency and maybe a second term. You're a dedicated, smart lawyer, who couldn't have envisioned our current predicament when my predecessor appointed you as director. Your term expires in fourteen months; the majority leaders of both houses and I want you extended until this mess is over, if you're willing. No one could lead us better than you. Take some time with them and recharge your batteries," the president insisted.

"Madam President, I'll admit, the attack has consumed us. The team we've assembled is remarkable, and I'm privileged to lead it. Thank you for your confidence. I'd be honored to see it through. As for Camp David, I'd love to go, and know we would enjoy it, but I . . ."

"No ifs, ands, or buts. We'll survive," she interrupted. "You've got good people working on this and they'll endure a few days without you. They're experienced. We need you at the helm. I don't want to lose you six months from now with a heart attack or another stress-related malady. In fact, I'll have my secretary schedule a physical at Walter Reed for you the Thursday morning before your Friday departure."

"Thank you, Madam President. I don't know what to say. This is a surprise."

"It will take a few days to unwind and relax. Don't take any of this with you. We'll keep you posted. Let's have our regular Wednesday meeting. Do the physical Thursday morning, wrap up loose ends and get out of here on Friday before the weekend traffic. Trust me, getting away from it all helps. Oh, our crew will be a little lighter tonight."

Officially the entire effort flowed through Homeland Security. Everyone with any information sent it there, where it was collated and prepared for the president. Unofficially, it all came from, or through, Director Townsend. His fourteen-hour days included being briefed by his own staff or briefing cabinet members, the attorney general, the Chairman of the Joint Chiefs, the NSA and CIA directors, congressional leaders, or the vice president.

Tonight's meeting in a small West Wing conference room included the vice president, the Speaker of the House, the Senate minority leader, the attorney general, and the Joint Chiefs' Chairman. The president called these weekly meetings 'filling in the blanks,' and included a light snack and a beverage of their choice. Tonight, it was beer and wings.

Ferguson would answer their questions of the how's and why's that didn't appear in the white papers and official documents. Being the 'go-to guy' for such an august group had not been lost on him, but he begrudged missing yet another of his daughter's swim meets or recitals, and dinner with them. It occurred to him these meetings played a role in his being asked to stay on as Director.

The President opened the meeting. "Let me start by thanking you for coming out in such inclement weather. Ferguson, can you give us a little regarding the chemical poisons they used? Do we know any more of where they came from?"

"We're sure the VX was stolen from Deseret Test Center, Dugway Proving Grounds in Utah a half century ago. At the time, the base housed over 45% of the total US stockpile," he began. "It's a chemical compound, but certain signatures unique to the source provide a strong indication of where it's made."

"KIS—keep it simple. Real English, please," the Speaker said.

Everyone laughed.

"Does anyone remember back in the late sixties there was an incident when two or three hundred sheep died while grazing adjacent to the proving ground?" A uniform shaking of heads around the table assured him no one knew what had happened. "They found when nerve gas was exposed to cool, dry air for a period, it can be modified, making it even more toxic. A finding not shared with the scientific community for many years. The modification is unique to Dugway VX. It was used in all three attacks.

"When Saddam Hussein unleashed nerve gas on his own people in the eighties, it surfaced there. We worked with the CIA and concluded the agent used in Iraq originated in Utah. There was no reported loss from the Test Center. They were surprised. We reviewed their records. Nothing was out of order. Still, the chemical compound was identical and, unless Hussein was lucky and managed to duplicate the exact temperature, humidity, and time of exposure, the agent had to have come from Utah."

Glancing over at the Speaker, Ferguson smiled. "How am I doing?"

Lowering his glass after a swallow of beer, Air Force Brigadier General Fred Higgins, the Joint Chiefs' Chairman, grinned. "Doing great. Keeping it simple and feeding him in tiny bits," he roared. The room erupted with laugher.

Ferguson continued, explaining how their investigation indicated the VX was stolen but CL-20 may well have been produced in a private laboratory. "If we're right and they made it or acquired it from a private source, we're more concerned. It's going to be the weapon of choice for lone wolf subway and airport bombings, risking many more lives. We're still working on the EEE."

Lightning flashed. *BOOM*!! The sound of the ensuing thunder shook the building.

The president ducked before realizing it was thunder. Smiling, she looked at the group. "It's like telling ghost stories on a campout when we were kids. You're in your tent and right at the scariest part, someone on the outside of the tent bangs the bottom of a pot with a metal spoon. Do we need a pontoon boat at the front steps to get you guys home?" she joked.

"Or pillows and blankets for a sleepover?" the Joint Chiefs' Chairman quipped.

"Give it an hour and the front will be gone," the Speaker replied. "Director, please proceed."

"You expect us to believe these people have been planning this for decades? Even before the 1993 World Trade Center bombing?" the president asked.

"Madam President, we don't make this stuff up. We ask the questions and follow the clues. But the more we find, the clearer it becomes this is a generational issue with deep roots. Remember, in the sixties there was no internet. Terrorism was what governments did to each other, and cybersecurity was in its infancy. Our computer security was naïve, focused outward. Our primary system was developed at Los Alamos and used by all the National Labs. They relied on vetting people in the system, believing anyone with access had proper security clearances and was accounted for.

"The age of their chosen technology reflects the length of their planning. Not the most current, but still effective. We've worked to determine if an incident occurred a half century ago and this group vowed revenge. Or did they think weapons acquisition would draw less attention if they used older technology? The U.S.-backed coup d'état deposing democratically elected Mosaddegh in favor of Mohammad Reza Pahlavi, the Shah, that brought back foreign oil firms under the Consortium Agreement of 1954? Or quandaries causing the nationalization of oil Venezuela in '71 or Saudi Arabia in '80. Was it drug related? We're working all these angles. But it's tough sledding."

"Ferguson, we all sit around, the president's taken off her jacket, even the minority leader has rolled up his sleeves as we eat wings, drink beer and pepper you with questions," the Chairman of the Joint Chiefs said. "Without notes or the blink of an eye, you tell us more than any of us can imagine, passing off the enormous amounts of work it has taken to unearth the details you've found. I for one want to stop and say thank you to you and all those working for and with you. You've been tasked with a monumental project and, with a great deal of professionalism and scrutiny, you're making progress. We all recognize these guys are smart. This was not a homegrown, paint-by-numbers group of zealots. The weapons of mass destruction, even the device intended to destroy Glen Canyon, are all thirty to sixty-year-old technology. These guys have had an agenda for a long time, burnishing their plan, waiting for the right environment to unleash this atrocity. I have no doubt that, sooner or later, you and your team's efforts will bear fruit."

"Speaking of that. I've spoken with Ferguson, and he's agreed to extend his time as director until this mess is concluded. So, Misters Speaker and Minority Leaders, let's get to work and make it official," the president suggested.

"Thank you, everyone," Ferguson said with a nod. "We don't know their identity or their motive. But I do know this. They grossly underestimated the will of this country. We have received tips from every walk of life. Tips regarding rail displacement and drone technology, tips from older folks, immigrants, and Boy

Scouts. Everyone in this room has played a role with resources, bolstering public support, even reducing red tape to help those in the field.

"We've found a few of their soldiers; we'll find others. As we speak, we're working on identifying people at the next level. We'll discover their agenda and determine the major players. I'm not sure we'll ever find the masterminds, the real people behind this. They've put lots of layers between themselves and us, which means they can do it again."

"Director, does the FBI or CIA believe another attack's coming?" the president asked, her alarm apparent.

Studying her pensive, sharp-featured face, Ferguson answered, "Madam President, I have no doubt they have the capability. We don't know why they attacked the first time. Whether or not they'll do it again, I can't answer."

43

Yes

0530 hrs. PDT San Francisco, California
Tuesday, July 25
Post Attack, Day 271

Thirteen months after David and Becca Mutschler's wedding, Maggie moved into Mike's house on North Point in the Marina District. Built in 1916, it was a 2,900-square-foot, four-bedroom, three-and-a-half-bath, two-story home on a 4,100-square-foot lot. Michael, as she preferred to call him, had purchased it four years earlier, updating the electrical wiring, kitchen, bathrooms, and wood floors. He retained the original character, removed two non-weight-bearing first floor walls to feature the kitchen, living room, half bath, study, guest room, master bedroom and bath. His baby grand piano sat in the corner of the living room.

At his suggestion, Maggie sold her Honda and began to drive his Ford Explorer. She had a key to his Maserati Quattroporte, which she enjoyed as a passenger when he drove. She didn't do well with a standard transmission on city hills. She enjoyed the Ford with its maneuverability through traffic, room for her cello, and their groceries. She was a good cook. They delighted in trying new recipes and cooking together. And he was great at finding the right wine to go with any meal.

A CPA and musician, Maggie intuitively learned the rules and followed them. Her brain interpreted the notes on the musical score, which moved her fingers, producing music, rhythm, tone, texture.

Raised a practicing Methodist, Maggie never expected to move in with a man or have sex outside the bonds of marriage. Michael was at home within himself. The way he described his time outdoors, the perfect melding of nature, she knew he had a strong faith in a Superior Being.

She enjoyed his company and looked for ways to be with him. She couldn't pinpoint what it was: the way he played the piano, or solved problems. If it was straightforward, Michael was direct and efficient. If not, he was expert at using the information at hand, the answer if you will, and working back to the question. He didn't take shortcuts or bend rules, but always found a working solution. In jazz: improvisation. Take the key, the beat, and all the other parameters, the listener enjoys the saxophonist's and trumpeter's different interpretations of the song.

Her way worked well for her. He used a different side of his brain, but sometimes, seriously perplexed by his "project," he would ask her to retell the story of how the almost deaf Beethoven composed his Fifth Symphony. How all the members of the orchestra knew their parts, when to come in and meld together for such a remarkable outcome. Different communications read off the same page, there was a pattern there, just not to the casual listener. They would talk, and he would thank her for helping him, which made her smile.

"Michael, do you like it when I put my hands on you?" she asked as she lay beside him, basking in a sensual afterglow unique to lovers.

He rolled onto his side and met her gaze. "It's great. Why do you ask?'

"I've never been in the same bed with anyone or had sex till you. I like to touch you, and I like your hands on me. I don't know what attracts you to me. It can't be my fried egg-sized breasts. When I was in high school, and it was apparent I was destined to leave an A cup but not fill a B, I talked to my mom, wondering if any boys would ever be interested in me. She told me to focus on what I did well, and at the right time in the right place everything would work out the way it was supposed to."

"Smart woman."

"She was right. I can't believe how great sex is. Thought it'd be 'wham, bam, thank you, ma'am,' and over. The whole experience with you is amazing. The foreplay, you know what I need, slow and gentle, passionate and intense, or deep and sensuous. If I'm in a hurry and need it now, or if I'm liking the playing, the kissing, the gentle touch, you're great at taking me to the top until my head explodes. At times it's hot and frantic, other times playful and fun. And then, like now, sprawled beside you and slowly coming down. The part of it I don't like, and I don't like it at all, is when you're in Boise and I'm here. When I want you and need you, and there's nothing I can do. I ache to have you near me.

"I wish I'd known Sally; we'd have been friends. I owe her. You're gentle, except when I'm not." She laughed. "You and she learned a lot together, and I'm the grateful beneficiary. I'm sorry for you she's gone. The pain and loss you've gone through. But I can't imagine my life without you and how happy you've made me. It's not just the sex. It's you, Michael. I like our quiet conversations, talking to you, listening to you, and being in the same room with you. Playing tennis, sailing, going out together. I like to cook for you, shop for you, and be with you," she added as she snuggled close and kissed his chest. "I'll be glad when you catch those guys, and we can have more time together."

"What? Have you got a grand plan where I die in bed? You then find a young buck and train him to meet your needs," he teased with a grin.

"Wrong! It'll never be any better than now. No interest in ever comparing you to anyone else. I waited a long time, and I'm batting a thousand. I still can't believe how good it is to have you inside me. When you are, I feel complete. Nothing compares to the moment you enter me. It's the most fantastic sensation in the world—the perfect fulfillment of all my desire when it happens. You're the only man I ever want to know intimately.

"Can we sail to the Farallon Islands? I want to go on a day when school is in session and no one's working. A day when we can have the place to ourselves. I want you inside of me on the deck when the waves move us back and forth and again below deck when we'll be in our own cocoon, you, me, and the water moving us."

"Sounds great! It's twenty-eight miles out there and twenty-eight miles back. For your sake we'll do a few six, eight, ten-hour trips closer to shore to increase your comfort being on board for longer periods. And evening and night sails to familiarize you with navigating by the stars, not the shoreline."

"Ever the engineer! Always planning, working the logistics, one of the hundreds of reasons I love you. It must be after midnight. I'm going to make us hot chocolate. Don't worry, I have an exercise we'll do afterwards to relax you enough the caffeine won't keep you awake."

She returned a short while later, mugs of hot chocolate in hand.

Looking at her, he said, "I've spoken to your parents and intend to make a legitimate woman out of you. This business with the FBI and Homeland Security is a jealous mistress. It nags at me and pulls at me and barks when I work on other projects. Steve has been a Godsend. Zia would have come to a standstill if he'd not stepped in to take up the slack. I told your folks you're the single thing keeping me sane. Finding another with whom to share my life again wasn't on my radar. I'd recreated my world. A world which kept me happy, and I thought, fulfilled. Hoped trying to do good through the foundation was enough.

"You came into my life and turned it upside down. I'm not complaining, but cohabiting isn't the way I was raised. Living in sin, as your mother calls it. I want you to have the kind of wedding you've always dreamed of and the honeymoon of your fantasies. It's a long, slow, hard slog. We're making progress, and we're going to find these guys. Your mom gave me a year. So, talk to her and find a date best for your schedule."

"Michael, are you asking me to marry you?"

He smiled broadly at her. "Yes, I am."

"The answer's yes! Yes! Yes!" she squealed as she put the mugs on the nightstand and dove into his arms. "You're amazing. We've shared many romantic times together. Sunsets on the water, sunrises in Idaho, candlelight dinners. Last Christmas Eve in Boise, sitting on the rug in front of the fire and you surprised me with two Giovanni Dollenz bows. We've celebrated so many milestones, but let me tell you, mister, this proposal was not textbook! But Michael, it was so you." She kissed him and hugged him close. "I do love you with everything in me. You make me happy. Tell me, when did you and my parents have this big, long talk?"

"I came back from Washington on Wednesday and took them to dinner. Your Dad and I are fine. Your Mom, of course, conducted the full 'where were you born, did you win the third-grade spelling bee?' interview. I skipped a lot, told her enough that I guess I passed. She'd like me better if I were a decade younger. I'm a year closer to her age than yours. All I got from your Dad was he hadn't seen you this happy since you were a little girl. By the way, your fried eggs fit your body perfectly. You're tall, slender, and graceful. Anymore and it would make you look top heavy, out of proportion. As it is, when people look at you, they see all of you, not just part of you."

44

Night Sailing

0530 hrs. PDT San Francisco, California
Sunday, August 15
Post Attack, Day 292

The fog had built across the entire San Francisco Bay area all afternoon, its gloom swaddling the bay and its grip not easing until well after midnight. The caravan of box trucks slowed, turned, and made their way onto a road lined on both sides with the foreboding high security fences of industrial storage units terminating at the sea. Nearing the wooden barrier at the road's end, the lead truck turned south and stopped; the driver entered the passcode and the gate opened. Pulling onto the property, a lane separating the two sections of storage units, the lead truck turned left behind the first row of units. In quick succession, the second, third and fourth trucks followed, turning into succeeding rows.

The passenger in the first truck jumped out, crossed the lane, opened the second unit, climbed onto a propane-powered forklift, and drove to the back of the first box. His driver and the driver of the second truck opened the back and were manually unloading the right wing of a large military-grade drone. The driver of the fourth opened the back of his truck and ran across the lane to open the doors of the three adjoining units before joining the others to steady the wing as it was transferred to the forklift. Once secured, the four drivers walked alongside, supporting the wing as the forklift made its way to the second storage unit where it was unloaded into its specially designed, protective wooden holder. The process was repeated for the second wing and fuselage, and then duplicated for the second and third trucks and their disassembled drones. Returning to the fourth truck, two men jumped in the back, while the third on the ground operated a hydraulic lift gate as they lowered a World War II vintage Howitzer to the ground. After attaching it to the back of the forklift, they pulled it into the remaining storage unit.

Throughout the process, the men moved with purpose but no sense of urgency as they returned the forklift, secured the storage units, and left.

Mike moved three quarters of a mile out from shore before turning on the running lights, throttling the inboard engine and heading to the Yacht Club. Crossing the bay, the night's blackness gave way to shades of orange, pink, amber, and rose, energizing him with a radiating hope the new day might shed light on the burden consuming his every thought.

After securing the boat, they drove to his house. Maggie, her head in his lap, slept as he hit the cellphone hands-free call button. "Frog, sorry for another early wakeup call. Maggie's been after me to sail to the Farallons. Says she wants to see the petrels and murres, humpbacks, and great whites. We've done six evening and night sails to familiarize her with being on board for longer periods and sailing in open water at night. We left the marina yesterday evening and sailed out the gate to Point Reyes Lighthouse. Came back in around 3:30. The fog, so thick when we left, was beginning to fade as we came back under the gate.

"On a whim, I took the north side, knowing I'd cross the bay to dock. We're three-quarters of a mile offshore, beyond the *USS Hornet* Museum. I'm tired, questioning the wisdom of my decision, and considering changing course to the marina when I saw the dim wash of a distant light that illuminated a self-storage unit. Except for our navigation lights, we were pretty much invisible.

"My question is this: what would bring four box trucks and five big bruisers out at what's now a quarter to four in the morning? I'm thinking maybe it's a robbery. Maybe we can move in a little closer, sort out what's going on, and call 911 if need be. Fog's still gloomy, the light's faint, and the sound muffled. I killed the lights and crept to within two hundred feet of shore."

"Pretty gutsy, or you were tired, and your brain was asleep. *Miss Jessie* is sixty-five feet long and big as a bus. If they're as bad as you suspect and had heard or seen you, you and I might not be talking right now," Frog said, concerned.

"You're right. Did it on impulse, didn't think it through. Our drone work helped me recognize the tail of the Boeing ScanEagle." Mike continued to describe the scene they'd witnessed. "With the fog and distance, my cellphone images aren't much. No idea who these big dudes are. Can't tell you the storage unit numbers, but I'll send the GPS location with the images. I'll get Maggie home and head your way. Let's see if we can find the place this morning."

"I'll look. It's an industrial locale. Stay home. The GPS will guide me."

"See who's paying rent on the units. Is there a direct correlation between what we saw and what's already happened? Probably not, but it's worth looking into. Let's build the case before talking to Ferguson. It may be nothing. If so, hell of a coincidence. Be nice to catch a break after all the work we've put in."

"We don't know much about the guys we've been chasing. They're pros. For them, it's a business. They're cold, calculating, careful. We've made progress, but it's a big haystack and a tiny needle. Serendipity is serendipity. I'll take every break," Frog replied.

"With regular business and as much of this as I dare load on them, Zia's running wide open. Can your guys look at it? If it's nothing, cut it loose and move on. Let's make sure we're solid before we take it to the feds. Need anything from me?"

"Good for now. Got your pictures. I'm going to work. You get some sleep."

45

Digging through the Rubble

2030 hrs. MDT San Francisco, California
Thursday, October 24
Post Attack, Day 363

"It's nice to hear, and a reflection on you. Thank you. Now get out of there, go home. Tell Mary I'm sorry for making her put your supper in the oven again. Good night. See you Monday," Mike said, finishing an extended call with Steve Nottrott and a review of a new Zia project for General Electric. He was pleased that, as he was pulled deeper and deeper into the quagmire, the senior staff and the rank and file of Zia had risen to the occasion and responded positively.

Feedback from existing clients was good and business was on track to outperform last year's record. He had settled into a routine of being in Boise Mondays and Tuesdays and working from his San Francisco office the other five days as at least part, if not all, of Saturday and Sunday were consumed with what Maggie referred to as his mistress, working with the FBI.

At the round table in his office making notes of the call and ready to call Maggie to say he was on his way home, his phone rang. David Eller's name popped into his caller ID. He looked at the old Fukien Tea Bonsai tree. *Hither, you've survived some hard times along the way, otherwise you couldn't have reached your ripe old age.*

"Hey, Mike. It's David. Got a minute?"

"What's going on? Are you working second shift? It's 8:30 here, 11:30 where you are."

"Yeah, well, we're working for the same task master. Lord, you should talk. Do you ever sleep?" He laughed before his tone shifted to business. "When we first started, we looked at all the female passengers with Arabic surnames and one-way tickets on flights out of the U.S. and Canada to Europe and the Mediterranean countries from two weeks before the attack till three weeks after."

"I remember. What did you find?"

"Not what we set out to. We logged passport data including their photos. The other day, I ran the list against all the names of females we've identified. No matches. Five women met the original criteria. Two were graduate students, an anthropologist went on an extended study to Egypt. The other, a restorative architect, worked in Tunisia and Spain. One's studying at the University of Chicago, the other Washu, St. Louis. Ferguson checked with both schools and their major professors. Both legit. Two of the other women went home to care for an ailing parent; one in Jordan, the other in Lebanon. The fifth went back to the Sudan to be married.

"Got to thinking. What if our girl's still here? What if she's hiding in plain sight? She's here, but she's not. She's a shadow person. She has an identity when she needs one, for renting the car in Houston, or a storage unit in Pocatello, a different identity. Otherwise, she has no address, no telephone, no driver's license, no social security number, no voter registration, and pays cash for everything. She moves with the wind when and where she wants, making her impossible to find."

"Good call. You're right," Mike replied. "There've been a lot of people traveling under assumed names. The three who failed at Glen Canyon, don't have their real names, but they're not the people who rented the cars at the airports in Salt Lake, Denver and Albuquerque and left them abandoned in Cortez, Farmington, and in the parking lot of the visitor's center. Phillip identifying all those locations used as 'way stations' for ordinance storage and hotel rooms allowed Ferguson's guys to authenticate all the renter/lessee names as legitimate. Addresses, driver's licenses, and phone numbers, they're real people, with solid alibis for their presence the day of the attack. Total strangers with no reported identity theft issues."

"Mike, you know where I'm going. Two hundred and seventy-three names. I couldn't believe these people, all at least second generation, Middle Eastern, American citizens from diverse backgrounds, education levels, and socioeconomic backgrounds living in southern California were picked at random. Turns out they all served in the military, all branches, all ranks, Coast Guard, Marines, Air Force, from Army corporal to Navy Lieutenant. The common thread, they're all patients at the VA Hospital in LA.

"If a list exists, chances are it contains additional names. Find the list, keep an eye out for all the unused names and when one appears, we're dealing with at least a mid-level terrorist. Can your guys access the VA system without their knowledge? Looking for a lower-level staff member, personnel type, an admitting or billing clerk who's compiled the list without the VA's knowledge. I'm betting the list's maybe three, four hundred, mostly men. It would take time to find the right people to fit whatever criteria they have. Bet it's a longer-term employee with the flexibility to collect data on their own. If we can find the list and its creator, we've found a player, not high-ranking, but a player," David said, reflecting both excitement and exhaustion.

"Entering the VA system, no problem," Mike answered. "May not be an employee of Middle Eastern lineage, maybe they have a grudge or are doing it for the money. Send me your names, and we'll find the list. If they've done it by hand, it'll be more of a challenge, but we'll find it. Hats off to you and your guys. Great catch, David."

46

The Aftermath
A Step Closer

2100 hrs. PDT San Francisco, California
Monday, October 30
Post Attack, 1 Year, Day 4

"Where'd you find this recipe? And the wine, perfect. I know you've had a long day, but if you'll come with me, I'm rather good at taking your mind off your troubles," Maggie assured him, rising from the table, grabbing his hand, and kissing him on the check. As if on cue, Mike's phone burst with Ferguson's now familiar ring. Exasperated, she rolled her eyes and collapsed on the couch before going to the kitchen to rinse the dishes.

"Sent you a link. Got it? Watch. It was on two LA local evening newscasts last night," the bass voice boomed loud enough for Maggie to hear as Mike sent the link to the living room television screen.

"In other news, Azadeh Ebadi, an admissions clerk at the Los Angeles VA Hospital, was killed this afternoon, the victim of a robbery gone bad. We warn you the surveillance video you're about to see is graphic. Two armed suspects enter the store where she'd gone to pay for her gas and buy a half gallon of milk. She's forced to the ground. The store clerk retrieves his gun and in the exchange of gunfire, Ms. Ebadi is killed. The suspects escaped. If you have any information regarding either of these two men, you're asked to contact the LA police."

"Azadeh Ebadi, our VA patient list person?" Mike asked.

"Right! Yesterday our agents met her in her supervisor's office where she denied everything. They walked to her desk. Wanted irrefutable proof the file was on her computer. Making their way to her workstation, she excused herself to go to the restroom and didn't return. Our guys found and copied the file and brought her computer back to our offices.

"LAPD issued an APB for her and obtained a search warrant for her apartment and car. She was dead before they got to her apartment. LAPD found her cellphone in her purse. She'd made a three-minute call to a 510 area code. 510 is Oakland and the entire east side of the bay. We identified the cell towers and traced the call to a central Oakland neighborhood. Two minutes after her call, a flurry of calls bounced back and forth between the 510 number and a prepaid Los Angeles number. The prepaid number called Oakland seven minutes after Ebadi died.

"Mike, watch that video closely. She wasn't an innocent victim. She was executed. We've touched a nerve. We're as close as we've ever been. We're working on the Oakland number and the others on her phone."

47

Phone Numbers

0730 hrs. EST Quantico, Virginia
Monday, November 22
Post Attack, 1 Year, Day 37

By any measure, it had been a tough three weeks. A freak tropical storm from New Orleans produced torrential rainfall throughout the southeast and up from Fredericksburg through Baltimore and on to Delaware City. Nine days later, Hurricane Rachel devastated the region. It had begun as a tropical depression near the Yucatan Peninsula. Intensifying as it tracked in a west-northwest direction, Rachel attained Category 5 status with peak winds of 165 miles per hour on November 11. It weakened to a Category 4 before making landfall at Virginia Beach and tracking northeast, the eye of the storm passing over Charlottesville.

The wet, dirty side of the storm churned the Chesapeake. Rain and wind caused monumental flooding and uprooted trees. In Washington, D.C., the strongest winds occurred during the night of November 15. Quantico, Virginia recorded a wind speed of 82 miles per hour. Reagan National Airport clocked a sustained wind of 66 miles per hour, with a peak gust of 74 miles per hour. Afterwards, FBI agent Inez Alexander, her family, and everyone in her subdivision were marooned, held hostage by the water and fallen trees. The ongoing loss of power complicated their world. Four days to escape her neighborhood. Two days ago, her first to the grocery store. Yesterday was her first day back to work.

"How did you guys do in the storm? Get water in your house?" Kelly asked as she and Inez rode the elevator to their floor at the FBI research center.

"Four inches in the house, might as well have been four feet. You?"

"No, we dodged the bullet, but like you we've been without power since the night the storm hit. What are you going to do with your house?"

"We've pulled together what we can, important papers, marriage license, insurance papers, and all, and the girls' clothes. We moved into Ben's parents' back bedroom. All four of us in one room. It's tight but we're thankful we have a place to go that has electricity. Most of our neighbors are in shelters. Ben, his brother, and their dad have spent the last two days ripping out the carpets and tearing out the sheetrock from the ground up four feet in every room in our house. All our furniture's lost. Our street looks like a garbage dump. Downed trees, carpet, padding, furniture, trash bags piled shoulder high. It's the pits. I called our insurance agent, and we've started processing the claim."

"You're smart, the claims will be massive and submitting a claim early will help. Is there anything I can do for you?"

"Thanks, depends how soon we can move back in. I may need help with work hours. Taking the girls back and forth to school may be a challenge. We'll see once school reopens."

"On the bright side, if there is such a thing, yesterday we got Azadeh Ebadi's phone back from the cyberlab vault in Manhattan. Even though it was an older model with only a four-digit passcode, it must have been weird, took 'em long enough to break it. See what you can do with the phone numbers."

48

Keeping It in Perspective

1630 hrs. PDT San Francisco, California
Sunday, October 30
Post Attack, 1 Year, Day 49

"Thank you, Michael. We haven't been out in the bay since the kids were little. I'd forgotten how relaxing it is to soak in the views of our magical city from the water. Sausalito, Belvedere, Angel Island, and the Golden Gate and Bay Bridges. Up close and personal with the dolphins was a plus. And Maggie, your lunch was a hit," her mother said as Mike helped her off the *Miss Jessie* and back onto dry land.

"Yes, thanks, Mike. I'd forgotten how calming sailing is. Even when the wind comes up, it helps you clear your head," said Dr. Barrington, a tall, balding man. "I've sailed with a few of the trustees, the president, and a dean or two over the last few years, but this is very nice, a step above. Let me help you tie her up."

"You're both welcome. I'm glad we finally found a weekend to do this. We'll do it again." Mike smiled as his phone rang with Ferguson's distinctive tone. He answered.

"Mike, filling in the blanks, not the big one, but blanks nonetheless."

"Afternoon, Director, what's up?" Mike asked, handing the picnic basket and car keys to Maggie as they all walked from the marina.

"It's Sunday afternoon. Know you have a life; hoped you might want to hear the latest."

"None of us will have a life till this is over. Whatever you've got, it's one more puzzle piece, and sooner or later, we're going to find enough to ID these guys," he said, a touch of tedium in his voice.

"Triple E. We've found the source," Ferguson said triumphantly.

"Great. Congratulations!"

"Thanks, it's a step, maybe only half a step. Need your help to make it a whole one."

"Of course. How can we help?"

"I just started talking, didn't even ask. Do you have a minute, are you in the middle of something?" Ferguson asked.

"Just got off the water, took Maggie and her folks sailing this afternoon," Mike replied.

"I'll cut to the chase, or fill you in later, if you like."

"You said you need our help, so give me the bare bones now and tell me the story tomorrow," Mike said.

"The University of Texas Medical Branch in Galveston is the oldest medical school in Texas. They're not flashy, do a lot of good solid meaningful research. And the students they teach turn out to be solid clinicians.

"They work on EEE where you've gotta have live virus and strict safety protocols. A lot like your world, protocols and safety standards are only as strong as the people using them. You've got to be bright to work there. If you do, and want to break the rules, you're smart enough to know how.

"Victor Torres was such a guy. Born and raised on the island. First in his family to go to college, smart, made good grades. Got his Associate Degree in math, wanted to be a chemical engineer and work for Big Oil. Started his third year at Texas A&M, mother was diagnosed with stage four cervical cancer. A month later his dad, a longshoreman at the Port of Galveston, had an industrial accident, and Victor's world imploded."

Catching up to his guests as Maggie finished loading their basket, jackets, and rain gear, Mike smiled and rolled his eyes. Pulling on his arm, she gave him a quick peck on the check. "Hold on, Director, caught up with Maggie. Like I said, coming in from sailing with her parents. Can I put you on speaker? We're all on our way to dinner."

"Sure. Hi Maggie, hate to eat into your time with this guy."

"Hi, Director. You guys have a job to do, and I appreciate how hard it is. I'll be glad when you catch them. I know your family will be, as well," Maggie said.

"You're right. My girls are ready to have their dad back. I'll cut this short."

Mike switched him off the speaker, giving Maggie a peck on the check. "Victor drops out of school and goes to work to help the family of eight make ends meet. He finds a job in a research lab at UTMB. Mom dies, dad's on permanent disability. He's the primary breadwinner. A younger sister becomes surrogate mom to the youngest three. Fast forward a decade and a half. The father has died. All the kids are on their own. He's continued to work for the school and is now a shift supervisor.

"Three years ago, Victor comes down with a serious case of midlife crisis and realizes he'll never achieve his dream of becoming an engineer. '*Without a degree, I'm limited in what I'll earn. My treadmill's not dissimilar to dad's. While not as physically demanding, it's nonetheless as limiting.*' He's managed his life and his money well. Still single, he spends all his free time at the Royal Purple Raceway in Baytown or Houston Motorsport Park, both NHRA sanctioned tracks, dreaming of what might have been.

"Long story short, Victor gets hoodwinked into trading live virus for what he thinks will be a sixties muscle car, a new Harley Davidson, and a quarter million dollars. Gets the car and 'cycle, and he sees the money in his bank account. That evening, he's found in his living room shot in the back of the head.

"Money transferred into the account came from a bank in Wisconsin. Overnight it was transferred out to a bank in Hanoi and on to a bank in the Cayman's. Galveston police called us. Our guys found the car owner and the Galveston Bank clear of any involvement. UTMB was eager to work with us. We're sure Victor is the source of the virus. That was three years ago, a cold case and the lead investigator has retired. We didn't put it together until yesterday.

"Mike, we chased the money from limited partnership to offshore accounts, to foreign assets. Honestly, it was incredibly convoluted, and we had other priorities. Need your help to track it to its source."

"Send me the file."

"Kelly, we found the 510 area code number from Ebadi's phone," Inez said, walking into her supervisor's office.

"Great! What's the story?"

"It's in a cache of hundreds of unassigned phones designated to seasonal work crews at the City of Oakland Public Works Department's temporary contractor's division. It hasn't shown on their inventory for four years. When they tracked it, it'd been gone for at least that long. Probably a temporary hire walked away with it.

"When the current supervisor started, she saw it on her inventory but couldn't match it to any hardware. She reported it and it was removed from her department asset listing. Property management or accounting didn't follow through, it wasn't returned or discontinued, the expense transferred to a general account and continued, and the number remained active.

"We've gone back seven years and have now identified all the numbers to and from this phone. An ongoing stream of communications with eleven numbers to cellphone subscribers we're investigating. Eight are in greater Los Angeles, two in Oakland, and starting a year ago, one in Detroit. The unique numbers which appear prior to the attack, incoming and outgoing, involve pre-paid phones. The kind you find at the supermarket or drugstore with a limited number of minutes. All purchased with cash or gift cards in Los Angeles. The records are incomplete, no straightforward way to tell who bought them.

"The records show sporadic use, long periods of inactivity followed by a flurry of action. In the months, weeks, and days prior to the attack, calls to and from Ann Arbor, Dover, Farmington, New Mexico, Houston, and San Antonio. The person using this phone was in Los Angeles the day of the attack. No activity from two days after the attack until Ms. Ebadi's call, nothing since her death. The guy who died at Glen Canyon called from the Salt Lake airport the day before the thwarted attack. The names on the rental cars in Denver and Albuquerque, and the hotel rooms in Moab, Durango, and Farmington are on Dr. Eller's list.

"Kelly, this is the number of the operational head of the Attack on America. We're working the Los Angeles numbers to identify their owners and the communication between them. Hope to finish in the next few days."

"Great job! What do you need? More people? Anything?"

"No. This was a challenge, but a chance to step away from the calamity and mess of a flooded house. My world's been crazy, living out of a suitcase, dealing with the loss of my home, all our meals, having no privacy, not knowing when or how our lives will come back together. I'm more than ready for this to be over. Still, nobody died at our house. In Ann Arbor, Dover, Texas, and Los Angeles, their nightmare will never end."

49

Control the Money, Control the Future

2230 hrs. CET Salzburg, Austria
Friday, July 2
Post Attack, 1 Year, Day 248

He'd been irritable all day, teething, a slight fever, diarrhea, making sleeping through the night impossible. At last Ana had gotten their thirteen-month-old down and joined Omar in bed when he turned on the television and switched the satellite to the American broadcast of *NBC Nightly News*. "Up next a story from Gaza City, Gaza, after these messages . . ."

"Here we go again," she said.

The television screen showed an image of two men, one in traditional Middle Eastern attire, the other in Western business clothing, shaking hands and smiling at the camera. "In a joint statement, Hamas, the governing body of Gaza, and the Chinese Minister of Trade, announced today the China Road & Bridge Corporation will build a deep-water port, a cruise ship terminal, and a shipyard capable of repairing the world's largest cargo ships: the new Panamax, Capesize and Chinamax class ships that must traverse the Cape of Good Hope and Cape Horn to travel between oceans; twelve hundred feet long, they're limited only by port infrastructures. And, of course, the Ultra Large Crude Carriers, the enormous supertankers."

Sliding close to Ana, putting his hand on her stomach, Omar said confidently, "We've worked hard. Parsa invested the money, had the vision of what to build, when to build it and the insight to know how to position it to lead the way into the future. He also moved all the money out of the U.S. and other stock markets and into hard assets without being detected before the *Hujum* was initiated. His Asha clients—we're all making money while the rest of the world is still reeling from the recession."

"The three of us had each other to bounce off ideas, refine plans and keep each other grounded," Ana replied. "He's incredible and has done it all on his own. His network includes economists and financial types, but also architects, engineers, and construction people. With the recession in full swing, he'll feed the money back into the world markets and we'll gain again."

Images of supertankers and mammoth container ships being loaded and unloaded appeared on the television as the commentator continued. "The three-part facility will be built on an artificial island, which will include both rail and road options. This is an expansion of what was first proposed by the Israeli government decades ago. It's been modified to allow for substantial expansion should the need arise."

"We could be seeing the new Amsterdam; the birth of the largest port in the world." Ana smirked.

"This morning's announcement follows last month's similar declaration between the Gaza government and France and Russia to build a state-of-the-art international airport. These two events position Gaza to communicate with other Mediterranean countries and the rest of the world despite severe disapproval from senior Israeli officials," the television commentator continued.

"Parsa's plan is right on track. The Jews are unhappy now; they'll be really pissed when we're done." Omar laughed and kissed his wife.

"They tried so hard to isolate Gaza," Ana said as she giggled. "We learned from them, control the money, control the future."

The camera focused on the commentator, who said, "Hamas's Ministry of Defense has petitioned the UN for maritime safety assurances for ships visiting Gaza's new terminal, asking for safe passage from all challenges from the Israeli navy. China and Russia have already contacted Israel, saying any interference of their ships will be considered an act of aggression and will be dealt with accordingly. An announcement from the White House is expected soon.

"The port's cruise ship terminal joins Barcelona and Rome as a Mediterranean port of departure for passengers wanting to visit Italy, Greece, the Mediterranean Islands, the Middle East, and the North African countries. For people interested in different cultures, and the essence of the history of mankind, this new port will also focus on ports of call in Turkey, Egypt, Israel, and other Eastern Mediterranean countries with a flavor for the exotic and unusual.

"We look at the wildfires continuing to rage in Arizona, New Mexico, and California right after these messages . . ."

Turning off the television, he rolled toward Ana and kissed her again, "It's been a long time coming but Allah has blessed us, and the fathers and grandfathers are pleased."

"You're right. This calls for a congratulatory celebration." She snuggled close before slipping off her nightgown. "The new baby won't be here for six and a half more months. She won't mind being a little crowded tonight, and we deserve to celebrate."

50

Susan

1740 hrs. EDT Washington, D.C.
Wednesday, September 15
Post Attack, 1 Year, Day 323

At 5:40, Ferguson was trying to finish his day and get home for dinner and his daughter's first violin recital of the school year. He was immensely proud of her, three years all-state, two years all East Coast with scholarship offers from Eastman, Juilliard, New England, and Cleveland Conservatories and a handful of others, including Berkeley School of Music. Mike and Maggie hosted her visit to the University of California and, of course, she received the cook's tour of the San Francisco Symphony Orchestra. Impressed, she was considering it.

Leaving his office, cane in hand, his computer pinged an email from Mike, which read:

Director—

Day one I told you we'd find information, tell you where it was, but leave it to you to ensure its useability in court. Attachment 1: the names, addresses, cellphone numbers, and email addresses of the individuals we discussed. Attachment 2: transcripts of representative conversations between themselves and others, and a list of several of their frequently visited websites.

These data are sufficient to request a search warrant for each one's personal computer. I leave it to you to work through how it was acquired when you talk to the issuing judge. I assure you there is much more incriminating evidence. Also attached are comments attributed to Niousha Rostami, and her role in the Attack. We're confident she was the Chief Operating Officer for the Attack. She has the credentials and experience, but it's curious they filled the position with a woman. Do not know her current whereabouts. We've not found direct electronic communication between her and Ahem Shehadi, the banker, or his son. We continue to look and if it's out there, we'll find it.

Lastly, links to sites in the Indian Air Force High Command and the personal email of one Bhupendra Mathur, an active-duty Indian Air Force captain assigned to the Unmanned Aerial Vehicle Control Center. Fifty thousand US dollars was deposited in his personal bank account the Friday before the Attack. An additional one hundred and fifty thousand deposited the following Monday. Those funds professionally laundered, tracing their source doubtful. Current account balance, 63K. We can extract the funds and see if and to whom he squawks.

Call when you have a minute.

Mike

He hit the reply button:

Great work!! Thank you and thank your guys. Take the money and see what happens.

Talk to you in the morning.

To her boss, she was FBI undercover agent Susan McDonald. To her colleagues, she was Susie Mac. Two weeks ago, she had made sure Ardashir Shehadi noticed her at the Alameda County Community Food Bank benefit. He learned she was Alice Havens, the great-great granddaughter of Frank Havens, a legendary Oakland founding father. Having returned from an extended stay in Paris, she was reacquainting herself with the socially elite while looking for community causes to support.

A senior vice president at his father's Bayside Bank, Ardy, the heir apparent, enjoyed a well-earned playboy reputation. He often represented his aging father at the civic fundraising galas the elder gentleman supported. Tonight, at Oakland Museum of California's Gala, Alice Havens' poise expressed both dignity and composure, thus positioning her as Ardy's stunning new challenge.

Unattended, she had planned to come with her cousin who became ill at the last moment. Her boss had manufactured a major traffic jam crossing the Bay Bridge, delaying his date by three hours. She sympathized when he mentioned it as why he too was there as a single. The result, Alice and Ardy found themselves sitting together, separated from the other guests at their table by an empty chair on either side.

At first it was small talk. He complimented her heart-shaped Judith Liebert evening bag, and her Jimmy Choo shoes. She smiled, placed the bag on the table between them and asked where he had attended school. Undergrad in Paris and grad school in London. A graduate of Vassar, she loved Paris, Vienna, and Budapest, London not so much. She enjoyed her time abroad and was sure she would travel more, but she'd missed America and was glad to be back home. Tonight's venue, Piedmont Community Hall, was a nice place.

"Wasn't your grandfather instrumental in developing the Piedmont section of town?" he asked.

She smiled and moved the conversation back to him, but soon shared that she was a published author, having written several short stories for English-language European magazines. She was working on a novel modeled after the terrorist attack the United States suffered two years ago. She had several pieces of the plot worked out but was troubled researching how her drug cartel villains could acquire enough explosives to destroy the Delaware and Catskill Aqueducts and the NYC water tunnels supplying the five boroughs. She was torn between the use of conventional TNT, or a Russian made 'suitcase' bomb like the terrorist had tried to use at Glen Canyon Dam.

"Have you thought of including a biologic like COVID?" he inquired.

Yes. She explained that her plot also included use of a biologic agent against the populations of Boston, Philadelphia, and Washington D.C. She wanted to use the H5N1 flu virus—the "bird flu"—but had no idea how to acquire it. Warming to him, she smiled and assured him the story writing would be straightforward once she completed her research. "It's important to do the research. It makes the story believable for your readers." This time her smile was flirtatious.

The meal served, entertainment concluded, and the announcement made—the evening's goal had been achieved—she smiled and readily accepted Ardy's invitation for a drink at the bar. Relaxed and in control at a quiet table in the back, second drinks in, third drinks waiting on the table, she watched him for cues and led the conversation by asking questions she either knew the answers to or wanted him to admit. "I can't speak as a terrorist, but I can talk as a banker. Russian 'suitcase' bombs, if they still exist—the logistics of obtaining them would be complicated by foreign countries, intermediaries, criminal elements, and risk. And lots of money."

Expecting pauses in the conversation, she didn't let them throw her off.

Instead, a knowing nod and smile told him she understood and was paying attention. She would bring up bits and pieces and he, like an idiot, filled in the rest with a rambling monologue ranging from how providing the financing for upgraded servers at Oakland International Airport gave him insight into the covert movement of TNT cross-country by rail, to how his older cousins' experience in the Iran/Iraq conflict had opened his eyes to chemical and biologic weapons of mass destruction.

Keep talking, sucker, I got you. "How do you know all this?" she cooed.

"Those large airport servers cost lots of money and when you loan the money you better know your risk," he replied.

The combination of her smile, starry-eyed gaze, hand on his thigh, and his fourth drink loosened his tongue. "As a banker, I tell you the key is money. TNT, bombs, chemicals, money is the most powerful. Everything is available on the black market if you know how to use the internet and the price is right."

Another drink, his arm around her shoulder, right hand cupping her breast. She snuggled close, put her head on his shoulder, looked up, smiled, and kissed his check. "Ardy, you are amazing and smart. You've been so helpful." Her hand stroked his thigh, slid to his crotch, and found its mark. In her best come-hither voice, she murmured, "Hold this thought. I'm going to the little girl's room, canceling my Uber driver, and depending on you for a ride home." Standing, she faced him, bent forward, breasts in full view, arms around his neck, leaned in and whispered in his ear. He smiled as she turned, took her bag and disappeared.

Witnessing the entire exchange at the table, her colleague also left the bar. Maintaining the chain of evidence, the two women drove to their office on Webster and logged in the bag and tape recorder. "The dumb jerk. He's chased more skirts than investments for his bank. Even after all these years, I'm still amazed how a smile, your hand on their thigh, a press of your tits on their ribs, a peck on the check, and they start thinking with their zipper instead of their head. He complimented my evening bag twice. Wait till he finds out all I had in it was the tape recorder."

"Quite a show, especially right there at the end. What did you whisper?"

"Told him to be thinking of how he liked it best. Promised he would never forget tonight."

"You look good, but you know you're wicked." She laughed, looking at her friend.

"If the judge issues the search warrant and Mike Paxton's people are as good as the director says, I didn't lie."

51

Who's Paying the Rent?

1730 hrs. EDT Washington, D.C.
Thursday, November 5
Post Attack, 2 Years, Day 10

"Director?" David Eller asked from his Washington office.

"Good evening to you, David. How are you doing?" Ferguson asked as he rose from the dinner table and moved to his home office.

"Doing well, thanks. I hate to disturb you at home, but you might want to hear this. Do you have a minute?

"For you, anytime."

"Yesterday, Mrs. Mary al-Khayr, an Army nurse when she served on active duty, bought a ticket on Turkish Airlines Flight 2632 from Istanbul to Montréal for tomorrow. A few minutes later, Mrs. Habibeh Rakhsha, a former Navy JAG officer, bought an Air Canada ticket from Montréal to Chicago O'Hare for later tomorrow evening, flight 2055. Both these names are on our VA hospital list. Your guys have vetted everyone on that list. Until now, these names haven't appeared anywhere. Mosharref al-Khayr lives in Thousand Oaks, California, and is a well-respected attorney working in the music industry. Mike told me Mrs. al-Khayr used her credit card for groceries yesterday afternoon. Tahmouress Rakhsha and his family live in Glendale, California. He's a licensed plumber. His wife cooked supper for him and their kids last night.

"Whoever bought the tickets paid cash, Turkish lira, at the Istanbul Atatürk Airport," David continued. "The person who bought them doesn't know we have the list, or they think we're no longer looking worldwide for names on it."

"So, what you're saying is both Mrs. al-Khayr and Mrs. Rakhsha are safe at home with their families, and our person, believing she's safe to travel, is returning to our country. At a minimum, she'll be a person of interest," Ferguson added. "David, you and your guys amaze me. Man, I'm glad you're on our side. Send me the proper spellings of the names and the flight numbers. Whoever she is, she'll have a welcoming committee when she arrives in Montréal. And thank you. I'll keep you posted."

"Maggie, that was a good meal! A woman of many talents, master musician, master chef. Thank you. And thank you both for having me." Frog smiled, pushing back from the dining room table at Mike and Maggie's home in San Francisco.

"Phil, you're always welcome here. You and fishing are the best medicine for Michael. You make him laugh."

Clearing the dishes, she moved to the back of the house to practice for tomorrow's string quartet performance at the Transamerica Pyramid. Finding a seat in the living room, Frog winked. "She's special, and you're lucky. This discussion's best had in person, and I appreciate her willingness to put up with me. Sailing around the bay in the middle of the night might turn out to be the biggest break of this whole exercise. If it proves to be the case, I'm giving her all the credit. You and I are bit players." He laughed a low, genuine laugh as he looked at his friend. "Somebody doesn't want anyone to know who they are or what they're doing,"

"That's what this is about?" Mike asked, a little surprised. "It's been a while. What's up?"

"The storage units. They rented four each under a different name: Sapp and Company, Freeman, Freeman and Giles, Inc., Doggett and Waters, and Green River Engineering Systems. Each incorporated in a different state, pay their taxes but show no financial activity. Rents are paid every month in cash, pushed under the door in unmarked envelopes, with unit numbers on a slip of paper. All four shell companies, including one owned by a South African holding company, have a common director, Babak Hartanto, the brother of Indonesian strongman Aziz Hartanto. Babak also sits on the board of Whittemore, Wiewandt, and Barron, a UK corporation based in Sussex. It's about to become complicated. Let me describe one to give you the idea."

"No wonder it's taken a while. You've got all this for each company?"

"Trust me, we have more than enough on all of them for any court."

Raising his wine glass, Mike mouthed, "More?"

On a roll, Phil declined with a shake of his head. Taking his pen, he drew a diagram on his napkin, illustrating how Whittemore was owned by an LLC in Sarajevo, Bosnia and Herzegovina, which was a subsidiary of a Chad limited partnership. "If you weren't dedicated to running this to ground, you'd throw in the towel and quit in frustration. It hasn't been an easy exercise, even for my guys. Here's where the real challenge began."

Continuing his diagram, he showed how the Chad limited partnership was held by a British Virgin Island unlimited company without shares. This entity was held by an Iranian trust. *Falah. Falah*, Arabic for success, was a trust established in 1939. The man who set it up, Yamani Shehadi, had been dead for over a quarter century. He had five sons. One was a banker in Tehran. One, an early member of Hezbollah, was killed along with his two older sons in the 1992 war with Israel. The third, a banker in Cairo, the fourth, a banker in Beirut, and the last, a banker and respected businessman in Oakland. They were all in their late eighties or nineties, had all been extraordinarily successful, and were well-connected both financially and religiously in their respective locations.

"Two noteworthy twists. First, Shehadi, the guy who established the trust, his best friend was a Shi'ite cleric named Antar. The two families have remained close. An Antar serves in a power position in the religious community of each bank location, and an Antar sits on every bank board. Second—and this one took serious digging—by establishing an international banking family through his sons, Shehadi managed to spread the family across multiple geographies and political spectrums—some in democracies, others in more centralized power structures. These are big banks focused on national and international issues and are much less impacted by local banking laws and political upheaval.

"Yamani Shehadi and his sons put their assets in financial instruments, circulating through the world as stocks, bonds, debts, and government notes. This allowed them to insulate their assets beyond the grasp of any regime. Keeping control of their banks within the family, they've been able to maintain secrecy of the size of their fortune. Through the effort of the Beirut banker, and, to a lesser extent, his oldest brother, their conservative banking practices, integrity, and financial skill, they have gained credibility with the international banking fraternity in the last half of the twentieth century and in this one. We've not focused on it; a rough estimate puts the family worth at over seven hundred billion dollars."

"The old man was a smart dude. And his kids seem to have embraced and expanded his vision," Mike remarked.

"The banks are all now overseen by the third generation. This is a tight-knit group. This third generation is well-schooled in their fathers' ways. They've even expanded by acquiring a bank in Bangkok, Thailand, a struggling bank now flourishing under their leadership.

"Mike, these large banks are quiet. Money's flowing in and out from other Middle Eastern banks, Africa, Europe, Asia, India, in the aggregate, these guys are a force. Bayside, the Oakland bank, has not been as actively involved as the others. It's as if by leaving it out of the mix, they hope to keep US authorities from considering the other banks' activities. Bayside is involved in international banking, Asia, Eastern Europe, Russia. I'll come back to this and the brother who runs it in a minute."

Standing, Mike raised his hand and started out of the room.

"Am I boring you? Where're you going?" Frog feigned concern.

"To get my laptop and take notes."

"Bring me more paper, I'm running out of room on this napkin. But don't bother with your laptop, I've got it all in laborious detail. I'll send you the file. We haven't found any overt activity. Nothing out of the ordinary or illegal in any way. Collectively, they're connected to Gaza, the West Bank and the Palestine issue. A substantial amount of the money for the improvements in those two regions has passed through one or another of those banks, including accounts of private investors."

Phil continued, explaining how the patriarch was Iranian and how Iran has supported both Hezbollah and Hamas, Shi'ite and Sunni militias as they've learned to govern. He warned many believe that as Hezbollah and Hamas go, will determine the Shi'ite Sunni relationship. They have hated each other for millennia, but they shared a loathing of the Jews and Israel. American support of Israel added fuel to the fire.

Leaving the couch and his diagram, Phil walked to the living room windows and took a moment to enjoy the lights across the bay. "Let's look at eighty-eight-year-old Ahem Shehadi, the Oakland banker and businessman. He's enjoyed a successful career since coming here from Iran in 1959. Fluent in four languages, he studied banking and finance at Oxford before earning his MBA at Harvard and becoming a naturalized US citizen in 1963. He started Bayside Bank in Oakland in 1965, and Marin Oil Tanking and Terminals the following year. Both are privately held. You've seen Bayside Bank's signs across the city.

"They're good corporate neighbors, supporting business development, the environment, and the community. They support the Oakland Food Bank, arts and education, and any local community need. He enjoys a well-earned reputation as a patrician community leader, served for many years as a director for the United Way and the Boys and Girls Clubs of America. He's also been a major contributor to the American Heart Association, a frequent member on the mayor's economic diversification committees, and even served as an adjunct professor in International Business at the University of San Francisco."

"Wait, the name's familiar. I met him last year! The bank made a major contribution to the foundation," Mike exclaimed.

"You may want to return the money. Soon. We found a tie between those storage units and Marin Oil Tanking and Terminals. The Marin Oil property includes acres of large oil storage tanks and warehousing facilities accessed on one side by rail and the other with loading docks near the Port of Oakland. They provide receiving and storage capabilities for several international oil companies and have completed an agreement with Russia's largest oil company and highest valued company. This follows the agreement they made two years earlier with Lukoil, the Russian oil company with service stations in Russia, Europe, and the United States. Marin is an approved supplier for the United States military and provides fuel to Fort Ord and the Presidio. As such, it's not uncommon for Marin Oil trucks to be on the base or for employees to associate with the enlisted men."

Walking back to the couch, Frog sat and continued with his diagram. "Let's go back to who's paying the storage unit rent. We've found no record of any financial activity for any of the storage unit renters. The California and Delaware state records show they pay their fees in cash. Not to be deterred, we found the company, Whittemore, Wiewandt & Barron, has a simple savings account at Bayside. They withdraw cash three times a month with no pattern of which branch or what day the withdrawals are taken. Expenses for the five months before the attack ticked up higher, which would make sense with the costs for travel, storage, and hotel rooms in advance of the rail dislocation. Afterward, expenses returned to previous levels before increasing from $9,100 to $11,300, which coincides with the move of our Mystery Woman from the Villa Gardens Apartments. She relocated from Los Angeles to an apartment in Lake Merritt Park, an upscale neighborhood in Oakland. She's been gone from there nineteen months and we're not sure she's still in the country. Other than the storage unit rental expense, there has been no account activity. We have no specific evidence, but my gut says there is a direct connection between this bank account, our Mystery Woman, the activity at the storage units, and the Attack."

As Mike stood, stretched, and refilled their wine glasses, Phil assured him, "We've known this story for two months. Have verified it. No possibility of a mistake. Substantiated from every angle. Emails documented having originated on one computer and received on another. Trust me, we're rock solid. We've followed the money. Ahem Shehadi, our Oakland banker, is guilty as they come. He's damn near ninety years old. No way he had the technical expertise to pull this off by himself. He's a banker and an oil guy. He couldn't have financed it on his own or with the help of his brothers without us knowing it.

"The drones are seven-and-a-half to eight million apiece if you're a government buying them from the Israelis. On the black market, they're way more. They used four and have seven in reserve. We've looked hard. No record he, his bank, Marin Oil, or any of the holding companies paid for any of this. He has ties to Russia. We have his emails, introducing their politicians to his banking brothers and they, in turn, to Gazan officials. We tracked emails and texts from his son's phone. The kid, Ardashir, is a player and not as careful as his dad. Working through intermediaries, Ardashir housed the drones and played a role in their transport to Ann Arbor and Dover. Bayside played no financial role in how the Glen Canyon bomb was acquired. Marin Oil was involved in bringing it into this country, storing it, and transporting it to the site. The old man's in over his head, but he's a facilitator, not the top dog."

Frog stood, heels even with the front edge of the couch, locked his knees, bent forward, and put his hands flat on the floor. Straightening, he brought his arms to his shoulders, hands extended, rotating his torso 170 degrees in both directions, ten times. "Not ready to cry uncle, but we're getting older." Returning to the couch, he continued. "Regarding 'State' involvement and the 'coincidence' of Gaza's rise with the timing of the attack, total cost of the new port will be nine billion, plus the cost of the artificial island at another 23.6 billion. The airport, 2.1 billion. No way Gaza pulls this off without serious help. The Arab nations rallied around their brothers and financed it. Whether for ethical considerations or their true hatred of Israel, I leave to the political types.

"My guys have chased more leads than you can count. Revenue has come into the Gaza governmental coffers without a trace of where or why. Slight amounts, large amounts, it started with the death of the Gaza City mayor, the same weekend as the attack here while they continued receiving UN and other promissory notes from nations who pledged help following the last Israeli bombing. Even after the negotiated peace, the Israeli embargo made life in Gaza miserable. Prior to the mayor's death, money trickled in. Afterward, the spigot was turned on, and money gushed in from several straightforward accounts in Libya, Morocco, Tunisia, Turkey, India, France, and Indonesia, even from people and privately held companies. The total's three-plus billion. These are straightforward accounts. Three billion's a lot, but construction of what we know is an order of magnitude higher.

"Since the mayor's death, we've found 137 new accounts in the Gazan banking system, which have received increasing amounts each year. I'm confident in finding many more. The first year was around thirteen billion, it's increased to this past year where those accounts received 29.9 billion. They total over seventy-eight billion and counting this year. Much of it's been contributed through the brother's banks or their bank in Bangkok.

"It's important to remember the funds are coming through their banks, not from them. Try and follow it back further and good luck. It comes from hundreds and hundreds of different sources. It's been professionally laundered. We've looked back ten years, haven't found a smoking gun in the money's origin. Can't prove a connection between the attack and Gaza's rise, or between the banks and the source of the money, but it's intriguing.

"Shehadi and his brothers are well-positioned between their banks and control of a European wealth management firm with an influential client list, heads of state or their surrogates, international industrialists, power brokers. There is no evidence of any wrongdoing. Too much money is flowing into Gaza and the West Bank for there not to be a connection. Unless they implode internally, we'll be a long time sorting it out.

"Time your Fed buddies joined the fun. I'm betting a search warrant for the four storage units and everything in the Marin Oil Tanking and Terminals facilities will yield fascinating information. With what we've given you, and what they find, old Ahem Shehadi is toast. His days as a free man are numbered. We aren't to the next level yet. We will be. My guys love a challenge, and this has been one. Trust me, it ain't over. He's an old man, we're in his personal computer and the personal computers of his brothers. If they're involved and communicate with each other in any incriminating way, we'll pick it up. Their security is topflight. Still, there's no protection from old and tired and taking shortcuts. When you've been as successful as these guys, you believe you're insulated from the rest of the world. If they make a mistake, and they will, we'll catch 'em.

"Oh, in a week, I'll send you some numbered accounts for a Guernsey bank. Guernsey's a British Crown-dependent island in the English Channel. They print their own banknotes and make their own tax laws. Tell the director to deposit 18.6 million. The guys have earned it, a nice, neat group of bad guys, all packaged with a bow on top.

"Lastly. When I called Maggie the other day and invited myself to dinner tonight, I told her we might have made a little progress. She thanked me for giving her back her husband. She's a sweetheart. You, my friend, have done very, very well. I'm happy for you."

52

Help From Our Friends

1143 hrs. EDT Montreal, Canada
Friday, November 6
Post Attack, 2 Years, Day 11

"*Mesdames et messieurs*," came the voice over the flight deck's loudspeaker. "Welcome to Canada. Once again, we thank you for flying with us today. We know you have a choice, and we appreciate the opportunity to serve you," the senior flight attendant announced in French as Turkish Airlines Flight 2632 touched down at Montréal's Pierre Elliott Trudeau International Airport. "Please remain seated with your seatbelts fastened and your seats and tray tables in their locked and upright position until we have taxied to our gate. We apologize for the walk from the gate to customs. We hope you've had a chance to rest on our flight from Istanbul and have arrived refreshed and ready to enjoy a beautiful day here in Montréal." He repeated the announcement in English and again in Arabic.

Niousha Rostami replaced her magazine in the seat pocket in front of her, checked around to ensure she'd left nothing behind, and prepared to depart her first-class seat.

"Excuse me, Mrs. Mosharref al-Khayr? Mrs. Mary al-Khayr?" the customs agent asked the petite Arab woman clad in a burqa.

"Yes?"

"Please come this way. These gentlemen have questions for you," the agent said, stepping out from behind his station. Holding her arm, he escorted her to two waiting inspectors with the Royal Canadian Mounted Police.

"Be seated, Mrs. Al-Khayr," Inspector Melvin Hoy said as he and a six-foot, six-inch Inspector Joseph Browning ushered her into a windowless room furnished with a simple table and three straight-back wooden chairs.

"We have a few questions, if you don't mind," Inspector Browning added in his clipped Canadian accent. "First, you have only now arrived from Istanbul, correct?

"Correct."

"And what is the nature of your visit today to Montréal?"

"Here for a few days of vacation. I've heard how beautiful the city and surrounding vicinity are, and I wanted to enjoy it for myself," she replied in her best California tongue.

"Are you here by yourself or meeting another party?" Inspector Hoy asked.

"Here alone."

"Do you live in Istanbul?"

"It was my home. Sadly, this time I was there to bury my father. I now live in Thousand Oaks, California. After my visit, I will be returning home," she stated matter-of-factly.

"Are you married? What does your husband do?"

"Yes. He's a physician, a surgeon."

"Do you have any children?"

"No."

"Mrs. al-Khayr, or whoever you are, forgive me if I don't believe you," Inspector Hoy interrupted. "I spoke with the real Mary al-Khayr this morning in her home in Thousand Oaks, California, and she assured me she's at home with her attorney husband and their children, does not have family in Istanbul, and has never been to Montréal. You'd better start over with who you are, where you're from, and what your intentions are here in Canada, or you'll face a long and difficult future."

"Well, there must be a mistake, I assure you I'm Mary al-Khayr, and I live in Thousand Oaks," she protested.

"Fine. Call your husband. Let me talk to him," Inspector Browning growled.

"I can't. He's on his way to a medical convention in Oklahoma City. He won't arrive for another hour or so."

"What flight's he on? If you don't remember, what carrier did he fly? We'll check the flight manifest. If you're not telling us the truth, you will not be seeing the sights of our city anytime soon," agent Hoy snapped.

"I don't remember. He usually flies United Airlines, I'm not sure of his travel plans."

"What's his cellphone number?"

"He's got a new number. Excuse me, I'll have to look it up."

"Fine. In the meantime, what's the number for his practice, and what are the names of the other doctors in his practice?" Hoy asked.

"Patrick Royal and Oscar DeYoung."

"Does he have a nurse accompany him into the operating room? What's her name?"

"Yes. Cindy Watts, she's been with him fifteen years," she responded coolly.

Looking into her eyes with penetrating, disturbing inquisitor's gaze, Hoy insisted, "I've tried it three times and the number you handed me isn't a working number. I wish to give you the following warning: You need not say anything. You have nothing to hope from any promise or favor and nothing to fear from any threat whether or not you say anything."

"Anything you do or say may be used as evidence," Browning said as he stood. "Please empty your purse here on the table."

"What's this?" Inspector Hoy asked, picking up a second US passport. "Who is Habibeh Rakhsha? Why do you have her passport and driver's license?"

"Stand up! Turn around!" Inspector Browning barked. "Put your hands behind your back. You are under arrest for entering this country under false pretenses. We will be moving to have you extradited to the United States," he said, handcuffing her.

Afternoon traffic triggered tardiness to his meeting. The old banker pulled his steel blue Mercedes SLS-Class Roadster in behind the dark brown van at the valet parking station in front of the Ordway Building. Leaving the engine running, he slipped from behind the wheel and handed the attendant a twenty-dollar bill, asking him to leave the car to the left of the driveway. As he entered the building, he was met by two FBI agents, spoken to briefly, and ushered back outside and into the van.

Calmly and with no ado, Ahem Shehadi was taken into custody.

53

Pay Off

0730 hrs. CET Salzburg, Austria
Saturday, November 7
Post Attack, Two Years, Day 12

"Papa! Papa!" sixteen-month-old Rami yelled as he ran from the stool where he was eating his breakfast toward his grandfather who, with his nephew Jamal, had arrived at his daughter's opulent apartment.

On one knee, he said, "Look at you! You're growing so fast. Soon you will be bigger than me and even your father." He grinned as the boy jumped into his outstretched arms and they hugged. "Are you helping Mommy with your sister?

"Yes, yes, I am. Now she can ride in the wagon when I pull her!"

"Good for you! Mommy loves all your good help." He stood to embrace his daughter. "They bring such joy. You and Omar are good parents and watching them grow brings much pleasure. Your mother sends her best. She continues to struggle with her health, but she thinks of you and prays for you and your family."

"Thank you, Papa," Ana responded. "She's always in my thoughts and prayers, as are you. Thank you for being part of our lives. I'm forever torn between serving you and TLS and being a good mother to my children like my mother. I'm thankful we have Adeleh here for the children. Her experience and wisdom give me assurance they will be safe and strong in the faith. But when I'm gone, I miss them dearly."

The children down for their naps and afternoon prayers concluded, father and daughter sat together in the darkened living room. "I have sad news. The American authorities took your uncle Ahem into custody late Friday. They've charged him with providing material support to those intent on doing harm to their country. This is serious. We're working to find him the best possible legal help. Right now, we have no idea who or what tipped them off. They had a search warrant for the terminal facilities and found the second Russian bomb and nerve gas reservoir, among other items. We hope they will stay focused on the oil company and not look to connect the bank. Connections between the bank and the attack, with Niousha or with any of us, don't exist. Nandi does not believe any cyber communications have been violated. She and her team continue to check. If we find a confidence was broken, the person and their family will pay to the fourth generation." He grimaced. "Speaking of Niousha, she was detained in Montreal coming through customs after her flight from Istanbul yesterday, as well."

"No!" Ana gasped.

"I know, Habib Albi. She is as your sister, our second daughter. Canadian authorities stopped her and turned her over to the FBI. As far as we can tell, she's in Washington, D.C. Her plan was to enter the U.S. under yet another name, believing she'd be less conspicuous coming from Canada than from the Middle East. We're not sure how authorities discovered she was on the flight. She was excited and ready to return and assume oversight of TLS American operations."

After spending the last thirty minutes working and reworking the rift between stanzas, Maggie walked from her practice room into the kitchen for a glass of cold water, flipping the television on as she did so.

"This just in as we come on the air with this special edition of *ABC News*. I'm Ron McNeil."

The breath left Maggie as she tried to suppress the shockwaves that swept over her as she took in what she was seeing on screen.

"After authorities fruitlessly pursued the world's most wanted criminal for more than two years, Niousha Rostami, believed to be a Lebanese national, was apprehended yesterday in Montréal as she tried to clear customs following a flight from Istanbul, apparently traveling under false pretenses. Canadian authorities questioned her after finding two additional aliases, using passports, driver's licenses, and voter registration cards to confirm the identities in her purse. Unable to identify herself to their satisfaction, she was handed over to the FBI and brought to Washington, D.C.

"Rostami is considered the primary operative of the Attack on America, which included the use of weapons of mass destruction, earning it the United Nations' recognition as the most abhorrent crime ever committed internationally. The allegations against her place her atop the world's Most Wanted list.

"The tip leading to her capture has not been disclosed. An FBI spokesperson credited multi-agency cooperation between the US Attorney General's Office, the Department of Justice's Counterterrorism Section, the FBI's Joint Terrorism Task Force, Immigration and Customs Enforcement, Homeland Security investigations, and the public with substantial support from Canadian federal authorities. The announcement of Ms. Rostami's capture was not made public until late this afternoon, in part because authorities wanted to verify her identity. What made her apprehension difficult was that on paper, she didn't exist. She had no known address, no telephone, no driver's license, no social security number; she was not registered to vote. Articulate and an impeccable dresser, she had lived under an assumed name in a multistory apartment complex in upscale Oakland. She paid cash for all her purchases and used different identities as she moved from location to location. She was positively identified from her fingerprints on file with Cal State Fullerton where she worked on a research project for NASA while earning a degree in chemical engineering over two decades ago while in this country on a student visa. Authorities have also learned she received a law degree from Harvard under an assumed name.

"Late Thursday evening, Ahem Shehadi, an Oakland banker and oil executive, was also taken into custody. A prominent person in the community for decades, his arrest shocked the city of Oakland. Supportive of civic activities, he was not one to be suspected of being involved with terrorism or any type of civil unrest.

"Announcements of the Rostami and Shehadi arrests were made at a news conference within the last hour. FBI Director Townsend told the media 'Ahem Shehadi is a top terrorist suspect, accused of using his oil company to acquire, store and distribute all manner of military and paramilitary weapons and equipment. Specifically, he stored the nuclear bomb used in the attempted destruction of Glen Canyon Dam, and the drones used in the attacks on Ann Arbor, Michigan, and Dover, Delaware, which resulted in the deaths of so many innocents. He'll be arraigned tomorrow morning in federal court in the Northern District of California and charged with fourteen counts, including providing materials, financial support, and resources to a foreign terrorist organization, being an enemy combatant, conspiracy, and having discussed terrorist targets with an alleged terrorist organization, conspiracy to kill US nationals, and destruction of government property. He's being held without bail pending trial, which is not expected until at least late spring of next year.

"In addition to Rostami and Shehadi, the FBI arrested fourteen people believed to be associated with the attack late last night and early this morning. All the suspects were taken from their homes, arrested without incident. Director Townsend is confident they have significant evidence against each and will be moving forward with their prosecutions. It's believed they're all either naturalized citizens, or in this country legally with green cards and other appropriate documentation. Eleven live and work in greater Los Angeles and are believed to have been part of a sleeper cell, which provided information and material support for the train derailments and other components of the attack."

Shock continued to resonate through Maggie as she sank into a nearby chair and listened to the reporter.

"Assistant US attorneys Curtis Boyer and Craig Reed expect all will be arraigned Monday morning in federal court. The Justice Department will bring an array of charges against each of them, ranging from conspiring to commit murder, planning to commit terrorist acts, conspiring to detonate a weapon of mass destruction and malicious destruction of property resulting in death, providing material support to terrorists, soliciting others to engage in acts of terrorism within the U.S., and being an enemy combatant. Those arrested range in age from twenty-five to fifty-one." McNeil went on to list each of the arrestees, along with their suspected role in the Attack.

"Elizabeth Morgan, US Attorney for the Southern District of California, indicated more arrests will be forthcoming with the extradition of Bhupendra Mathur, an active-duty captain in the Indian Air Force charged with piloting the drones in Michigan and Delaware. Morgan emphasized while those arrested all played significant roles in the attack, they are not the ones who designed or financed it. Those investigations continue.

"In making this announcement, US Attorney Gary Hacker stated, 'The prosecution of these cases is the result of the continuing effort to find and bring to justice those who perpetrated the atrocities against our nation over three years ago. The president has defined a foreign terrorist organization as the term is used in Title 18, United States Code, Section 2339B (g) (6) and Section 219 of the Immigration and Nationality Act by the United States Secretary of State and has made it clear we will not rest until those responsible have been apprehended and prosecuted. This office continues its active pursuit in all cases involving those engaged in these illegal activities. Today is a great day for the rule of law and for those who believe in justice.' We'll have much more on these and other related breaking stories at the start of *ABC World News* in ten minutes. We now return you to your regularly scheduled programming. For *ABC News*, I'm Ron McNeil."

54

Passing the Torch

0900 hrs. SGT Singapore
Wednesday, October 26
Post Attack, 5 Years

Singapore: a gathering at another well-appointed luxury hotel.

As though a silent consensus had been reached among the cousins, Parsa's success with Asha, its financial growth and international clientele expansion made him the obvious heir apparent and leader of his generation upon the passing of the last 'Uncle.'

Farhad Antar stepped to the front of the room, summoned Parsa, and said, "Let us pray."

Oh Allah! You are our Lord.
There is only You, sustainer of all worlds.
You created us and we are your servants.
Praise be to Allah, who has guided us to today.
Never could we have found guidance,
had it not been for the guidance of Allah.
Continue to bless us.
Let us show our thanks in our daily actions.
In the name of the Most Merciful One
Continue to show us the straight way.

"Brothers, we are here to commemorate the fifth anniversary of the initial *Hujum* effort. Its success was due to the efforts of many. Today, our brother Parsa will tell us of the ongoing implementation made possible because of that great day. What he won't tell you is how he has used Asha, its member clients and his own international network to help lessen the impact of the worldwide recession and speed the recovery of the United States, because he knows a strong US economy is essential in balancing the world economy.

"America will play an important role in repositioning the Middle East on the world economic stage and help to keep China and Russia in check in the region. He has worked tirelessly on the international monetary front to enact monetary policies aimed at increasing the money supply and encouraging lending. Together, we have convinced our Arab brothers to stabilize the production and cost of oil. Restoration of American ports in Los Angeles and Houston and the recovery of their rail system and petrochemical industry are ahead of schedule, in no small measure because of Parsa's behind the scenes leadership. Parsa, if you will."

The medium-sized, slightly overweight man with a prematurely lined middle-aged face, more from the responsibilities he carried than of the accumulated years, stepped up to the podium to address the small group of cousins, fathers, sons, and daughters, Antars and Shehadis.

"This year's meeting date is intentional. Five years ago, today, our plan to isolate Israel was initiated with the *Hujum*. Today, the combined GDP of Gaza, the Golan Heights, and the West Bank is more than triple Israel's. Gaza's multi-billion-dollar petrochemical complex and port is now the fifth largest in the world. Renewable energy exports rank fourth. The new joint air base and naval station north of Jabaliya ensures a Russian military presence for the foreseeable future and has ended Israeli bombing of Gaza. The naval base has enabled a ten-fold increase in the fishing industry.

"Asha and Asha clients now own 72% of the businesses and 53% of the land in the Golan Heights and the West Bank. The new owners do not hire Israelis. Within the next decade, Arabs will be the predominant nationality, because the Jews will not be able to find work. The nations surrounding Israel will continue to strengthen their borders and trade with Arab-owned businesses." All traces of his smile left Parsa's lips as he looked up and studied the assembled group.

"We've gathered these few days in celebration, reverence, and anticipation. Celebration of the lives well-lived by our fathers and forefathers and their example of steadfast trust in Allah. Reverence regarding the April passing of Amir Antar and the recent death of my father, Jalil. Now, all of Sayyad Antar and Yamani Shehadi's children have perished. The night before I left for Harvard my freshman year, my father and Uncle Amir told me this story, one I've never forgotten, and one I hope you never will. It goes like this." Taking a drink from his water bottle, and looking out at his audience, he recited the tale.

"There was a moment after the Great War as the Ottoman Empire began its dissolution, hemorrhaging its European territories and its retrenchment in Turkey as a twentieth-century state, when Great Britain, France, and the other colonial colossi took their eyes and constraining fists off the Middle East, allowing those countries a glimpse of freedom and independence.

"Persia, released from Ottoman control, enjoyed several heady, invigorating years, and looked forward to regaining its historical glory from the time of Cyrus the Great. In the central city of Khomeyn, two young men came into their own personal freedom. Sayyad Antar and Yamani Shehadi, inseparable since their first year of school. Their families worked, played, and worshipped together through the Ottomans' possession, continuing as the Russians and British made their presence known, and without interruption into the disastrous alliance with Germany.

"The Sykes-Picot Agreement pillaged the region more brutally than all its previous conquerors. The land, arbitrarily cleaved with straight lines and sharp angles, ignored the labyrinth of incumbent populations, their history, geography, and cultures. Shi'ites were split between Iran, Iraq, Kuwait, Bahrain, and the eastern provinces of Saudi Arabia. Their smaller sects splintered in isolated pockets along the coast and throughout the region, rendering any hope of sustainable political stability and self-governance virtually impossible.

"In the spring of 1928, Sayyad and Yamani set off for a glorious future and education in Qom and its university. There, Sayyad received advanced religious training, and Yamani trained in the secular, business and accounting. They studied, grew, and learned while governments, borders, names, flags, allegiances, and republics came, flourished, disintegrated, and began again. They wanted to ensure their families survived and prospered, regardless of what transpired at the regional, national, or international level.

"Surrounded by the sights, sounds and competing aromas of congested traffic, crowds making their rounds, and beasts of burden delivering goods, the two men sat in the back of an open-air café in Qom's business district near the intersection of Chamran and Metri, finishing a lunch of dates, figs, fresh fruits, and Turkish coffee, coping as best they could with the stillness and oppressive heat of a 1935 August afternoon. Sayyad looked at his friend, saying, 'The Shah has changed the world our fathers knew. He'll change it more. Our children have and will benefit from the basic education he has established but will learn more out of the classroom than in it.'

"Yamani smiled, 'Help me, my friend. If our families are to survive to generations yet unborn, we must compete with other cultures and other nations on their turf. We must protect our holdings, ensuring they are unattainable by any one man or government. I will train my children in the ways of banking and finance, and I shall rely upon you to help me if there is an issue with their faith. I foresee a time when we add banks in Russia and China. My children, with my guidance, your support and the blessing of Allah will have the same religion, albeit different cultures. They will eat different foods and listen to different music. Their clothes and, of course, their languages will differ. And they will have certain cultural and traditional practices not derived from the Islam of their childhood. In the end, they will not waver. They're brothers, they're Persians, they're Muslims.'

"Sayyad replied, 'A boy goes into the forest and sees a drop of water land on a flat rock. The water ricochets into a thousand tiny droplets, the rock undaunted, another drop and another, and another. The rock is unfazed. The next year, the boy returns, *drop, drop, drop,* a slight indentation forms in the rock. Years later, a cavity appears in the stone. In his old age, he sees the water passing unscathed through a hole in the rock.'"

Looking up, Parsa paused. "My cousins and I are the third generation. We have and are continuing the vision of our fathers and grandfathers. We have remained true and pass on to you, our children, patience, perseverance, and persistence. My brother, Ehsan Antar, please come, join me, and lead us in prayer."

Bowing his head, Ehsan prayed.

"Allah, we thank you for the gift of our fathers and grandfathers,

For their examples shared with us through their lives of faith.

Thank you for the lessons they taught, and the trust placed in us.

We here and now rededicate ourselves, to continue the path they set before us, to help all Muslims, Shi'ite, and Sunni, focus on the common goal of diminishing Israel's place in the region. We trust the plans we have developed meet with your approval and with their successful completion, the families will continue to be made whole.

Our hope is to pass the torch to our children with the same confidence our fathers had in us. Above all, we hold our trust in you, Allah, and pray these efforts serve to your glory."

"Thank you, Ehsan." Parsa looked up. He took another long drink from his water bottle before congratulating the Antars for making the *Hujum* a success. He told the group that the ongoing cooperation of the Middle Eastern nations was a constant reminder of the remarkable efforts of their work. Manifestation of Sunni cooperation was seen with the improvements in the lives of those in Gaza, the West Bank and Golan Heights and how the new banks in Amman and Riyadh, the ending of conflicts in Syria and Yemen were all made possible because the Antars developed an open dialogue and maintained a good faith relationship with the Sunnis.

Shifting topics, Parsa spoke of what had changed since their grandfathers had first envisioned their path forward, lessons learned from the *Hujum,* and the coming transition in generational leadership of Asha. "When Sayyad Antar and Yamani Shehadi set the course for the future of our families, they did not anticipate the success we now enjoy. They were honest, open men. Look around the room, a third of you are women. A few here for the first time. Something our founding fathers could not have imagined. Asha is stronger, more competitive because of you. You stand on the shoulders of Anosha and Niousha, without whose exceptional work you would not be here or hold the responsible positions you do."

Parsa explained that most Antar and Shehadi cousins were not there. They were established clerics and high-ranking managers in the corporate holdings of the family, believing those in attendance were involved with Asha, which to them was a nebulous financial management company.

"It's not for them to ever know of TLS, the cash cow that made all this possible. Secrets are not healthy, but no one outside this room must ever hear of TLS. We were careful to build layers between ourselves and those who carried out the *Hujum*, and as careful to insulate Asha and its holdings. Our cousin Ardashir's carelessness cost him and his father their lives. He destroyed our American presence and brought unnecessary scrutiny. A reminder, Nandi and her team have updated the network architecture for our HORNET browser, enabling high-speed end-to-end anonymous channels. It is imperative all Asha, Antar, and Shehadi communication be done on our HORNET browser. Make no mistake, America continues to search for those involved in their Attack on America.

"Jamal, Omar, Anosha, and I have worked to provide the funding for Gaza's infrastructure and oil and gas industry and the forthcoming improvements in the West Bank and Golan Heights. They have succeeded in the world's most brutal and unforgiving environment by adopting new technologies, paying unbelievable attention to detail, learning from their mistakes, and watching those who must stay out of the grasp of governmental authorities, and ever greedy suppliers.

"In their industry, those apprehended fall into one or more of three categories. They get greedy, get lazy, or get sloppy. Result: they get caught. TLS never 'got' any of those. But they did get old." He smiled, glancing over at them as a slight titter crossed the room. "They know the secrets, instinctively staying ahead of the authorities. But there is a time and place for everything. The need to generate large sums of money at considerable risk and exposure has passed. TLS has closed."

Another pause, a long drink, and Parsa stepped in front of the lectern as he told his audience about Jamal, Omar, and Anosha's new fivefold assignment. They and the TLS senior leadership would focus on Israeli society, using the internet, social media, and smart phones to spread turmoil and discord in their daily lives.

First, attacks on Israeli infrastructure with outages, disruptions and shutdowns of their water, power, and internet. Complicating their lives would give Israelis reasons to be dissatisfied with their leaders. Second, frequent, ongoing quality, performance, and customer service issues will undermine customer trust and satisfaction in every facet of the Israeli economy. Third, pirating research data from Israeli universities and companies developing new technologies, products, or medical treatments will sabotage work and provide Arab companies time to develop competition.

"Fourth, they will target local, regional, and national political and industrial leaders, corrupting them with cash and expensive gifts before threatening to leak their financial and personal information unless they alter their decision-making votes on key issues. Finally, using local social media to question every action, agitate every issue, fuel tension, and create chaos, they'll exploit rivalries that will pit Russian Jews against German Jews against American Jews, secular Jews against the ultra-Orthodox, to cause as much continuous civil and international unrest as possible."

Parsa paused to let his words sink in. "The transition of Asha and the expansion of new banks is well underway with locations in Istanbul, Hong Kong, Toronto, and Montreal. Long term, we'll have banks in North Africa, Indonesia, and Eastern Europe, providing funding for developing nations with substantial populations of our brothers, and emerging economies. We'll continue to invest where Asha's clients live and work, while also exerting substantial influence.

"As I step away from the operational components of Asha, I'll focus on identifying and monitoring the next generation of Russian, Chinese, and American leaders and, to a lesser degree, those in India and Japan. We'll engage and help build personal fortunes beyond their imaginations. Wealth and financial holdings that will keep them close and seeking our help with international stability. The *Hujum* expedited the transition of power in the Middle East from America and its allies to a united Arab block supported by Russia and China. We must be vigilant and not allow America to sow discord among us with our Sunni brothers. We must also position ourselves to take full advantage of China's expanding economic presence while holding them at bay. We have more oil than Russia, lead the world in renewable energy technology, and their dependence on America and our international agriculture production can keep them in check should the need arise.

"Years ago, when the Uncles set us on the path to become Asha and TLS, The Lasting Solution, with more than mere moral pedagogy, they reminded us of the story of our father Abraham and his trust in Allah. They understood the generational nature of the tasks at hand and how success depended on a coordinated, constant effort applied over the long-term. The twentieth century was fraught with the meddling of colonial Europe, and later both Russia and the United States spilled blood to retain the arbitrary and capricious borders drawn for Western interests. We can never lower our guard. The Americans won't stop looking for those responsible for the *Hujum*.

"Our forefathers were wise men. We are blessed. They taught us we are first and foremost family. We are Persians. I pray they are pleased with the progress achieved and with our efforts to provide you guidance. May your generation care for your children, raise them faithful to Allah, not losing sight of His will for us. Work in unity and with integrity to move our grandfathers' vision forward," Parsa concluded.

55

Shifting Sands

1930 hrs. EST Washington, D.C.
Sunday, March 14
Post Attack, Seven Years, Day 138

"Welcome. We continue our BBC Special Series, 'The Shifting Sands of the Middle East.' I'm Erin Mulvaney, reporting from BBC Headquarters, Studio 3 in London.

"Previously, we've talked of the region's long history as the birthplace of three of the world's major religions, the role it played in cultural exchange as a major trade route from China to Egypt and Europe to India. Tonight, we look at the extraordinary transformation taking place in Gaza.

"Gaza has enjoyed opulent prosperity and endured devastating desolation. For most of the last century, militant groups with no experience in governance have ruled this region. Corruption and infrastructure neglect are two of the many problems plaguing Gazan civilization as it struggles with the difficulties of incumbent populations displaced by the creation of modern Israel."

Music played as the television screen showed scenes of ancient ruins, bombed out buildings, raw sewage flowing into the Mediterranean Sea, barefoot children playing in bomb-cratered streets, patients waiting for hours for simple first aid, and gangs pillaging and looting. The scene shifted to the sun shining through a grove of trees, an aerial view of a busy, thriving downtown Gaza City, a high-end hotel lobby and candlelit fine dining. A narrator, speaking off camera, began, "The transformation of Gaza has been nothing short of spectacular. Gaza City, a city of five hundred thousand, is again on the rise. With a history stretching back five thousand years, it's among the oldest cities in the world. Enjoying the favor of Egyptian pharaohs, Alexander the Great, and Roman emperors, it has witnessed its share of prosperity and devastation. The most recent of which has come at the hands of Israel, whose latest bombing resulted in piles of destruction and rubble, an impoverished, disabled, and wounded population with an unemployment rate in the 40% range, 60% among young people. Reconstruction costs are estimated to exceed 300 billion dollars."

The television screen shifted to new high-rise office buildings and commercial amenities, bustling streets, busy major highways, and construction of new hospitals, schools, and water treatment plants. The narrator continued.

"What makes this most recent resurgence impressive is the amount and sources of support. For decades after its assumption of political power in the Gaza Strip, Hamas was plagued by internal greed and corruption as it tried to learn how to govern. Following what has been called the 'cleansing,' the assassination of the prime minister, several members of his cabinet, three of the five Governorate administrators, and the Gaza City Mayor seven years ago, governance has been a picture of efficacy and efficiency with improvements in city and regional infrastructure, the economy, jobs, healthcare and education. Gaza has become a picture of prosperity and an example of what a united Arabic effort can produce."

Images on the television showed a thriving agricultural industry, a busy Yasar Arafat International Airport, container ships loading and unloading on the docks and oil tankers taking on refined products at their new port, children in classrooms, and students walking across a new university campus.

The narrator resumed. "In a remarkable show of uniformity, every Middle Eastern nation from Egypt to Lebanon has supported this transformation with money, increased aid and trade. Following the 'cleansing,' Gaza officials announced an agreement with China Road & Bridge Corporation, to oversee construction of a deep-water port south of Gaza City, on the coast north of Deir al-Balah.

"This was followed by the signing of a long-term agreement with Russia as a tenant of the new port. In return, Russia promised to provide substantial berth, warehousing, crane, and rail support for the new port. The port has been under continuous construction with expansion undertaken prior to completion of the original scope of work. Those expansion plans have been added to again as they now include a state-of-the-art dry dock for tanker and supertanker ship repair for international shipping fleets. The port already competes with the other Mediterranean Sea deep water ports for price, port facilities, and services, and will soon be headquarters for a new international fishing, marine security, and oceanographic research center. Officials have also signed agreements with three cruise ship lines, which become effective next spring following completion of their new dedicated cruise ship terminal."

Aerial and ground level views showed two new sprawling oil refineries. Additional auxiliary utility units and storage tanks tied together with miles of pipes. The audio continued. "Port construction was followed with the construction of a new international airport, two massive oil refineries and four new chemical processing facilities. Iraqi, Iranian, and Saudi Arabian oil now flows through a new pipeline along the Jordanian-Saudi Arabian border under the Gulf of Aqaba into Egypt. The pipeline turns north-northeast, feeding a new bulk terminal for an Egyptian rail line dedicated to the transport of this crude. It continues, terminating in Gaza at the refineries.

"These refineries produce 275,000 barrels of gasoline per day, regular, premium unleaded, and low sulfur reformulated and conventional gasoline for their own use and international markets. Natural gas and crude oil are converted into feedstock for plastics and other products. Commercial jet fuel, kerosene, diesel fuel, lubricating and heating oils are among the hundreds of products exported daily. They have produced all the asphalt used to resurface and improve their own roads and highways. In addition, chemical feedstock of ethane, propane and butane, major building blocks for chemical products, are produced in massive quantities and fed to the adjoining chemical plants for production of benzene, toluene, ethylene, plastics, polyesters, acetone, and phenol. Reduction in transportation costs to Houston and other US refineries are already being experienced there and on world markets as OPEC oil production costs decline. Their petrochemical industry, still in its infancy, moves forward at an incredible pace. Within the next fifteen months, they'll be producing a litany of products, an entire array of adhesives and sealants, cleaning products, food additives, inks, paints and coatings, pharmaceuticals, textiles, building and construction supplies, plastics and synthetic rubbers."

The screen depicted a busy port with super tankers taking on refined petroleum products for worldwide delivery. Tugboats and barges expedited the activities.

"The cooperative effort of Saudi oil moving through an Egyptian pipeline to multinational refineries and petrochemical plants in Gaza for sale to new trading partners has provided the money and jobs to reposition Gaza as a tourist attraction and sent a message to the US and the West that their influence in the region has diminished," the narrator said.

Scenes of children drinking from water fountains in city parks, freshwater irrigating acres and acres of fresh fruits and vegetables, and videos of agriculture workers working in the fields played across the television screen. "The booming economy has had wide ranging implications for everyone. Construction has prompted a major overhaul of the region's infrastructure, including building four new desalination plants, allowing, for the first time, 100% of Gaza's residents to be connected to the public water supply and sewage system. This reduced a major public health hazard where half the city with no water was forced to rely on 'salty wells' and daily dumped millions of tons of raw sewage and untreated water into the Mediterranean Sea. This, in turn, resulted in the breeding of insects and an uncontrolled explosion in the population of mice and rats. Construction of nine wastewater treatment plants throughout the region has eliminated this problem and improved air quality and living conditions in large sections of the city.

"There is an active effort to reclaim the 200,000 square kilometers of land most suitable for farming destroyed by Israel. Desalination has provided sufficient water to re-establish the agricultural industry lost after the last Israeli conflict. Vegetables, berries, flowers, dates, figs, olives and olive oil, and fruits like apples, oranges, almonds, and grapefruit have made a remarkable comeback. Production of cotton, wheat, and a fledgling wine industry have progressed enough for Gaza to export their excess, putting 100,000 people once again back to work on 35,000 farms. Since the beginning of this century, Israel has implemented a policy of bulldozing land and uprooting trees, creating what they call a buffer zone of self-defense. In a recent communication, Russia informed Israel any buffer zone must be created inside their own border. All cross-border activity in Gaza will be considered an act of aggression against the sovereign state of Gaza and dealt with swiftly and appropriately by their new ally."

Street festivals and active social evening scenes flashed across the television as the narrator observed, "For the first time this century, Gaza is power independent, providing sufficient power for its own needs and now selling power to Lebanon. They have also invested in their solid waste management with state-of-the-art, environmentally responsible recycling of concrete, steel, and other items, resulting from Israeli bombardments. This project will take several years. It serves the dual purpose of eliminating the huge quantities of rubble and debris left from the aerial bombings, naval shelling, and artillery fire, while creating usable space in its place.

"All the hospitals in Gaza are now equipped with their own emergency power generators and access to sufficient fuel to ensure their safe operation for seven consecutive days. The government and private sector have worked together to ensure access to local clinics, regional and tertiary hospitals. Serious cases are no longer transferred out of the region for care.

"The Yasser Arafat International Airport, near Rafah, twenty-five miles south of Gaza City, has been repaired and refurbished, including a state-of-the-art terminal and control tower, additional gates and improved runways. The original airport opened in 1998. Israeli aerial bombardments damaged its runways and facilities in 2001 and 2002, rendering it unusable. With three hundred flights arriving every day, regional travel, flights to Europe, North Africa, Russia, China, and Indonesia are now a daily occurrence.

"Flights to North America are scheduled to begin in the spring. The addition of the new airport gives them two international points of departure and positions them as a key tourist destination. Coupled with the deep-water port, these international airports provide Gaza a link to the region and beyond, thus destroying the isolation stranglehold the Zionists in Israel have used to keep the Palestinians at bay for much of the last century.

"Improvements on all major highways and roads have been completed or soon will be, making travel from Egypt to Lebanon easy and fast. Traffic now moves in and around Gaza City at a much more efficient pace." Scenes inside manufacturing facilities, white collar office workers and construction workers appeared as the narrator concluded. "The result of this, unemployment is at an all-time low—in the low single digits. The standard of living is up, as is tourism. The new port has forced Israel to withdraw its control of no-fishing zones and restricted passage sectors off the coast of Gaza. Trade agreements with Russia and China and the unified support of all the Middle Eastern countries have established a new normal for the entire region," the video concluded.

The scene returned to Erin Mulvaney in studio as she turned to the camera. "This past Wednesday, Gaza, Russia, and Indonesia signed a long-term agreement to build a new joint military base north of the city of Jabaliya. The base will include an air base and a naval station. The air base will be jointly operated by Russia and Indonesia with the Russian Air Force providing three Multi-Role Strike Sukhoi Su-34 jet fighters and three Utility Mi-8/17 transport/patrol helicopters and training and maintenance for the personnel responsible for this equipment. The Indonesian Air Force will provide three Russian and two French fighters, and a Chinese KJ-500, the third-generation airborne early warning and control aircraft.

"The new air base will have two runways and sufficient ground support to service Russian bombers. This new development, combined with their existing relationships with Syria and Iran, increases Russia's military presence in the region, ensuring their ability to deploy forces in the region for the next half-century.

"Regarding the naval station, Russia will provide three armored, guided missile cruisers and a guided-missile destroyer equipped to carry out anti-submarine, anti-air, and anti-surface operations. Upon completion, the new port more than doubles space for Russian warships in the Mediterranean, providing them with a second port.

"In an expansion of Gaza's efforts to establish their own military capability, last year they created a military academy in Khan Yunis and now have a standing army of ten thousand men with tanks, traditional artillery, and surface to air missiles. Although slight in number, they continue training a combat air assault force like the United States Army First Cavalry Division.

"This and Gaza's improving trade relations with several African nations, their Middle Eastern neighbors, and China tips the balance of power with Israel in Gaza's favor.

"A furious Israeli government on Thursday protested these developments as further poisoning an already toxic atmosphere between Israel and Gaza, Russia, and China, raising questions of further direct actions against Israel. Israel's Parliament released a statement yesterday, decrying these developments as a presumptive act of aggression, seeking action from the UN to nullify the agreements. However, China and Russia's presence on the Security Council guarantees no action from the UN regarding these new developments. Instead, late Friday, the UN warned Israel not to incite any violence.

"Egypt, the lone Arab member of the Security Council, responded, saying Gaza, the Golan Heights and the West Bank are focused on improved infrastructure issues and increasing trade with Africa, China, Asia, Russia and others, and they have no interest in activities in Israel. Gaza's active participation in the fossil fuel revenue stream and their newfound trade and military connections bring a whole new dynamic to the turbulent region. Gaza and the Middle East have let Israel and the West know they will no longer be bullied by a militarily superior neighbor.

"Next time, we'll look at the mining interests in Jordan and the West Bank, and we'll explore how new industry there has improved the lives of so many. These new efforts take advantage of robotics technology, are more efficient, and can produce at a higher rate than the current Israeli potash mine. With lower operating costs, they compete favorably with their neighbor and will, at a minimum, cut into the profits of their Israeli competitor. Is this the beginning of a united Arab economic front capable of competing head-to-head with every industry in Israel? In every market Gaza and Arab-backed industries in the Golan Heights and the West Bank have entered, they bring newer technologies, strong marketing, solid financial backing, and what analysts see as a strong commitment to establish a firm client base to expand their market share.

"Future programs will focus on the massive Arab repopulation of the West Bank and Golan Heights in response to jobs and a growing economy in those regions, which begs the question, will residents there one day choose to align themselves with Syria or another Arab nation? And we'll look at the Shi'ite-Sunni struggle for regional hegemony. With Russia's increasing economic and military presence in Gaza and Syria, Syria's Shi'ite sect Alawite government, and Hezbollah in Lebanon, Iran has established a direct link to the Mediterranean for the first time in more than two millennia. The Sunni alliance counters with Saudi Arabia, the Gulf states, Egypt and Jordan and United States support.

"This has been a BBC special series, 'The Shifting Sands of the Middle East.' I'm Erin Mulvaney. We hope to see you next time. Good night."

56

Always Remember

1630 hrs. MDT Idaho
Tuesday, October 26
Post Attack, Ten Years

Maggie stood at the kitchen sink window of their Idaho summer home, looking out across the pasture to the river's edge. Washing her cake pan and cookie sheets after having made chocolate chip cookies for the twins, oatmeal cookies for Michael, and the chocolate cake she would serve for dessert after dinner tonight, a sense of serene happiness came over her. She loved this view, this place, her world.

Her first trip to Idaho had been at Michael's invitation when she and the San Francisco Symphony's Director of Development spoke with the Idaho Philharmonic leadership about increasing the subscriber base. Proud of his adopted state and its many scenic venues, Michael brought her here. Four square miles of undeveloped land, split in half by the river, it had been in a family trust for decades. She had fallen in love with its grandeur and tranquility. It helped her see the draw which pulled him away from San Francisco. He bought the land and presented it to her as a wedding gift. Together, they'd designed the house and Bob Mutschler had built it for them.

The 3,100-square-foot, story-and-a-half home gave no indication of the elegance within. It had wood floors throughout, four bedrooms and three and a half baths. The home's double front doors opened into a large, appealing room with a grand piano to one side, a grand, inviting fireplace on the other, glass across the entire back and an elegant, descending staircase. A modern kitchen, dining room and well-appointed study completed the first floor.

The house sat atop a naturally occurring three-ton granite outcropping. Its towering windows provided a magnificent view of a landscaped, grassy backyard with well-established purple leaf plumb and common smoke trees and a variety of flowering perennials, including coleus and ornamental kale. The flagstone patio and walking paths bordered with rows of dahlias, snapdragons, asters, pampas plumes, tulips and larkspur gave way to a manicured lawn with rose trellises on the south side and a well-worn wooden swing hanging from the branch of the majestic, hundred-year-old Shumard oak standing at the back—all surrounded by a weathered jack fence whose presence helped keep the cows out rather than anything in.

Michael worked to intersperse flowering trees beyond the jack fence. Dogwoods, oriental cherry, English hawthorn, eastern red cedar, Rocky Mountain maple, and tulip trees provided a great show of color without encumbering the view. Below the knoll, a mile of scrub oak, greasewood, and sagebrush intermingled with salt grass, and other native grasses in plentiful supply provided pasture for their cattle. Beyond the North Fork of the Payette River, further still, the Sawtooth Mountains provided a majestic sentinel.

It had taken a few years, but Michael sold Zia, invested wisely, and now spent his time working on projects for the foundation and being a willing and able full-time father to their twins. On occasion, he consulted for the FBI, DOJ, or Homeland. He was determined the foundation's efforts would find meaningful answers and was pleased with their investigators' advances in stem cell applications for infants born with congenital heart defects and how bacteria attached to healthy cell walls before infecting them.

Watching now, she could make out her returning crew this side of the water's edge. Michael, the twins, Jack, and Emma made their way back on their horses, Phillip following on the 4-wheeler and old Jake and his young son Charlie, the boys' dog, running and playing alongside. In her mind's eye, she could hear the banter between her five-year-olds and their favorite cousin. The absolute joy of riding their horses, knowing Daddy had their fish, and Mommy would cook them for supper painted a vision in her mind she would cherish forever. She knew the boys had had a grand time fishing, catching grasshoppers, and watching the dragonflies, all the while learning lessons of wildlife conservation, fair play, and an ever-increasing love of the outdoors.

Life was hectic but good. They lived in San Francisco where she worked for the Symphony. With funds from the foundation, they'd identified a full-time teacher to work at the Children's Hospital to help kids write and record music, and they'd implemented the program in several other hospitals. With foundation seed money, the San Francisco United School District had adopted many of her ideas to expand the elementary school curriculum to include music and art.

They'd sold their Boise home. Keeping three houses wasn't practical. With the twins starting school, it was clear the opportunities in San Francisco outnumbered any other option. Grandma and Grandpa Barrington were an integral part of their lives. They spent extended time in the summer and as many long weekends as possible at this house. And Walt Duncan, Sally's father; Michael made sure he could enjoy the boys, his grandchildren. They visited his summer place in Maine each year, made frequent trips to New York and hosted him in San Francisco. She appreciated his warmth and genuine affection for her and the boys. Occasionally, she played with the Boise Philharmonic Orchestra. As a birthday present to Michael, the orchestra and Boise Philharmonic Master Chorale would perform Gustav Mahler's Symphony No. 8 in E-flat major tomorrow night.

"Nancy, thanks for setting the table and frosting the cake. Will you put it on the credenza? We'll feed the gang cookies and milk here on the kitchen table," Maggie said as the two worked together to prepare dinner. "I'm glad you could join us. "

"Oh, look at this picture of the four of us," Nancy Plummer said from the dining room. "The day we all sailed under the Golden Gate Bridge. Six months before he got sick. You guys have been so kind, and I love you more than you know. I still can't get my arms around tomorrow's ceremony, Don Plummer Children's Hospital. He'd be so proud."

"Michael said I could tell you, there will be one more announcement tomorrow. He has worked with UCSF Benioff Children's Hospitals to implement a teaching relationship between the two hospitals. They rank among the nation's best and now they'll have medical students, residents, fellows, and faculty here in Idaho."

Sitting on a kitchen stool, she smiled. "Oh, Maggie, I can't believe it."

"Don was very special to Michael and you guys were a couple. I can't tell you how often he would tell me how Don was the older brother he never had. Michael always appreciated his honesty. His word was his bond, and he never pulled any punches. He, Phil, and Jack were Michael's go to guys. They were always straight with him and kept his feet on the ground. We still can't believe the cancer took him so quickly."

Fifteen minutes later, all the boys in her life were seated around her kitchen table, eating cookies and drinking ice-cold milk. "So, tell me, Toby, what was your favorite part of fishing?"

"I already told you, Mom, catching the fish. Daddy said we could eat her for supper. Can we, please?" he pleaded.

"Yes, we may, but you have to help Daddy clean him and take his scales off."

"It's not a boy fish, Mom. It's a girl. When Daddy cut her open to take out the insides, he showed us this little bag inside all full of eggs. If I hadn't caught her, she was going to have baby fish for us to catch next year. Daddy let me take out her eyes. At first it was kind of yucky, then it was really neat."

"Enough already, and no more cookies or no one will be hungry for dinner. By the way, can everybody have a bite of your fish or are you going to eat him all by yourself?"

"Everybody gets some, Mom. I wouldn't have caught her if Daddy hadn't taken us fishing and shown me how to put the grasshopper in the place for the fish to bite it. And Phil, 'cause he caught both grasshoppers and the fish bit his hook but slipped off and got away. Maybe next time he'll catch the fish, and mine will get away. And Uncle Jack because he brought Emma, and Uncle Frog because he brought Jake to play with Charlie. And Mrs. Plummer because she is your friend."

"Sounds like a good plan. Phil, what was your favorite part?" she asked, turning to her other boy.

"I liked it when this big ol' bird swooped down and grabbed this little rabbit and flew away. Daddy showed him to us when he was way up in the sky. We had to be quiet and not move. All of a sudden, he came down fast, then he jumped up and flew away and when he did, he had the little rabbit in his claws. Daddy told us that the big bird took the rabbit back to his nest to feed his family. And Daddy knows him. He looks for him every time he goes fishing, but he hasn't seen him since before Toby and I were even born. Boy, he must be really old."

The kids asleep, Mike, Frog, Nancy, Jack and Emma settled into their respective easy chairs after dinner.

Maggie turned on the television. "We all remember this weekend's anniversary. Let's see if anyone else does," she said.

Concluding her national newscast for what had been another difficult week, Mary Ann Holland looked into the camera. "This concludes my final broadcast as the evening anchor here at CBS. For the past twenty-two years, it has been my pleasure to be invited into your homes to report the day's happenings. We have witnessed a lot together: a worldwide pandemic and its impact on our economy, healthcare delivery systems education, and technology. Seismic changes in the workplace regarding space, attire, commute times, and travel. Major societal shifts in attitudes toward people of color and sexual orientation. A reworking of the role and responsibilities of our police force. Immigration policy changes, political upheaval and divisiveness, fake news, and a social media explosion have changed the way we relate to one another. But the Attack on America has been the most impactful." She paused for a brief moment.

"I leave you with this. In our nation's history, the Attack on America stands alone. Not the carnage of our own Civil War, nor the war to end all wars; not the fight to stop fascism in Europe, nor the prolonged wars in distant lands with no military objective, costing thousands of lives; not economic recessions, natural disasters, nor international pandemics, not the senseless killing of our own by our own with assault weapons. Nothing has gripped this country like the Attack on America, which occurred ten years ago today. The assault on our people, our way of life, shocked us out of our sense of security, awakened us to our own vulnerability, penetrated our homeland with a gaping hole of grief, and changed our lives forever.

"Terror isn't a foreign problem. It no longer happens in isolation in Oklahoma City, New York, or Las Vegas. It can happen anytime, anywhere, in our cars, on the train. It can fall from the sky. Domestic violence of recent years had been based on race, sexual orientation, ideology, and anti-government sentiment. In every case, it had been a person or modest group of people fueled with deep-seated anger, frustration, revenge, or hatred, which resulted in the deaths of innocent victims. The Attack on America was all that and more. The importance of educating each new generation about the Attack and the dangers of hatred, bigotry, racial discrimination, intolerance, and violence cannot be overstated.

"As they have for the past decade, today, across our country in Dover, Ann Arbor, Houston, and Los Angeles, survivors, victims' families, and ordinary citizens gather to pay tribute and grieve the lives lost and those forever altered. A decade ago today, generations of families were lost," she reminded her audience.

"Wherever you are, whatever you do, stop for a moment today and every day, promise to never forget, and care for yourself and your neighbors."

About the Author

Domestic Violence was inspired by the events of 9/11 and takes the reader on a feasible journey into what could happen if a group dedicated to reestablishment of their homeland as an international power were to obtain adequate funds, sufficient political influence, and access to technology to impose their will.

Chuck Edmonds is a scientific writer whose military experience includes the evaluation of weapons of mass destruction. Most recently, his work has focused on mechanical circulatory support systems (partial and total artificial hearts), his field of specialization at one of the nation's leading cardiac centers. His research has appeared in national medical and surgical journals. He draws from his background of deep scientific knowledge to create his fictional works, which often incorporate apocalyptic and war themes.

Chuck and his wife live in Houston, Texas, where they enjoy spending as much time as possible with their kids and grandkids.

Acknowledgments

Thanks to Claire Anderson, Mary Janicke, Christi Jones, Victoria Lightman, Helen Mann, Michelle Shedd, Evelyn Snow, and Beth Whittemore for their generous aid and encouragement in the writing of this book.

Special thanks to Lindsey Carter for editing and Laura Taylor for bringing expertise, focus, clarity, and energy.

And to Dee Pipes, without whom the story never would have been told.

Made in the USA
Middletown, DE
03 January 2023

21236547R00188